PB

The BLUE BOTTLE CLUB

PENELOPE J. STOKES

WESTBOW
PRESS

A Division of Thomas Nelson Publishers
Since 1798

visit us at www.westbowpress.com

Published by WestBow Press, a Division of Thomas Nelson, Inc., P.O. Box 141000, Nashville, Tennessee 37214

WestBow Press books may be purchased in bulk for educational, business, fundraising, or sales promotional use. For information, please e-mail SpecialMarkets@ThomasNelson.com.

This novel is a work of fiction. Names, characters, places, and incidents are either the product of the author's imagination or are used fictitiously. Any resemblance to actual events, locales, organizations, or persons, living or dead, is entirely coincidental and beyond the intent of either the author or the publisher.

ISBN 1-5955-4051-2 (repak)
ISBN 0-8499-1573-2 (HC)
ISBN 0-8499-3780-9 (TP)

Printed in the United States of America

05 06 07 08 09 BTY 5 4 3 2 1

ACKNOWLEDGMENTS

With appreciation to all the people who made this work possible, especially:

Sister Antonette and Sister Janet,
who endured my endless questions about convent life;

Mary Patton, who lives the music;

My parents, who freed me to follow the dream;

And my own Blue Bottle Club—Cindy, B. J., and Catherine—
who enrich my life by believing in me.

PROLOGUE

Christmas Day 1929

In the watery dimness of a December afternoon, the attic looked dismal and a little spooky. High gabled windows on either end provided the only light, and very little heat filtered to these upper reaches. In an alcove near one of the windows, four girls gathered in a circle around a rickety table.

"It's cold up here." Adora Archer shivered.

"You should have thought of that," Eleanor James snapped, slanting a glance at her friend's thin gauze blouse. "The rest of us had the good sense to wear sweaters."

"Here, take mine." Mary Love Buchanan stripped off her wool sweater and handed it to Adora. She pinched her own chubby forearm and grinned. "I've got plenty of natural insulation."

Adora muttered, "Thank you," turned up her nose just a little at the worn gray sweater, and slipped it on.

Letitia Cameron arranged a trunk and three packing crates around the scarred wooden table. She lit a candle in the center and motioned for them to sit. "Now," she said in a brisk, businesslike voice, "we all know what we're here for."

Mary Love leaned forward, gazing intently into the candle flame. "We're here," she intoned, "so our dreams won't die."

"That's right," Eleanor added. "Times are likely to get difficult for all of us. Mother is afraid that—"

"Your mother is afraid of *everything*," Letitia interrupted. "Daddy says that it took a great deal of convincing to get her to invest with him after your father died, and look how well she's done." She settled back on her crate and smiled benignly. "Daddy says that all we have to do is bide our time; this stock market problem will straighten itself out if people just don't panic."

"I hope he's right." Eleanor's voice was faint. "But if he's not—"

"If he's not, everything's going to change," Mary Love put in matter-of-factly. "My papa says that business has gone down like a rock in the river since October. Mama prays constantly night and day—she goes to Mass every morning, and she's used up enough candles to light the city for a month."

"Everybody seems pretty upset." Adora adjusted the sleeves of Mary Love's sweater and patted her hair. "People are beginning to flock into my father's church—not members, but people right off the streets." She shrugged. "I suppose a little prayer couldn't hurt."

"Well, it's hurting *me*," Mary Love shot back. "If Mama would spend some of that time on her knees cleaning the kitchen floor, I wouldn't have to do all the work. As it is, I'm cooking most of the meals and taking care of the little ones after school."

"Girls!" Letitia interrupted. "We're here to make a pact, remember?"

Eleanor nodded. "A pact that we will always be friends, no matter what. That we'll support each other. That we'll see our dreams fulfilled."

Letitia drew a folded paper from her pocket and opened it with a flourish. "Then let's get on with it. I'll go first." She squinted in the candlelight and began to read: *"'I, Letitia Randolph Cameron, on this twenty-fifth day of December, 1929, here set forth my dream for my life—to marry Philip Clifton Dorn and bear three children and give my life to make them happy and productive members of society.'"* She creased the paper in half and sighed. "Philip and I have it all planned," she said. "When I turn eighteen, we'll be married, and he'll join Daddy in the firm. We'll live in a big house and start a family. He's going to be very successful, you know, and—"

Adora snorted. "Tish, sometimes I can't believe you and I have been best friends since we were ten years old." She shook her head. "That's it? Your *big dream*? To marry into the Dorn dynasty and raise a litter of society brats?"

Mary Love put a restraining hand on Adora's arm. "We *promised* to support each other," she reminded Adora. "If that's Tish's dream, we have no right to question her about it."

"Thank you, Mary Love," Letitia murmured. "I think being a wife and mother is a perfectly respectable ambition."

"Okay, okay, I a-*po*-lo-gize, all right?" Adora whined. Her tone of voice, however, indicated that she did not feel particularly repentant and that she still thought Tish was aiming pretty low. "So, Mary Love, what's your dream?"

Mary Love fished in her skirt pocket and came up with a sheaf of papers, folded lengthwise.

"Good heavens!" said Eleanor. "That's not a dream—it's a whole book."

"I won't read it all," Mary Love conceded, her round cheeks flushing. "I guess I got a little carried away." She scanned the pages in front of her. "First—no offense to you, Tish—I don't *ever* want to get married. I want to live *alone*, in a place that's all mine. I've had it up to here with a big family, all the responsibility, the noise, the distractions. No children. And—" She lowered her eyes. "I want to be an artist. That's my dream."

"Really?" Tish raised one eyebrow. "I knew you liked to draw, but—"

"Not just drawing," Mary Love corrected. "Painting too, and maybe even sculpture."

"Do you think you can make a living at it?" Adora raised her eyebrows.

Ellie shut her up with a glare. "Of course she can. She's good at it—really good."

"I put in a sketch of mine," Mary Love added shyly. "I hope you won't mind." Hesitantly she passed the small pen-and-ink sketch around the circle.

"Look, everybody, how realistic it is!" Ellie said. "A child opening a package under the Christmas tree. You can almost feel his excitement."

"It's very good," Tish agreed.

Adora gave a cursory glance at the picture and handed the sketch back to Mary Love without comment. "*I* want to be an actress," she declared. "On the stage, on Broadway. Or maybe out in Hollywood, in those new talkies."

"Your father will have a fit," Letitia stated flatly. "I know for a fact that no Presbyterian minister in his right mind would let his only daughter flit off to California to be in the movies. I've heard him preach about the reprobate lifestyles of those actresses in Hollywood. He'll never let you do it."

"It's not a matter of what my father will *let* me do," Adora sniffed. "It's my dream, and I'll do it—you wait and see. And when I'm famous, you can all come visit me."

Eleanor cleared her throat nervously. "You'll probably all laugh at my dream," she whispered. "I want . . . to be a social worker, like Jane Addams. I want to help people who are less fortunate." She gave a weak smile. "Sounds pretty silly, I guess."

"It sounds," Letitia answered, "like something that would horrify your mother. Little Eleanor, namesake of the great Eleanor Fadiman James, doing welfare work?"

Eleanor shrugged. "I'm not like my mother."

"An understatement if ever I heard one." Mary Love squeezed her friend's hand. "But a noble dream, Ellie. Truly."

"All right," Letitia said, all business again. "We're agreed. We put our dreams together in this bottle—" She held up a cobalt blue bottle, shaped like a log cabin, with little doors and windows pressed into the glass. "And leave them hidden for posterity." She removed the cork and set the bottle on the table next to the candle.

"Dreams in a bottle," Mary Love whispered. "It sounds so poetic—like a song."

"It's like a time capsule," Eleanor corrected. "I read about it—"

"Let's just do it," Letitia snapped, "before my mother catches us up here."

Each girl, in turn, handed over her papers, and Letitia rolled them up and slid them solemnly into the bottle. Together they repeated in a whisper, "Our dreams . . . for the future."

"Shouldn't we pray, or commit them to God, or something?" Adora asked suddenly. She didn't pray much, personally—her father was the professional pray-er in the family. But some kind of closing ceremony seemed to be in order, and she couldn't think of anything else.

"Spoken like a true preacher's daughter." Mary Love shook her head in dismay. "With a mother like mine, I've had enough religion to last me a lifetime. But—" She thought for a moment, and her round face brightened. "How about a moment of silence, so that each of us can commit our dreams to—to whoever—in our own way?"

Apparently satisfied with the compromise, Adora nodded. She laid her hand on the bottle, and everyone else followed suit, touching the blue bottle and each other in the center of the circle.

It was a magical moment. In the dim stillness of the Camerons' dusty attic, with their dreams captured in a cobalt blue bottle, the four friends joined hands and reached out toward the unknown.

"We commit our dreams to the future," Letitia said quietly.

"To the future," the others echoed.

After a moment Letitia stood, stuck the cork into the neck of the bottle, and clambered up on the steamer trunk to lodge the jar high in the rafters above their heads. It couldn't be seen from below, but they all knew it was there. Hidden from view, holding their dreams, secret and sacred, awaiting the future.

Silenced by the awe and mystery of what they had done, they crept down the stairs and out of the house into the cold December afternoon.

BRENDAN

1
DEMOLITION DAY

October 10, 1994

Brendan Delaney pulled up the collar of her coat, held up three fingers, and began the countdown for the cameraman: "Three, two, one, roll!"

She raised her hand mike and looked into the camera. "Asheville witnessed the end of an era today as the dismantling began on Cameron House, one of the oldest and best-known homes in the Montford historic district. Cameron House, originally built in 1883, took its name from Randolph Cameron, a wealthy stockbroker who purchased and renovated the house in 1921. It was a showplace in the twenties, but as you can see behind me, Cameron House has seen better days. It was made into apartments in the sixties and just last month was condemned by city inspectors."

Brendan adjusted her scarf as the cameraman shifted to the house, panning in for a closeup of the rickety, rotting porch, the front door hanging off its hinges, the broken windows. As the camera came back to her, she cleared her throat and wrapped it up.

"Neighbors in the Montford district expressed mixed feelings about the demolition of Cameron House. Most were sorry to see the landmark go, but admitted that the vacant building was an eyesore and a public health hazard. As one neighbor summarized, 'None of us lives forever.' For WLOS, this is Brendan Delaney." She gave a brisk nod and smiled into the camera.

The red light blinked out. "We're clear," the cameraman said, and Brendan heaved a sigh of relief.

"Let's pack it up and get back to the station," she suggested. "It's getting colder."

Buck, the cameraman, nodded. "Sounds good to me. Want to stop at Beanstreets and get a cup of coffee?"

"Not today, thanks," Brendan murmured absently. "I've got work to do." The truth was, she didn't feel like company—not even Buck, whose friendship she had counted on for almost six years. The demolition story had depressed her, and she wasn't sure why.

She was good at her job, that much she knew. The station vault was full of outtakes from the other reporters, mistakes worthy of a spot on that Sunday night bloopers show. Every year at the station Christmas party, someone inevitably dragged out the most recent composite of editing scraps and gleefully played it, much to the chagrin and humiliation of the reporters. But Brendan Delaney's face was rarely seen on the cutting room floor. She almost always got her spots right on the first take—even that horrible, hilarious report at the Nature Center, when a pigeon landed on her head and pooped in her hair.

If nothing else, Brendan Delaney was composed.

She was a good reporter, and regular promotions at the station confirmed it. But she didn't feel as if she was getting anywhere. What difference did it make if she did an outstanding job of on-the-scene coverage of traffic accidents and spring floods and the demolition of a hundred-year-old house in Montford? Nothing she did seemed to have any lasting significance.

But that was the news business, she reasoned. Today's lead story went stale by midnight. It was like manna in the wilderness—if you didn't get it fresh every day, it rotted on you.

As the image flitted through her mind, Brendan shook her head and gritted her teeth. If she lived to be a hundred, she'd probably never be completely free from the religious stuff her grandmother had drummed into her. Gram had spent her life trying to get Brendan to see the benefit of believing in God. But God hadn't been there to protect her parents from a drunk driver—why should she give the Almighty the time of day now that she was grown and on her own?

Brendan Delaney was no atheist. She called herself an agnostic, but if she were to be perfectly truthful, she supposed she was more of a combatant. She admitted the possibility—even the probability—that God might indeed exist. But the idea brought her no comfort. She didn't disbelieve; she just didn't like God very much.

And so she had come to an uneasy truce with the Almighty. She pretty much left God alone, and God, in turn, didn't bother her.

Gram would have told her, of course, that if she was in doubt or uncomfortable with the way her career was going, she should pray about it, seek God's direction. Well, Brendan didn't want God's direction; she was doing just fine on her own, thank you very much. She would discover her own way, make her own destiny.

In the meantime, however, she had better get to the bottom of this depression that came over her every time she went out to do a field report. This was an ideal job—why wasn't she happy with it? Why did she feel as if her life, like Cameron House, had been condemned and was just waiting for the demolition team to show up?

She couldn't go on this way. She had no passion for her work, no enthusiasm. And it was bound to show sooner or later.

Brendan watched as Buck got into the big white van and drove away. Maybe she should go to Beanstreets after all. It might do her good to sit in that crowded little corner cafe, have a cappuccino, and try to sort out the warring emotions that were assailing her. Her assignment, such as it was, was wrapped up. She still had to do the edit, but that wouldn't take more than an hour. She could spare a little time for herself.

She got behind the wheel of her 4Runner, pulled down the visor, and stared at her reflection in the mirror. Her appearance was okay, she supposed, for thirty-three. People were always telling her that she looked ten years younger, that she had the perfect "image" for TV: a kind of healthy, natural athleticism, she supposed—dark hair, dark eyes, not too many crow's-feet. She had a promising future. And she was, in the words of LaVonne Howells, her best friend from high school, "living her dream." So what was wrong with her?

Vonnie, of course, would have mocked her depression, as surely as Gram would have advised her to pray about it. But then Vonnie was a confirmed optimist, the kind of person who got up every morning excited about the day, anticipating the wonderful developments to come. Vonnie was a psychologist, with a booming private practice, and Brendan secretly wondered how she could be an effective therapist if she loaded her Pollyanna tripe onto her clients.

She couldn't have explained it to Gram or to Vonnie, but Brendan was feeling . . . well, stuck. She was successful, certainly, but everything—her job, her life—seemed so predictable. She could sum it all up in one sentence: *She wanted something to happen.*

Anything.

But it wasn't going to happen here, on Montford Avenue, in the middle of an unseasonably chilly October afternoon. She'd better just shake it off and get back to work.

She rummaged in the bottom of the huge leather bag that served as both purse and briefcase, found her key ring, and shoved the car key into the ignition. But before she had a chance to start the car, a knock on her driver's side window arrested her attention. She looked up to see a big burly man in a plaid jacket. Dwaine Bodine, his name was. He was one of the demolition crew. She had tried to interview him for a spot in the Cameron House piece, but found him too eager, too camera-hungry. Maybe he was just trying to be helpful—he was, after all, what people called a "good old boy." But if Brendan let some uneducated clod hog the spotlight, she'd be the laughingstock of the newsroom—and the main event at this year's Christmas outtakes showing.

That well-meaning, earnest enthusiasm filled Dwaine's simple face now, and Brendan shuddered. He tapped on the window again and motioned for her to roll it down. Might as well see what he wanted. At least Buck had taken the cameras, so Dwaine Bodine wouldn't have any success getting his face on the six o'clock news—no matter how hard he tried.

Brendan cranked the 4Runner and pushed the button for the window. Before it was all the way down, Dwaine had his face inside the car and was yammering excitedly about his "discovery." The man had obviously had a meatball sub for lunch; his breath filled the car with the pungent scent of garlic.

"What discovery?" Brendan asked, leaning as far away from him as she could get.

"Look," he said, reaching into his jacket and drawing out a blue glass bottle. "Lookit what I turned up in the attic."

He handed it over and crossed his arms, looking immensely pleased with himself. "I thought it might, you know, be something you'd want to use in your story. I could tell how I found it, way up in the rafters—"

"Sorry, Dwaine," Brendan muttered absently, turning the bottle over in her hands. "Buck's already on his way back to the station with the film, and we've wrapped up for the day. But thanks. Do you mind if I keep this?"

"Naw, go ahead." His broad smile deflated, and he laid a hand on the car door. "Guess I'll get back to work."

"Me too." Brendan smiled and patted his hand. "Thanks for everything, Dwaine. You've been a big help."

"Really?" The grin returned. "I'll watch you on TV tonight, Miss Delaney. You're my favorite." He lowered his big head and gave her a sheepish look. "Do you think I could have an autograph?"

Brendan suppressed a sigh. She was, she supposed, a celebrity of sorts, especially to a guy like this. Even local newspeople had fans now and then. "Of course."

He fished in his pocket and came up with a stained paper napkin. Marinara sauce, it looked like. She had been right. Meatball sandwich.

"How about a picture instead?" He was a nice fellow, and he had tried to help. She could afford to be generous. She slipped a publicity photo and pen out of her bag and wrote across the corner: *To Dwaine—Thanks for your invaluable assistance, Brendan Delaney, WLOS.*

He took it, read the inscription, and beamed. "Thanks a bunch. Hey, maybe we'll work together again sometime."

"Maybe." Brendan raised the window, put the 4Runner in gear, and pulled away with a wave. "In your dreams," she muttered.

⌒

For once, Beanstreets was almost empty. Brendan sat at a small corner table sipping cappuccino decaf and doodling in a notebook. On the other side of the small cafe, a man with a ponytail and three gold earrings sketched on an art pad, looking up at her every now and then.

She had been here an hour. The first page of her notebook was filled with journaling—a practice she had begun in her early teens when she imagined herself going off to New York and taking the publishing world by storm. This afternoon's entry, however, was more literal than literary—an attempt to get at the root of her depression, to map out strategies for the future, to determine some kind of direction.

Brendan was a planner; always before she had been able to write her way into hope, to chart out a course and follow it. But today nothing seemed to work. She just kept writing around in circles and finally abandoned the exercise altogether. The only conclusion she had reached was that she needed a change, something that would hold her interest and give her life and work some meaning beyond a thirty- or sixty- or ninety-second spot on tonight's newscast.

But how was she supposed to do that? She couldn't just march into the news director's office and declare that she needed more meaningful assignments. It didn't work that way. A reporter—a good one, anyway—made her own drama, discovered for herself the kinds of stories that would touch the pulse of her audience.

She thought about her piece on Cameron House—an ordinary, unremarkable stand-up, with background shots of the decrepit old house and herself in the foreground spouting clichés about "the end of an era." Not exactly Emmy-nomination material. Good grief, the story didn't even interest *her*—how could she expect it to interest an audience? She envisioned a citywide drop in water pressure at 6:26 tonight as toilets across the county flushed during her forty-five-second demolition spot.

Brendan glanced at the bill the waitress had left—$2.75. Well, she wasn't doing herself any good here. Might as well go back to the station, get her tape edited, and call it a day.

She reached into the bag at her feet, groping for her wallet, and her hand closed over something cool and smooth. The bottle Dwaine had brought to her from the attic of Cameron House. The blue glass bottle.

⌒

Brendan sat on her bed in the dark and stared out the bay window at the multicolored lights that twinkled below her. Sometimes, late at night, it was hard to distinguish the stars in the sky from the lights on the mountainside. It was like having the whole midnight firmament for a blanket—above, below, and all around.

There were perks, certainly, to this "ideal job" she held. This house on Town Mountain, for one. Five minutes from the station, overlooking the historic Grove Park Inn and the western mountains. Four bedrooms, a vaulted great room with a glass wall facing the view, a state-of-the-art kitchen, a hot tub on the back deck. She could never afford this house if she left broadcasting to search for a more "meaningful" career.

But the airing of tonight's spot on the demolition of Cameron House convinced her that she had to do something. She could have phoned it in, for all the impact it made. She had watched it three times in editing, once at six, and now again on the eleven o'clock wrap-up, and it got worse every time. She looked catatonic, bored out of her skull, with a smile so phony it threatened to crack her face. When she heard herself intone those hideous words "the end of an era," she cringed and hit the mute button. The screen filled with images of Cameron House, once a showplace, now seedy and dilapidated. Its last moment of glory. By this time tomorrow, the Montford mansion would be a mass of rubble—nothing left except this blue bottle.

Brendan turned off the television, flipped on the bedside lamp, and scrutinized the cobalt glass. It was junk, probably—might bring a buck or two from an antique dealer—but it was unusual. Ten inches high, made in the shape of a small house, with a long neck. The outlines of a door and two windows were pressed into the sides; her fingers absently traced the image. The glass was filthy from years in the attic, and the cork was stuck tight.

She set the bottle on the bedside table and leaned back against the headboard, sighing. She wouldn't be able to sleep for a while; she might as well watch Letterman. Where had she put that remote?

Out of the corner of her eye she spied it on the edge of the table and turned. The light from the lamp streamed through the clouded bottle, casting a blue glow over one side of the bed. Brendan squinted and picked up the bottle, moving it closer to the light.

There was something inside. . . .

She gripped the cork and pulled, but it wouldn't budge. After trying vainly for a minute or two, Brendan took the bottle into the kitchen and rummaged in a drawer for a corkscrew. Maybe she could pry it out.

On the third twist of the corkscrew, the dried-up cork split into a dozen pieces, scattering debris over her counter and kitchen floor. The remnants of the cork dropped into the bottle. Brendan held it up and peered inside.

There were papers of some sort, rolled up and squeezed in through the neck of the bottle. Her pulse began to race, but reason immediately stepped in to quell her excitement. This wasn't an SOS floating on the ocean, for pity's sake. It was just an old glass jar. Still, she was determined to find out what was inside.

After ten minutes of fiddling with the papers, she managed to extract them using a table knife and a pair of needle-nose pliers. She took them back to the bedroom, spread them out on the bed, and began to read.

The first page sent chills up her spine. *I, Letitia Randolph Cameron, on this twenty-fifth day of December, 1929, here set forth my dream. . . .*

Good grief, Brendan thought, *this stuff was written sixty-five years ago.* Letitia Cameron. Middle name Randolph. She must be related somehow to Randolph Cameron, the stockbroker who renovated the house in the twenties. His wife? No, more likely his daughter. Christmas Day 1929. Two months after Black Friday, the day of the stock market crash that brought on the Great Depression.

Brendan shuffled through the rest of the pages. There were similar declarations from three other people named Eleanor James, Adora Archer, and Mary Love Buchanan. None of the rest of the names meant anything to Brendan, although she vaguely remembered something about a clothing store called Buchanan's, down Biltmore a block from Pack Place. The building, she thought, that now housed the Blue Moon Bakery.

She scrutinized the papers. Letitia Cameron's was written in a fine, feminine hand. Eleanor James's penmanship was more angular, a no-nonsense style. Adora Archer's was a back slant full of flourishes, and Mary Buchanan's a legible, down-to-earth print. A small pen-and-ink sketch was included, a representation of a child opening a Christmas package. *Amazingly lifelike,* Brendan thought. The picture was signed with the initials MLB.

Clearly, they had all been young—teens, perhaps—when these statements had been written. The ink was faded and uneven, the paper coarse and brittle. Unless Brendan missed her guess, these pages had been hidden away, untouched, behind a rafter in the attic of Cameron House, for more than six decades.

Her imagination latched onto the image and would not let go. Four young girls, best friends, writing out their dreams for the future and placing them in this blue glass bottle. There had to be some kind of ceremony, of course—girls that age loved drama. She could envision them sitting in a circle, solemnly committing their dreams to one another, promising to be friends forever.

It was an intriguing scenario that raised an even more compelling question: What had happened to those four girls? Had they, indeed, realized their dreams, lived out the fulfillment of the destinies they had envisioned for themselves? They would be in their eighties now—were they even still alive to tell the story?

The story.

Brendan's heart began to pump, and tears sprang to her eyes. Here it was, right in front of her. The demolition of the historic Cameron House wasn't the real story. *This* was the assignment she had been looking for. The human narrative that had been building, layer upon layer, for the past sixty-five years.

She gently fingered the yellowed pages and traced the lines of faded ink. This was what had been missing in her life—passion. This was a story that could change her future, that could put meaning and significance back into her work. This was the direction she had been searching for.

She didn't know how she knew it, but she knew. She would find these women, track them down, tell their stories. She would do profiles, a whole series, maybe. If—

Please, God she thought suddenly—the first genuine prayer she had uttered since her parents' deaths when she was twelve. *Please, let them still be alive.*

2
FILM AT ELEVEN

Under normal circumstances, Brendan despised archives research—especially searching for the kind of obscure information that dated back to the twenties. All the old newspapers were on microfilm, which translated into motion sickness, eyestrain, and terminal sciatica as she sat in the downtown library and peered into a microfilm reader for hours on end.

But this time, at least, she wasn't just doing her duty, logging facts to supplement another dull story. This time she was a detective, searching out truths that had been hidden for more than sixty years.

Norma Sully, the reference librarian, brought out an armful of reels and dropped them on the desk with a clatter. "That's all of 'em."

"Thanks, Norma." Brendan shuffled through them and pulled out the reel dated 1930.

"What did you say you're looking for?" Norma hovered at Brendan's side and peered over her shoulder.

Brendan looked up. "I'm not sure, exactly." She pulled her notepad out of her bag and held it up. "These four women. They were teenagers, probably, at the outset of the Great Depression."

"Cameron, Archer, James, Buchanan." Norma read the list aloud and scratched her head. "Cameron. Is that the Cameron of Cameron House, the report you did on the demolition over to Montford?" She grinned and pushed her glasses up on the bridge of her nose. "Real nice piece, Miss Delaney. Caught it on the news the other night."

Brendan sighed and suppressed an urge to throttle the old gal. Even though that report had set her on a quest that might bring her the story of her life, every time she was reminded of it, she could hear that sappy "end of an era" comment. She clenched her teeth and said, "Thanks. And yes, it's the same Cameron. Right now I'm looking for anything on the family, or any of these other names."

"Well, I'm not old enough to remember the Depression, but I've lived here all my life, and it seems to me I remember Mama talking about those days."

Brendan closed her eyes and braced herself for a trip down memory lane. Norma Sully was a competent reference librarian and had on occasion been extremely helpful to Brendan. But the woman could talk a blue streak, and once she got going there was no stopping her.

Norma, however, didn't seem to be in a garrulous mood. She reached over Brendan's shoulder, threaded the tape, and made a dizzying run through the reel until she found the place she wanted. She pointed a gnarled finger. "Might try startin' with the obits," she suggested cryptically. "Lots of suicides around that time."

Then she was gone, and Brendan was left staring at the dimly lit screen that bore the obituary column:

LOCAL FINANCIER TO BE BURIED MONDAY.

Whether Norma was a genius or a psychic, Brendan didn't know and didn't care. But one thing was certain: She would get a dozen roses and a big box of chocolates for her efforts. For there on the faded screen was the obituary of one Randolph Cameron, dead at the age of forty-six, survived by his wife, Maris, and daughter, Letitia. Services to be held at Downtown Presbyterian Church under the direction of Reverend Charles Archer.

Brendan sat in the parking lot of Downtown Presbyterian and held the photocopy of the obituary in trembling hands. The pastor who had conducted Cameron's funeral was named *Archer.* Another clue; another connection.

She tried to calm her racing heart. She knew from experience that this would very likely turn out to be a dead end—no pun intended. The chance of anyone knowing anything about the Camerons, or even about this

Reverend Archer, a former pastor of the congregation, was slim. Still, it was the only lead she had, and she intended to follow it.

Brendan's stomach clenched, and for a minute she thought she was going to be sick. The last time she had set foot in a church was for her grandmother's funeral three years ago, and—except for Christmas and Easter, when Gram forced her to go—nearly twenty years before that, when her own parents, or what remained of them, were buried in a closed-casket service.

She remembered that funeral as if it were yesterday—her grandmother holding her hand, stroking it until little Brendan thought the skin would rub off. She could still hear the preacher talking about God's loving purposes. But what kind of love took a twelve-year-old child's parents away in a senseless, violent accident?

It had been raining when they went to the cemetery, and Gram had tried to console her with an image of God weeping for her loss. But Brendan, wise beyond her years, knew better. God didn't cry. God let a drunk driver walk away unharmed while her parents, who had never done anything but love her, lay dead on the highway. If God was, as the preacher was saying, all-knowing and all-wise and all-powerful, then God must have known it was going to happen and had done nothing to stop it.

Brendan had decided, right then and there, that a God like that didn't deserve to be worshiped, and that she would never speak to him again. On the rare occasions when her grandmother insisted she go to "God's house," she complied, resigning herself to the sentence like a convicted but innocent felon, counting the days and months and years until she was old enough to be reprieved.

By the time she was thirty and attending Gram's funeral, Brendan had revised her childhood theology somewhat. She no longer held God accountable for the deaths of her loved ones—at least not consciously. She simply accepted the reality that if there ever had been a divine Presence behind the creation of the world, that Presence had long since vanished from the universe. Things happened because they happened. God could neither be blamed for bad fortune or adored for imagined blessings.

The imposing edifice that loomed over her now, impressive with its stonework, stained glass, and spires pointing heavenward, was, she reminded herself firmly, merely an empty shell, a mausoleum to the memory of a deity who no longer inhabited the place. She felt the emptiness clutch at her heart, a visceral, palpable reaction. Bile burned her throat, and she took a deep breath to still the churning in her stomach. It was a building, nothing more. Why then did she feel such apprehension about going in?

From the cavernous depths of her leather bag, her cell phone began to ring. Brendan pulled herself together and groped in the bag until her hand closed around the phone. She flipped it open, jerked out the antenna, and snapped, "Yes?"

"Where are you?" a strident voice demanded. It was Ron Willard, the station manager.

"I'm in my car, sitting in the parking lot of Downtown Presbyterian Church. I got my first lead on the blue bottle story, Ron, an obituary for Randolph Cameron that says—"

"Hold it," he interrupted. "Are you telling me that you're following that red herring when you're due at the Parkway mudslide in fifteen minutes? Buck's already on his way with a camera crew, and if you're not there to interview the Parkway official, you'll be writing your *own* obituary—you can entitle it 'Death of a Promising Career.'"

Brendan glanced at her watch and let out a gasp. "Ron, I'm sorry. I forgot all about it. Call Buck and tell him to stall for me. I'm on my way now."

"You'd better be, or—"

Brendan snapped the phone shut before Ron could get off another threat. This was so unlike her, so unprofessional. She never forgot an assignment, never arrived late for a shoot. The mudslide that had closed the Blue Ridge Parkway was all the way up past Craggy Gardens, a good twenty minutes north. It would take her another ten minutes just to get down 240 and onto the Parkway.

Randolph Cameron and Pastor Archer would just have to wait. If she wanted to keep her job, that is.

She started the 4Runner, slammed it into gear, and sped out of the parking lot toward the 240 loop.

C~

All the way through town and north along the Parkway, Brendan seethed—not so much at Ron, who was just doing his job, but at herself, for not doing hers. And at circumstances, which seemed to be conspiring against her to keep her from pursuing the one story she really wanted to investigate.

The day after the Cameron House demolition piece, she had sat down with Ron and told him of her discoveries—the blue bottle, for one, and the potential for a human-interest series that resided there. And her own passion, for another. Something she thought she had lost years ago in the accumulated blur of miles of videotape—stories brainstormed, researched, taped, and edited, then forgotten as soon as they were aired.

But *this* story—that haunting image of four elderly women looking back on their dreams—had gripped her imagination and would not let go. She had felt her pulse accelerate as she told Ron about it, sensed the adrenaline surge that rose with her excitement.

Ron, the consummate pragmatist, had heard her out with a mixture of amusement and intrigue. When she finished, he nodded and waved one hand—a gesture not quite condescending, but just this side of patronizing. "All right," he said with a long-suffering sigh, "go on and track down your old ladies, if any of them are still alive. But don't overspend your expense account. And promise me—promise—that you won't let your other work slide while you're doing the Jessica Fletcher bit."

Brendan had promised. Now here she was, not two days after that vow, late for a taping and careening wildly around the curves of the Blue Ridge Parkway in a frantic attempt to save herself from professional suicide. In TV news, nobody gave you much room for error. If you did your assignments well enough to get your tape on the air, you got the accolades, the promotions, the viewer shares, the opportunities. An Emmy nomination, maybe— or even a Pulitzer. But the show went on at six and eleven, whether you were ready or not. No matter how well you did yesterday, if you fouled up today, your job was on the line.

At this moment, however, Brendan Delaney couldn't have cared less. Her foot was on the accelerator and her camera crew was waiting at the top of the mountain, but her mind was sixty-five years in the past, crouched with four teenage girls in the drafty attic of a big old house on Montford Avenue.

The house was gone now, but its story still lived—in the carefully-photocopied dreams of those four young girls, and in the hearts of the old women who waited to tell her whether those dreams had ever been fulfilled.

3
MANY MANSIONS

A t three in the afternoon, Downtown Presbyterian was dim and quiet. Brendan stood at the end of the center aisle and looked down the long nave toward the altar, elevated on a three-foot dais. Behind the altar, an enormous stained-glass window depicted the Crucifixion, and with the afternoon sun slanting through the glass, the dark sky behind Jesus' head took on the same hue as the cobalt bottle that had brought her here.

Clearly, the building had originally belonged to the Catholics, not the Presbyterians. All along the sides of the nave, curved alcoves lined the stone walls—alcoves obviously intended for statues of saints. But when God had vanished, the saints had vacated the premises along with him. The alcoves sat empty now, like the hollowed-out eyes of a skull.

Brendan turned again and considered the crucifixion scene. The crown of thorns, the spikes through the hands and feet, the wound in the side, the deeply recessed, shadowed eyelids, closed against the pain. The corpus mocked her with its silent suffering. No matter what Gram had tried to teach her, she found no grace here, no hope, no purpose. What purpose could there be in such a brutal act of God?

All the old hostility came flooding back, rage she thought had long since been whipped into silence. She could feel her heart beating against her rib cage, hear her pulse pounding in her ears. And above the din, the whispered words, "May I help you?"

For all her anger and disappointment with God, Brendan never thought twice about the source of the question. She shook her head in fury. "It's too late for that. Long ago I needed your help, and where were you? You missed your chance."

"I beg your pardon?"

This time Brendan realized that the voice was coming from behind her, in the doorway to the narthex. All the blood rushed from her face and she turned to find herself facing a tall, rangy man with graying hair and watery hazel eyes.

"I'm sorry—I was—" Brendan stopped. "What did you say?"

"I asked if I might help you."

Brendan looked at him, then glanced over her shoulder at the empty cross. She closed her eyes and let out a deep breath.

"It's all right," he said. "People often come in here to pray. If I'm disturbing you, I'll just go back to my office."

"I wasn't—" What could she say? That she wasn't praying? But she had been talking to God, hadn't she? Or at least to the shadow of the God who had made his exit from her life years ago. "Are you the pastor here?"

The man stepped forward. "Yes. I'm Ralph Stinson." He extended a hand, narrowing his eyes at her. "And you're Brendan Delaney, the TV reporter."

"I am. Thank you for recognizing me." Brendan relaxed a little. She was moving back into familiar territory now—the interview, where her natural composure and people skills served her well. "Actually, I came to speak to you."

"To me?" His eyebrows arched upward. "Well, I am flattered. Do come into my office."

He led the way down the hall into a spacious, book-lined room dominated by a large antique desk. Behind his leather chair, in an alcove of the bookcase, a computer screen saver scrolled a Bible verse in neon green across a darkened background: *Ask, and you shall receive.*

Brendan took the seat across from him and tried to position herself so that she couldn't see the computer screen. *Holy e-mail,* she mused. *Wonder if God ever gets snarled in cyber-traffic on the information highway?*

She collected her notes and looked at him. "Pastor Stinson—"

"Call me Ralph."

"All right then, Ralph. I'm doing a follow-up story on the demolition of Cameron House in Montford—"

"Yes, I saw that spot the other night. It was very good," he said. "I especially liked the part where you compared the destruction of the house with the inevitability of death."

"Well, that wasn't exactly me," she hedged. "It was the neighbor. But that's not why I'm here. In doing follow-up research, I discovered that Randolph Cameron's funeral was held at this church, under the direction of a Pastor Charles Archer."

He frowned. "And this was when?"

"Early 1930. January."

"Well, of course, I wasn't the pastor then." He grinned and winked at her, as if Brendan should think this funny. She smiled politely. *He must be a riot in the pulpit.*

"And to tell the truth, I haven't lived in this area all that long—only about three years. There was a Pastor Archer here in the thirties, I know that much, but I'm not much of an expert on this church's history."

For someone who "wasn't an expert," Pastor Ralph Stinson had plenty to say. He droned on about church growth and development, the new building program for the educational wing, and the rising costs of everything. He even asked if Brendan had a church home, gave her a fistful of literature, and invited her to worship with them. *Not likely,* Brendan thought, *especially if his sermons are this long-winded.* She had been here over an hour and gotten absolutely nothing she could use. This was a waste of time. She had no choice but to go back to the archives and try again. If she could ever get away from the loquacious Pastor Stinson, that is.

At last she interrupted as politely as she could. "I appreciate your valuable time, Ralph, but I should be going."

He rose from his chair and shook her hand. "Thanks for coming by. If I can ever be of further help, just let me know. Maybe you'd like to do a piece on the Asheville religious community? I could—"

"I'll keep that in mind." Brendan gathered her things and backed toward the door.

"Oh, by the way," Pastor Stinson said just as she was making good her escape. "I did think of one person who might be helpful to you."

Brendan turned.

"Our oldest member, Dorothy Foster. She's in her nineties and in a nursing home over in Chunn's Cove, but she's still sharp as a tack." He scribbled something on a Post-it note and extended it in Brendan's direction. "Here's the address. Dorothy loves visitors."

༄

Brendan shuddered when she saw the name of the nursing home, *Many Mansions Presbyterian Retirement Community*. The place was a complex of condominiums, assisted-living apartments, and common areas, with a nursing home wing attached to the back—and not a single street of gold. If this place was a reflection of the many mansions of heaven, Brendan believed she'd better look for other accommodations. It reminded her more of a rabbit warren, although she supposed that "in my Father's house are many cubicles" lacked something in charm and elegance.

In one of the central common areas, Dorothy Foster sat in a wheelchair at a window overlooking an autumn-hued mountain. Her white hair was so thin on top that, from the back, the pink scalp showed through. When the old woman turned, Brendan saw a face seamed like folded parchment, with just a touch of pink rouge—the old kind that came in a tin, no doubt—applied in precise little circles on her cheeks. Dorothy smiled and extended a frail, spotted hand.

"Hello, dear," she said in a whispery voice. "Do sit down."

Brendan lowered herself into a creaky vinyl chair while Dorothy, still holding her hand, patted her fingers and smiled. "My name is Brendan Delaney, Mrs. Foster, and I've come to talk to you."

"That's nice, dear. I do so love to have a little company of an afternoon." She smiled broadly, and her teeth slipped a little. "You're a friend of my pastor?"

"Just an acquaintance, actually," Brendan corrected. "May I call you Dorothy?"

"Of course, dear."

The old woman went on patting Brendan's hand, and for a moment Brendan was twelve again, standing at her parents' graveside in the rain, feeling Gram stroke her fingers in a vain effort at consolation. She shook off the memory and squeezed the fragile hand gently. "Pastor Stinson suggested I come to see you. I'm doing research for a story about the Cameron family, who used to attend Downtown Presbyterian. Your pastor said you might remember them."

"I remember everybody," Dorothy whispered. "It's all I have left, my memories. Everything else—everyone else—is gone." Tears filled her rheumy blue eyes and she shook her head. "It's not natural, outliving your own children, you know. I'll be ninety-four my next birthday. Don't know why the Lord just doesn't go on and take me."

"So you were a member of Downtown Presbyterian during the thirties?"

Dorothy nodded. "Grew up there. Got married there. Baptized my babies there." She paused and swallowed hard. "Buried my husband and those same babies there too—although they weren't babies by the time they died."

Something in Brendan wanted to forget about time and the necessity of research and just let this dear old woman ramble about her past and the people she loved. But the reporter in her couldn't wait for Dorothy Foster to get around to telling her what she needed to know. "Do you remember the Cameron family?"

"Nice folks," Dorothy murmured. "Mr. Cameron, he was some kind of financial wizard—worked in stocks, I think. Owned a big, beautiful Victorian mansion over on Montford Avenue. Real well off. Gave his share to the church too."

"And Pastor Archer, the one who conducted Mr. Cameron's funeral?"

"Archer," Dorothy repeated. "Yes, that's right. Had a daughter name of Dora, or something like that."

"Adora?"

Dorothy's eyes lit up. "That's it. Adora. Odd name, don't you think?"

"And she would have been a teenager in the early thirties."

"Yes." Dorothy frowned and looked into Brendan's eyes. "Why do you want to know about these folks who lived so long ago? They're all dead."

"All dead?" Brendan's heart sank. So much for answered prayer.

"Well, yes, child. Folks don't live forever, you know." She smiled wistfully. "Except for me. I guess the Lord doesn't want a dried-up old woman like me."

"I'd think the Lord would want you most of all," Brendan said. The sentiment felt foreign on her tongue, especially the words, *the Lord,* but she couldn't help herself. Dorothy Foster was an absolute delight, and if God didn't want her, then it was God's loss.

"You're very sweet, child," Dorothy murmured.

"Could you tell me more about them—the Camerons and the Archers?"

"Rumor was that Mr. Cameron killed himself after the stock market crash—you know about Black Friday and everything that followed it?"

"Yes, ma'am."

"I thought so. You seem like a smart girl." Dorothy resumed patting Brendan's hand. "You should see the kids who come in here visiting their grandparents and great-grandparents. Those children know nothing about their history. What do they teach them in school nowadays, anyway? Computer games?"

Brendan laughed and shook her head. "I have no idea, Dorothy. Now, about Randolph Cameron?"

"A couple of months after the crash, Mr. Cameron turned up dead. No explanations, just a quiet funeral. Mrs. Cameron lost everything—the big house, the money, everything. It was a real shame, although, let me tell you, they weren't the only folks hit hard by the Crash. She moved somewhere else—I don't recollect just where. Quit coming to church."

"And what about the Archers?"

"The pastor stayed on for a while. His girl—what was her name again?"

"Adora."

"Yes, Adora." Dorothy frowned as if trying to imprint the name upon her memory. "Adora left town a few months after graduation—went away to college, they said. But there was something funny about it."

"Funny? What do you mean, funny?"

"Well, for one thing nobody had money during the Depression, hardly even enough for food and a roof over their heads. The Archers lived in the church parsonage, of course, so they weren't out on the street. And even without much salary, the parishioners saw to it that they didn't go hungry. But money for college? No one had money for college." She paused and wiped a trembling hand over her eyes. "And then there was that other thing."

Brendan could see that the old woman was getting tired, but she pressed on. She had to. "What other thing?"

"The girl died. They announced it in church one Sunday and had a real quick memorial service. Died of the influenza, they said, and was buried up east, wherever it was she had gone for college."

"Is that so unusual?"

Dorothy smiled and nodded. "To lose a child? No, I'm afraid not. I outlived two of them. But the uncommon thing was this: That man, that Pastor Archer, never shed a single tear that anyone could see. The wife grieved, grieved herself right into her own grave. But not him. And to my knowledge, no one ever talked about that child again. Never spoke her name. Maybe that's why I had such a hard time remembering it."

Brendan sat back in the vinyl chair and considered Dorothy Foster's words. The old woman was, as Ralph Stinson had indicated, sharp as a tack. She could remember the thirties like it was last night's news.

And Dorothy's memory had just brought Brendan's research to a brick wall.

The Camerons were gone. The Archers were gone. Most of Brendan's hope was gone. She had prayed one genuine prayer, and it had not been answered. Maybe some things never changed. Maybe this story was never intended to see the light of day.

Brendan glanced at her notebook and saw the four names listed there—four young girls whose dreams had probably died long before they had breathed their last breath. It was an exercise in futility, this story she had taken on so obsessively.

She retrieved her pen and drew a line firmly through the first two names on the list: Letitia Cameron and Adora Archer.

"What are you doing, dear?"

Brendan stood up and held the notebook where Dorothy could see it. "These are just my notes on the four girls I was trying to track down. I've crossed off Letitia and Adora. If they're dead, I can't very well interview them, now can I?"

"Letitia?"

"Letitia Cameron, the daughter."

"Tish Cameron is dead? When?"

"Well, I'm not sure." Was the old woman losing touch with reality? Brendan eyed her cautiously. "You told me she was dead."

"I told you no such thing. For a reporter, Miss Brendan Delaney, you don't listen very well. You never *asked* me about Tish Cameron—just about her daddy and about the Archers. Get your facts straight, dear."

Dorothy lifted a gnarled finger and pointed toward the east door. "Unless something's happened since dinner last night, Letitia Cameron is alive and well and living in Apartment 1-D of the East Mansion."

Brendan sank back into the vinyl chair, reeling as if she had been struck by a left hook to the jaw. "She's alive? *Here?*"

"Of course. Some of us old Presbyterians don't die, honey. We just go on forever at Many Mansions."

"Why didn't you tell me?"

Dorothy smiled broadly and adjusted her upper plate with an unsteady hand. "If I had told you right off, would you have spent all this time talking to me?"

Brendan narrowed her eyes at the old lady. "You're a sneak."

"Maybe so. But now that we know each other so well, you'll come back and visit me, won't you?"

"I wouldn't miss it for the world." Brendan stood, gathered her notebook and bag, and gave Dorothy Foster a gentle kiss on her weathered cheek. "Thank you."

"You know," Dorothy murmured as Brendan started to leave, "maybe the Lord didn't forget about me, after all."

Brendan turned and leaned down over the wheelchair. "What do you mean?"

"Maybe he left me here just for you. So you could find Letitia—and whatever else you're looking for."

"Maybe." Brendan sighed.

"You have doubts about the purposes of God?" The old woman cocked her head to one side.

"You might say that, Dorothy. You might even say I don't believe in God anymore."

"That's all right, child," she murmured. "God still believes in you." She reached up and patted Brendan's cheek with a hand as soft as old flannel. "Go on now and find Letitia. Find your destiny."

The words—an odd parting, to be sure—dogged Brendan's steps as she made her way through the maze of sidewalks and finally stood at East Mansion, Apartment 1-D. She tried to push them out of her mind, but they echoed inside her like a haunting refrain:

Find Letitia. Find your destiny.

"It's only a story," she muttered under her breath as she stood on the tiny square stoop in front of Letitia Cameron's door. "Only a story, like a thousand other stories."

Why, then, could she not still the hammering of her heart?

4
TIME IN A BOTTLE

Yes? What is it?"

Brendan's head snapped up as the door to Apartment 1-D jerked open. A broad, square woman in white towered over her, completely blocking the doorway. Her florid face pinched in an expression just shy of a snarl.

"If you're selling something, we're not buying."

"No, no, I'm not selling anything—" Brendan fumbled in her bag and handed over a business card. The woman took it gingerly between a thumb and forefinger and held it away from her as if it might be contaminated. "I'm Brendan Delaney, of television station WLOS," she stammered, pointing at the card.

The woman gave no ground. "So I see."

"This is Letitia Cameron's apartment?"

"What if it is?"

Brendan took a deep breath and met the narrowed gaze of the solid woman who stood before her. "Miss—" Her eyes focused on the small brass name tag pinned above the left pocket. *Gertrude Klein, LPN.* "Miss . . . Klein, is it?"

The woman nodded and said nothing.

"Miss Klein, as I said, I'm Brendan Delaney, and I'm here to talk with Letitia Cameron, if you don't mind."

The nurse raised one eyebrow. "Miss Cameron is not available."

"This is very important to me," Brendan insisted.

"Miss Cameron's health is very important to *me*," the nurse countered. "And she will see no visitors."

Brendan took a step back. When Dorothy had told her—finally!—that Letitia Cameron was alive and within reach, Brendan had assumed that at least this first step of the journey would be a relatively easy one. But Dorothy hadn't mentioned the rather formidable presence of Frau Klein. Now Brendan felt as if she were facing down a snarling Doberman, trained to kill and eager to take a chunk out of anyone who took a step in its master's direction.

But she wasn't about to give up without a fight. If you couldn't outmaneuver a Doberman, at least you could outwit it. And Brendan had developed plenty of tricks, over the years, to get unwilling subjects to talk.

They stood there toe-to-toe, waiting to see who would make the first move. And suddenly it occurred to Brendan that the prayer she had uttered out of sheer desperation had, in its fashion, been answered. Letitia Cameron *was* alive. She wasn't willing to accept the idea that God necessarily had anything to do with it—she, after all, had been the one to find the obituary, follow the lead to Downtown Presbyterian and then to Many Mansions. But *something* had led her here—if not divine Providence, then instinct, or as Dorothy Foster had implied, destiny. Whatever the source, it was a good sign, and it bolstered her hope and courage. Now if she could just get her foot in the door.

She kept her eyes firmly fixed to Frau Klein's impenetrable gaze and sent up another experimental prayer for help and inspiration. "Miss Cameron *will* want to talk to me," she said with more confidence than she felt. "Please tell her I'm here."

At that moment a voice drifted out from the next room. "Gert? Who's at the door?"

Brendan's heart leaped, and she leaned forward to peer around the nurse's bulk. "Miss Cameron?" she called out.

Frau Klein shifted her weight to block Brendan's view and answered over her shoulder, "No one, ma'am. Just a reporter. I'll get rid of her."

Then, just as the nurse began to close the door, the inspiration came. Brendan reached into her bag, came up with the cobalt blue bottle, and held it up with a triumphant flourish. "Show her this," she demanded. "If she still doesn't want to talk to me, I'll leave."

⟡

"You must forgive Gert's lack of manners," Letitia Cameron said with a wan little smile. "She can be rather overprotective."

Brendan nodded and took a sip of coffee. "So I noticed."

She watched in silence as Letitia Cameron sat on the sofa, turning the blue bottle over and over in her trembling hands. The old woman wore a pale pink housedress and soft slippers, and her hair, an odd shade of bluish white, cascaded over her shoulders like foam from a waterfall. Her eyes, a faded gray-green, bore a lost, faraway expression, and between the eyebrows, a deep frown line made a permanent furrow in her brow.

"Oh, dear. I must look a fright," she muttered. One spotted hand went to her neck, pushing the hair into place. "I just got up from my nap, and Gert hasn't had a chance to put my hair up."

"You look just fine," Brendan assured her.

The pale eyes fixed on Brendan's face. "What was your name again?"

"Brendan Delaney. I've come to talk with you about the bottle."

The faraway expression returned. "I remember this," she said, stroking the glass. "I remember it all so well. It must have been fifty years ago."

"Sixty-five."

"Ah. Time does pass, doesn't it? While you're not paying attention, while you're busy with other things, it just slips away. And then it's gone, and you can never get it back." She paused. "And who are you?"

Brendan cut a glance at Gert, who hovered at the bar in the kitchen. "Arteries," the nurse said curtly. "Short-term memory loss. Some days she's pretty lucid, and other days—" She shrugged.

"But I've had a good day today, haven't I, Gert? Haven't I?" Letitia's voice went soft, like a child pleading for affirmation.

"Yes, honey, today was a good day."

"We had macaroni and cheese for lunch. I remember that."

"I know, honey, it's your favorite."

Brendan listened to this exchange and watched the obvious affection between the two women. "Do you think you could talk to me, tell me about the bottle, and about your friends?" she asked gently.

"The bottle? Oh, yes, the bottle." An indignant expression washed over the old woman's countenance. "I'm old, child, but I'm not crazy. I might not remember lunch, but I remember 1930 like it was yesterday. I can never forget that, no matter how much I might try."

She looked up at Gert and nodded. "You go on to the grocery store. I'll be just fine. We'll sit here and have ourselves a little talk."

"Are you sure?"

"Of course I'm sure. Brenda here will stay with me until you get back, won't you, Brenda?"

"Yes, ma'am." Brendan suppressed a smile.

Gert gathered up her purse and car keys. "I won't be long."

"You take your time, now," Letitia said. "Brenda and I have got lots to talk about, I think. And bring me some of those little cupcakes, please."

"I always do." Gert came over and kissed Letitia on the top of her head. "There's more coffee in the kitchen," she said to Brendan, "and cookies in the jar."

"We'll be all right." Brendan smiled up at Gert. Frau Klein wasn't so terrifying after all. The killer Doberman was just a puppy at heart.

When the front door closed gently behind Gert, Letitia settled back on the sofa. "I get so mad sometimes," she said, clenching her fists in frustration. "Some days everything is so clear, like I was forty again. And other days—" She waved a hand in the air. "Other days aren't so good." She sat up straight and fixed Brendan with an intense gaze. "Don't ever let anyone tell you it's a blessing to live a long life," she said fiercely. "It's a curse, old age—not what you forget, but what you're condemned to remember."

"And what," Brendan prodded gently, "do you remember?"

"I remember that bottle. I remember making a solemn promise. And I remember, every day, that I failed to keep that vow. It's my one regret in this life."

The old woman let out a heavy sigh. "Getting old wouldn't be so bad, I suppose, if it weren't for the loneliness. Except for Gert, bless her soul, I think I'd go mad." She shook her head, and an expression of deep sadness filled her rheumy green eyes. "The hearing fades and the eyesight dims, and the old body just won't obey any longer. But you can endure all of that with grace as long as you have friends." She pointed a shaky finger at the blue bottle. "Friends like that."

"Do you mind talking about it?" Brendan asked. "It's not my intention to cause you pain."

"Pain is a fact of life," the old woman muttered. "Besides, I'd think about it whether you were here or not. It's just when you showed up at my door with this bottle, everything came rushing back like a flood." She picked up the bottle from the coffee table and caressed it with arthritic fingers. "The house is gone, you say?"

"I'm afraid so. It was condemned by the city. I covered the story of the demolition."

Tears swam in her eyes. "It was a wonderful old house, full of memories."

"Yes, it was. A landmark. I was sorry to see it torn down."

"Some of the memories aren't so good," Letitia whispered. "But the memory of that day, that Christmas—" She smiled and closed her eyes.

Brendan reached into her bag and brought out her notebook, a small tape recorder, and the photocopies of the papers she had found in the blue bottle. "Would you like to read what you wrote and put in the bottle?"

Letitia shook her head. "I don't need to read it. I know it by heart, every word. I was seventeen that Christmas, and so sure of everything. Sure of the future. Sure of the man I was destined to marry." She let out a long sigh. "*I, Letitia Randolph Cameron, on this twenty-fifth day of December, 1929, here set forth my dream for my life. . . .*"

LETITIA

5
O HOLY NIGHT

December 24, 1929

La-tish-ahhh!" The familiar screech echoed up the stairway and careened around the doorpost into Tish's room. She winced. Philip was coming up the walk—she had just looked out her bedroom window and seen him—and no doubt he, not to mention the rest of the neighbors, had heard that banshee wail.

Letitia wished, for the thousandth time, that her mother would make an effort to be a little more refined. Daddy had all the class in this family, and why he had married Mother was a mystery not only to Tish herself, but to most of the rest of Asheville society. She had seen people whispering behind their hands at parties or the symphony. Mother was too outgoing, too eager—what people derisively called New Money. She laughed at her own jokes, readily admitted her ignorance of social customs, and actually seemed to enjoy the social faux pas she committed with alarming regularity. In short, Mother embarrassed Tish. She was too real, too down-to-earth.

Some of Tish's friends—especially Eleanor and Mary Love—adored her mother, thought she was funny and wonderful and easy to get along with. But then Eleanor was entirely too liberal for Tish's tastes, and Mary Love was, well, if not common then at least middle class. She could hardly be blamed for not knowing any better.

Adora, Tish's best friend, of course favored Tish's father. Adora had style and grace and a sense of propriety. And Philip Dorn, the boy Tish fully intended to marry when she turned eighteen, gracefully ignored Mother and cultivated a relationship with Daddy. The two of them could talk for hours about stocks and bonds and what investments would yield the most capital growth. Both of them were convinced that this downturn in the market would spring back and right itself if people would just be patient.

Tish didn't understand finance, but she did understand that Daddy wholeheartedly approved of Philip. And Philip, on his part, idolized Daddy. There was a partnership in Daddy's firm with Philip Dorn's name on it, just waiting until Philip finished college. By the time their first child came along, the sign on Daddy's office door would read *Cameron, Matthews, and Dorn*. Philip would be a bona fide financial adviser and commodities broker, and they would raise their children to be responsible, profitable members of polite society.

"*La-tish-ahhh!*" Mother squealed again. "Your young man is here!"

"He has a name, Mother," Tish muttered under her breath. She shoved the last pin into her hair and turned to survey her appearance in the full-length mirror. Oh, yes, Philip would be pleased. The green velvet dress she had wheedled out of her father set off her gray-green eyes to perfection and made her waist look smaller than it actually was. Her hair, a pleasant enough shade of strawberry blonde, glistened in the light, and she had filched a bit of rouge and lipstick from her mother's cosmetics drawer. She would do, she thought. Tonight she would be a suitable adornment for Philip's arm . . . almost.

Not for the first time, Tish thought what a cross it was for a girl to bear the knowledge that her intended was better looking than she was. Philip was so thoroughly handsome, with his dark hair and eyes, his muscular shoulders and slim hips, and that million-dollar smile. He always upstaged Tish wherever they went.

But what she lacked in natural beauty, she made up for in grace and charm and social poise. Tish made sure of that. No one was going to talk behind her back the way they talked about Mother when she wasn't around. She would be a fitting wife for Philip Dorn—and an acceptable match in the eyes of the Dorn family—if it took her last ounce of energy and imagination.

When she descended the stairs to find Philip waiting for her, Tish smiled to herself at the look of admiration that settled on his handsome features. His eyes lit up and he smiled, showing the little dimples that always took her breath away.

They were going to have a wonderful life, Tish was sure of it. And beautiful children.

The sanctuary of Downtown Presbyterian Church was already beginning to fill up with the Christmas Eve crowd by the time Tish and Philip made their entrance. But the music hadn't started yet, and a ripple of hushed admiration ran through the congregation as the handsome young couple made their way down front to the second pew.

Adora Archer slid over to make room for them, and when they were seated, Adora squeezed Tish's hand. "You look beautiful!" she whispered and reached over Adora to pat Philip on the arm.

"Thanks." Tish smiled and winked at Adora. "I worked at it. Believe me, it isn't easy when you've got a fellow like Philip."

"Well, you make a lovely couple," Adora said. "Are your parents coming?"

"They'll be here. Mother had some last-minute preparations for the party. You are going to join us, aren't you?"

"I wouldn't miss it. Daddy will be late, of course, because he has another service after this one." She nodded toward her father, who sat in his customary seat on the platform looking over his sermon notes. "Mama will come with him. What about Little Eleanor?"

Tish craned her neck around and waved a hand toward the back of the church. "Here she comes now. Oh, gosh, you don't think her mother intends to sit with us, does she?"

"Big Eleanor? Your favorite person?" Adora giggled. "I'll just make sure she sees us." She stood up and started to motion to Ellie's mother, but Tish grabbed her hand and jerked her back down into the pew.

"Stop that! Sit down, will you? Ellie will find us. I'd rather her mother sat somewhere else."

"You don't like Big Eleanor much, do you?"

"She's so stuffy. And so pretentious. She's always talking about her money. And she's always riding Ellie. I don't agree with everything Ellie believes, but does her mother have to nag her all the time?"

"Your father talks about money all the time too."

"That's different. That's professional. He's supposed to talk about it. Big Eleanor is just a snob about her wealth."

"But she will be at your parents' party, won't she?"

Tish sighed. "I don't see any way around it. She is one of Daddy's most important clients. We'll just keep our distance."

Ellie, minus her mother, slid into the pew on the other side of Adora just as the organ music began to play. "I love Christmas," she whispered to Tish and Adora. "It's such a sacred time. Listen."

The organist was playing "O Holy Night," and as she concluded the interlude, a young man stood up and began to sing. His voice, a clear, effortless baritone, rang out over the hushed congregation with such power and warmth that Tish almost imagined she was hearing an angel's song.

Adora poked Tish in the ribs with an elbow. "Who is he?"

"His name is Jack something—Bennett, I think. He's the new music director."

"Shhh," Ellie reprimanded.

"Shhh yourself." Tish turned her attention back to the singer. "He's wonderful."

"Leave some for the rest of us, how about it?" Adora muttered. "You're practically engaged."

"I didn't mean it like that," Tish protested. "I just—"

"Sure you didn't." As the last notes of the song died away, Adora turned and grinned at Tish. "Take my word for it; you're better off if you steer clear of professional Christians."

Tish settled back in the pew and laced her fingers through Philip's. From everything Adora had told her, it was probably good advice. People like Pastor Archer, Adora's father, tended to be strait-laced and unyielding. And most of them were married to the ministry. They were at the beck and call of their parishioners twenty-four hours a day, and their own families often got left behind to fend for themselves.

Tish wasn't sure how much of this information had been filtered through the grid of Adora's ongoing conflicts with her father, but of one thing she was sure: Philip would never let her take second place to his career. Philip would always care for her and protect her.

⌒

By midnight, the Christmas Eve party was winding down. The Archers had made an appearance after the late service but only stayed a few minutes, and Adora had gone home with them. Mary Love Buchanan had arrived, at Ellie's invitation, around eight and stayed until she had to leave for midnight Mass. Over Big Eleanor's objections—which were none too vehement since she was embroiled in an animated discussion with Tish's father over how to ride out the storm of the current stock market problem—Ellie went to Mass with Mary Love.

That left Tish and Philip alone, pretty much ignored by the adults.

It had been an unseasonably warm week. Even in winter, the temperate mountains of North Carolina sometimes surprised folks with a gentle turn. On this particular Christmas Eve the temperature hovered in the low fifties and every star shone bright and distinct against a cloudless velvet sky.

Philip took Letitia's hand and led her out onto the stone patio, away from the noise and clamor. Christmas carols drifted faintly on the breeze, and the conversations inside muted to a low hum. He took off his coat and placed it around her shoulders, then sat beside her on a wrought-iron bench.

"Tish," he said solemnly, "there's something I need to talk to you about."

She tried to shush the hammering of her heart. "All right, Philip."

"You realize, I suppose, that everybody says we were made for each other."

Tish nodded.

"And everyone—your father included—assumes that we'll be getting married as soon as you're of age."

She wanted, at that moment, to throw herself into his arms and shout, "Yes! Yes, Philip, I will marry you!" But that wouldn't be proper. The gracious thing to do was wait, at least, for him to finish his proposal.

"Well, I'm not very comfortable with those kinds of assumptions," he went on hesitantly.

What was this? Was he going to reject her, right now, on Christmas Eve? Letitia's stomach clenched and she braced herself for the worst. She lowered her eyes and fought back tears, but when she raised her head again, he was smiling.

"I'd like to make it official, to go back in there and announce it to everyone." He reached in his pocket and drew out a small velvet box. "Letitia Cameron," he whispered, flipping the box open to reveal a huge diamond solitaire—at least a carat and a half, Tish thought. "Would you do me the honor of consenting to become my wife?"

A squeal of glee rose up in Tish's throat and pierced the night air—a noise that sounded, much to her dismay, exactly like her mother's banshee shriek. But Philip didn't seem to notice. He was still smiling, fumbling to put the ring on her hand, reaching to embrace her.

She leaned toward him, and their lips met in a kiss that was more passionate than proper.

"I take that as a yes?" he murmured into her hair.

"Yes, yes, YES!" she shouted.

"Then let's go tell our parents." He got up and extended a hand to help her to her feet. "We're going to have an incredible life together," he said as he wrapped his arm around her. "We'll have a big, beautiful house and lots of children. Your father and I will build the business together, and I'll be a partner, and—oh, Tish, it will be just wonderful."

Tish took a deep breath and steadied herself against his side. It was all happening, just the way she had planned. Just as she had dreamed.

6
NOT MY WILL

January 1, 1930

Letitia Cameron awoke with a delicious feeling of well-being. She could vaguely remember dreaming about Philip, about a starlit night on the patio, and him proposing in a most romantic way.

Then she sat straight up, jerked her left hand from under the covers, and let out a squeal of delight. It was no dream! The proof was there, on her ring finger—a carat and a half of absolute brilliance, casting rainbow prisms around the room as it reflected the morning sun.

It was the first day of a new year, a new decade. And, for Tish, a whole new life.

Adora had mocked her a little for having no other dream than to marry Philip and live happily ever after. But Tish didn't care. She possessed everything a girl could want—a handsome fiancé, a father who doted on her, a best friend who, despite her own wild dreams of becoming an actress, would support Tish and serve as her maid of honor, and a future that spread out before her with glittering promise.

Tish lay back under the quilt and sighed. It had been the perfect Christmas. Perfect. First Philip's proposal on Christmas Eve, then the gathering on Christmas Day, when she and her friends had committed their dreams to each other's keeping. Never mind Adora's ridicule; never mind Ellie's gloomy practicality about what *might* happen because of this stock market setback. Tish was seventeen and engaged; nothing could stand in the way of her happiness. Nothing.

Besides, Adora hadn't really meant to belittle Tish's dreams. And Ellie was just being . . . well, her usual pessimistic self. The fact was, Tish knew she could depend upon her friends. The ceremony in the attic had been like a blood bond, joining them as sisters forever. You fought with sisters, sometimes, but you always loved them.

In her mind's eye Letitia could see the blue bottle that held all those dreams, wedged high in the rafters amid the dust and cobwebs. It gave her a feeling of safety and security, as if she had committed her future into someone else's hands, someone who could be counted on to cherish and protect her.

Perhaps it was God, after all.

Tish didn't think much about God, if truth be told. She went to church, but mostly because her friends were there and Adora's father was the pastor. She had been baptized and confirmed, just like everybody else, and she figured that was enough religion to keep her on God's good side. Daddy gave a great deal of money to the church—there was even a plaque on the wall acknowledging his contributions for renovations when Downtown Presbyterian purchased the old cathedral from the Catholic diocese in 1924.

Letitia had only been a little girl when the Presbyterians moved into the huge old stone church, but she remembered her reaction the first time she had gone into the place. The renovations had not yet begun, and the sanctuary had been full of statues set into curved alcoves along the walls. Dark and cool, with huge stained-glass windows backlit by the sun.

She hadn't heard a word of the service that first Sunday; she had been too preoccupied with the unfamiliar sights and smells. The scent of old incense permeated the stone walls and wafted back an odor that made her eyes burn. All around, the statues stared down at her as if piercing through to the core of her young soul. And above the high marble altar, from the stained-glass window that dominated the sanctuary, the eyes of the crucified Christ scrutinized her every move. It was eerie and frightening, seeing that broken and bloody form hanging there on the cross. She didn't know how Mary Love stood it, week in and week out, being reminded of sin and suffering. Maybe that was why Catholics spent so much time in confession; every time they went to church, they had to look into those eyes.

Downtown Pres was different now. Thanks to her father's money, the statues had been removed, and at Christmas or Easter, poinsettias or lilies sat in the stone alcoves like bouquets on a gravestone. The dark confessional boxes in the back of the sanctuary—which had reminded Tish of big coffins stood on end—were also gone. The stained glass stayed; it was much too valuable to be replaced, so she still had to confront the face of Jesus every Sunday. But eventually she got used to it and hardly even noticed.

Now Tish thought of that face and remembered everything she had heard over the years about God's love and grace and about Jesus' sacrifice. She was getting older—for heaven's sake, she was almost a woman, engaged to be married. She would have to raise her children, when she had them, to believe *something*. Maybe it was time she thought about God a little more.

And what better time than on New Year's Day—the beginning of a new decade, the outset of a new life as a woman headed toward the ultimate fulfillment of womanhood? Tish smiled to herself and thought again of the blue bottle hidden in the attic. The cobalt glass reminded her of the dark sky behind Jesus' head in the crucifixion window.

"God," she whispered, "I guess you saw us in the attic when we shared our dreams—you know, me and Adora, Ellie and Mary Love. We didn't pray then, not really, so I'm going to pray now. If you're up there, would you watch over our dreams and help them come true?"

Her mind wandered back to the church, to the left side of the nave where another window depicted Jesus praying in the garden. She had always liked that one—the dark burgundy color of his robe, the iridescent light shining from heaven on his face. Snatches of Bible verses flitted through her mind, words that had lodged in her subconscious through sheer repetition. "Into thy hands I commit that blue bottle," she added, feeling pretty spiritual. "And not my will but thine be done."

Her prayer finished, Letitia clambered out of bed and pulled on the new quilted dressing gown her father had given her for Christmas. The scent of bacon wafted up to her from the kitchen, mingled with the aroma of fresh coffee. Mother was undoubtedly cooking up a fancy breakfast to celebrate the new year—fresh mushroom omelets, probably, with pancakes in the shape of stars and animals.

They could afford a cook, of course, but Mother wouldn't allow anyone else "messing in her kitchen." She did it all herself—meals for the family, birthday cakes and holiday pies, even the huge spreads of canapés and aspics and petits fours necessary for the parties Daddy put on for his clients.

This little eccentricity of Mother's would have been another source of gossip among Asheville's high society—except that she was so good at it. Everyone raved over her cooking; it was the one contribution she could make to Daddy's success, and she did it brilliantly. Now, if Tish could only make her understand the necessity of being a little classier, a little more reserved.

Letitia entered the kitchen and gave her mother an obligatory hug, then poured herself half a cup of coffee and sat down at the big oak table.

"Coffee?" Mother asked with a quizzical smile. "And when did you start drinking coffee, young lady?"

Tish shrugged. "I am not a child, Mother. I am a woman engaged to be married."

Mother set a platter of bacon on the table and kissed Letitia on the forehead. "Do forgive me, madam," she replied. "For a moment I thought you were my daughter."

Despite herself, Tish giggled. She poured milk into the cup and added three teaspoons of sugar, enough to dilute the bitterness and make the coffee palatable. To tell the truth, she didn't like the taste one bit, but if she intended to be treated like a woman, she had better learn to drink coffee like one. "Where's Daddy?"

"He got up early, I guess. He was gone when I woke up." Tish's mother frowned and shook her head. "If I live to be a hundred, I'll never understand how that man can sleep for three hours and be ready to go again."

"That's probably why he's so successful. I just hope Philip can keep up with him."

"Your young man will do just fine, dear. I'm sure of it."

Tish stared into her coffee cup and smiled. Mother really was a dear soul, always encouraging, always doing her best to make other people feel important and valuable. When it was just the two of them, when Mother wasn't surrounded by their aristocratic friends and putting her foot in her mouth, Tish could actually be proud of her. She was slim and attractive and devoted to her family; she just wasn't—well, elegant. Maybe now that Tish was engaged, she could approach her mother on a more equal basis, help her with her hairstyle and clothing choices, train her a bit in how to fit in. Or maybe Ellie's mother could take her under wing, teach her the finer points of social decorum. As much as Letitia despised the way Big Eleanor treated her daughter, the woman did possess a certain charm and grace. If only she could communicate the style without the snobbery. . . .

Tish's coffee had grown tepid, and she grimaced as she took a sip. It was worse cold than hot. She got up and dumped it in the sink, ignoring her mother's grin at her expense. "Do we have any orange juice?"

Mother nodded. "Fresh squeezed. I'll pour it for you. Go up to your father's study, will you, and tell him that breakfast is almost ready. We'll eat right here, in the kitchen."

As she passed the open doorway on her way to the stairs, Letitia cast a longing eye at the formal dining room. A brightly decorated Christmas tree—one of three in the big Victorian house—sat in the corner, and the mantel and windowsills were draped with greenery and ribbons. The Dorns, she was certain, would be having *their* New Year's breakfast in the dining room, served from silver platters by white-gloved attendants. Unless they were having company, *her* mother favored the kitchen, where she could talk to everybody while bustling about with her preparations. So gauche. Something had to be done about her, really. Especially if Tish expected to be welcomed into the circle frequented by Philip and his parents.

The door to her father's study was open a crack, and Tish knocked lightly, then stepped inside. The stained-glass banker's lamp on the desk burned, and every horizontal surface in the study was covered by piles of papers and files in disarray. The glass-domed stock ticker sat idle in the middle of the room, its narrow paper printout curling across the carpet like an impossibly long tail.

Daddy was nowhere to be seen.

He was probably in the library downstairs—a room designed for formal reception of his clients, but far too large and imposing for a working office. She backed out of the study, closed the door, and started toward the stairs again.

On the landing, however, something stopped her. A cold breeze, a draft that raised goose bumps on her arms, even through the warmth of her quilted robe. She turned and looked. The door to the attic stairs stood open, just a little. The musty smell that drifted down into the house tickled her nose, and she suppressed a sneeze.

Just like Daddy, she thought ruefully, to leave the door open and let all the heat out of the house. Honestly, sometimes that man got so preoccupied that he'd forget his own name. He kept his old records up there, in a tall filing cabinet against the far wall. She could almost see him rummaging through the drawers, then coming downstairs and leaving the door ajar.

Tish reached for the doorknob, then paused. Surely he hadn't found the blue bottle they had hidden up there on Christmas Day! She knew you couldn't see it unless you got up on a chair or trunk, but the very thought of her father discovering their secret and reading those papers sent a chill up her spine. There was nothing incriminating in what *she* had written, of course—Daddy already knew that she intended to marry Philip. But what about Adora's dreams? If he read how Adora intended to leave home and go to New York or Hollywood to become an actress, would he feel obliged to warn Pastor Archer of his daughter's plans? If he read Ellie's dreams of becoming a social worker, would he tell Big Eleanor, toward whom he had what he called a "fiduciary responsibility" so that she could nip Ellie's liberal notions in the bud?

Tish shook her head in dismay. She didn't have any reason to believe her father had found the bottle and read its contents, but a sense of betrayal washed over her nevertheless—as if someone had discovered her diary and violated her privacy by divulging her deepest secrets. If Daddy did find the bottle, it could spell disaster for Adora—and probably for Ellie too.

She had to check. Mother's pancakes and omelets could wait a couple of minutes. Daddy was probably at the table already, sneaking bacon from the platter and talking about how the market was going to bounce back any day now.

Tish opened the door and crept up the stairs. Daylight came through the gable windows and illuminated the attic in shades of gray. She went immediately to the little alcove where she and her friends had gathered a week before, climbed up onto the trunk, and groped in the rafters.

When her hand closed over the smooth cold glass, she heaved a sigh of relief. It was still there, right where they had hidden it, untouched.

Letitia turned to step down, but her slipper caught in the hem of her robe, and she tumbled hard against a stack of boxes. She struggled to her knees, dirty but unhurt, and set about rearranging the boxes that had fallen. Why had they been piled up so high, anyway? They should be over against the wall, out of the way. . . .

She felt it rather than saw it—a slight movement, a shifting shadow. She looked up.

Beyond the boxes, hanging from a rope tied around the rafters. A body. Her father's body.

7
NIGHTMARE

Letitia sat on the sofa in the front parlor, squeezed between her mother and Adora Archer. Everyone was there—Pastor Archer and his wife; both Eleanors, Big and Little; Philip and his parents; Mary Love Buchanan; even the Buncombe County sheriff. She had barely had time to dress, let alone tend to her hair. But this was not the time to be concerned about her appearance.

Tish took in the activity around her as if she were peering through a thick fog. Mother rocked back and forth, her tears now dry, squeezing Letitia's fingers so tightly that Tish could see fingernail marks on the back of her hand. Philip sat to one side, flanked by Mr. and Mrs. Dorn—*Stuart and Alice,* Tish reminded herself. Adora patted her back and shook her head. Big Eleanor just sat in the chair and stared at the carpet; Little Eleanor held on to Mary Love for dear life, while Mary Love fingered a worn rosary. The sheriff paced back and forth across the parlor.

"Mrs. Cameron"— he spoke as gently as he could, but it still came out gruff—"I'm sorry to question you at a time like this, but I do need to know everything that's happened here."

"She's already told you everything," Pastor Archer interjected. "The daughter found her father in the attic."

"Did he leave anything behind?" the sheriff persisted. "Any note, any word of explanation?"

"He said things would get better," Big Eleanor moaned. "If only we would bide our time, wait this thing out—"

"Hush, Mama," Ellie chided.

"But he *said*—"

"I know, Mama." Ellie let go of Mary Love long enough to pat her mother's hand. "We'll get through this, all of us." She fixed a look on Letitia that said she knew what it was like to lose a father. "The important thing right now is to support Tish and Mrs. Cameron."

Tish watched it all as from a great distance. Odd, what you thought about at a time like this. The boxes, still scattered where they lay across the attic floor. Mother's omelet, blackened to oblivion, still sitting in its pan on the stove. The acrid odor of burned mushrooms that pervaded the house.

Concentrate, she told herself. Her eyes fixed on Mary Love's pudgy fingers, moving deftly through the beads on the rosary. *Think about the mushrooms, the bitter taste of the coffee.* Even the blood drawn by her mother's fingernails digging into her hand was a welcome diversion—anything to keep her mind off the body in the attic.

The Body. That's how she had to think of him now. Not Daddy, not the man who doted on her and adored her and treated her like his little princess. It wasn't Daddy who fell to the attic floor like a limp rag doll when the sheriff cut the rope. It wasn't Daddy who was carried out the back door with his face grotesquely blue and his eyes wide open. It was The Body.

The Body was now at the undertaker's, being prepared, she supposed, for their friends and acquaintances to view in all its mortal finality. She hoped they could cover up the angry red burn around the throat, could close its eyes and restore its color and make it back into a semblance of the man so many people had depended upon.

She would grieve later, she expected, but right now the prevailing emotions were horror and emptiness. Would she ever be able to purge her memory of the sight of him hanging over her? And what would happen to them now? Who would walk her down the aisle and give her away to Philip Dorn on her wedding day?

A shudder ran through her, and her mother squeezed even tighter.

The sheriff was still at it. People who committed suicide usually left a note, he said, and that brutal word, *suicide,* sliced through her like a razor. At last Pastor Archer stood up and cleared his throat. "With your permission, Maris, I'll go up to Randolph's study and see if I can find anything."

Mother nodded, and the pastor left the room, followed by the sheriff.

Adora rose and went to sit next to her mother, and Philip took the seat next to Letitia. He put one hand on her shoulder, and she could feel the warmth of his touch through her blouse.

"Now, Maris," Stuart Dorn began, "we need to talk about how we're going to handle this."

"I don't know how I'm going to handle it," Mother whispered.

"What my husband means," Alice Dorn put in, "is how we're going to *present it* to other people."

Tish looked up, and suddenly her mind registered the emotion that filled her future mother-in-law's face. It wasn't sympathy, or even compassion. It was *fear*.

"You know how people talk, Maris," Stuart continued. "If word gets out that Randolph, well, took his own life, the gossipmongers will never let it go. Your life will be ruined."

"What life?" Mother muttered viciously. "I have no life without Randolph."

Startled, Tish looked into her mother's face. She meant it, every word of it. With a flash of recognition, Tish saw her parents not from the viewpoint of a child, but with the eyes of an adult. Mother had truly loved Daddy, not for his money or his status, but for himself. Everything she did—the elaborate parties, the attempts to fit into polite society—she had done for him, out of love. Tish had known for a long time that this wasn't Mother's world, this world of aristocratic propriety and social decorum. She would have been happy in a modest little house with a picket fence and middle-class neighbors. She had done it all for Daddy.

"I know you feel that way now, dear," Alice crooned. "But eventually you'll move beyond the grief. Life goes on, you know. And you wouldn't want to be known as the widow of a man who was—well, not right."

"Not right?" Mother flared. "Crazy, you mean? Randolph was not crazy. He was troubled, certainly, by all this upheaval in the stock market, but he was not—"

Big Eleanor moaned loudly and closed her eyes.

"Maris," Stuart resumed softly, "let me say this as gently, but as directly, as I can. You must hear me, now. *You* know that Randolph was not insane. *We* know it. But people automatically assume that when a person takes his own life, there must be something wrong with him. Mentally."

Whatever progress Mother had made over the years in developing the social graces vanished in that instant. "Just spit it out, Stuart. What are you suggesting?"

"I'm suggesting," he answered smoothly, "that we keep the cause of Randolph's untimely demise right here, in this room. Given the circumstances, I'm sure the sheriff would agree not to disclose the manner of death."

"You're sure the sheriff would agree to what?"

Tish looked around. The sheriff and Adora's father had returned, and Pastor Archer was carrying a thick file folder.

"Ah, Sheriff. We were just discussing the necessity of keeping this as quiet as possible. For the sake of the family, of course."

"Of course." The sheriff turned toward Mother. "If that's your wish, Mrs. Cameron, I certainly understand." He took the file folder from Pastor Archer and opened it. "We did find something that helps explain this, ah, situation."

Big Eleanor roused herself and fixed a gaze on the sheriff. "Found what?"

Pastor Archer shook his head. "It's not good, I'm afraid. Everything's gone."

"What do you mean, *everything*?" Philip demanded, the first words he had spoken since his arrival.

"It appears that your husband," the pastor said with a nod toward Mother, "had all his personal assets in stocks, except for a small amount of cash we found in his desk. The business—" He retrieved the file folder from the sheriff and studied the first document. "The business is bankrupt."

"But he told me the market would bounce back!" Big Eleanor wailed. "He promised!"

Pastor Archer's eyes flickered toward Eleanor. "And he was right. The market *is* beginning to rebound. Unfortunately, if these reports are any indication, he didn't wait quite long enough. He tried to comfort people like you, Eleanor, to give them hope. But apparently he didn't take his own advice. Two months ago, when the initial panic set in, he sold everything, at rock-bottom prices, just trying to hang on. Your stocks, too, Eleanor."

"He was *lying*?"

Pastor Archer sighed. "He was just trying to get through Christmas."

The sheriff hooked his thumbs in his belt and nodded. "We found a will too, leaving everything to Mrs. Cameron. But I'm afraid it's all but worthless. Even the house had been mortgaged, and the money put into stocks."

"The house?" Letitia heard herself speak as if she were floating outside her own body. "Not the house."

"You don't have to do anything about it right away, of course." The sheriff tried to sound reassuring, but it came across hollow and unconvincing. "There's a little money, enough to get by for a while. No one is going to throw you out on the street."

Tish felt Philip's hand lift from her shoulder, and a chill went through her.

"We're agreed, then, that we remain quiet about the circumstances of Randolph's death?" Alice asked with a note of panic in her voice.

"Fine by me," the sheriff agreed, and Mother nodded mutely.

"It'll be for the best; you'll see," Stuart murmured.

Philip and his parents got up to leave, followed by Mary Love and Ellie and her mother. Pastor Archer came over and took Mother's hand. "Maris, I'm so sorry about all of this. You and Letitia probably need some time alone. I'll come back later this afternoon and we'll make arrangements for the service. In the meantime, if you'll get a suit ready, I'll take it to the funeral home."

"I'll do it." Tish got up from the sofa and left her mother sitting there. She had to get away, anywhere, just to relieve herself of the sight of Philip's face. He couldn't look at her, wouldn't meet her gaze. He just moved woodenly toward the door without a word.

Tish went into her parents' bedroom and shut the door behind her. Everything was so infuriatingly *normal*—Daddy's slippers side by side under the bed, his navy dressing gown hanging on the back of the door. A pair of gold cuff buttons and several ivory collar stays scattered across the top of the dresser.

She opened the door of the wardrobe and took out his best suit—a dark charcoal-gray wool with a matching vest—and pressed it to her face. The scratchy fabric reminded her of all the times she had greeted him at the door, flinging herself into his arms and burrowing into his shoulder. The wool still bore his smell, a tantalizing mixture of pipe tobacco and the spice-scented Macassar oil he used on his hair.

Carefully Tish laid the suit on the bed and brushed off the lapels. She collected a freshly starched white shirt, her favorite wine-colored tie, under-shorts and undershirt, black shoes, and socks. She picked up the gold cuff links from the dresser, but after a second thought dropped them into her pocket and rummaged in the top drawer for some ordinary bone ones. There was no telling what might happen next; she and her mother might need the gold in those cuff buttons.

At the thought of pawning Daddy's gold cuff links, a rage rose up in Letitia that threatened to overwhelm her. How could he *do* this to them? Make his escape and leave them alone with nothing, not even a house to live in?

She wanted to scream at him, to shake her fist in his face and demand an explanation. But when she tried to conjure up the memory of her father, all she could see was the limp rag doll hanging from the rafters over her head. The blue, distorted countenance, attached to the neck by a wide red rope burn.

Daddy was gone. Only The Body remained. And the memory of The Body would be with her, she was grimly certain, until the day she died.

8
WORKING WOMEN

March 1, 1930

For two full months Letitia felt as if she had been drowning, fighting frantically to heave herself to the surface and pull a deep breath into her aching lungs. But the sheer effort of going on with life weighed at her limbs and dragged her down. She slogged through the days in slow motion, reluctantly helping her mother pack the few possessions they hadn't sold, sort through her father's things and dispose of them, and move, at last, to a tiny cottage on the other end of Montford Avenue—a converted carriage house with two small bedrooms and a postage-stamp garden.

Then she awoke one morning to find everything changed.

For one thing, her mother wasn't crying. Instead, she sat at the little kitchen table looking out over the fallow garden, jotting notes on the back of an envelope.

Tish watched from the doorway for a few minutes and then said, "Mother?"

Her mother glanced up and smiled—really smiled. "Good morning, darling! Wonderful day, isn't it?" She gestured out the window to the sun-drenched plot of ground. "Look—it's almost spring."

Tish looked, but all she could see were high weeds, dried and brown, left over from last year's planting. "Look at what?"

"See, over there in the corner next to the wall—crocuses. Yellow and purple crocuses."

Now that her mother had pointed them out, Tish could discern a flash of color low to the ground amid the weeds. A surge of hope rose in her heart, that breath of air she had been struggling to find since January. But her mother's smile had more to do with it than the blossoming crocuses.

Tish poured herself a cup of coffee and sat across from her mother at the table. "What are you doing?"

"Figuring." Mother raised an eyebrow. "Coffee?"

Tish shrugged. "I'm getting used to it. You okay?"

"I'm fine, honey. But we need to talk, if you're awake enough."

"I'm awake."

"All right. Now—" She turned the envelope so that Tish could see the columns of figures listed on it. "Here's what we've got, from the sale of the furniture and the little bit of money we had left after your daddy's funeral expenses."

Tish felt her chest tighten, and she turned away. "Mother, I don't think this is the time to—"

"Yes, it is the time," Mother said firmly. "According to my figures, we have enough to rent this house for almost a year."

"A year!" Tish thought wistfully of her huge, bright bedroom in Cameron House, with its fireplace and canopied double bed. Here she had a room no bigger than a closet, with a narrow single bed, a small chest of drawers, and a tiny window. She couldn't live here permanently; she'd die of sheer claustrophobia. "Surely you don't intend to stay here for a year?"

"I intend to stay here forever, if need be."

"Mother, you can't mean it. We're in the servants' quarters, for heaven's sake! We've barely got room to breathe."

Tish's mother cleared her throat and shifted in her chair. "We have plenty of room, Letitia. The parlor is spacious enough, and what do we need bedrooms for except to sleep? There's a nice bath, and a workable kitchen—"

"Mother, there's not even a proper dining room!"

"And just who, pray tell, do we expect to be entertaining?"

The question drew Tish up short. She looked at her mother and saw on her face an expression of benign amusement. "You're actually enjoying this!" she snapped, dismayed at the accusing tone in her voice but unable to stop herself. "What—do you think I need to be taught a lesson in humility?"

"It might not hurt," her mother replied softly. But her tone was gentle, without rancor, and Tish felt a wave of shame wash over her. "Let's be realistic, daughter. We have very little left, and we were fortunate enough to find a place that's warm, dry, and comfortable."

Against her will, Tish found her mind wandering to images she had seen in the newspapers—people who, displaced by the looming Depression, lived in tarpaper shacks next to the garbage dumps of large cities. Homeless, jobless people with haunted expressions and tattered clothes. Mothers on the streets, with dirty children in tow. Perhaps she and her mother didn't have it so bad, after all.

"You're aware of what's happening around us," Mother said as if she'd read Tish's mind. "Many, many people are worse off than we are. People who were like us, once, with good jobs and nice homes and a bright future."

"If you're trying to get me to be thankful for all of this, Mother, you're wasting your breath," Tish muttered. But the images had taken their toll. She *was* thankful. Thankful, at least, that they weren't completely destitute. They had a place to live. And she, of course, had a future. A future with Philip Dorn.

Daddy had been right, in the long run. The market had begun a gradual recovery. And Stuart Dorn hadn't panicked, the way Daddy had. The Dorns still had their fine house, their place in society. They stood to regain most of what they had lost in the initial crash. There would be no partnership for Philip in Daddy's firm, of course—there was no firm left. But Philip would find another position, they would be married, and things eventually would get back to normal.

The worst of the damage had hit not the wealthy, who would recover their losses, but the middle class—people whose jobs had suddenly terminated in the panic as factories and businesses shut down and banks went under. They were the ones standing in interminable bread lines, wandering the city streets. They were the ones whose pitiful life savings had vanished in the bank closings, whose homes had gone into foreclosure, whose lives were devastated.

Letitia Cameron still had hope. Still had a future to look forward to.

It was true that Philip hadn't been around very much. He had been busy, undoubtedly, trying to get his own future prospects in order. But she and Mother, too, had been occupied with the grim business of divesting themselves of the house and other possessions. Now that they were moved, once everything was settled, she would begin seeing Philip again on a regular basis.

And in seven months she would turn eighteen. They would be married immediately. Surely she could hold out until then.

"This is, I think, our best option," Mother was saying when Letitia's attention returned to her. "We have to be practical."

Tish stared at her. "What did you say?"

"I said, we have to be practical."

"No, before that. About options."

"Letitia, please pay attention. This is important."

"I'm sorry, Mother. Now, what options?"

"Several women we know—Alice Dorn, for one, and a few of her friends, have approached me about doing some work for them. Preparing food for dinner parties—rather like what I used to do for your father's business gatherings. They would pay me well, and—"

Tish shook her head, unable to believe what she was hearing. "You'd be a—a *servant*—for other people's parties? A *cook*?"

"It wouldn't exactly be like that," Mother hedged. "I would prepare food and serve it, yes. But I'd do the preparations here, in our own kitchen, then take it to the party, serve, and clean up afterward."

"And how do you intend to manage that?"

"We still have your father's car. I'll learn to drive. Pastor Archer will teach me."

"Mother, you absolutely cannot do this. Alice Dorn is my future mother-in-law!"

"Yes, and she's been generous enough to offer—"

"This is not generosity, Mother!" Tish interrupted. "It's—" The word stuck in her throat, and Tish fought back tears. "*Charity!*"

Mother clasped her hands on the table and looked Tish squarely in the eye. "It is not charity to do honest work for honest wages. Besides, I love doing this, and you know I'm good at it. I will do it, Letitia. For myself. For you. You have to finish school."

"I graduate in three months, Mother. And then Philip and I will be married, and you won't have to worry about anything, ever again."

"And you think taking the Dorns' money and living off my son-in-law is not charity, just because my daughter marries into their household?"

"That's not charity, Mother. Be sensible."

"I am being sensible, Letitia. And you're right. It's not charity—it's prostitution."

Tish sat back in her chair. She wasn't certain what shocked her more—her mother's use of the word *prostitution,* or the backbone Mother had shown by coming up with this idea in the first place. Either way, it was completely out of the question.

Letitia had to do something and had to do it fast.

⤳

The Dorn residence, a sprawling brick-and-stone home off Edwin Avenue, lay like a jewel against a vast lawn, bright green with new growth. In the carefully-sculpted flower beds, crocuses bloomed, and the first blades of the daffodils pushed through the mulch.

Tish had been here any number of times, both for parties and for private family dinners. But as she stood before the massive double oak doors, she felt small and strangely out of place. She knocked, timidly at first, and then with more boldness. She was the fiancée. She belonged here, if anyone did.

The door creaked open to reveal Miles, the ancient butler who had been with the Dorn family for ages on end. When he saw her, he raised his bushy eyebrows, then composed himself and said somberly, "Miss Letitia."

"Hello, Miles," she said as brightly as she could. "I've come to see Philip. Is he home?"

"Master Philip is expecting you, Miss?"

Tish faltered. "Ah, no, I don't believe he is. But if you'll announce me, I'm sure he'll make time for his fiancée."

She followed Miles through the massive entryway into the formal parlor and waited, fidgeting, as her eyes took in the opulence of the place—the imported marble fireplace and hearth, the crystal chandelier, the custom-loomed English floral rug in shades of ivory and pink. There had been no selling of possessions in the Dorn household, that much was obvious. But then Stuart Dorn had wealth that was unaffected by the price of stocks. He could afford to bide his time.

"Letitia?"

Philip's voice, when it came, sounded odd—strained and distant. Tish turned.

He stood in the doorway, tall and handsome as ever, his broad shoulders thrown back and his hand resting casually on the doorpost. She waited for the smile that did not come and finally whispered, "Philip, I need to talk to you."

"All right."

He took her hand and led her to the settee, then sat in a chair adjacent to her and crossed his legs. Tish scanned his face for any hint of warmth, any sign of affection, but there was none. Only a practiced graciousness, an aristocratic lift to the eyebrows, a thoroughly Philip-like composure.

"What is it, Letitia? Is something wrong?"

Tish pushed from her mind the awareness that he never called her "Letitia"—only when he was rebuking her for some infraction of social protocol or introducing her to some superior being far above her own social standing. She reached for his hand, but he was too far away, and he didn't reciprocate. With a flush of shame for her forwardness, she let the hand fall into her lap.

"You haven't been to see us since we moved." The words weren't consciously intended as an accusation, but he obviously took offense. He drew back in his chair and his eyebrows went up another notch.

"I didn't know I was expected to report my whereabouts," he answered smoothly. "But since you asked, I've been out of state for a few weeks. Father has some business associates in Atlanta, and I've been negotiating with them about an opportunity in their firm. It looks like a very promising possibility."

Atlanta! Tish shuddered at the thought. She had been to Atlanta once or twice and remembered it as a teeming, noisy place with a pace that made her head spin. She couldn't possibly move to Atlanta, couldn't possibly . . .

But she'd deal with that later. One thing at a time. Right now, the important thing was getting Philip to understand her predicament without demeaning herself.

"Well, isn't that wonderful, Philip!" she forced herself to say. "Imagine, Atlanta!"

"But I gather you didn't come here to talk about my future possibilities."

Ah! He had given her the perfect opening. "No, Philip, I came to talk about *our* future possibilities." She took a breath and rushed on before he had time to comment. "Since Daddy's—ah, passing—Mother and I have been forced to face some difficult decisions. Now, I know that we had originally planned to wait until I was eighteen to marry, but given the circumstances, I'm sure Mother would give her permission for us to go ahead."

He stared at her blankly. "Excuse me?"

She held out her arms and gave him her most brilliant smile. "Let's get married, Philip—now, this spring. It would only be pushing the ceremony up a few months, and I'm certain we could get ready by May, or—"

"Married? *Now*?"

"Well, not now as in today, Philip. But soon. I never considered the possibility of moving, especially to a place as big as Atlanta, but I'm sure you have other offers as well, maybe right here in Asheville. We could—" She looked up at him, and his face had gone hard as iron. "What's the matter, Philip?"

"Tish, I'm sorry. I just can't discuss this. Not right now."

"But we *have* to discuss it," she protested. "We have to make a decision. Do you know that Mother is planning—"

She stopped short. She wouldn't bring Mother into this, wouldn't humiliate herself by telling him how her own mother had every intention of hiring out to the people who had once been their peers, their social equals. But he was nodding. He knew. He already knew all about it.

"You know?"

"Yes."

"But how?"

"Listen, Tish," he said with a dismissive gesture. "Things have changed."

"They haven't changed for *you*," she shot back. "Look around. Everything here is the same. Everything between us is the same." She fixed her eyes on his face, but he wouldn't meet her gaze. "Isn't it?"

"I don't know, Tish. It's a confusing time for everybody. I'll admit, it was my idea for my mother to hire yours. I wanted to do something to help."

"This is *helping*?"

"I thought so. Your mother does enjoy that kind of thing—cooking for fancy dinners and parties. She's a natural at it. And, well, I just thought—"

Suddenly it all came clear to Tish, and Philip Dorn didn't look so handsome to her anymore. He looked, instead, like a pampered, arrogant rich boy more concerned about his reputation among the elite than about his intended's feelings, or any empty promises he might have made.

"You don't have any intention of marrying me, do you, Philip?"

He blanched. "Letitia, as I said, this isn't the time to discuss this."

"It is the time. It's the only time. Now, answer my question."

"I've been wondering if it might not be the best for both of us if we waited a while—you know, postponed the wedding until—"

"Until what? Until some miracle happened and we were rich again, suitable to your station in life?"

"You're raising your voice, Letitia. Please don't shout."

"I'll shout if I want to!" she countered. "And don't talk to me about what's best for *both* of us. You're thinking about what's best for you, admit it!"

"Letitia, I beg of you, don't make a scene." He turned his face from her and muttered under his breath, "Mother was right. You are just like Maris."

"Just like Maris?" she repeated. "The woman, you mean, who is only good enough to serve canapés at your fancy parties? Just like Maris, who was just a little less sophisticated than you and your type wanted her to be?"

"You have to admit, Tish, that our circumstances have changed since your father died."

"Yes, circumstances have changed. *You've* changed, Philip. Or maybe you haven't changed at all. Maybe I'm just seeing, for the first time, what an insufferable snob you really are!"

"There's no need to be nasty."

"Of course not," Tish sneered. "God forbid that we should say what we really think. Why don't you, Philip? Take a chance. Say what you mean; for once in your life be honest. I was an acceptable match for you as long as my father had the money and the big house and the reputation. I was stupid enough, and awestruck enough, that you were sure you could mold me into your little image of what a society lady should be. But then something happened. Daddy died." She paused. "No. Daddy *killed himself*. And you couldn't be expected to sully your good name by marrying the daughter of a man who committed suicide. The daughter of a woman who now has to work for a living."

Philip opened his mouth to protest, but she kept on.

"Well, let me tell you something, Philip. My mother has more class than all your uppity society people put together. And she has something else too. She has courage. Moral courage. She tried to fit into your world because she loved my father. Now that he's gone, now that the money is gone, she *will* make it on her own, mark my words. And I can only hope, Philip, that you're right—I hope to high heaven that I do turn out to be *just like Maris.* Because she is the finest, bravest, most loving, most compassionate woman God ever created."

Philip got to his feet and looked down his nose at Letitia. "Fine. Go on, become like your mother. Cook for a living, or do whatever it is you working people do. But don't come crawling back to me after this little exhibition of temper."

She stood up, gathered her bag, and stalked to the door. "Good-bye, Philip."

"Haven't you forgotten something?"

She turned. "What?"

He extended one hand, palm up, and sneered at her. "The ring?"

Tish looked down at her finger, still adorned by the diamond solitaire Philip had given her that magical Christmas Eve night on the patio. For a brief moment, a wave of regret washed over her. This had been her dream, her one shining hope for the future. Now, as the diamond winked in the light of the chandelier, she felt the regret subside, replaced by an overwhelming sense of purpose and power. She stiffened her spine, jerked the ring off, and held it out toward him.

"This ring, Philip? The ring that represents all the promises you made to me, all our hopes and dreams for the future?"

He took a step forward. "Let's have it."

"A real lady would return it, I suppose," she said softly.

"Certainly." He smiled at last, showing his white, even teeth and deep dimples. "No hard feelings?"

"Of course not, Philip." She returned his smile and dropped the ring into her handbag. "No hard feelings. I do hope you enjoy Atlanta." She turned on her heel and jerked the door open.

"Wait a minute!" he called after her as she ran down the steps and out into the street. "What about the ring?"

Tish paused and gazed at her surroundings. Spring was coming. Birds were singing, the sun was shining, and the sky was a bright Carolina blue. She wheeled around to see him standing on the porch, his handsome face a bright shade of red.

"I earned it, Philip!" she shouted, loud enough for the neighbors to hear. "I'm just a working woman, remember? Just like Maris."

Then she swung the bag high over her head and began the long walk home, laughing all the way.

9
THE PRICE OF FREEDOM

You did *what*?" Mother stopped in the middle of chopping onions and stared at Letitia as if she had grown two heads.

"I went to see Philip Dorn," Tish repeated. "To ask him if we could get married right away."

"Tish, no!" her mother wailed. "I know things are difficult for you right now, and all this is a big adjustment, but how could you go crawling to him? His mother has hired me to do the food for her parties, for heaven's sake!"

"I thought that maybe, if we could go ahead and get married, you wouldn't have to—"

"Wouldn't have to humiliate myself in front of our former friends?" Mother pushed a lock of hair out of her eyes and sank wearily into a chair at the table. "Whether you marry Philip, and when, is your business—once you're of age," she sighed. "But you might as well know one thing, Letitia Randolph Cameron. I'll not be taking one dime of the Dorn money unless I work honestly for it. Not if you married Philip and became the wealthiest woman in Buncombe County."

Tish waited until the tirade had subsided. "I'm not going to marry Philip, Mother."

"And furthermore, if you think for one minute—" She stopped. "What did you say?"

Tish smiled. "I said, I'm not going to marry Philip."

"You're not?"

"I'm not."

Tish's mother cocked her head and gave her daughter a quizzical look. "When did all this happen?"

"This afternoon. If you'll just keep quiet for a minute or two, I'll tell you about it."

Mother wiped her hands on a dishtowel and nodded. "I'm listening."

"As I said, I went to see Philip, intending to suggest that we push the wedding up. But he was so . . . so snobbish, so superior! He didn't say it right out, of course, but it was clear enough he had no intention of marrying me now that—" She paused, groping for words.

"Now that your father is dead and we aren't rich anymore?"

"That's pretty much it, I guess." Tish smiled and shook her head. "You always have been direct and to the point, Mother."

"One of my many failings as the wife of a wealthy aristocrat."

Tish gazed at her mother as if seeing her for the first time. Flushed from the warmth of the oven, her cheeks bore a rosy glow and her hair, slightly disheveled, curled in disarray around her forehead. She looked at once ordinary and beautiful. And happy. Tish didn't think she had ever seen her mother happier.

"Was I like that—you know, self-important and snobby—when Daddy was alive and we were part of that circle?"

Mother bit her lower lip as if considering her answer. Then she said, "Yes."

The truth stung, and tears sprang to Tish's eyes.

"I'm sorry if that hurts, honey, but it's the only answer I can give. I love you—I've always loved you—but you did tend to get caught up in the aristocratic way of life. I prayed, almost every night, that you would come to your senses before it was too late, before you became like—well, like Alice Dorn. But of course a mother can't say such a thing; you wouldn't have listened anyway. You had to find out for yourself."

"Well, I certainly found out some things today." Tish went on with the story, telling her mother how Philip had treated her. She considered leaving out the part where Philip insulted Mother and accused Tish of being *just like Maris,* but in the end she related that part as well.

Much to her surprise, Mother laughed. "He said that? Said you were *just like Maris?*"

"He didn't mean it as a compliment, Mother," Tish protested. "But I'll have to admit, it's exactly what I needed to hear."

"And what did you tell him?"

Tish felt a flush of warmth creep up her neck. "Well," she said hesitantly, "I wasn't very, ah, ladylike. I told him that you had more class than all the uppity society people in his circle put together. And that you had something else—courage. Moral courage, I think I said. And that I hoped to high heaven I *was* just like you, because it was the best thing that could ever happen to me." Letitia averted her eyes as embarrassment washed over her. She had never admitted such feelings to herself, let alone to someone else. But she knew, just as she had known when she shouted the words in Philip Dorn's handsome face, that they were true.

When she looked up again, Mother was sitting there, dabbing at her eyes with the dishcloth.

"Are you crying, Mother?" Tish reached out a hand.

Her mother's strong, lithe hand closed over her fingers, and she shook her head. "It's just the onions." She smiled. "Did you really say all that to him?"

"Yes." Tish looked into her mother's eyes, no longer ashamed. "I did. And I meant it. Every word of it." She shrugged. "I don't know, Mother, I just saw something today, something that made me so mad. Philip didn't care about me; he just cared about having a girl who fit into his mother's plan of what a society lady—his wife—should be like. I was the same person—exactly the same person—he had claimed to love. The only difference was that now I didn't have Daddy's money to back me up. And in his eyes, that put me on a level with some scullery maid. I saw disgust in his eyes, Mother, and heard a condescending, smug tone in his voice that raked over me like fingernails on a blackboard. Suddenly he didn't seem so handsome, so desirable. And when he insulted you, well, that was the final straw. I knew I could never be the girl he thought I was, what he wanted me to be. And to tell the truth, I didn't want to be. I just wanted to be—to be loved for myself, to be—"

Without warning, tears welled up in her throat and choked her. For the first time since Daddy's death, the full force of her losses overwhelmed Tish, and she began to sob. When she felt her mother's arms go around her, her initial reaction was to resist, to steel herself against the embrace, to be strong. But she couldn't do it. At that moment she was not a young woman nearly grown, old enough to be on her own. She was a child, a little girl who needed her mommy's love. She let go, buried her face against her mother's shoulder, and wept.

Tish didn't know how long she sat there, crying. But when the tears at last subsided, she felt her mother's hand stroking her hair, heard a quiet voice whispering in her ear, "It's all right, honey. I'm here. Let it out."

Exhausted, Tish struggled to sit upright. Mother pressed a handkerchief into her clenched fist and pushed her hair out of her eyes. "I'm sorry," she gasped. "I don't know what that was all about."

"It's about loss," her mother said softly. "You've lost so much, darling—your father, the only way of life you've ever known, and now Philip—"

"Philip!" Tish snarled. "I can't believe I ever thought I loved him!" She blew her nose and exhaled heavily. "I won't miss him, that's for sure."

"Yes, you will," Mother said firmly. "You will miss his attention and feel keenly the loss of all the plans the two of you had made. But you'll get over it. Eventually."

She pulled Tish's head to her shoulder and began stroking her hair again. "Grief is a difficult process, honey. It doesn't happen all at once, but in stages, a little at a time. You think you're over it, that you've moved on, and suddenly it comes on you again—the sadness, the anger—"

Tish sat up a little and looked at her. "You were angry? With Daddy?"

Mother nodded. "I still am, sometimes. Oh, not because of the money. But because he took away the one thing that I really wanted—his presence." She gazed out the kitchen window to the edge of the garden plot where the purple crocuses grew. "I loved your father a great deal, Letitia. I still do. But sometimes I also hate him. Hate him for leaving like that, without a word of good-bye." She hugged Tish tighter. "We'll be all right, honey. But we both know things will never be the same."

Tish straightened up and swiped at her eyes. "But you seem so—so happy. So content here, in this little house."

"In some ways, I am. This kind of life is much more to my liking than the opulent society your father introduced me to. Your young man was right, honey—I don't belong in that world."

"He's not 'my young man,' Mother," Tish corrected. "He's an overbearing, spoiled rich boy who doesn't know the meaning of love. I never want to see him again."

"Perhaps. But you'd better prepare yourself for the fact that you *will* see him again. And you *were* engaged to him, so you'll have to get used to the idea of people talking about it. Especially since your mother is now"— she grinned broadly—"a low-class working woman."

In spite of herself, Tish smiled in return. "With a low-class working daughter." She squeezed her mother's hand. "I just want you to know that I will help you," she said. "With the catering, I mean—the food and parties and all that."

"I know you will, honey. And I suppose we should start making some firm plans. After all, you'll be graduating in a few weeks."

"The first thing we need to do," Tish said, "is learn to drive Daddy's car."

"Both of us?"

"Both of us." She raised one eyebrow at her mother. "I'm not going to be a society wife carted around by a chauffeur. I'm going to be doing the chauffeuring. Do you think we can afford one of those little billed caps and a dark suit?"

Both of them began to giggle, overcome by the ridiculous thought of Letitia Randolph Cameron in a chauffeur's uniform. They laughed together until tears came again, and Tish found herself amazed at the camaraderie—the *equality*—she felt with her mother. How much had she missed, all those years of thinking they had nothing in common? How much hurt had she caused by her own attitudes toward her mother's lack of sophistication?

Sophistication didn't seem nearly so important any longer. What mattered was that they were in this together.

At last her mother's laughter subsided and she grew serious. "Tish, we do need to talk about what you're going to do after graduation."

"I'm going to help you."

"I appreciate the offer, but I don't think so. I mean, I may need your help on the larger parties, but I want you to have the opportunity to do more than that. Have you thought about what you'd like to do?"

Tish shook her head. "Not really. I put all my eggs in Philip Dorn's basket, I'm afraid. The only real plans I made were to marry him and have children. It seemed like a wonderful dream at the time, but now—"

"Now you're starting over. We both are."

Tish thought for a minute. "I do love children. And I've been a pretty good student. Maybe I could teach."

A shadow passed over her mother's face. "I hate to throw cold water on your idea, honey, but—" She paused. "Well, I'm afraid that right now we don't have the money for you to go to college, even if you went to the University here. We're barely getting by, and even when I start earning more—"

Suddenly Tish let out a squeal. Why hadn't she thought of this sooner? She jumped up and raced into the parlor.

"What is it, honey?" her mother called from the kitchen. "Are you all right?"

"I'm just fine, Mother," she shouted over her shoulder. "Wonderful, in fact." She retrieved her bag from the settee and came back to the kitchen. "Philip Dorn is going to pay my way through college."

"Absolutely not!" her mother protested. "Even if he were willing to pay, to make amends for his broken promises to you, I couldn't allow you to—"

"Just hold on, will you?" Tish rummaged through the bag and came up with the diamond engagement ring. "I said I put all my eggs in Philip's basket. But I was wrong. I forgot about one egg. The golden egg." She picked a piece of lint off the stone and held it up to the light. "*This* is my ticket to college, Mother."

Her mother stared at the sparkling stone as if hypnotized. "You didn't return it?"

"I did not." Tish began to laugh, a low rumbling chuckle. "He wanted it back, all right. Nearly wrestled me to the ground for it. But I told him that I was a low-class working woman, just like my mother. And that I had earned it."

"He'll find a way to get it back."

"No, he won't. Philip's too proud to admit that I got the better of him. He'll never mention it again. And in the meantime, I'll be enrolling in college to get my teacher's certification."

Letitia's mother took the diamond ring and examined it. "It's very valuable, you know."

"Money's only valuable for what it can buy, Mother," Tish said. "A very wise woman told me that—about a thousand times in the past seventeen years."

"So you did listen?"

"Once in a great while. But I promise I'll pay attention more carefully in the future."

Mother squinted at the stone and turned it this way and that. "And what is this diamond going to buy, my darling daughter?"

Tish shrugged. She knew the answer, but she pretended to think about it before she answered. After a long silence she said, "Liberty, Mother. Freedom."

And she knew it was true. How many women in this world chose gilded shackles and gem-encrusted prison cells rather than taking the risk to be true to themselves? It had almost happened to her. On her finger, that ring represented bondage to a life—and a man—completely unsuited to her. Without it, she was free to become the person she wanted to be, to do what she was destined to do.

Free, she silently hoped, to become *just like Maris*.

10
ENGAGEMENT PARTY

April 5, 1930

Tish stood in the kitchen doorway and peered into the huge dining room of the Dorn residence, fighting back tears. She hadn't expected this to hurt so much.

The massive mahogany table groaned under the enormous spread she and Mother had laid out—cakes and pies and petits fours, little sandwiches of watercress and cucumber and chicken salad, homemade sweetbreads and her mother's famous tomato aspic. Fresh flowers overflowed from silver urns on the sideboard, and a hundred candles, at least, shed their wavering, romantic light over the scene.

It had taken Philip Dorn exactly one month and four days to find himself a new fiancée, and this was their engagement party. But instead of being the center of the festivities, as she should have been—decked out in a golden dress and smiling with happy promise—Letitia Cameron had been relegated to a gray maid's uniform and stationed in the kitchen.

In the parlor beyond the dining room, the sounds of music and laughter drifted to her ears. She recognized Adora Archer's high-pitched giggle and the low, rumbling voice of Pastor Archer. A champagne cork popped, and everyone applauded. "A toast!" someone shouted. "To the happy couple!"

Tish couldn't see Philip, but she could imagine him, tall and handsome in his tuxedo, grinning broadly and showing his dimples while Marcella Covington hung on his arm and gushed with pride. Marcella? How could he! Marcella was just a homely little wallflower with pallid skin and huge dark eyes—the girl who couldn't get a date to save her soul. She wore her mouse-colored hair pulled back like a skullcap, and she was so painfully thin that on her, even custom-designed dresses looked like charity castoffs.

But her family had money and connections. Her grandfather, people said, had been some crony of George Washington Vanderbilt's and had been a frequent guest at that ostentatious monstrosity, the Biltmore House. Old Mr. Covington apparently liked the mountains and decided to take up residence here, and Vanderbilt sold him a plot of land that made him a bundle as the city expanded. The rumor now circulating was that Cornelia Vanderbilt Cecil, current resident of Biltmore, had been approached by the city fathers about opening the house for public tours. But before that happened, there would be a wedding to end all weddings in the atrium—the nuptials of Philip Dorn and Marcella Covington.

It was just the kind of thing, Tish figured, that Philip would go for. Lots of glitz and glamor. High-profile guests, in the country's largest and most elaborate private home. Never mind that Marcella had the looks of a ferret and all the charm and personality of a slab of Swiss cheese. She had social acceptability, and that was enough for Philip.

Through the doorway Tish caught a glimpse of a skeletal form swallowed up in a blue satin gown. That would be Marcella. The dress looked as if it were still hanging on the rack.

Tish tried to drum up some ill will toward her—if not outright hatred, at least a little rancor. But all she could feel was pity. The girl might have money and prestige and a permanent place on the social register, but she also had Philip. And that was bound to cause her no end of heartache.

"Are you all right, honey?"

Tish turned to see her mother slicing cake at the kitchen counter. "I guess so."

"Feeling left out?"

"A little. At first it hurt, being here and seeing Philip's engagement party. As if I should be the one being the center of attention—even though I wouldn't want to marry him, you know?"

"I know."

"I wanted to hate Marcella, Mother. I'm ashamed to admit it, but it's true. But now, seeing her with him, I just—well, I just feel sorry for her."

"No regrets?"

Tish shrugged. "Well, I wouldn't mind having *my* wedding at the Biltmore. Is it true, that they're going to have the ceremony in the atrium?"

"That's what I've heard," her mother said. "Cornelia Cecil is here, you know. She's fawning over Marcella as if the girl was a long-lost niece."

Tish sighed. "What really hurts, I think, is seeing Adora out there with the guests while I'm stuck in the kitchen."

"Adora is still your friend, Letitia," her mother countered. "Did you expect her to turn down the invitation?"

"As much as Adora loves parties?" Tish laughed. "I don't think so. But did you notice who's *not* here?"

Mother nodded. "Eleanor James and her daughter."

Tish backed into the kitchen and began helping her mother arrange cake slices on a crystal platter. "I didn't expect Mary Love to be invited, even though she and Marcella are in the same class. But Ellie has known Philip nearly as long as I have, and Big Eleanor has been a pillar of Asheville society—and a friend of the Dorns—forever."

"Times change, honey. Mrs. James is having a difficult time adjusting, I understand."

"So Ellie says. The loss of their money was bad enough. But to be snubbed like this—"

"She blames your father, doesn't she?"

Tish averted her eyes. "Maybe just a little. But it's worse than that, Mother. Ellie says she's just—well, not right."

What Ellie had actually said was that Big Eleanor had gone over the edge. She had stopped eating and almost never slept. She wandered the house at all hours of the day and night and once Ellie found her in her nightgown out in the street at three in the morning. Maybe it was for her own good, Tish mused, that Big Eleanor had ceased receiving invitations to society functions.

The kitchen door swung open and Alice Dorn entered under full sail. "Everything is wonderful, Maris! Our guests are absolutely ecstatic over those petits fours!"

Mother blushed. "Thank you, Alice," she murmured. "We worked very hard on them."

"Mrs. Dorn," Alice corrected.

Tish looked at her mother and saw the flush fade. Mother's face had gone stark white. "Excuse me?"

Alice gave a high, tittering laugh. "Well, even though we've known each other for a long time, I don't think it's quite proper for you to call me by my given name, do you? All the servants call me 'Mrs. Dorn'—what would Cornelia Vanderbilt say if she heard me being overly familiar with the help?"

"Cecil," Mother corrected tersely. "Her married name is Cecil."

Alice's eyes narrowed, and when she spoke again, her voice was like ice crystals. "A Vanderbilt is always a Vanderbilt," she said haughtily. "You may serve coffee now. And do keep your daughter out of sight; we wouldn't want her presence upsetting Philip and Marcella."

Tish could tell that her mother was beginning a slow burn, but Mother didn't say a word. She simply poured coffee into the silver serving urn and nodded. "Yes, ma'am."

"And make sure you clean up thoroughly. The parlor rug will need sweeping."

With that, she was gone, the door swinging shut behind her.

"Can you believe that?" Tish fumed when Alice was gone. "The way she treated you, Mother—how could you just stand there and take it?"

"Times change," Mother repeated quietly. "And we have to change with them."

⟡

Times had changed, all right.

At noon on Sunday, the day after the engagement party, Tish and her mother stood in the fellowship hall after church, sipping punch and nibbling on the leftover petits fours Alice Dorn had brought. Everyone was milling around, as usual—chatting and smiling and being friendly.

Except, Tish suddenly realized, to them. She saw it as if she had been lifted bodily into the rafters and could survey the whole room at a glance. Over there, against the far wall, the women's circle that normally met at their house clustered with their backs to the room, and every now and then one of them would turn and look in Mother's direction. Pastor Archer, who usually made a point of speaking to every single one of his parishioners, steadfastly avoided the corner where she and her mother stood. Twice she saw people point at the two of them and whisper behind their hands.

Only Adora actually came over and spoke to them—and even then it wasn't the kind of natural interaction born of long friendship. Tish couldn't remember what she had said, only that her voice was high and tense. Defiant, Tish decided finally. As if she were deliberately flaunting their friendship for the benefit of someone looking on.

She didn't understand it. The Camerons had been members of Downtown Presbyterian for years. Mother was head of the social committee and hosted one of the women's circles in their home. When the church had purchased the Catholic cathedral, Daddy had supported the renovations with generous financial gifts and a good deal of time and effort. These people were, well, family of a sort—the folks they depended on, socialized with. Nearly every person the Camerons had ever called "friend" was in this very room—with the exception of Ellie and her mother, who hadn't been to church in weeks.

Now it seemed as if they were standing on the outside of a clear glass bubble, able to see in but unable to get past the barrier that separated them from the goings-on inside.

Tish caught a glimpse of movement out of the corner of her eye and turned to see Alice Dorn bearing down on them. The expression on her face, halfway between a smile and a grimace, showed all her teeth and half her gums. Funny how Tish had never noticed what a terrible underbite the woman had.

"Maris, dear!" Alice fastened a hand on Mother's elbow and steered her farther into the corner.

"Mrs. Dorn." With an arch of one eyebrow Mother extracted her arm from Alice's grasp.

"The girls and I have been talking, dear. They're all aware of how hard you've been working and"— her eyes darted to the group across the room— "how difficult it must be for you to keep up. We've decided that you shouldn't bear the burden of heading up the social committee any longer. Roberta Weston is going to take that job over. Now, I'm sure that little house of yours is very sweet," she went on in a rush before Mother had time to interrupt, "but of course you no longer have room to host the women's circle properly." She let out a piercing little giggle. "No, now, don't thank me, dear—we're just trying to be considerate of your busy schedule. Don't worry your little head about it."

Alice began to move away before Mother could respond. "Oh, by the way," she called over her shoulder, "we'll be changing the day of the circle meeting too, but I don't know just when or where at the moment. I'll let you know, all right? All right, then. Bye-bye."

Letitia moved closer and put an arm around her mother's shoulders. "She'll never call you about that circle, will she?"

"No." Mother sighed. Tish followed her gaze toward the door, where Pastor Archer stood with his wife at his side, shaking hands with people as they left. He looked up, and for a moment his gaze fixed on them and froze, as if time had stood still. Then he lowered his eyes and turned a brilliant smile on Philip Dorn and Marcella Covington, clapping Philip on the shoulder and giving Marcella a kiss on the cheek.

Mother looked around. The fellowship hall had begun to empty out, leaving behind a litter of punch cups and napkins and crumbs from the petit fours. "Someone else can clean this mess up," she muttered under her breath. Then she took Tish by the elbow and headed for the side door.

"Where are we going?" Tish whispered. In all the years they had been attending Downtown Presbyterian, her mother had never left the fellowship hall until the last plate had been washed and the last crumb swept away. "The fellowship hour isn't over yet."

"It's over for us," her mother hissed through gritted teeth. "It was over the minute your father died. Now come on—we're going home."

11
COMMENCEMENT

May 18, 1930

Letitia stood next to Adora Archer and adjusted the neckline of her new dress. Mother wasn't nearly as adept at the treadle sewing machine as she was in the kitchen, but she had done an admirable job, all things considered. The dress was just a shade off white, with a lace-overlaid bodice and cap sleeves.

"That's a beautiful dress, Tish," Adora said.

"Thank you. Mother made it." Tish offered the confession boldly, without a twinge of embarrassment in the admission. Time was, and not so long ago, that she wouldn't have been caught dead in a dress of her mother's making, or at the very least, would never have admitted it. Now, it seemed, her mother's ingenuity was a source of pride, not shame. Things change, Mother said. Indeed they did.

Adora reached up and adjusted the gold locket around Letitia's neck—a graduation gift purchased with her mother's hard-earned money. "I've missed you at church."

"You're no doubt the only one." Tish smiled to take the edge off her caustic reply. "Sorry. I just meant—"

"I know what you meant, and you're right. I wouldn't want to go there and be snubbed every Sunday, either. But I miss you, all the same."

"Ellie and her mother haven't come back either, have they?"

Adora shook her head. "Big Eleanor never leaves the house, and most of the time—when she's not in school, anyway—Ellie is stuck there with her. Daddy went to visit a couple of times, but apparently his efforts to get Big

Eleanor out of her depression didn't work. Besides, he's got his hands full with everything that's going on."

"Such as?"

"You wouldn't believe it, Tish. All sorts of people are coming, more of them every Sunday. People in rags, practically, who stand in the bread lines during the week. Some of the ladies have actually come to Daddy to complain about the smell."

Letitia suppressed a laugh. She could just see Alice Dorn holding a lace hankie over her nose and trying to escape before her designer dress was soiled by brushing shoulders with the unwashed multitudes. The past few months had instilled in Tish a sense of empathy with the poor souls who had no jobs, no food, no decent place to live. And she rather enjoyed the idea of Alice's discomfort at being forced to fraternize with the down-and-out in the name of the Lord.

"Tish! Adora!" Ellie and Mary Love appeared, as if from nowhere. "You both look so *beautiful*! Are you nervous?"

"Nervous about what?" Adora asked. "You go up, get your diploma, and that's all there is to it. I was *nervous* about final exams. Once you get past them, graduation is a cakewalk."

"Well, I'll be nervous next year when it's my turn," Eleanor admitted.

"That's because you'll be valedictorian and have to give a speech."

"Oh, but it's a wonderful time, a watershed event," Mary Love said. "It's one of the biggest moments of your life. The commencement of adulthood. It's like a rite of passage, the dawning of a new day, where—"

Ellie laughed and clamped a hand over Mary Love's mouth. "If we went to the same school, you can bet I'd let *her* give the speech."

The music started, and the graduates began to shuffle to find their places in line. "I've got to go back to the C's," Tish said. "Now, don't forget—we're having a little party at our house afterward. Mother's been cooking all weekend."

"We'll be there!" Ellie and Mary Love ran off to take their seats.

Adora put a hand on Tish's arm. "I am sorry about the church thing. And sorry we haven't seen more of each other lately. Forgive me?"

"There's nothing to forgive," Letitia murmured. "It wasn't your fault." She drew Adora into a hug. "You're my best friend, and nothing can change that."

"I hope not."

Tish made her way to her place in line and stood waiting as the strains of "Pomp and Circumstance" moved them forward. She had missed Adora too—and Ellie and Mary Love. So many things had changed since Christmas Day, when they shared their dreams and made their pact of friendship. Less than five months ago, everything had seemed so perfect, so well planned out. But times were changing, almost more quickly than they could keep up with the changes.

There would be no society wedding for Tish, no big house, no Philip, no children to give herself to. The society she had grown up in had rejected her. All of it had unraveled in a single moment with her father's death.

And not just for Tish, either. Now Eleanor spent most of her time taking care of her mother, and Mary Love worked harder than ever to help the family make ends meet. Adora's world was changing too, in a church that didn't know quite how to accommodate an influx of desperate, destitute people.

But for a little while, this afternoon, they would all be together again. And it would be just like old times.

⟡

Mother had worked miracles with the tiny garden. The last of the pink tulips bloomed in beds along the low stone wall, and tall purple irises rose up against the side of the house. Yellow pansies overflowed from a crumbling stone planter, and a terraced rock garden boasted pink, blue, and white creeping phlox and clumps of yellow and purple Johnny-jump-ups.

In the center of the garden, on a small brick patio, a table was spread with a lace cloth and adorned with a vase of wildflowers. It was perfect. Absolutely perfect.

Mother set out the food, let the girls fend for themselves, and disappeared into the parlor.

At two o'clock Ellie and Mary Love arrived together, and Adora appeared a few minutes later. Letitia gave them a quick tour of the house and then led them out into the garden.

"This is beautiful!" Mary Love said. "Why, it's like a little dollhouse."

"It's home, and it's enough for me and Mother." Tish heard her own words as if someone else had spoken them. And she knew them to be true.

The little carriage house, despite its limited space and modest furnishings, had become more truly home than the big house on Montford Avenue had ever been. It was the space she and her mother had created for themselves, the place in which they had found each other again—as mother and daughter, and as friends.

"Why haven't we done this before?" Ellie said as she bit into a flaky cream horn.

"Eat everything in sight, you mean?" Mary Love laughed and wiped a dollop of cream off Ellie's nose.

"No, silly. I mean, it's been months since we all got together like this. I'm ashamed, Tish, truly ashamed, that we haven't been to visit you before now."

Letitia brushed the comment aside. "We've all been busy. And, well, life seems to be a little different now than it once was."

Her comment sobered the group of friends, and they fell silent. After a while, Mary Love leaned forward and said, "I'm sorry about you and Philip, Tish."

"Sorry?" Tish burst out. "Don't be!" At Mary Love's astonished look, she went on. "Oh, it was hard at first, I'll admit. But once I saw what Philip was really like, I felt a little like Houdini escaping from that underwater coffin." She grinned. "Everybody thought Philip Dorn was such a catch. And I guess he is"—she paused—"if you want to catch the plague."

Laughter broke the ice, and soon they were all talking at once, as if the past five months had never happened. Letitia looked around the circle and smiled. *Fiancées come and go,* she thought. *But good friends are forever.*

"So," Ellie said, "Adora tells us you're going to college now?"

Tish nodded. "Part-time, at least. I'll still be helping Mother with her catering, but I'm going to get my teaching certification."

"A spinster schoolteacher, is that it?" Adora winked at her.

"Well, I wouldn't go quite that far," Tish protested. "Just because Philip Dorn is out of the picture doesn't exactly mean I am. I'll find someone, someday. Someone a great deal nicer than snobby old Philip. But in the meantime, a girl's got to make a living."

"I think a lot about that day we all put our dreams in the bottle," Mary Love said wistfully. "I know things have changed, but I agree with Tish—it's too soon to give up those plans."

Eleanor smiled pensively. "I still have hopes," she murmured, "of becoming a social worker like Jane Addams. Mother needs me right now, of course, but when she gets better—"

Adora chose a sandwich from the platter and held it up, surveying it with a faraway gaze. "Well, I've made a decision to follow my dream right now, no matter what."

"And just what does that mean?" Mary Love demanded.

Adora reached in the pocket of her dress and drew out a slim folder. "This," she said dramatically, "is a bus ticket. To Hollywood, California." She waved it in the air. "I'm leaving, girls. I'm going to the West Coast to find my destiny."

"To *California*?" The reality hit Tish like a body blow. Her best friend was going to get on a bus and go all the way across the country to become an actress in the talkies! She had dreamed about it, Tish knew—they all knew—but now she actually intended to *do* it. To defy her father, to leave everything behind, including her friends. Panic gripped her, accompanied by a sudden overwhelming sense of loss and loneliness. "When will you be back?"

"Never, I hope." Adora put the ticket back in her pocket and leaned over the table. "You have to promise—all of you—that you won't tell my father. I'm leaving tomorrow night. Mama has her women's circle, and Daddy has a church board meeting. I'll be halfway through Arkansas before they even know I'm gone."

"Your father will have a stroke." Ellie's dire prediction echoed Tish's thoughts.

"He'll get over it. I'm not a child. I'm eighteen years old, with a high school diploma. I can go where I want and do what I want, and no one can stop me."

Tears sprang up in Tish's eyes, and she blinked them back. "We'll never see you again?"

"Don't be silly," Adora scoffed. "I'll write to you—to all of you. And when I'm famous, I'll send you a ticket and you can come see me."

"But where will you live? What will you do?"

"I've got it all planned." Adora let out a long breath. "I read about this boardinghouse that caters to young actresses. I've got the address and everything. I have a little money saved up—not much, but enough for a

month or two. By then I'll be working and—you'll see, it will be wonderful!
A real adventure, with no one to tell me what to do or how to behave."

"Adora, you're so brave!" Mary Love sighed. "You're really going to follow your dream, just like you wrote for the bottle."

At Mary Love's words, a stab of envy shot through Letitia's heart. It might
be a foolhardy stunt borne of rebellion against her father's conservative
ways, but Adora was, at least, taking the risk. You had to admire her for her
courage.

"So then," Ellie summarized in her no-nonsense manner. "This is a
farewell party as well as a graduation celebration. Let's make the best of it,
girls." She lifted her lemonade in a toast. "To our dreams," she said. "May
they all come true."

"To our dreams."

Letitia raised her glass with the rest of them and cut a glance at Eleanor.
She was smiling, but her eyes held the haunted look of one who knew too
well the hopelessness of her own cherished dreams.

12
COUNT YOUR BLESSINGS

November 24, 1943

"Miss Cam-*ron*! Miss Cam-*ron*!"

Letitia turned from the window to see a dark-haired boy bouncing in his seat, his hand waving frantically. "You have to go to the bathroom *again*, Stuart?"

"No, no, no!" he said impatiently. His eyebrows met across his forehead like the wings of a crow, furrowing his little face into a scowl. "I just can't—" He threw his crayon onto the desk and folded his arms in front of him. "What's a *blessing*, anyway?"

Tish moved to the center of the room and leaned against her desk. "A blessing," she said as a dozen heads lifted to look at her, "is something good in our lives. Something we give thanks for." She paused. "Tomorrow is Thanksgiving Day, the day we celebrate our blessings. Can anyone give Stuart an example of a blessing?"

Timmy Marshall—in her mind Letitia called him "Timid"—raised his hand cautiously. "You mean, like, we don't have to come to school tomorrow? That's a blessing, isn't it?"

Everyone laughed. "Yes, that's a blessing," Letitia responded with a chuckle. "What else?"

"Our homes are a blessing," Cynthia Tatum chimed in with a toss of her head. She patted her blonde curls in a gesture Letitia recognized all too well. "And the food we have to eat, and our brothers and sisters—"

"My little sister ain't no blessing," someone called.

"*Isn't* a blessing," Tish corrected automatically.

Cynthia, however, was not to be deterred by the interruption. "And our mothers and fathers, and our friends, and the big turkey we'll have for dinner tomorrow, and—"

"Very good, Cynthia. But let's give someone else a chance, all right?"

"My daddy says it would be a blessing if somebody shot that Hitler guy in the head." This came from Mickey Lawhead in the back of the room, a little hoodlum-in-training who was always going on about killing something or someone. It would be nothing short of a miracle, Tish thought, if that boy didn't end up in the federal penitentiary before he ever graduated from high school.

"Yes, Mickey," she said with an exaggerated sigh, "I've heard others say that. But let's try not to talk about killing people, just for today." She looked around the room. "Anyone else?"

"Mama says being a wife and mother is her greatest blessing," tiny Anna Shepherd ventured shyly. "She's going to have another baby in January."

Tish turned back to Stuart. "Does any of this help, Stuart?"

"I dunno." He shrugged. "I don't think I *have* any blessings, and I wouldn't know how to draw one if I knew what it was."

She patted him on the shoulder. "Well, give it a try, okay?"

Tish turned back to the window as her students resumed their artwork. Blessings. How do you communicate to a ten-year-old about blessings and thankfulness? Half these children were so poor that they barely had shoes on their feet and clothes on their backs. A few, like Stuart, came from wealthy homes but didn't comprehend the privileges they took for granted.

Still, every time she laid eyes on Stuart, her heart swelled with a mixture of conflicting emotions. He was so like his father—well-built and handsome, with dark hair and eyes, white, even teeth, and dimples that appeared when he smiled. But the smiles were few and far between, she realized. Stuart Dorn seemed like a very unhappy child.

His unhappiness manifested itself in a number of ways that stymied her as his teacher. He had an arrogant streak—one he came by honestly enough—and tended to bully the other children. And where learning was concerned, Stuart was his own worst enemy. He read well enough, but if he didn't catch on to a new concept right away, he became frustrated, even hostile. She could almost see the walls go up. With very little provocation, Stuart could sabotage the simplest of tasks—like this art assignment, to draw a representation of your blessings. Ever since the beginning of the year she had been racking her brain to find a way to help him, but to no avail.

A voice drew her out of her reverie. "Miss Cameron," Anna said in her whispery voice, "do you have any blessings?"

"Well, yes, I have lots of blessings." She turned to find every eye trained on her.

"Are you gonna have a turkey tomorrow?"

"Yes, we are—a small one. It will be just the two of us—"

"You and your *hus-band*?" Cynthia drew out the word in a singsong voice and grinned slyly, as if she knew all about what husbands and wives did on their days off.

"Me and my mother," Tish corrected.

"Your *mother*!" Mickey scoffed. "You still live with your *mother*? But you're so *old*!"

"Of course she lives with her mother," someone called from the back. "That's what spinster schoolteachers do."

Letitia flinched at the word *spinster,* but she supposed it was true. Just turned thirty-one and still single, she would, to these ten-year-olds, seem like an old maid. A very old one.

"You're not married?" Cynthia pursued the issue like a cat toying with a mouse. "Why not? Didn't anybody ever ask you?"

Letitia considered her reply. She probably should nip this discussion of her personal life in the bud immediately, but something in her balked at the idea of putting a stop to it. Children were naturally curious; she had spent the past ten years defending that curiosity, encouraging it. Former students, now nearly grown, had written letters to her, expressing gratitude to her for teaching them how to think, how to explore for themselves. A few had even come back to thank her face to face.

"No, I'm not married," she said at last. "Some people, both women and men, choose not to get married. But single people can live fulfilling, productive, happy lives, just like married people."

"Not all married people are happy," Stuart muttered under his breath.

Letitia gazed at him, and tears filled her eyes. So that was it. Rumors circulated freely in a town this small, especially when they concerned one of the community's wealthiest and most visible citizens. She had heard the gossip about Philip's drinking, about other women, about shouting matches in the middle of the night and slammed doors and unexplained bruises on Marcella's arms and face. She had even seen Marcella a time or two—thinner than ever and deathly pale, with dark circles under her eyes.

No wonder the child showed up at school dead tired and barely able to focus. And no wonder he couldn't think of a single blessing for his Thanksgiving picture, despite the money and the social status and the big house. None of that mattered to children. What mattered to them was love.

Tish took a deep breath and composed her thoughts. "All right," she said at last, "let's talk about it." She fixed her eyes on little Stuart, who gazed up at her with an expression of unutterable pain and hopelessness. "When I was very young—"

The class came to immediate attention, and she smiled. She didn't know whether it was because they couldn't imagine her being young, or because they simply liked to be told stories, but they waited eagerly, as if they were sure this was going to be interesting.

"When I was very young," she repeated, "I was engaged to be married."

A gasp went through the room. "Really?"

"Really." Letitia slid up onto the desk and sat quiet for a moment. "I thought the most wonderful thing in the world would be to marry this young man and have children."

"Like my mama," Anna interjected.

"Like your mama." Tish nodded. "But then some very bad things happened. My father died, and life got difficult for my mother and me." She shrugged. "We didn't have a lot of money, and we both had to work very hard. The marriage never happened."

"Did your heart get broken?" Cynthia asked.

"My heart hurt for a while," Tish admitted. "And I was very angry at God. I had prayed, you see, that my dreams of marrying this young man would come true. When they *didn't* come true, I blamed God. But later on I found out that God had something even better in mind for me."

"Somebody even better to love you, like the prince riding up to rescue Sleeping Beauty?" Cynthia, a confirmed romantic, was totally absorbed in the story. Clearly she wanted it to come out happily ever after.

"Yes, but not the way you mean." She looked toward Stuart and smiled. "Life doesn't always turn out the way we hope," she said softly. "Stuart is right: Sometimes married people aren't happier. I discovered that I could be happier unmarried than married, that even when bad things happen, there are blessings to be enjoyed and appreciated. We just have to open our eyes to see them."

"But you never got to be a mother," Anna protested.

"I never had the opportunity to have children of *my own*," Letitia corrected. "But look around. How many children do I have, right here in this class?"

"Twenty," Timothy answered. "I counted."

"Yes, twenty. And I've been teaching for ten years. How many does that make?"

Tish could almost see the calculations going on in little brains. A few students even scratched the numbers in crayon on the side of their art paper. At last Mickey Lawhead called out, "Two hundred!"

"Very good, Mickey. Two hundred children. That's a lot of blessings."

Stuart looked up at her, and tears stood in his eyes. "We're your blessings?"

"Oh, yes, Stuart." Letitia swallowed against the lump that had formed in her throat. "You're my blessing. All of you—and you're the best blessings anyone could ever want."

⌒⌒

The three o'clock bell had rung, signaling the end of the school day. Letitia had said her good-byes and wished them a Happy Thanksgiving, but now, as she erased the blackboard with her back turned to the desks, she could feel a presence in the room.

She turned. Stuart Dorn still sat at his desk, his little feet banging against the legs of the chair.

"Stuart? It's time to go."

"I know."

She came to him and perched on the back of a chair. "Is something wrong?"

"Did you mean it when you said we were your blessings?" His eyes searched hers, looking for something.

Tish squeezed his arm. "Of course I meant it, Stuart. I became a teacher because I love children. At the time, I thought I would teach for a few years and then get married and have children of my own, but as I told the class earlier, that just didn't happen for me. Still, it turned out even better than I could have dreamed. I have so many children, and every one of them a blessing."

She watched his face for some sign of understanding, and her heart wrenched with love and pity. She couldn't tell him, this bright, anxious child, that he might, under different circumstances, have been her own son.

And what would she do if he *were* her own son, if *she* were the one married to Philip Dorn instead of poor Marcella? Would she have the courage to take him away, find a safe place for him and for herself, leave behind the terror and security of Philip's big house and the Dorn fortune? She'd like to think that she would protect this fragile child, that she would be the mother he needed, a tigress of a mother who would defend him and shield him from harm, no matter what the cost.

But to be perfectly honest, Letitia wasn't sure. Fortune and social status and financial security were powerful, seductive forces. Had she married Philip, she might have allowed him to browbeat her into silence and submission, as he obviously had done to Marcella. And even without the money, she might have stayed just to spare herself the humiliation of admitting the truth.

She couldn't lay the blame at Marcella's feet. And she couldn't do much about the fear and hopelessness that haunted this poor child's young life. All she could do was be his teacher—and, perhaps, his friend.

"Things are pretty tough at home, aren't they, Stuart." It wasn't a question.

His eyes widened. "It was him, wasn't it? My father. The man you almost married."

How could he have known that? Had Philip said something, in an argument with Marcella, perhaps, that the boy had overheard?

Stuart answered the question before she had a chance to ask it. "Mama said so. They were yelling, and she said that if he wanted a pretty wife, he should have married you when he had the chance." He looked up at her, and tears pooled in his big brown eyes. "Is it true?"

Letitia hesitated, but she knew what her answer had to be. She would be honest with this child if it tore her heart apart. "Yes. It was a long time ago."

A tear rolled down his cheek. "I wish—" He paused, obviously apprehensive of speaking his mind.

"Wish what?"

"I wish you were my mother." He frowned and swiped at his eyes. "Well, I sort of wish it. For me, not you. It would be awful for you."

Tish put her hand under his chin and lifted his face to meet her gaze. He was so like Philip in some ways—when he grew up he would be handsome and charming, the most eligible bachelor in three counties. But he was unlike his father too. He was sweet and sensitive and sad. Even at this young age he worried about other people's feelings.

"Stuart, I want to tell you something."

"Yes, ma'am?"

"We all have wishes—dreams and ambitions and longings—for our lives. Some of them come true, and some of them don't. When they don't, try to remember that God may have something better for you than what you asked for."

His expression grew fierce. "Isn't God supposed to protect us from bad things?"

Letitia suppressed a smile. Where had such wisdom, such insight come from in a child so young? "Some people believe that," she said. "They believe that God is supposed to keep us from ever getting hurt. But think about this, Stuart. You have a little sister, right?"

"Uh-huh. She's five."

"Do you remember when she was learning to walk?"

He scratched his head. "Yeah. She was terrible at it. She kept falling down."

"Then why did your mother allow her to keep trying? If she fell down and hurt herself, kept scraping her knees and crying, why didn't your mother just pick her up and carry her?"

He looked at Tish as if this were the dumbest idea anyone had ever come up with. "Because then she'd *never* learn to walk! Somebody would have to carry her around for the rest of her life."

"Exactly." Letitia nodded. "And God doesn't always protect us from getting banged up and bruised, either. God doesn't always let our wishes come true. And sometimes that's for the best."

A memory surfaced, an image she hadn't thought about in years. A cobalt blue bottle, holding the dreams of four young girls, secreted away in the rafters of Cameron House. A prayer that God would make those dreams come true. That prayer hadn't been answered—or had it?

Tish smiled and tousled the dark head. "You'd better be getting on home now." She peered at him intently. "Are you all right?"

He nodded. "Thanks, Miss Cameron. And I guess I don't really wish you were my mother, 'cause then you couldn't be my teacher."

He lifted the top of his desk, pulled out a sheet of art paper, and with a sheepish grin handed it over to her. "See ya," he said.

Then he was gone.

Tish took the paper to the window and held it up to the watery afternoon light. It was a rather good likeness, she thought. A picture of her sitting at her desk with the blackboard behind her and a big red apple in front of her. He had gotten the colors almost right—her hair a little more vibrant shade of strawberry blonde than its present faded color, her eyes a bit more brilliant than the natural gray-green she saw in the mirror every morning. But there was no doubt who it was.

And just in case she didn't recognize herself, a message printed in a careful, childish hand across the bottom:

My Thanksgiving Blessing is Miss Cameron. Love, Stuart D.

13
LETITIA'S DREAM

October 12, 1994

A nd so," Letitia finished, "I guess that's all there is to tell. I don't know
where the years went. They just slipped away, I suppose, while I was
teaching all those children. I never felt old, not once, as long as I stood in
front of a classroom and saw those eager little faces looking up at me. Then,
out of the blue, they came one day and told me it was time to retire. And I
was still . . ." She sighed. "*Miss* Cameron."

Brendan reached to turn off the tape recorder, then thought better about
it and left it running. Sometime during the story—Brendan didn't know
when—Gert had returned with the groceries and now hovered in the background like a protective angel. The light outside was fading, and all her
muscles had gone stiff from sitting on the sagging couch.

Letitia reached over and patted her arm. "I suppose it's a pretty unevent-
ful story, considering the kind of work you do. You know, murders and car
wrecks and all that." She waved a trembling hand. "Quite a disappointment,
I'd expect."

"Disappointment?" Brendan chuckled. "No, Miss Letitia, I wouldn't call
this a disappointment. It's a fascinating story."

Letitia smiled. "They gave me a wonderful life, my children."

"I wonder whatever happened to little Stuart Dorn."

"Oh, you don't have to wonder, child. I know what happened to him."

Brendan sat up, her weary mind suddenly thrust into full alertness.
"Well?"

Letitia rubbed at her forehead with one arthritic hand. "He was ten years

old when he attended my class—that was in '43. Right out of high school
he enlisted in the army and went overseas—Korea, I think. Yes, Korea.
Anything to get away from home." Her faded green eyes took on a faraway
expression. "Came back three years later"— she began to laugh—"with a
Korean bride."

Brendan let out a gasp. "Not really!"

"Yes, he did. Prettiest little thing you ever did see. His father was livid."

"I can imagine, given what you've told me about Philip."

"Philip disowned him on the spot. The two of them eventually moved
out to Washington state and never, to my knowledge, returned again. When
Marcella passed away a year or two later, Brendan's little sister, too, shook
the dust of this town off her feet and never came back."

"And Philip?"

"Philip died in 1982, all alone in that big house on Edwin Avenue. Liver
disease, I think they said, from years of alcoholism." She let out a sigh. "He
was a broken, bitter man."

"So you have no regrets about not marrying him."

"Heavens no, child. I came to peace about that a long time ago." Her head
bobbed up and down. "As my children might say, I dodged a bullet. I say—
well, that God kept me from making the biggest mistake of my life."

"Even though your dreams were never realized?"

Letitia's head snapped up and fire flashed through her eyes. "Haven't you
been listening? I had my children—hundreds, maybe thousands of them.
I loved them, I taught them, I helped them grow into good, upstanding men
and women. God answered my prayers—well, most of them, anyway. All
but one."

"And that was—?"

"You reporters can't help but focus on the negative, can you? It must be
something in your constitution." She gave a little huff of disgust and went
on. "After a while, I didn't care so much about being married. It was the
other part of the dream that bothered me the most."

Brendan leaned forward. "Go on."

"The girls, of course. Adora and Ellie and Mary Love." She shook her
head despondently. "We made a solemn vow always to be friends, to care
for each other and support each other. But we lost touch. We drifted apart.
That's the solitary thing I regret in this life—not keeping that vow."

Brendan looked at the old woman and saw in her face an expression of deep sorrow and longing. She wanted to comfort Letitia, to assure her that her God didn't hold her accountable for what had happened to the others. But the words wouldn't come. Instead she just moved to Letitia's chair, perched on the arm, and stroked the old woman's hair. It was soft and white, like cotton candy, and just touching it brought back memories of her grandmother, the love and safety Gram had provided when Mama and Daddy died, the years of encouragement for her to follow her own dreams, to fulfill her own destiny.

At last she said, "It must have been difficult for you when Adora Archer died. She was so young, and she had been your best friend—"

Letitia jerked around and stared at Brendan as if she had lost her mind. "Adora didn't *die*," she spat out venomously.

"But I was told that she died of influenza as a young woman, up east, where she went to—" Brendan stopped as the truth sank in. Adora hadn't gone up east. She had gone to *California*. There had been no body, no funeral, Dorothy Foster had said. Just a brief memorial service and a father who never again spoke her name.

"You mean her father—"

Letitia nodded. "Her father concocted the story about her going to college in an attempt to protect his own reputation. After all, what would people think of him if he couldn't control his own daughter? Then he lied and told people she had died—had a service for her and everything. I didn't go, of course—Mother and I had long since left Downtown Presbyterian and joined a little Methodist church where the people at least made an effort to act like Christians. I didn't even see the obituary in the newspaper until it was all over and done with."

Brendan closed her eyes and tried to imagine what kind of father would turn his back on his daughter like that. Then a thought struck her—a long shot, but a possibility nevertheless.

"Did you hear from her—Adora, I mean? Once she went to California?"

Letitia nodded. "Fairly regularly at first, long newsy letters full of her hopes for becoming a star. Then suddenly, a few months after she left, they stopped."

"Just like that?"

"Like turning off a faucet. I tried to write to her, but my letters kept coming back, so eventually I gave up. It was like she had dropped off the face of the earth."

Brendan's shoulders slumped. "And you never heard from her again."

"Did I say that? Child, you must stop putting words into other people's mouths. It's not an attractive habit for anyone, let alone a reporter." She waggled a finger under Brendan's nose and continued. "A few years back—maybe ten or fifteen years ago—I started getting Christmas cards, but with no return address. Then this—"

She motioned for Brendan to help her up and shuffled over to a small desk. After rummaging through a couple of drawers she came up with a picture postcard and handed it over. It had been forwarded three times before it finally got delivered.

"Flat Rock Playhouse?" Brendan held the card to the window and tried to make out the spidery writing. "It says—"

"*Old dreamers never die,*" Letitia supplied.

"Do you suppose she's alive, living in Flat Rock?" Brendan's heart raced as she made two circuits of the small living room. "That's less than forty-five minutes from here!"

Letitia came back to the chair and eased herself to a sitting position. "I'm not stupid, child. I tried to call, but Information didn't have a number for her. And I'm too old to go wandering all over Henderson County trying to find a needle in a haystack."

Brendan grinned. "But I'm not."

Letitia's face brightened, and suddenly she looked ten years younger. "You'd do that? For me?"

"For you," Brendan said, squeezing Letitia's wrinkled hand. "And for me."

The old woman closed her eyes and let her head sag back against the chair. She was clearly exhausted. After a minute or two Gert came over and helped her to her feet. "She needs to rest now."

"I'll be going, then," Brendan whispered. "Thank you, Miss Letitia, for everything. I'll be in touch."

Brendan gathered up her keys and put her notebook, her tape recorder, and the cobalt blue bottle in her bag. She, too, was exhausted, her muscles tense and knotted. But none of that mattered. What mattered was that something—or Someone—had led her here, and for reasons that were

probably beyond her comprehension. For her part, she was more determined than ever to follow.

She didn't know if it was prayer or instinct that had led her to Letitia
Cameron. Her own feeble attempts at communicating with the Almighty
paled in comparison with Letitia's down-to-earth faith.

But between the two of them, maybe God would listen one more time.

14
FLAT ROCK

November 17, 1994

Brendan sat on a bench in front of the Park Deli and put her head in her hands. For the past month she had spent every free minute and most of her work time—except for one deadly boring story about deceptive practices of local auto repair shops—scouring Flat Rock, Hendersonville, and the majority of Henderson County for some clue to Adora Archer's whereabouts. But the Playhouse was closed for the season, and the whole thing had turned out to be little more than an exercise in futility.

She kept seeing Letitia Cameron's face, remembering the hope that had flared in the old woman's eyes when Brendan promised to go looking for Adora. But she had let Letitia down. She had let herself down. And if she didn't find something soon, Ron Willard was sure to pull her off the story and send her to do one of those on-the-scene bits about some mother cat who was nursing orphaned baby possums or a rat frozen into a package of bagels.

"Miss Delaney? Brendan Delaney?"

Brendan opened her eyes to see a pair of enormous feet in gray wool socks and clunky Birkenstocks. Her gaze traveled upward past an ankle-length flowered skirt in shades of tan and black, past a black knit T-shirt and rag wool sweater, to the smiling, intense blue eyes of a rangy middle-aged woman with long straight hair, ash blonde mixed with gray. Brendan sighed. All she needed right now was the effusive cheerfulness of some granola hippie throwback. A big fan, no doubt.

"Yes?"

"You don't remember me, do you?" Granola asked. Without waiting for an answer, she plunked down on the bench next to Brendan and went on. "I'm Franny Carpenter-Claymaker. You interviewed me last year when you did that piece on the Carl Sandburg farm."

Ah, Brendan thought, *the goat lady.* She should have remembered; after all, it was the first time in her life she had ever seen a human kiss a goat on the mouth. And the last time she ever wanted to.

"Well of course, Franny," she answered smoothly. "So good to see you again. How are the kids?"

Franny threw back her head and laughed. "Kids! Oh, that's a good one!" She even sounded a little like a goat, Brendan thought. And the kid joke wasn't that funny.

"To tell the truth," Franny was saying, "I'm no longer at the farm."

She shifted to face Brendan on the bench and began to give a detailed account of how she had developed an allergy to goat hair and had to make a major life change because of it. "I just kept sneezing and sneezing, and my throat kept closing up until—well, until I just couldn't go on. It was very difficult, you know, leaving the goats in someone else's care. We had become so close, bonded—like family, you know."

"Terrible," Brendan muttered absently. The way this woman went on, you'd think that goat-hair allergy was on a level with cancer or AIDS or cardio-myopathy and that turning over the care of Sandburg's goats to some other granola-head was a tragedy equal to losing a child.

"Anyway," Franny said, brightening, "I'm sure you don't want to hear me ramble on about goats and allergies."

The understatement of the decade, Brendan thought, but of course she didn't say so. She glanced at her watch, wondering what she'd have to do to extricate herself from Franny Carpenter-Claymaker. But before she had a chance to think up an excuse about some phantom appointment, Franny grabbed her arm and twisted it around. "Is it twelve-thirty already? My goodness! I'll bet you're waiting to meet someone for lunch!" She waved a hand toward the deli. "I do hope I'm not keeping you."

"No, not at all." Brendan's response came out automatically, before it registered that the woman was giving her the perfect out. She could have kicked herself.

"Well, then, how about joining *me*? I'd love to treat you—"

"That's not necessary," Brendan hedged.

"All right, we'll go Dutch, then. But at least let me buy dessert. The Park has the most wonderful pastries and pies—"

Before she knew what had happened, Brendan found herself seated on the upper level of the Park Deli, ordering a grilled chicken salad. Franny opted for the vegetarian lasagna—no surprise there—and spent the next nine minutes (Brendan timed it) chattering about the benefits of tofu and her personal aversion to eating anything that had once had a face.

"So," Franny said when their iced tea arrived, "what brings you down here? A follow-up story about the Sandburg home?"

"Not really." Brendan stirred artificial sweetener into her tea. "I'm doing background work, actually, for a future story. I'm looking for an elderly woman, and my last clue to her whereabouts was a postcard from the Flat Rock Playhouse. But I've been all over Flat Rock and Hendersonville and haven't found her—or anyone who knows her. I'm about ready to give up."

Franny gave a little squeal and gripped Brendan's wrist until the skin turned white. "I *work* at the Playhouse now!" she gushed. "Maybe I can be of some help—you know, see what we can track down together."

"I thought the Playhouse was closed for the season."

"Well, yes, the plays run through mid-October—you just missed our last musical, in fact. But during the off-season we're making preparations for the coming year. The offices are open, and planning is going on." The food arrived, and Franny attacked her lasagna as if it might scuttle away. "When we're done here, we'll go down and see what we can find."

Brendan picked at her own salad and silently urged Granola Franny to hurry. It might be a long shot, but it was the only shot she had.

⁓

"This is so much fun," Franny said as she waited for the computer to boot up. "Like detective work and television all rolled into one."

Brendan was tempted to ask if the woman even had electricity in her house, much less a television set. Franny seemed the type who would find intrinsic value in outhouses and oil lamps. But Brendan kept her mouth shut. Despite her eccentricities, this woman just might give her something to work with. At that moment, Brendan would have swapped her fine house on Town Mountain for a hillbilly cabin in the woods—if the trade would lead her to Adora Archer.

"Okay," Franny was saying. "We're ready to go. What's the lady's name?"

"Adora Archer," Brendan replied. "A-D-O-R-A."

"Odd name." Franny typed in the name and punched a few keys. "Nope. Nothing here."

"Where are you looking?"

"Ticket sales—both season tickets and individual."

Brendan thought a minute. Letitia didn't have much information about Adora from later years—only a few Christmas cards and the Flat Rock postcard. Maybe Adora had gotten married, taken her husband's name.

"I don't suppose the gift shop keeps computer records of sales," she suggested.

"For a postcard? I doubt it. Not unless it was paid for by credit card." Franny grinned at her little joke and tried again. "Nothing. Sorry."

"Can you run a search on *first* names? She might have gotten married."

"If we just knew more about her—"

"I don't know much more than what I've told you. She'd be in her eighties by now—82, 83, somewhere around there. She was originally from Asheville and left in 1930 to go to California. Wanted to become a movie star."

"An actress?" Franny warmed to the chase. "Why didn't you tell me? Let me check—"

"Check what?" Brendan interrupted, but Franny held up a hand for silence.

"Just a minute. I'll do a cross-link. There!"

Brendan felt her heart race with the clicking of the keys. "Did you find something?"

"I just thought—well, no. I guess not."

"What?"

"There is an Archer here, but it's a middle name, not a last. C. Archer Lovell. Bought two sets of season tickets the last three years in a row. Oh, wait. There's another Lovell."

"More tickets?"

"No, this one is in the actors' workshop—or was. Name: Addie A. Lovell."

Date of birth, 1912. Had a bit part two years ago, apparently, in one of the crowd scenes in *Carousel*." Franny turned. "Not your gal, apparently, but can you imagine being eighty years old and still on stage?" She flipped her long hair away from her face. "Guess they do it all the time, though—look at George Burns."

Brendan turned away from the computer screen and sighed. "Well, thanks for trying anyway, Franny. I appreciate your time."

"If there's anything else I can do for you, Miss Delaney, just give me a call." Franny clicked a key, and the screen saver came up. "Want me to send you a brochure for next season? We've got a good lineup."

"That'd be nice," Brendan murmured as she closed the door behind her.

She sat for a long time in the 4Runner, with the cobalt blue bottle in one hand and the postcard Letitia had given her in the other. Brendan examined the postcard one more time, although she didn't know why—she had practically memorized it by now. *Old dreamers never die,* the message said. No signature, just that wavering, spidery hand. Postmarked Flat Rock, NC, April 9, 1992.

She turned the card over and looked absently at the photo. A stage scene, with the words *Flat Rock Playhouse* superimposed across the bottom. Rather dark, in fact—not a very good picture. The stage was crowded with costumed people, all circling around a life-size merry-go-round. . . .

Carousel!

Addie A. Lovell, Franny had said. Addie. Could it be . . . Adora? And the other Lovell, the person with the middle name of Archer, who bought season tickets—

Brendan shoved the bottle back into her bag and bolted for the office. "Franny!" she yelled as she slammed through the door. "Get those names back for me, will you?"

In the space of two minutes—an interminable two minutes, by Brendan Delaney's internal clock—Franny had the lists up on parallel screens: the season ticket holders on one side, the actors' workshop people on the other.

"Can you isolate Addie A. Lovell and C. Archer Lovell?" Franny nodded. "Now, what about addresses?"

Franny clicked the mouse on a pull-down menu and said, "Oh, wow."

"What?" Brendan snapped impatiently.

"Same address." She clicked on an icon in the upper left of the screen and poised her hand over the printer. A page slid out, and she handed it to Brendan. "I know this place. Take the road past the Sandburg house. After you pass the access drive that goes into the goat barns, it'll be the next drive-way on the right."

૮૭

"I owe you," Brendan called over her shoulder as she dashed for the door. "The juiciest porterhouse in town." She stopped and grinned at Franny, who was making a face. "Or a big hunk of hummus. Your choice."

15
GRANMADDIE

Brendan held her foot on the brake and peered through the windshield at the house to which Franny Granola had directed her. It had to be a mistake.

The long driveway, flanked by ancient oaks, evergreens, and rhododendron, had shrouded the home with a living curtain of privacy until she came around the last curve and broke into the clearing. Then the full impact of the place assaulted her senses, as the architect and landscaper had obviously intended. The house stood like a magnificent pearl against the green of the lawn. Three stories high, all white, with massive turrets, twin spires, and Victorian gingerbread, it was a palace, not a private house.

Brendan looked around for some kind of historical marker, some indication that the place was open for tours. But she saw nothing. Only a silver-blue BMW convertible parked next to a three-tiered fountain at the end of the front walkway.

She drove forward another hundred yards, stopped, and got out. The estate was totally secluded, surrounded by gardens and woods, and so hushed that it gave her the odd sensation that she should tiptoe up the brick walk to the door.

She took a deep breath, shouldered her bag, and rang the bell.

A pleasant-looking young woman answered the door, dressed in faded jeans and a Vanderbilt sweatshirt. "May I help you?"

Brendan fumbled in her bag and handed over a business card. "I'm Brendan Delaney with station WLOS."

"I see. I'm sorry, Miss Delaney, but you see, I simply don't give interviews."

Brendan regarded the young woman. She seemed like a gracious, well-brought-up girl in her twenties—a college student, perhaps. She had straight blonde hair cut very short and brown eyes behind gold-rimmed glasses. There was nothing pretentious about her, either in her tone or her manner. And she was smiling—but she clearly did not want a reporter on the premises.

"I—I'm sorry," Brendan said. "I'm afraid I didn't make myself clear. I'm not here for an interview. I'm looking for someone, and I was given this address. An elderly woman, in her eighties. Perhaps I've made a mistake. Forgive me for disturbing you."

"Wait." The girl stepped out onto the porch and peered at Brendan. "What's her name, if I might ask? The woman you're looking for?"

"Archer. Adora Archer."

The brown eyes flitted away for a moment. "And why are you looking for her?"

Brendan considered her answer. Gut instinct told her that this young woman was more likely to be swayed by personal motives than professional ones. Never mind the story. She could get to that later. "Letitia Cameron sent me. She's a very old friend of Miss Archer's, and she—"

A transformation swept over the girl's face, a look of wonder, almost awe. "I can't believe it. After all these years. Please, come in, Miss"—she looked at the card again— "Miss Delaney."

Brendan followed the girl through a marbled foyer into a high-ceilinged room on the left. A library, with tall bookcases flanking an enormous fireplace. Comfortable, overstuffed chairs and a love seat circled around the hearth, and the girl waved a hand. "Have a seat. Would you like something to drink? Coffee or iced tea?"

"Not right now, thanks." Brendan sat down and placed her bag on the oriental rug at her feet.

"Letitia is alive, then?" the girl said eagerly. "Granmaddie will be so thrilled."

"Granmaddie?"

"My grandmother. Adora Archer. Or, rather, Adora *Lovell*." She took one look at the expression on Brendan's face and began to laugh. "Oh, I'm sorry. I didn't introduce myself, did I? I'm Dee Lovell."

For a minute all Brendan could focus on was the truth that Adora Archer was still alive. That she was sitting across from the old woman's grand-daughter. That even if Adora didn't live here, this young girl obviously kept in touch with her and could set her on the right track.

Then her mind came to attention. *Dee, the girl had said.* Her name was Dee. But the receipt for the Playhouse tickets had been under a different name. C. Archer Lovell. Who, then, was C. Archer, the mystery Lovell whose American Express Gold card had paid for the tickets? Not this fresh-faced youngster, surely.

The reporter in her kicked in. "You live here? Not just you." This house had to be eight thousand square feet, minimum. Brendan had seen whole apartments smaller than the library they presently occupied.

"Some people would consider this a little excessive, I realize," Dee admit-ted. "But I wanted a peaceful place, somewhere I could write and not be dis-turbed. And when I found this on the Internet, in the very mountains where Granmaddie grew up, well, I just fell in love and couldn't resist it. It gives me"—she grinned broadly— "a sense of place, you know?"

Suddenly something clicked in Brendan's mind, like the tumblers of a lock falling together, a door swinging open. *A Sense of Place.* Wasn't that the title of a novel that won the Pulitzer a couple of years ago? By some new, rel-atively unknown writer—what was her name? Cordelia something.

"*You* are Cordelia A. Lovell, the Pulitzer novelist?" Brendan knew her jaw was hanging open, but she couldn't help herself.

Dee laughed. "Guilty as charged. I thought you knew."

"Forgive me. I had no idea. I simply didn't make the connection." Briefly Brendan told the girl how she had come to find them, from the C. Archer Lovell on the credit card slip and the cross reference to Addie Lovell in the Playhouse workshop records. "I'd heard rumors that Cordelia Lovell had moved to this area, but you—well, I expected—"

"Someone much older?" The girl grinned. "I'm not as young as I look, Miss Delaney. I'm thirty-seven. But I have to confess that I allow the mis-conception to go uncorrected—I even encourage it, on occasion. The truth is, I don't like being a celebrity. I value my privacy. And thankfully, my small measure of success has made seclusion possible." She ran a hand through her hair. "I write under the name Cordelia. But friends know me as Dee, and my credit cards are issued in the name C. Archer. It helps keep me from being recognized too often."

"I can't believe it," Brendan repeated. "Cordelia Lovell." She shook her head. "And Adora Archer is your grandmother? And she's alive?" Brendan knew she sounded like a complete idiot, but she couldn't seem to stop herself.

"Yes, and yes." Dee chuckled. "Very much alive. You'll see soon enough."

"She's here?"

"She lives here, yes. With me. But she's out at the moment. If you don't mind waiting, she should be home before long." She kicked her shoes off and tucked her feet under her. "Now, tell me about the story you're working on."

Brendan started. "Story?" She hadn't said anything about a story, she was sure of it. Only that Letitia had sent her to look for Adora Archer.

"I'm no fool, Miss Delaney. I know there's a story here somewhere. Heaven knows I've felt often enough what I see in your eyes right now. And unless I miss my guess, it's a story that won't let go of you. A destiny of sorts."

So she did know, Brendan mused. And she understood. Of course she would understand. She was a writer. Good stories were her bread and butter too. Her passion. Her life.

As Brendan related to Dee Lovell the events of the past few weeks—finding the blue bottle in the attic of Cameron House, and how enamored she had become with the idea of finding these women and discovering the outcome of their lives—she could see the young woman's excitement mounting. At last she finished, reached into her bag, and drew out the clouded glass bottle.

Dee reached for it, holding it carefully, touching its surfaces as if it were an icon from a sacred oracle. "This bottle holds my history too, you know," she said reverently. "And there's so much I don't know. I wonder—"

Just then the front door slammed shut. "Cordelia?" a woman's voice called out. "Sweetie, where are you?"

"In the library, Granmaddie," Dee called back. "Come in here—we've got company."

Brendan's heart began to pound.

Adora Archer had come home.

⁓

Brendan would have sworn that nothing could ever take her off guard as much as meeting Pulitzer Prize–winning author Cordelia A. Lovell. But she was wrong. Granmaddie—Adora Archer Lovell, now called Addie—was an even bigger shock.

She stood in the doorway, a diminutive woman no more than five feet tall, clad in a purple and green silk running suit and bright purple high-topped tennis shoes. Dazzling platinum blonde hair curled out wild and windblown from her forehead, and she paused only for a moment before dashing into the room and plopping down on the love seat next to her granddaughter.

"Hi, sweetie," she said, giving the girl a kiss on the cheek. "Sorry I'm a little late. You know how those old geezers at the center love to talk."

"Granmaddie goes to the senior center at Opportunity House on Thursdays," Dee explained.

"Yes, and I don't know for the life of me why I bother. Half of those folks are fifteen years younger than me, and still all they want to do is sit around on their keisters playing bridge. I did get Davis McClellan to dance with me today, but I practically had to drag him out onto the floor, and then everybody kept yelling at us to turn the music down."

"Not everybody stays as active as you do, Granmaddie."

"Well, they should, and that's the truth. Use it or lose it, that's my motto. I can't wait till the Playhouse starts rehearsals again. I've heard they're going to do *Camelot* this year. I may audition for the part of Guinevere." She threw back her head and laughed, then snapped to attention and fixed her gaze on Brendan. "Who in blazes are you?"

Dee stroked the old woman's arm. "Granmaddie, this is Brendan Delaney. She's a reporter with WLOS, the television station."

"Caved in, did you?" She patted Dee on the cheek. "I thought you said you had absolutely no intention of doing interviews." The old woman nodded in Brendan's direction. "She's a gifted one, my granddaughter. But I guess you know that, or you wouldn't be here."

"Brendan didn't come to interview *me*, Granmaddie. She's here to talk to *you*."

"Yes, Mrs. Lovell," Brendan began, "I—"

"Oh, posh. None of that 'Mrs.' stuff. It's Addie. If you can't manage to be friendly, you can just run along."

"Yes, ma'am. Addie, I mean," Brendan faltered. "The reason I'm here—"

Addie held up a hand, and Brendan stopped mid-sentence. The old woman's attention focused for the first time on the cobalt blue bottle, sitting on the table next to Brendan's chair. Her hand began to shake, and tears welled up in her eyes. "It can't be," she breathed. She turned to Brendan. "Where did you get that?"

Brendan repeated the story she had told to Dee just a few minutes earlier—how the bottle had been discovered, and how she had determined to track down the four women and find out the end of the story. When she got to the part about Letitia Cameron, Addie took in a quick breath.

"Tish," she whispered. "Alive?"

"Yes." Brendan smiled. "I spoke with her last week. You sent her a postcard from the Playhouse—"

"*Carousel*," Addie finished. "I didn't know where she was—I just used the last address I had, from oh, fifteen years ago, maybe. I really didn't know if it would ever reach her."

"It was forwarded several times, but yes, it was finally delivered. Letitia said she had tried to call, but couldn't get a number from information."

"Our telephone is unlisted," Dee explained. "Otherwise—"

"I understand." Brendan leaned forward toward Addie. "I would like it very much if you would tell me your part of the story, Addie. You went to California, Letitia said, to follow your dream. But she didn't know much of anything after that."

"It was such a long time ago," Addie murmured, looking from Brendan to Dee and back again. "Such a long time. I tried to forget, but I couldn't. And now you come here with that—" She pointed at the bottle. "It's a sign, I think. A sign that maybe it's time, once and for all, to let the truth be told. Some of it I have never told anyone—not even my granddaughter." She paused and passed a hand over her eyes. "There have been too many secrets over the years, secrets I'm tired of keeping to myself."

Brendan got out her tape recorder and pad and moved her chair closer to the love seat.

"Are you sure you want to hear this? All of it?" Addie reached out a hand toward Dee. "It might make a difference in your feelings about your old grandmother."

"I'm sure." Dee smiled and squeezed the hand. "Nothing will ever change my love for you, Granmaddie." She motioned to Brendan, who handed her the glass bottle. "You and Letitia actually wrote out your dreams and put them into this bottle?"

Addie nodded. "And two other friends too—Eleanor James and Mary Love Buchanan." Her eyes took on a distant, faraway look. It was Christmas Day 1929. . . ."

ADORA

16
THE ACTRESS

December 24, 1929

Adora sat in the second pew, craning her neck around to watch for Letitia and Philip's grand entrance. Tish had been her best friend since grade school, and Adora loved her like a sister, but she couldn't for the life of her figure out what she saw in that insufferable snob, Philip Dorn. She didn't tell Tish that, of course. The girl was absolutely smitten.

Because of her own father's position as minister of Downtown Presbyterian—and the fact that the church catered to a lot of wealthy and influential congregants—Adora often found herself thrust into that aristocratic circle. But she had no intention of staying there. She had bigger fish to fry. Fish her father would throw back if he ever found out about them.

But he wouldn't find out . . . at least not right away. And by the time he did, it would be too late, and he wouldn't be able to stop her.

Most other girls, Adora realized, would doubt their ability to pull it off. But she wasn't most other girls. Acting came naturally to her. Her mother called it lying, but it wasn't deception, really. It was research. Playing a role, disappearing behind the facade of a different persona, was at least equal parts gift and skill. She had the gift, and, given a chance, she could develop the skill.

Take Tish, for example. In most instances, Adora was completely honest with her best friend. But when it came to Philip, and to that aristocratic circle of the Dorns—even to Tish's daddy—Adora could put on a front with the best of them. If truth be told, Adora favored Tish's mother. The woman had something special, a brightness that surrounded her like a halo. She was funny and generous and loving—all the things Adora's mother was not. Maris Cameron generated an atmosphere of welcome, so that even at the mature age of seventeen, Adora had to restrain herself from running to her motherly embrace every time she saw the woman. But in Tish's presence, Adora feigned a preference for Randolph, Tish's father. It pleased Tish and made her feel as if Adora understood her, when in fact Adora could never comprehend why her best friend was so blind when it came to discerning the true nature of those around her.

She looked up to see Tish, resplendent in a green velvet gown that brought out the green in her eyes, squeezing into the pew with Philip in tow. If only Philip had the sense to appreciate what he had in Letitia Cameron. Despite her best efforts to cover it up, Tish had inherited her mother's generous nature and loving heart. And while Tish truly did love Philip, Adora suspected that Philip did not return that love, that he only wanted a trophy—a beautiful socialite who would hang on his every word, produce offspring as handsome as himself, and serve as hostess for the parties he would give when he became a financial bigwig like Tish's father.

Adora greeted Tish and Philip with the effusiveness that was expected and settled back into the pew. Her eyes wandered to the platform, where her father sat in his holy robes, his gaze fixed on his sermon notes. Soft organ music filled the sanctuary with the sounds of Christmas, and candles lit the room with a pulsing glow. For a moment Adora could almost sense a presence, a peace beyond human comprehension. Her father, she knew, would have called it the Spirit of God.

The problem was, this Spirit that Dad talked about from the pulpit didn't seem to have much effect on the way people acted in everyday life. Adora had read the Bible—you didn't grow up in a preacher's home without absorbing a thing or two—and from what she read, Christians were supposed to show love and compassion toward everybody. Jesus, after all, spent most of his time with prostitutes and sinners and lepers and poor people.

If Jesus had been pastor of Downtown Presbyterian, however, his ministry would have looked a lot different. In the two months since the Crash, a whole lot of those sinners and poor people had been coming to the door. Maybe not prostitutes and lepers—there weren't many of those in Asheville—but people who certainly did not fit the image Downtown Pres had cultivated over the years. And the church members hadn't exactly welcomed them with open arms. The women's society, in fact, including Alice Dorn and her cohorts and even Adora's own mother, had approached her father about taking steps to curb the influx of these people that "didn't fit in."

The whole thing appalled Adora. She wasn't exactly a social work do-gooder like Little Eleanor James, but she did find herself disgusted at the idea of so-called Christian people expending so much time and energy to try to exclude whole classes of outsiders. If that's what Christianity was all about, she was just about done with the whole idea.

If she could just hang on a few months longer—play the game, act out the role—she would be free from all of it.

Forever.

CO

Christmas Day 1929

Adora said her good-byes to Tish and Ellie and Mary Love and left the Cameron house with a smile on her face. What a glorious thing it was, to have the future spread out before you like a beckoning road! That afternoon, as they shared their dreams and slid them into Tish's blue bottle, Adora had felt more of God's presence than she had ever known in church.

She didn't call it that, of course. She wouldn't, lest she jinx the sense of well-being that now infused her. But she had to admit to an overwhelming feeling of *rightness* about the ceremony, a conviction that somehow the four of them had connected on a deep and lasting level, committing their futures to a power greater than themselves, a power that could—and would—oversee the fulfillment of those dreams.

Tish had appeared wearing Philip's ring, a development that both surprised and dismayed Adora. But what could she say? This was Tish's big dream, and who was Adora, even as Tish's best friend, to second-guess it? Besides, Tish wouldn't be eighteen until November; maybe by then the girl would see the light on her own, without Adora having to risk their friendship to tell her that she was being an idiot.

Ellie, bless her heart, had come up with the idea of becoming a social worker and helping people. No surprises there, although she would be in for a battle with Big Eleanor, who valued money and social position above all else. And Mary Love wanted to become an artist, to live *alone*—she emphasized the word—and give herself to her work. No wonder the girl didn't want to marry. With ten other children at home in that chaotic Irish Catholic family, she had probably done enough diaper-changing and bottle-feeding to last three lifetimes.

In many ways, Adora had the least in common with Mary Love. The girl was rough around the edges and—as a middle-class Catholic—not part of the social circle Adora had grown up with. But she had a good heart. And on one thing they did agree—that an excess of religion made everybody miserable.

Mary Love's mother, apparently, was good at two things: conception and prayer. Once she had given birth, she turned over the babies' upbringing to the older children, but she evidently did not have the same capacity to let go when it came to praying. According to Mary Love, she was on her knees all hours of the day and night, lighting candles, saying the rosary, interceding for everything she could think of—her husband's business, the pope's health, the horrible predictions about the recent stock market crash. She went to Mass every single day unless she was in the last stages of labor, and one of the younger children—her name was Bernadette, Adora thought—had nearly arrived right on the church steps. Mrs. Buchanan had almost cut that prayer session too close.

Adora, fortunately, did not have to endure that kind of fanatical fervor at home. Presbyterians were more circumspect about their religion. There was very little God-talk in the Archer household—Dad saved that for the pulpit—but her father's commitment to his calling affected the family every bit as much as Mrs. Buchanan's fevered faith. Dad made it clear that his flock came first, and his wife and daughter got the crumbs that fell from the table. He never said this; he simply lived out his calling in a way that left no room for discussion.

Adora had no idea whether or not her father genuinely believed what he preached. He approached the church—and his position as pastor—as a business. Whatever fostered expansion, whatever resulted in greater fiscal growth, he would do. Generally that meant that he never preached about anything controversial, and he focused his time and energies on the church members who were able to make the greatest financial contribution to the life of the congregation. People like the Dorns, Big Eleanor James, and Randolph Cameron. When they sneezed, he was there with a prayer and a pat on the back. When they expressed an opinion, he listened. When they donated huge sums of money, he made a public display of thanking them profusely for their largess. He was always gracious and kind to the "little people," of course—that was expected of a man of the cloth. But he and Mother were regulars at the Camerons' parties, and clearly they preferred dining in the opulent surroundings of the Dorn home, waited on by quiet, black-clad servants, to a rustic meal at the kitchen table of less fortunate parishioners.

For as long as Adora could remember, Downtown Presbyterian had followed its pastor's lead. It was known as an "upper-class" church, and most of the longtime members expected it to stay that way. What was Dad to do, then, with the less-than-upper-class multitudes, the victims of the Crash who now seemed desperate to return to their religious roots?

His answer, Adora realized, was to do nothing. Her father couldn't stand at the door and forbid them to come to worship. He couldn't overtly cave in to the pressure Alice Dorn and her ilk were imposing upon him. Somewhere, Jesus had said—Adora couldn't remember exactly where—that "the poor you shall have with you always." Dad didn't deny the truth of those words; but apparently he thought if he ignored the poor long enough, they might—despite the Lord's opinion—eventually go somewhere else, and he wouldn't have to deal with them.

Adora felt at odds with herself about the whole matter. She loved the parties, the privileges, the acceptance as much as anyone else—and that part of it, at least, wasn't an act. But something in her, deep in her heart or soul or mind, rebelled at the way people were treated if they didn't have money or a name or social position. Maybe, she was vaguely aware, it was because she would soon be giving these things up, voluntarily abdicating her own place in society to follow her dreams.

She didn't know for a fact how her father would respond to her when she did it. But she had a pretty good idea.

And the very thought sent a chill up her spine.

17
NEW BEGINNINGS

May 20, 1930

Adora stared out the window and watched as the sun rose like a great golden coin surfacing on the currents of the mighty Mississippi. Twelve hours ago she had boarded this bus in Asheville; it had just now reached the bridge that spanned the river into West Memphis, Arkansas. In the middle of the night, at a greasy little diner in Nowhere, Tennessee, she had purchased a pocket-size map, and her smudged pencil mark confirmed the dispiriting news: Adora Archer was less than one-quarter the distance to her ultimate goal.

She had slept little, despite the lulling rocking motion of the bus. Her mind was too filled with questions, her heart too agitated about the enormous risk she had taken. Had her parents gotten any sleep at all? She wondered.

The note she had left gave them precious little information—only that she had gone, that she was no longer a child and had to pursue her own dreams, her own destiny. That she would, at some point, find a telephone and let them know that she was all right. *Please don't worry,* she had added as an afterthought. *I know what I'm doing.*

They wouldn't come after her, of that much Adora was certain. Her father adhered to the "you've-made-your-bed-and-now-you'll-have-to-lie-in-it" school. Besides, he had his hands full with church. The controversy over the presence of the Bread Line People, as they had come to be called, had escalated to all-out war, with Alice Dorn leading the charge on behalf of the Haves to rid Downtown Presbyterian of the Have-Nots.

Everything had changed so quickly since the day she and Tish and Ellie and Mary Love had entrusted their dreams to each other and the blue bottle. In her mind, Adora marked that day as the last moment of their childhood. Within a week, Tish had found her father dead in the attic, a grisly suicide, and all of them had been thrust into adulthood almost overnight. Now Tish was living with her mother in that tiny cottage and helping her work for the very people they had once called friends. Enduring the scorn and ridicule of the church—or at least the Alice Dorn crowd— while Adora's own father kept silent and did nothing to stop it.

One good thing, at least, had come from Randolph Cameron's demise. Philip Dorn had finally show his true colors. Tish's place had been usurped by that mousy little creature Marcella, a girl Philip never would have looked at twice had her daddy not been a friend of the Vanderbilts and a very rich man.

A wave of shame crested over Adora, and she struggled to break the surface of her own self-reproach. She never should have attended Philip and Marcella's engagement party, not when she knew Tish would be in the kitchen with her mother. Tish was gracious about it, of course. She always was, these days. In fact, she was becoming increasingly like her mother— another blessing hidden behind the barbs of reality. Still, it had to hurt, seeing her best friend mingling with the Vanderbilts like royalty, while Tish herself, the erstwhile fiancée, was given no more respect than a day servant.

Adora sighed and shifted in the seat, leaning her head against the cool window. She hadn't been a very good best friend to Letitia, if she was going to be brutally honest with herself. Until two days ago at graduation, and afterward, at the party at Tish's house, they had seen little of each other except in passing at school. For months Adora had simply accepted the changes as the inevitable outcome of the struggles that had assaulted all of them. But then on Sunday, at the graduation party, she had gotten a glimpse of the way it used to be. The four of them, together, laughing, as if the tragedies of the preceding months had never happened. As if it had all been a bad dream, scattered to oblivion by the morning light.

And now, just as things were beginning to get back to normal, she was leaving.

But she wouldn't let it end there. She couldn't. She had made a vow, a solemn promise, that she would uphold her friends and encourage them to fulfill their dreams. Adora wasn't sure quite how she could be true to that commitment; even now every bump in the road put more distance between her and the three friends she had vowed to support.

Prayer was the first idea that came to her mind, but she immediately dismissed it. She had experienced quite enough of religion—the Alice Dorns of the world defending their turf, the Pastor Archers abdicating responsibility by their silence. Adora had seen too much. And as the minister's daughter she had seen it much too closely. The underside of Christianity didn't look nearly so appealing as its public face.

No, prayer wasn't an option. If the Almighty wanted to communicate with her, he'd have to give her more to go on than what she had seen so far. The Christ her father represented wasn't a god she was willing to serve.

She'd have to settle, Adora concluded, for holding Tish and the others consciously in mind, writing letters to them, keeping in touch. Letting them know what was going on in her search for stardom.

And no pretense, no acting. Complete honesty.

It was the least—and the most—she could do.

Miss McIlwain's Hollywood House for Young Ladies didn't turn out to be quite what Adora expected. A looming brick mansion on a dead-end street, it hulked out of sight behind high shrubbery and a heavy iron gate, as if forbidding anyone to enter uninvited.

Caroline McIlwain, the proprietress, incarnated the house's austerity in flesh and blood. The stereotypical missionary spinster, Miss McIlwain had pale, pinched features, suspicious eyes, a bun at the nape of her neck, and an impassioned certainty about her calling—which, she told Adora in no uncertain terms, was to serve as guardian to protect the chastity and honor of "her girls" while they sought employment in the City of Sin.

Mother Mac, as the other residents called her, laid out the house rules for Adora: The gates were locked promptly at 10:30 P.M. All residents were to be in their own rooms with the lights out by eleven. There would be no drinking of alcoholic beverages or smoking, and absolutely no visitors of the male gender except in the front parlor on Sunday afternoons between two and four. Two meals per day were included: breakfast at six-thirty, supper at seven. No refunds were given for missed meals. No Victrolas in the rooms, and absolutely no dancing on the premises, except for young ladies studying classical ballet, who could use the sunroom off the back parlor for rehearsing.

Wonderful, Adora thought. *Just like home.*

"You say your father is a minister?" Mother Mac asked as she led Adora up three flights of stairs to her room. She opened a door at the end of the hall and ushered Adora into a tiny cell furnished with a single bed, a dresser, and a small desk. A high dormer window looked out over the enclosed gardens. "How lovely. It's always a blessing when I get good Christian girls who know how to behave themselves. Sets a good example for the others, don't you know?"

"Don't I know," Adora muttered. She laid her suitcase on the bed. After four days on a bus, all she wanted to do was lie down beside it and sleep.

"You met Candace and Emily as you came in. Candace is right down the hall, and Emily is on the second floor. The rest of our little family you'll meet at dinner tonight. Seven sharp, remember?"

"I remember."

"Oh, and—Adora, is it?"

"Yes ma'am."

"Just what are your intentions here in Hollywood? Ballet, perhaps? Or opera?"

"Acting," Adora said. "I want to become an actress—in the talkies."

Miss McIlwain's hand flew to her skinny neck. "Oh, my. I had no idea."

"Is this a problem?"

"Well . . . usually I only take in girls who are studying the serious arts. Actresses tend to be—you know. Unmanageable. But since your father is a minister of the gospel, I suppose I could make an exception this one time." She peered into Adora's face. "He must be a very . . . *liberal* man of the cloth, to allow you to pursue acting."

"Indeed," Adora sighed. "Very liberal."

"And he must trust you a great deal."

"Implicitly."

"Ah. I see. Well, I suppose we need devoted Christians in all venues," she murmured. "Who's to second-guess the Lord about his calling?" She gave a tight-lipped smile and backed out of the room.

As soon as the door shut behind her, Adora kicked off her shoes, flung herself on the bed, and heaved a sigh of relief.

Never mind that she found herself—at least temporarily—a ward of Miss Caroline McIlwain, self-professed guard dog of virtue. Never mind that her room was cramped and dark and smelled a little like mildewed shoes. Never mind that she was exhausted, hungry, and utterly alone. She had made it. She was here.

The City of Sin, Miss McIlwain had called it.

Sin be hanged. This was Los Angeles. Hollywood.

The City of Angels, Adora thought.

The City of Dreams.

◌◌

Adora awoke to find the room bathed in a blue glow. The sun had set, and a rising moon came through the curtains and cast an eerie light over the bare floorboards. What had awakened her? And what time was it?

A knock sounded on the door—again, Adora realized. It was the knocking that had roused her from a very deep sleep. Her suitcase lay beside her, open but still packed, and her legs were numb from hanging off the edge of the bed.

"Come in."

The door opened, and two female figures entered. One of them carried a tray, and the other reached over to the bedside table and snapped on the reading lamp. Adora blinked and tried to focus.

"You slept through supper." The first girl, a tall blonde with a lithe figure and very large breasts, set the tray on the foot of the bed.

"We told Mother Mac you were probably exhausted from your trip, so she made an exception and let us bring a tray up." The other, a tiny slip of a thing with bright red hair, smiled at her. They looked familiar, vaguely, but Adora couldn't place them.

"Thank you," she managed, rubbing at her eyes in an attempt to wake up. "I'm starving."

The tall blonde smiled. "I'm Candace—Candace Mannheim. We met downstairs when you arrived."

"And I'm Emily Blackstone."

Adora sat up and propped against the head of the bed and took the tray in her lap. Candace moved the suitcase to the floor, and both she and Emily sat on the foot of the bed.

"Adora Archer," Adora said, eyeing the meatloaf and mashed potatoes. "Do you mind?" She gestured with her fork.

"Of course not, go right ahead." Candace smiled and motioned for her to eat. "So, where are you from? And what are you in for?"

Adora frowned. "I'm from North Carolina. Asheville."

"Ha! A Cracker!" Emily burst out. "Or is it a Southern Belle?"

"Neither, actually," Adora hedged, not knowing whether they were making fun at her expense or simply didn't know the difference. "What did you mean, what am I in for?"

"Just a little prison humor among the inmates," Candace chuckled. "What brings you to Hollywood?"

"I want to be an actress."

"You and everyone else on the planet, honey." Emily shook her head. "I've been here for six months. Candy's been here almost a year. I've gotten two callbacks, but no jobs. Candy's been in two talkies, as extras, for base pay."

"Two films?" Adora stared at Candace. "But I thought Miss McIlwain didn't take in actresses—that she made an exception for me because my dad is a—" Adora stopped suddenly. For some reason she couldn't articulate at the moment, she didn't want these two knowing she was a preacher's daughter.

But they didn't seem to notice her hesitation. "Let us tell you something, Addie—can we call you Addie? Every girl in this house—all nineteen of us, now twenty counting you—is pounding the sidewalks looking for work. This town is full of us—we meet ourselves coming and going. All alike, all wanting the same thing—to be a star. As for Mother Mac, as long as you carry around a pair of toe shoes and do a plié now and then on the back porch, she'll convince herself that you are a 'student of the serious arts' and leave you alone."

"What's your plan?" Emily asked.

"My plan?"

"You've got to have a plan. Do you—wait, I'm afraid to ask. Do you have any contacts? Any connections with a studio?"

Adora felt a wave of embarrassment wash over her, and she pushed her dinner aside. "No, I didn't know—"

Candace patted the blanket. "It's okay. Stick with us, kid. We know the ropes, and we'll help you get on your feet. I hope you've got a little money to tide you over."

"A couple months' worth."

"That'll get you started. Em and I work three nights a week at a club on the west side. It's pretty dismal, but the tips are good, and they're looking for more part-time help. We can get you in—eight to midnight."

"But Miss McIlwain said the gates are locked and we're supposed to be in our rooms by—"

Candace threw back her head and laughed. "You'll learn this eventually, so you might as well hear it right up front. For every rule, kid, there's a way around it. In this case, it's a hole in the hedge and a trellis on the back wall of the house. Just make sure to leave your window unlocked."

Adora nodded.

"Now, eat up and get some rest. There's a cattle call tomorrow morning at eight. We'll come get you and we can all go together."

Adora didn't like the way these two made her feel—stupid, naive, and just a little prudish. But if she didn't ask, she'd never learn. "A cattle call?"

"For bit parts, you know, extras in a movie. You don't have to have an agent or an appointment. You just show up, and if they like your looks, you might get a job." Emily studied Adora with a scrutinizing gaze. "Good facial structure, nice cheekbones. Lips are a little full, but we can correct that with a little cosmetic deception. You're lucky, kiddo. Blonde hair and blue eyes are popular these days." She fluffed at her wild red curls. "I can't tell you how many jobs I've lost because I stand out too much."

"Cattle call, huh? And just what does that make us?" Adora smiled. Maybe she had been wrong in her initial reaction to Candace and Emily. They were trying to help, after all, and they obviously knew a great deal more than she did about the way things were done in Hollywood.

After they left, she finished off her dinner, unpacked her suitcase, and got ready for bed. Tomorrow was the big day—her first audition. Maybe by this time tomorrow night she would be writing Letitia to tell her that Adora Archer was on her way to being a star.

Or if not a star, she mused wryly, at least a legitimately employed cow.

18
WHITMAN HUGHES

July 4, 1930

Adora blotted perspiration from her forehead and went to the other side of the pool to seek out a little shade. Candy and Em had insisted that she come, said it would be a good opportunity to "mingle with the magic-makers of Tinsel Town." But so far the only star she had seen was Rudy Vallee, playing tennis, and he was so far away she couldn't be sure it was him until she asked someone. The entire party seemed to be populated by hopefuls like herself, mostly young men and women preening for the cameras and trying desperately to get noticed.

For the fifth time that afternoon, Adora refused the drink offered to her by a white-coated waiter. Obviously no one in Hollywood had heard about Prohibition; everywhere she went, liquor flowed as freely as self-aggrandizement. To be honest, it had taken her quite some time to become inured to the sight of a woman with a cigarette in one hand and a highball in the other. And in trousers, some of them, swapping crude stories with the men as if they were born to it. If that's what it took to be a success in Hollywood, Adora despaired of ever realizing her dream.

She had lost count of the number of cattle calls she had attended in the past month and a half. Enormous, chaotic gatherings of hundreds, sometimes thousands of starry-eyed ingenues waiting to be discovered. Of those thousands, one or two lucky ones would be chosen, and more often than not their two seconds of fame would end up on the cutting room floor. The only hope for most of them was a bona fide miracle. And her father, she was certain, would say that God wasn't in the business of doling out miracles for lewd and immoral purposes.

Adora went to the bar and asked for a glass of water "on the rocks"—she had learned that much about drinking, anyway—and then turned back to survey the crowd. What would Letitia and the others think, she wondered, if they knew what Hollywood was really like? She had written letters, just as she had promised—one every week since she arrived. But one promise she had not kept. She had not been honest about the way things really were.

She hadn't lied, exactly—she had just put a positive spin on reality. Referred to the cattle calls as "auditions" and neglected to mention that there were hundreds of others "auditioning" for the same two-second spot in a crowd scene. She reported that Miss McIlwain's boardinghouse was a nice, clean, respectable place to live, that she had made some good friends (though none who could ever take the place of her friends back home), and that she had some "promising possibilities" in the works.

The truth was, Adora's money was almost gone. Most mornings she was out of the house by six and didn't come home until well after seven, so she rarely got to take advantage of the meals she was paying for. She subsisted by sneaking coffee and sweet rolls from the tables set up for the real actors—a crime punishable by eviction from the lot if the studio ever caught her—and crashing parties like this one, where she wolfed down hors d'oeuvres and fruit salad and strawberries dipped in chocolate as if it were her last meal. As indeed it might be, if she didn't find something soon.

So far she had steadfastly avoided joining Candy and Em in their late-night carousing at the Westside Dance Club. They worked, certainly, serving the forbidden drinks and sometimes dancing with the customers. But more often than not, they came home with liquor on their breath and cigar smoke permeating their clothes, and once or twice Candy didn't come home at all. When she showed up the next day waving two fifty-dollar bills, Adora didn't dare ask what she had done to deserve that kind of tip. She knew, of course—or at least she suspected. She just wasn't ready to have her suspicions confirmed.

If nothing turned up for her in the next week or so, however, she might just have to abandon that last stronghold of morality and take the waitress's job at the Westside Club. She didn't want to; it represented some final capitulation to the seduction of Sin City. But what choice did she have? Her options were rapidly running out.

Adora felt a presence next to her and turned to see a devastatingly handsome man in a white summer suit lounging on the bar stool to her right. "Some party, isn't it?" he said languidly, his eyes running up and down as he surveyed her. He shifted his drink to his left hand and held out his right. "Whitman Hughes," he said in a low rumbling voice. "And you are—?"

"Adora—Adora Archer," she stammered. She stared at him and wondered what magazine cover he had stepped off of. Tall, at least six-two, and broad-shouldered, with wavy brown hair and dark eyes, a cleft in his chin, and a jaw that looked as if it had been chiseled from marble.

"Are—are you a movie star?" she asked stupidly. Great. Now he would think she was a complete idiot, some hick who just fell off the turnip truck.

To her surprise, however, he threw back his head and laughed heartily. "No, no," he said when he had regained his composure. "But aren't you the refreshing one? Most people in this town would drop dead in their tracks rather than say what they're really thinking."

"I'm sorry," Adora whispered.

"Don't be." He leaned forward and looked into her eyes. "I'm tired of women who play the game. You never know quite what you're getting." He extended a long brown finger and ran it tantalizingly up and down her arm. "And what, Adora Archer, is a nice girl like you doing in a place like this?"

She took a deep breath and decided to opt for the truth—partly because he had already said he liked it, and partly because she didn't have the presence of mind to come up with a believable lie. "I'm trying to be an actress," she said frankly. "And my friends seemed to think I might meet someone here who would notice me."

"*I* noticed." He arched one thick eyebrow.

Adora could barely breathe, and her heart pounded painfully in her chest. She took a gulp of water and set her glass on the bar so he wouldn't see the shaking of her hand. "Mr. Hughes, I—"

"Whitman," he corrected. "My friends call me Whit." One hand reached out and captured hers. "And I would be deeply honored if you would consider me a friend."

"Why are you here?" Adora blurted out. She was intensely conscious of his fingers stroking hers, but she couldn't have drawn her hand back if her life had depended upon it.

"I'm here," he rumbled, "because I saw that the most beautiful woman at the party was sitting unescorted at the bar."

"No, I mean, what are you doing at the party?" Suddenly his words registered, and she faltered. "Beautiful? You think I'm beautiful?"

"I think you are the most exquisite creature I have ever seen. Hollywood is a town filled with beauties, but you, my dear, outshine them all." He smiled into her eyes. "As to why I'm here, at this party? Why, I think I was destined for it—just to meet you." He gave a low chuckle. "Besides, I really had no choice. This is my home. My party. It would have been rude of me not to be here."

Panic swept over Adora, and her heart sank. His house. His party. If she had been an invited guest, she would have recognized him. For all his flattering words, he had found her out. She was sure to be ejected on the spot. She just hoped he'd do it quietly, with a minimum of uproar. Maybe she could still salvage a little of her pride, avoid being seen—

"Clearly, you don't know who I am," he was saying, still with that infuriating smile playing about his lips. Why didn't he just throw her out and be done with it? But no, he seemed determined to toy with her like a cat with a baby bird.

"Forgive me, Mr. Hughes. My friends brought me; I don't know why I came. Maybe it was just for the food—a girl has to eat, after all. I'll leave right now, before—"

"Hold on!" He fastened a hand on her arm. "Who said anything about leaving?"

"But-but—" she stammered. "It's clear I don't belong here, and I'm sorry for crashing your party, and—"

"I don't care about that!" he snapped. "I've never seen half these people, and the other half are only here because they think they might get on my good side." He peered at her. "Are you really hungry?"

"I was," Adora murmured. Despite herself, she liked him. Maybe he wasn't going to throw her out after all. "But your buffet was very good." She opened her handbag and peeled back the edges of a linen napkin to reveal several croissants and a selection of canapés. "I—I took a few for later."

Whitman Hughes nearly fell off the bar stool laughing. He laughed until his handsome face turned red and his breathing came in short, shallow gasps. At last he righted himself, swiped the tears from his eyes, and took her hand. "Let's go inside, my dear," he said. "I think we need to have ourselves a private little talk."

⊂⌒⌐

For all Adora's experience with the social elite in western North Carolina, nothing she had ever seen, except perhaps the Biltmore, came close to Whitman Hughes's house. It was a low-slung, white stucco ranch home that seemed to go on forever. The kitchen rivaled anything she could have imagined in the finest restaurant, and on the back side of the house, far away from the outdoor swimming pool and the tennis courts and the incessant chatter of party guests, was a second indoor pool, flanked by bubbling fountains and palm trees. There they sat, at a small table adjacent to a statue of Neptune, and sipped orange juice from champagne flutes.

Whitman Hughes, Adora discovered, was a producer of some reputation in Hollywood. He had gotten in on the ground floor of the talkies and made a fortune when most of his colleagues were still debating about whether or not the idea of talking pictures was feasible. Now he was exploring another radical idea—a concept called Technicolor, which would bring the movies to life in a way that no one had ever seen before. George Eastman had first introduced color film a couple of years ago in New York, he said. It would take years to perfect it, but this process would bring lifelike color to the silver screen and would have an even greater impact on the industry than the death of silent films.

"I'm backing a new project right now that's about to go into production," he said. "It'll be bigger than *Broadway Melody*." He leaned forward and gave her a wink. "Even bigger than Mickey Mouse."

Adora sipped her juice and nodded. How on earth had she gotten here, sitting poolside with a great Hollywood producer—and a handsome one, at that?

"I only have one question for you, Adora Archer," he went on. "How much do you really want to be a star?"

Adora inhaled suddenly and sucked orange juice into her lungs. She began to cough uncontrollably until he got up and pounded on her back. At last she caught her breath. "What did you say?"

"I asked how committed you were to being an actress. And not just an actress, mind you—a *star*. A constellation in Hollywood's firmament."

"Of course I want it. That's why I came here."

"Are you willing to work hard—and do exactly what I tell you to do?"

"What are you saying, Mr.—ah, Whit?"

"I'm saying that if you want it, it's yours. The brass ring, the dream. The whole thing. Provided, of course, that you are as talented as you are beautiful."

"You're offering me a job?"

"Not a job." He shook his head. "The chance of a lifetime."

"What do I have to do?"

Whit laughed. "You have to be an actress, of course. You have to learn lines, follow directions. You have to put yourself aside and become the role. Can you do that?"

"I—I think so."

"No, don't think. Be positive, confident. Say, 'Yes, I can do it.'"

"Yes, I can do it," Adora repeated.

Whit got up and began to pace around the pool. "You'll be magnificent! With that face, that voice—ah, the world will be at your feet. You will be my greatest discovery, my—" He leaned down and gave her a kiss on the cheek. "My creation!"

He looked at his watch. "It's nearly six. Are you hungry?" Without waiting for an answer, he snapped his fingers and a white-gloved waiter appeared. "Put some dinner together for the two of us, Yates. A little pâté, some of that cold chicken—" He paused and looked at Adora. "Do you like caviar?" She shrugged. "All right, it's time you learned to like it. Caviar, Yates. And champagne on ice."

"Oh, no," Adora protested, "I don't drink."

He cut a glance at her. "Please tell me I'm not going to get a speech about Prohibition."

"No, of—of course not," she stammered. "I just—"

"You'll love it. Guaranteed." He waved Yates away. "Now, let's get to work."

"Work? Now? Here?"

"No time like the present." Whit took her hand and led her back inside, to the den, where a large leather sofa faced the fireplace. He settled her in one corner of the couch and started pacing again. "The first thing we have to do is decide on your name."

"What's wrong with my name?"

"Not your first name. I love that—Adora. Sounds very sensual, very romantic. But we need a last name to complement it. Something equally romantic. Adora Love. No, that's too obvious. Adora Loveless. Nope. Sounds like a jilted bride. Adora . . . Adora . . . *Lovell*. Perfect!" He slid to the sofa next to her and brought his face up close to hers. "Adora Lovell. What do you think?"

To be honest, Adora thought Archer was a perfectly good name, but she didn't say so. Besides, given her father's disapproval of what she was doing, it might be better if she kept the Archer name out of it. It wasn't hiding, really. It wasn't deceptive. It was just . . . well, just the way things were in Hollywood.

"All right," she said.

"I knew you'd go for it."

Dinner arrived—an enormous spread of cold roasted chicken, pâté, caviar, and fruit. Adora didn't like the caviar at all, but ate it anyway just to please her new benefactor. The rest of it, including the pâté, was delicious. Whit mixed champagne into her orange juice to make what he called a mimosa, and she didn't even notice the champagne. By the time dinner was finished and the evening was over, she was growing accustomed to the taste of the champagne all by itself. The bubbles tickled her nose and created a wonderful fizzy warmth going down. She had to admit to a bit of lightheadedness, but surely that was from the excitement of the day, not the alcohol.

"Let's go out to the pool," he said when the last of the champagne was gone. "I have a surprise for you."

She followed him through the house and out to the patio, where guests were still milling around the bar and stuffing themselves at the buffet table. No one even seemed to notice that their host had been gone for hours.

"Attention, everyone!" Whit called out. He picked up a spoon and rapped it on the edge of a glass, and the crowd settled down. "I'd like to introduce all of you to my newest discovery, the young woman who, when my next picture is released, will be hailed as a genuine sensation. Ladies and gentlemen"—he pushed her forward—"may I present Hollywood's newest star, the most astonishing new actress ever to burst upon the scene. Miss Adora Lovell!"

Applause rippled through the crowd, and then, as if on command, a rocket launched from somewhere behind the trees, and a dazzling display of fireworks began. Whit ushered her to one of the deck chairs and drew his own chair up beside her. As the crowd oohed and aahed over the fireworks, he placed an arm around her and drew her close.

"When the fireworks are over, I'll send a car around to take you home," he whispered. "Then my driver will pick you up at seven in the morning." He nuzzled her neck and planted a fervent kiss on her ear. "You won't disappoint me, will you, Adora? I've got a lot riding on this. And so do you."

Somewhere in the depths of her champagne-fuzzed brain, a faint warning bell went off. The words sounded almost like a threat. But of course she must be wrong. Whit believed in her talent, enough to make her a star. This was her dream come true, the miracle she had hoped for, the big break most young actors never got.

It didn't matter that he had never seen her act. She would prove herself to him, prove that he hadn't made a mistake.

No matter what the cost.

19
TRUE LOVE

August 1, 1930

"Listen, Addie," Whitman Hughes said for the fifth time that evening, "just consider it. Promise me that you'll think about it."

Adora looked into his eyes, illuminated to a rich glow by the candle that sat between them on the table. He seemed so sincere, so completely open and honest with her. He genuinely did want her—and it was a feeling that was almost irresistible.

But you've known the man for barely a month, her mind protested. Her heart, however, sang a different refrain: *He is so gentle, so sweet. He only wants what's best for you . . .*

"I really want you to move in with me," Whit was saying. "It just makes sense. I hate to bring this up, Addie, but your money is almost gone—you told me so yourself. And your income from the movie part won't start coming in for several months yet."

"I just don't know, Whit. It seems so—so sudden."

"Things happen fast in Tinsel Town, sweetheart." He winked at her and reached for her hand. "I fell in love with you the first night we met. You were so green that you didn't even know who I was."

"I know," she hedged. She had fallen in love with him too, but she had resisted admitting it to herself, much less to him. Now that she had finally said the words, her relationship with Whit was gathering speed like a runaway train.

"This house is plenty big enough for both of us," he went on. "Big enough for a whole family of squatters, in fact, with room to spare. And you're here most of the time anyway."

It was true. Adora already spent nearly every day and most of her evenings here, working with Whit on the part and socializing with him after the workday was over. Her friends at Miss McIlwain's were green with envy over her big break and begged her to put in a good word for them with the famous producer.

"I—" Adora paused. How could she communicate to this sophisticated, worldly man her unsophisticated, unworldly hesitations? She thought she had left all that behind when she got on the bus bound for California. But apparently a lot of it had stuck in the crevices of her mind like spring pollen—her father's frowning disapproval not only of his daughter's dreams but of her very self, the haughty aristocratic air her mother wore like a protective shield, the unspoken *thou shalt nots* that formed the core of her life before her liberation.

Whitman had carefully skirted any discussion of physical intimacy between the two of them, had avoided talking about sleeping arrangements once she moved into the house, but Adora wasn't naive enough to believe the subject would stay buried. Their relationship had become increasingly physical over the past couple of weeks, and Adora had to admit that she hadn't done much to resist his advances. The fact was, she loved it when he touched her. She welcomed his kisses and caresses as a desert dweller welcomes the rain. His expressions of love fell on a dry and thirsty soul, and she absorbed his affection with joy and abandon. She knew well enough what would happen if she moved into the house with him.

Now she had a choice. If she said no to Whit's offer, she might risk losing not only him but the movie role she so desperately wanted. But if she put the past behind her once and for all, with its trivial limitations and old-fashioned morals, she could have everything she had ever dreamed of— fame, fortune, and the love of an exceptionally handsome, wealthy, and talented man.

They would most certainly not approve, of course—neither her parents nor the friends who had promised to support and encourage her dreams. To live with a man apart from the blessing of the church and the approbation of society? It was unthinkable.

And yet here she was thinking about it. Seriously considering it, if truth be told.

Whit's voice jolted her back to the present moment. "You're worried about how they might react—your friends and family back home?"

Adora smiled wryly and shook her head. "Are you reading my mind?"

"It doesn't take a mind reader to know that a young girl from Arkansas might still be influenced by her parents' opinions."

"North Carolina," Adora corrected.

Whit shrugged, as if the exact location was irrelevant. "Addie, this is Hollywood. People do things differently here." He arched one eyebrow and appraised her with a cool, measured glance. "You came to California to follow your dreams. I guess it's time for you to decide whether those dreams include me. And whether you're ready to quit being a country girl and start being a career woman."

The implication wasn't lost on Adora. It wasn't a threat, exactly, just an objective evaluation of her situation. And she couldn't bear the idea of Whitman Hughes thinking of her as a naive little girl who didn't have the courage to follow through when her dreams were presented to her on a silver platter.

What difference did it make, in the long run, whether the marriage happened before or after what her father would call "cohabitation"? By the time her parents found out about her new living arrangements, she and Whit would be married. In the meantime, she wasn't about to lose him because of some outdated notion of morality. She loved him, and he loved her. Nothing else mattered.

True love was a rare commodity in this life, a godsend. When you found it, you did anything you had to do to hold onto it.

Anything but question whether God really sent it.

                       *

October 5, 1930

Addie settled back in the deck chair and gazed out over the Pacific Ocean, a champagne mimosa at her fingertips and the foaming waves of Malibu at her feet. Whit's "beach cabin," this glass-and-cedar luxury home on a jutting rock overlooking the sea, had become her second home. Her first, of course, was his house in Beverly Hills.

"How are you doing, darling?" he called from the kitchen, his voice drifting onto the deck through the open sliding glass doors. "Need another drink?"

"Not now, sweetheart." She raised her champagne flute over her head and waved it languidly to show him that it was still half full. Most Sundays they spent here at the beach house—Whit's one day away from the pressures of producing, the one day they had all to themselves. And without fail, he pampered her by making brunch for them—one of his famous omelets, with Belgian waffles and sliced strawberries. And more champagne, of course. A star like Adora Lovell, he said, should always drink champagne.

Addie wasn't really a star, of course—not yet, anyway. Delays in the production of Whit's new movie were still dragging on. First problems with getting the necessary financial backing, then difficulties in casting and finding the right director. It would be spring before they ever began shooting. But she didn't mind. The delays gave her more time—time for learning the part, for drama lessons, for diction classes. She had just about overcome her accent; by the time the cameras started rolling, she would have it conquered. One of the many things she had put behind her.

Addie sighed and shifted in her chair. It didn't feel like Sunday, and it most certainly did not feel like October. She glanced at her watch. Back home, church would be out by now and her mother and father would be sitting down to dinner at someone else's table—Alice Dorn's, perhaps. Or now that they had been married for a while, Philip and Marcella's. The trees on the mountains would be just about at peak, gold and red and russet brown, with a backdrop of that intense Carolina blue sky. She envisioned Tish at college, attending classes and planning for her degree, and Mary Love and Ellie in their final year of high school.

She felt so far away from them, so set apart, in a different world and time. Did they miss her? She wondered. Did they ever think of her? She couldn't imagine herself in their place, still living as . . . well, as girls. Addie herself wasn't a girl any longer—Hollywood grew you up fast, whether you were ready or not. Not yet twenty, and yet here she was, living the life of a starlet, in love with a man nearly twice her age.

Sometimes she missed it, that camaraderie the four of them had, when life seemed so much less complicated. It wasn't simple, of course. The Crash and the resulting Depression had tangled everything up—and not just finances. Relationships, too, and values and morals and dreams.

Out here in California, the Depression didn't seem quite so real, or at least not so immediate. Compared to the rest of the country, Hollywood was an enormous playground, surrounded by a high wall. The world outside could be falling to pieces, but the children inside kept on laughing and playing and enjoying themselves.

People needed entertainment, Whit had reasoned on more than one occasion. The worse things got, the more people needed a way to escape their misery, and Hollywood offered that escape. They were providing a great service, painting portraits of hope and a better time to come. But every time he said it, Addie harbored a dark suspicion that he was rationalizing and had to push from her mind the picture of Tish and her mother in that tiny carriage house, of Little Eleanor James and her commitment to helping the less fortunate.

"Brunch is served." Whit's voice behind her startled Addie out of her reverie and caused her to jump. He was setting out omelets and waffles on a patio table and filling two glasses with pale champagne. "More bubbly?"

"Sure, why not?" Addie got up and settled herself in the chair opposite him. "It looks delicious, as always. I don't know how you do it. You're a genius."

"Darling, didn't your mother ever teach you how to cook?"

"She tried," Addie admitted. "But I wasn't interested."

"Ah." He gave a light laugh. "I suppose you always knew you'd find your-self a man who would take care of you and never let you rough up those lovely hands with kitchen drudgery." He picked up her hand and kissed her fingers gently.

"Actually, I never intended to *find myself a man* of any kind," she countered. "My best friend's big dream was to marry her high school sweetheart and raise a brood of kids. Mine was to come to Hollywood and become a star."

"And you got both," he mused. "The stardom and the man."

"I guess I did." Addie took a bite of omelet and regarded him. He was, indeed, *the man*—the kind of man she would have dreamed of if her dreams had taken her in a domestic direction. Handsome, confident, respected . . . and totally in love with her.

Why, then, had she not written to her friends about her good fortune? Her last letter to Tish had been penned a full two months ago, only a few weeks after she had met Whitman Hughes. At the time she had told herself that it was best to downplay her hopes for the relationship, and for her future as his "brightest star." But the truth was, she couldn't bring herself to admit to her friends back home that she was in love with—and living with— a married man.

Whit was only *technically* married, of course. He had told her about the situation, somewhat reluctantly, the first time she had ever raised the issue of marriage with him. According to Whit, he and his wife had been separated for almost a year by the time he and Addie met. The divorce, he said, was a difficult process, complicated by her demands on his money and a lot of ugly mudslinging. She didn't understand him, had no desire to be a part of his world. They married too young, he explained—if he had only waited, he would have been a free man when Addie came into his life.

When she first heard this confession, Addie had regarded Whit with some skepticism. A man like him—gorgeous and successful and wealthy— had to have women throwing themselves at his doorstep. She would be a fool to think that he would actually wait for someone like her to come along.

But the first time Whitman Hughes had taken her in his arms, all her reservations melted away like ice under the warm California sun. Whit's lovemaking confirmed his words, that she was the only woman he could ever really give himself to. Whenever he touched her, she felt a renewed sense of his commitment to her, a commitment that didn't need formal words or a legal document for verification.

None of that would matter to her parents, of course, particularly to her father. He would say that she was living in sin and condemn her to the fires of perdition. Just look at her life—she had abandoned the church, left home and hearth, broken her mother's heart, and given her virginity away to a man who was not her husband. That's what he would say.

But she would never have to hear it, except in her own head, because he didn't know.

Addie had written exactly two letters to her parents—one the first week she arrived at Miss McIlwain's Hollywood Home for Young Ladies, and one in response to a brief note Mama had sent wrapped around a five-dollar bill:

Thank you for letting us know you're safe. Take care of yourself and keep in touch. Your father sends his love.

Her father had sent no such thing, Addie knew. And her mother's hurried scrawl left her with the distinct impression that Dad didn't know Mama was writing at all—he had probably forbidden any contact.

Addie had written back, thanking Mama for the money and giving a glowing report of the promising possibilities that waited just over the horizon. When no response came, all correspondence between them ceased.

Shortly after that she met Whit, fell in love with him, and moved out of Mother Mac's dismal boardinghouse into his big home in Beverly Hills. She had, in her mind, followed her destiny over the hill and out of sight of the life she had once known.

There was nothing more to say.

20
TROUBLE IN PARADISE

March 1931

pring came—although in California, you could hardly distinguish spring from any other season—and shooting began on Whitman Hughes's new film. The director worked them all brutally, but Addie most of all, making her do her scenes over and over again until she got them right. Once or twice Addie overheard the director arguing with Whit, yelling about some "she" who just didn't have what it took to play the part, and why didn't he get his mind back where it belonged and look for a *real* actress. "You'll never learn, will you, Whit?" he yelled. "You keep bringing me these brainless beauties who can't learn their lines and think that acting is simply a matter of standing there and flaunting their wares!" He followed this accusation with a series of invectives pertaining to the producer's body parts, and Addie took herself out of earshot lest she hear something that would completely unnerve her.

A week later, Whit fired the director and went on a search for someone who, he said, would "understand his vision" for filmmaking. The set was shut down, and everyone went home.

For Addie, the additional delay could not have come at a more opportune time. She had contracted some sort of influenza, she thought—an illness that made her feel drained of energy and queasy. She could barely stand the sight or smell of food. Even when Whit made his wonderful Sunday brunch for her, she could only get down two or three bites. Worst of all, she no longer felt like making love. She tried to explain it to Whit, but he obviously took it as a personal rejection.

One Saturday morning shortly after Whit had hired a new director, he turned his anger on her. He had brought her breakfast in bed, but was obviously more interested in bed than breakfast. Addie, for her part, felt her insides churning and attempted to resist his advances without hurting his feelings. It didn't work.

"You are going to the doctor immediately," he snarled. "Monday morning, and no arguments. Shooting resumes at noon on Monday. Be there." He stalked out of the room and left her to wonder what had happened to the gentle, loving man she had fallen in love with. Maybe he was just under stress about the new picture, she rationalized. He wasn't the kind of man, after all, who would put his needs before hers.

Monday morning Addie did as she was told and drove one of Whit's cars to a clinic frequented by actors and their families. At noon she arrived on the set to meet the new director, only to find that filming had already begun.

She watched from the wings as a young blonde woman she had never seen before spoke *her* lines and acted out *her* scenes. When the director called "Cut!" Whit came out to the set and turned on the charm, praising the blonde and fawning over her, touching her arm, and giving her a lingering kiss on the cheek.

Then, out of the corner of his eye, Whit spotted her in the shadows. "Darling!"

Addie drew back a bit. "What's going on here, Whit?"

"Everyone has been anxious about you, sweetheart. They all know you've been sick, and—"

"And so you replaced me? Just like that?"

"You haven't been replaced, darling," Whit soothed. "But Richard—he's the new director, and he's dying to meet you—discovered this young woman and thought she'd be perfect for the part."

"I thought *I* was perfect for the part."

"You are, sweetheart. Or at least you were. But you *have* put on a few pounds in the past couple of months, and—well, since you have been ill, we thought you might be better in a different role, something not quite so . . . so *central*."

"If I've *put on a few pounds*, it's thanks to your waffles and omelets," she shot back. "And I'm not sick. Not so sick, anyway, that I can't do the lead."

Whit took her arm and steered her away from the set. "So what did the doctor say?"

"Don't try to change the subject, Whit. He said he'd have the results of my tests by noon, and he'd call here. There's nothing wrong with me that a shot or two won't cure—but apparently we have a bigger problem than a little bout of influenza—"

Just then the backstage telephone rang, and Whit jerked the receiver up on the second ring. "Whitman Hughes," he snapped into the mouthpiece. He listened for a moment and then said, "I see. All right. Thank you very much."

For a minute after he hung up, he said nothing, then he turned toward Addie. A strange expression filled his handsome countenance, a mixture of anger and . . . what was it? Fear.

"You're right," he said at last, grating out every word. "You do have a bigger problem than the flu." He shook his head and narrowed his eyes at her. "That was the doctor's office."

"And?"

"Unfortunately, you don't have an illness that can be cured with a prescription."

Addie felt her heart sink, and a thousand worst-case scenarios came rushing into her mind. Cancer, maybe, or kidney disease. She didn't want to ask the question, but she had little choice. "Am I—am I going to die?"

Whit shook his head. "I doubt it—unless I strangle you with my bare hands, that is. You're pregnant."

Addie's mind raced. She had never been very careful about keeping track of her cycles. It was an inconvenience, nothing more—a fact of life she genuinely wished God had had the foresight to plan some other way. She hadn't been thrilled, as other girls were, when she had matured, had never felt the longing some girls had for bringing new life into the world.

Not once in her life had Addie seriously considered the possibility of having children. She had always been too focused on her dream—making it big as an actress, building a career. She had even mocked Tish, just a little, for limiting herself, wanting nothing more than to be a wife and mother.

Now, in a single moment, all that had changed. A little someone was growing inside of her, the product of her love for Whitman Hughes . . . and his for her. A baby. A miracle. Instinctively she laid her hand on her abdomen and closed her eyes. A surging joy welled up in her, and a single tear streaked down her cheek. She reached out a hand toward the man she loved and grabbed a fistful of air.

Addie's eyes flew open. Whit was standing there, his arms crossed over his chest, watching her. And it was obvious that he did not share her joy.

"Whit—?"

He took a step back. "How could you let this happen?"

"Whit, I didn't intend—"

"Didn't you? Surely you're not so stupid or naive not to know where babies come from, or how to prevent them."

If he had slapped her full across the face, Addie could not have been more shocked. He had never used language like that toward her—calling her stupid and naive. He had always been the tenderest, most considerate of lovers. Had always treated her with gentleness and respect and solicitude. He had loved her, been devoted to her. . . .

Or had he?

Suddenly Addie saw the truth reflected in his eyes. An old saying returned to her, something she had heard back in North Carolina from one of the less genteel girls in school: *No fella buys the cow when he can get the milk for free.* At the time it had seemed to her a crude vulgarism, even though it was a sentiment she knew her father would agree with. Nice girls didn't talk about sex.

But her mind resisted. It wasn't that way with Whit. He loved her, wanted to be with her. He was just surprised, that's all. Once he got used to the idea—

"So what are you going to do about it?"

"It?" Addie stared at him.

"The baby. What are you going to do?"

"I don't know what you mean, sweetheart. This is—" she began, but he cut her off.

"I mean," he said deliberately, as if talking to a very stupid child, "that you've gotten yourself into a real mess here. Do you think this town is full of parts for pregnant actresses? Do you really believe anyone is going to hire you?"

"But Whit, I thought that you and I would—" She burst into tears.

He looked down at her, and at last his arms went around her, soothing her, whispering in low tones. "It'll be all right. It's not the end of the world."

Addie sighed and nestled against this chest. "Thank you, Whit. I knew you wouldn't let me down."

"Of course not. I'll help you through this. Before you know it, it'll all be over. You have your career to think about, after all."

Addie leaned into his embrace and tightened her arms around his waist. It would be all right, he said. It wasn't the end of the world. Then her mind registered his next words:

"There are people who can take care of this sort of thing. It won't be cheap, but I'll pay for it. And then things can get back to normal. The way they used to be."

She stiffened in his arms and pulled back. "Are you suggesting that I—?"

"Of course." He tightened his hold on her. "People do it all the time. You don't want to lose everything you've worked for, do you?"

Addie jerked away, and the words that came out of her mouth shocked her as much as they did him. "I haven't *worked* for anything, Whitman Hughes. You've *given* me everything. The clothes, the image, even this movie role—"

"And more roles to come, if you do the right thing," he added.

"If I kill my baby, you mean, and go on living in sin with you?"

Whit's lip turned up in a sneer. "Listen to you: *'Living in sin.'* You're still the little preacher's daughter, aren't you, no matter how much you try not to be." He took her by the shoulders and held her, putting his face so close to hers that she could feel his breath. "Pay attention, Addie. Face reality. Was I using you? Maybe. But no more than you've been using *me* to get what *you* wanted."

The truth stung, and a wave of shame washed over her. She had been so proud of herself, of how she was just about to break out in Hollywood, become the big star. And so proud that a man like Whitman Hughes had chosen her, had fallen in love with her. But she hadn't been able to do it honestly, to rid herself of all the vestiges of morality her parents had instilled in her. Instead, she had lied to herself, justified her actions, told herself that his divorce was just around the corner, that before long they could be married and—

None of it had to do with talent or gift or skill or even hard work. He was right: The only acting she had done was the act she had put on to deceive herself. And no amount of rationalizing could minimize that truth.

"All right," she said at last. "If we're telling the truth, let's tell it all. Your wife—"

"What about my wife?"

"You're not filing for divorce, are you?"

Whit chuckled. "Do you really want to know?"

"Yes."

"Okay, here's the truth: No, I'm not filing for divorce." He looked at her. "I'm not married. Never have been."

"But you said—"

"I said what you wanted to hear, Addie, that my vindictive, unreasonable wife was holding out on me. That she didn't understand me."

"But why?"

"Would you ever have moved in with me if you knew that I wasn't married and never intended to be?"

"Of course not."

"My point exactly. Marriage complicates things. Once we're done with this—this little problem—we can go back to the way we were. No commitments, no complexities."

"And if I refuse?"

He shrugged, and his eyes drifted to the set, where the makeup people were dabbing powder on the new blonde's lovely face. "There are other fish in the sea."

"But what about our baby?"

"*Your* baby, Addie," he corrected. "If you go through with this, you're on your own."

Addie fought for breath. She had asked for truth and had finally gotten it. But she wasn't sure, even now, whether she was better off with truth or with a beautiful deception. "One more question."

"Fire away."

The words wrenched up out of the depths of her soul. "Did you ever love me?"

"Addie, Addie." He brushed a hand over her cheek and leaned down to plant a kiss on her lips. "Of course I loved you"—he paused—"in my own way."

She watched through her tears as he walked back onto the set and began talking with the director and the blonde who had taken her place. Would she be the next one Whitman Hughes would serve brunch to on the deck of the Malibu beach house?

Probably. But Addie wouldn't be around to see it.

She had already seen enough. She had lost herself along the way, had gotten caught up in the pretense of a world that had no reality at its core. Everyone around her was putting on a show, even after the curtain came down. Adora Archer had bartered her heart for a chance at success, a shortcut to the fulfillment of her dreams.

But more than just her own life hung in the balance now. She had someone else to be responsible for—someone who was totally dependent upon her.

21
GODSEND

September 1931

Addie peered through the glass door of Grace Duncan's Hometown Cafe. The smell of fresh bread and a savory stew drifted out to her, and her stomach rumbled.

It had been six months since Whitman Hughes had turned his back on her and she had walked away. She had moved back to Miss McIlwain's, but when her condition began to show, Mother Mac had sent her packing. For weeks she had searched in vain for a job, any job, only to return at night to a seedy hotel in West Hollywood where the manager leered at her and made crass remarks under his breath.

Three days ago the money Whit had given her ran out. She had taken to the streets, standing in bread lines and sleeping under bridges with other homeless, desperate, destitute people.

But she couldn't go on like this indefinitely, Adora knew—not without risking the health and safety of her unborn child. Every kick, every tiny movement within her womb reminded her that she was no longer alone, responsible solely for herself. And despite her present wretchedness, she was determined to do better for this child than she had done for herself. She would find a place for the two of them, no matter what the cost.

And so, this morning, for the first time in a long time, Addie had prayed. Really prayed. She had laid her hand on her swelling midsection and asked—no, begged—for God to intervene on their behalf.

She doubted whether her father's God would condescend to listen to a woman like her, a woman who had flaunted convention and now was paying the price for it. But she held out a slim hope—just a glimmer—that perhaps another God, one more compassionate and forgiving, might listen to her plea and take mercy on her. Jesus did, after all, offer hope and forgiveness to the woman taken in adultery.

Dad had never preached on that one much, Addie mused, and the one time he did he had put most of the emphasis, as she might have expected, on the "Go and sin no more" part. But her father wasn't Jesus, and Jesus wasn't her father.

The truth rushed over her in a wave that left her breathless, and suddenly Addie realized that she had stumbled onto something important. All her life she had been judging God by the church—by the arrogant, uncompassionate attitudes of people like Alice Dorn and the spineless indifference of her own father. She had decided that if God was like that, she didn't want anything to do with him, ever.

But what if she had been looking at things from the wrong direction? What if God was less like her own father and more like the images of Jesus that she remembered from early childhood—the compassionate Savior who embraced children, touched lepers, and made the blind to see? What if God really was concerned about her, about her weakness and hunger, about the unborn child in her womb who was the innocent victim of her foolishness? Maybe she had been guilty of the worst kind of blindness, a self-inflicted darkness rooted in her own bitterness and rebellion.

"Look, God," she muttered as she leaned her hand against the glass door of the restaurant, "if you really do exist, and if you really do care, you're going to have to show me. And now would be a very good time . . ."

She waited, but no answer came. Then her head began to swim, and she crumpled into a heap on the sidewalk.

⌒∂⌒

"Honey, are you all right?"

Addie felt a gentle slapping against her cheeks and opened her eyes to see a hazy form leaning over her. Her eyes focused, and the image of a tall, broad woman with a homely face and bright red hair came into view.

"Where—where am I?"

"You're in Grace Duncan's Hometown Cafe." She grinned. "I'm Grace. And you are—"

"Addie. Addie—" She closed her eyes.

"How long has it been since you ate, hon?"

"I don't know. Couple of days, I guess."

"Well, come on, sit up. We're going to get some food into you pronto."

Addie struggled to a sitting position and then realized she had been lying across the seat of a booth in the back corner of the restaurant. She propped her chin in her hands and rested her elbows on the table. The redhead had disappeared.

But not for long.

"Here, now, eat up." The woman set a big bowl of stew in front of Addie, along with a wedge of homemade bread and a tall glass of milk. She slid into the booth and watched Addie while she ate. "You got family?"

Addie shook her head. "No."

"Husband?"

"No." Addie eyed her over the stew and gave her a scathing look.

"Nobody to take care of you?"

Addie bristled. "Why should I need anyone to take care of me?"

Grace threw back her head and laughed. "Well, just look at you, hon. You look like you've been sleeping in the streets and standing in the bread lines." She narrowed her hazel eyes. "But you sure don't look like it suits you much."

"I'm okay."

"Sure you are. You're just peachy." Grace reached out a work-roughened hand and fingered the lapels of Addie's filthy coat. "Nice fabric. Expensive. You haven't been out there for very long, have you?"

Addie let out a little snort of contempt. "You certainly ask a lot of questions."

"And you certainly don't seem to have many answers." Grace laughed again and leaned forward to peer over the table at Addie's swelling abdomen. "When's the baby due?"

Addie shrugged. "Couple months. Maybe three."

Grace eyed the empty soup bowl. "Would you like some more?"

"I—I don't have money to pay," Addie said. The admission shamed her, and she felt a hot flush creep up her neck.

"I know that." Grace left the table and came back with a second bowl of stew and more bread. "Drink your milk. It's good for the baby."

It was midafternoon, and the restaurant was deserted and quiet. "Why are you doing this?" Addie asked after she had eaten several more spoonfuls of stew.

"Doing what?"

"Giving me food, being so nice to me."

Grace chuckled. "Angels," she replied cryptically.

"Angels?" Addie shook her head. Just her luck, to be cooped up in a deserted restaurant with a madwoman who hallucinated about celestial beings.

"In the Bible. It says if you give help to strangers, if you feed the hungry and shelter the homeless, you just might be entertaining angels unawares."

Addie's stomach wrenched, and she laid the spoon aside. "Well, go out on the sidewalk, then. There's hundreds of angels everywhere you look. Are you going to 'entertain' them all?" She knew the words sounded harsh and cynical, but she couldn't help herself.

Grace, however, didn't seem to take offense. "Don't I know it," she said. "Too many, far too many." Her eyes took on a distant expression. "Too many to help them all."

"Then why help me?" Addie peered at the woman. She didn't look crazy, to tell the truth. She looked like a woman with a sense of purpose.

"Because you were the one who was sent." She said it simply, matter-of-factly, as if she were repeating the daily specials.

"Nobody sent me," Addie objected. "I just wandered by and apparently fainted in front of your door."

"You were sent, all right," Grace repeated firmly. "You got a job? A place to stay?"

"Do I look like I have a job?" Addie snapped.

"Well, you've got one now." Grace stood and gathered the empty dishes from the table. "There's a small apartment upstairs. It's not much, but it's clean, and it's yours if you want it. Go on up there, wash up, and get some rest. You can start tomorrow morning."

"Just like that?" Addie gaped at her. "You don't even know me."

"I know enough," Grace said. "Now, shoo. I've got work to do."

November 1931

Addie finished wiping down the last of the tables, turned the sign on the door so that it said "Closed," and eased her bulk into the nearest chair. Grace, sitting on a high stool next to the cash register, looked up from the till and smiled at her. "You doing okay, hon?"

"I feel like a watermelon on duck feet," Addie responded. "Do you think my ankles will ever be normal size again?"

"You're asking the wrong person." Grace shrugged. "Ask somebody who's had a baby." She chuckled. "But, yes, I think you'll get it all back soon enough. The ankles, the face, the figure—everything."

"How do women do this over and over again?" Addie asked, half to herself. "I had a friend back home who was the oldest of eleven children. Eleven! Can you even imagine it?"

"I can't, but then some women seem to feel differently about childbearing. Take my mama, for example. Best mother you'd ever hope to meet. Had six of us, and treated every one of us like we were the most special gift the good Lord had ever given her."

"Is that where you learned your faith, Grace? From your mother?"

"You don't learn faith, hon, at least not the way you learn arithmetic or grammar. Yes, you can be taught some principles of good living, but the real thing goes a whole lot deeper. It's like—well, it's like having a baby. You can know all the facts—where babies come from, and what those changes do to a mother's body when she's carrying her child. You can even imagine some of the pain and joy of delivering that baby and holding it in your arms for the first time." She sighed wistfully. "But until you do it for yourself, you never really know. You never really understand."

This wasn't the first discussion Addie'd had with Grace about religion, not by a long shot. But with Grace it wasn't really about *religion*. It was about something far more personal, something that had little to do with doctrines and worship styles. Personal relationship, she called it. Faith that makes a difference in the way you live your life.

And Addie had to admit that Grace's faith did make a difference. The woman lived as if she was accountable to God for everything she said and did and even thought. But the accountability she talked about wasn't some kind of hard-handed justice, meted out by a God who was just waiting for

her to step out of line. It was more like a marriage, like being in love. Grace
adored Jesus and didn't want to let him down.

The woman's faith was unlike anything Addie had ever witnessed, even
though she had grown up in the church as the daughter of a minister. Grace
Duncan took the Bible to heart, not quoting it or using it as a weapon, but
letting it guide her actions and attitudes. She provided food to those who,
in her words, "were sent to her," not as haughty charity, but as lowly service,
an honor placed upon her by the Lord who valued "the least of these." She
spent free time serving in bread lines and working in shelters. When she
could afford it, which wasn't often, she hired men off the street to do odd
jobs—and wept when they were gone because she couldn't do more for
them.

And what she had done with Addie had been nothing short of a miracle.
She had opened herself, heart and soul—taken her in and treated her as a
member of the family. Addie suspected that Grace was more thrilled about
the baby than she was. A new life, imprinted with the stamp and image of
God, she said. To Grace, every child was the Baby Jesus in the manger.

"Think about it," she had told Addie more than once. "We make Christmas into something it was never intended to be. When Jesus came, he was
born to a poverty-stricken, homeless woman who wasn't even properly
married at the time. Just like—"

"Just like me," Addie finished.

Before, Addie had always perceived the mother of Christ the way she was
portrayed in the crèches and stained-glass windows of her childhood—a
serene, bright-faced angel of a woman, her clothes unstained by the blood
of childbirth, her son quiet and smiling and holy, surrounded by a halo of
light and an array of heavenly choristers lulling him to sleep with a celestial lullaby.

But now, thanks to Grace's down-to-earth faith, Addie could identify with
Mary. A stranger in a strange land, with little more than the clothes on her
back and scant hope for the future, giving birth in a dank stable. A terrified
girl facing the blood and agony of delivery alone, attended only by a cadre
of animals who had been ousted from their place and one panic-stricken
man who was probably less than useless.

The difference was, in Addie's case there had been room at the inn.

Not only room, but an innkeeper who showered her with love, protection, and assurances that everything was going to be just fine.

Addie looked up and smiled fondly at Grace. The woman stopped counting money and raised an eyebrow. "Something on your mind, hon?"

"No, just thinking." Addie wouldn't tell Grace, at least not yet, but she was beginning to suspect that the woman's faith was rubbing off on her. It was so real, so right. If her father and Downtown Presbyterian represented Christianity, Addie didn't want it, not in a million years. But if Grace's kind of Christianity was a reflection of the true nature of God, Addie found herself drawn to it, and to the Lord Grace loved and served.

It was too soon to talk about it, of course. But it gave her hope. Hope for her own future, and hope for the child who waited to be born.

Addie felt a kick—a strong one. Then something gave way, and she looked down. Wetness flowed over the chair and onto the hard tile floor, gathering in a puddle under her feet.

"Grace—"

"Just a minute, hon." The woman held up a hand and kept counting.

"Grace, now!"

Grace looked up and suddenly she was all action.

She stuffed the uncounted bills into a bag and shoved it into her purse, then raced around the counter to Addie's side.

"Oh, my heavens!" Her eyes took in the puddle at Addie's feet. "Just keep calm. I think we should get the midwife, don't you?"

Addie laughed out loud. "That might be an idea."

"All right. Now, first I'll get you upstairs, and then I'll go for her. Or should I go for her first and let her help . . ."

Addie struggled to her feet and headed for the stairs.

"Right. Upstairs first." Grace took her arm. "There's plenty of time, hon— first babies usually take a long time coming."

"Like you know anything about babies?" Addie grinned.

"Okay. Point taken." They got to the top of the stairs, and Grace settled her on the bed and made a beeline for the door. "I'll be back as soon as I can. You need anything?"

"Yeah," Addie said. "I need you to shut up and get going."

"Right. Okay. Don't get up, all right? Just stay there."

"I'm not going out dancing, Grace. Now, go!"

When the door closed behind her, Addie lay back on the bed and sighed. Another contraction came, and she winced against the pain, but when it subsided she found herself giggling at Grace's panicky fussing. Everything would be all right. Grace would get back here with the midwife, the baby would be born, and her life would take on a whole new direction.

What direction that was, only God knew.

But in the meantime, she could count her blessings. She wasn't alone on the streets. She didn't have a dark and smelly stable for a delivery room. Grace and the midwife would at least be more capable attendants than Joseph and the cows and sheep.

And despite all her questions and uncertainties, Addie felt something else with her in the room. A presence, warm and comforting. A sense of joy and hope and possibility for the future.

"Thank you," she whispered as a tear seeped past her closed eyelid. "Thank you for sending me here . . . for Grace . . . for everything."

22
IN MEMORIAM

May 15, 1932

Addie sat on the sofa in the upstairs apartment and gazed down at the infant asleep in her arms. Was it possible that he was six months old? Nicholas A. Lovell. *A* for Archer.

Addie still wasn't sure why she had given him that middle name. It was a name she had fled halfway across the country to escape. Despite her abysmal failure as an acrtess, she had held on to the stage name, Lovell—a new identity she supposed. A new life unmarked by the past. And yet when the moment of truth came, when the midwife asked the name for the birth certificate, she'd returned to it like a compass seeking magnetic north.

Maybe, even after all this time, she still held out hope. Hope that little Nick would someday know his grandparents and be loved by them. Hope that *home* was still an option.

She had put it off for a long time, writing the letter that burned in her soul. She loved Grace Duncan, of course—the woman had given her everything, and most of all a place to belong. But now that this baby was a reality, a living, breathing, flesh-and-blood extension of herself, Addie couldn't shake the feeling that she owed it to him, and to her own soul, to try to reconnect with her parents.

A soft knock on the door interrupted her thoughts. Grace stuck her head into the apartment. "You busy?"

"Come on in. Nick went right to sleep after his feeding, and I was just about to put him in his crib." Addie got up and went into the small bedroom, settled her son with his blanket and teddy bear, and returned to the living room.

"You're really taking to this motherhood thing," Grace said with a smile.

"Do you think so?" Addie sighed. "Sometimes I wonder. Nick is such a good baby, and I love him with all my heart." She paused. "I never knew I could feel this much love. But I'm not sure it's enough. A child needs more than that . . . doesn't he?"

"More than love?" Grace frowned in thought. "I don't know. Seems to me love is the most important thing a person can have in life."

"But more than just—well, a mother. Doesn't a child—especially a boy— need a father too?"

"You're wanting to get married?"

Addie let out a cynical little laugh. "Be serious, Grace. Who would want to be saddled with me—an unmarried mother with a six-month-old son?"

"Surely you're not thinking of giving him up for adoption?"

A shock of pain knifed through Addie, and she closed her eyes against the thought. "I've wondered if it might be the best thing for him. But I couldn't do it—not now."

"That's a relief." Grace leaned forward and took Addie's hand. "You know I love you—both of you—like my own, don't you?"

"Of course I know that. You've been so good to me—to us. But I was thinking that maybe I should, well, at least let my parents know that they have a grandson. I've tried to avoid it, Grace, but the idea won't go away. It's like—"

"Like God is telling you something?"

"Yes." Addie chuckled and shook her head. "Can you imagine me saying such a thing a year ago?"

"You've changed," Grace said simply. "You've let God into your life, and now you can't ignore the urgings of the Spirit in your heart."

"I guess not. Do you suppose it means that my parents have changed too? That they—especially Dad—would be willing for me to come home with my baby?"

"I don't know." An expression of pain and resignation washed over Grace's face, and she averted her eyes. "I don't want you to leave, of course. I'd miss you something awful. But you have to follow your own heart, and far be it from me to stand in the way of what God's doing." She raised her head, and Addie saw the unshed tears that threatened to overflow. "The Lord's got purposes we can't fathom," she went on. "The same hand that brought you here might lead you away again. But you probably won't know the purpose until you've been obedient to what God's telling you to do."

Grace stood up and laid a hand on Addie's head. The simple touch communicated a depth of love that shook Addie to her roots. It felt as if all the love in Grace's heart, all her commitment to God, all her strength and compassion, flowed through her fingertips and into Addie's body. It was a silent blessing, a benediction.

"I'll leave you to your letter," she said at last. She leaned over, kissed Addie on the cheek, and was gone.

June 17, 1932

Addie was just finishing cleaning up after the lunch rush when the letter came.

It was a plain envelope, addressed to Addie in care of Grace Duncan's Hometown Cafe. No return address. But Addie knew where it had come from. She would recognize her mother's handwriting anywhere.

She sank down in a chair, trembling, holding the unopened envelope in one hand. For two weeks after she had mailed her letter, she had eagerly awaited a response. But as the days dragged on with no word from home, her hope flagged. And now that the long-awaited letter had finally arrived, she found herself unaccountably agitated. This letter held her future in the balance.

Grace came out of the kitchen and sat down beside her. She didn't need an explanation—one glance at the envelope in Addie's hand was sufficient.

"From your folks?"

Addie nodded. "From Mama, actually." She turned toward Grace and frowned. "It's odd, you know. Mama always supported Daddy, always agreed with him. I never once felt any sense of approval or encouragement from her. But the few letters I've received since I've been in Hollywood were from her. Not both of them. Her. She even sent me money a time or two."

Grace nodded. "I've seen all kinds of mother-daughter relationships in my time. Some of them good. Some of them not so good. None of them perfect, the way people would like to make you think. But during difficult times, even the worst mother usually stands up for her children. Think about Nick. What if he grew up and made some decisions you didn't think were very wise?"

Addie smiled. "He would never do that, of course. He's going to be the sweetest, kindest, most intelligent, wisest young man the world has ever seen."

"Certainly. But what if he made some choice that you didn't like?"

"I would do my best to trust him, naturally. And to support him. And no matter what, to make sure he knew I loved him."

"Maybe that's what your mother is doing, even though she doesn't know quite how."

"Oh, I hope so." Addie looked from Grace's face to the envelope she held in her hand. "But what if this is bad news?"

"Then you'll deal with it, just like you always have." Grace gave a resolute little nod. "Are you going to open it?"

Addie heaved a deep sigh, picked up a knife from the table, and slit the envelope. She pulled out the contents—a single page bearing a rumpled newspaper clipping. And across the top, three words: *I'm sorry. Mama.*

For a minute Addie couldn't speak as she scanned the contents of the article. Then she began to weep, huge hot tears of disappointment and despair. Grace waited, patting her arm and stroking her fingers. When she finally got control of herself, Addie handed the paper over. "It's worse than I thought."

Grace looked, but said nothing. At last, without a word, she laid the article on the table and put her arms around Addie.

Addie leaned into the embrace and gave a shuddering sigh. And over Grace's shoulder, the words from the newspaper clipping jumped out at her, mocking her, tormenting her wounded soul:

LOCAL PASTOR'S DAUGHTER DIES
Adora Archer, daughter of Reverend Charles Archer of Downtown Presbyterian Church, died last week from complications of influenza.

Miss Archer, a university student, was taken ill with the disease two weeks ago. A memorial service will be held at Downtown Presbyterian on Saturday, June 25, at 2:00 P.M. The family requests no flowers.
June 25 was Addie's twentieth birthday.

⟨∂⟩

June 25, 1932
The sanctuary of Downtown Presbyterian seemed different to Addie—dark and cloying and claustrophobic. She had waited in the alley around the corner until a little after two, then slipped in unnoticed to stand at the back of the nave and watch her own memorial service.

Addie didn't know why she was here—only that she had to come, to witness it for herself. Unless she saw her own father standing in his pulpit delivering his daughter's eulogy, she would never be able to believe him capable of such outright deception.

But oh, was he capable! He stood tall and erect, in a dark suit—without his holy robes—and intoned in a somber voice what a wonderful girl his daughter had been and how much everyone would miss her. "You all know," he said with a catch in his voice, "that after graduation, Adora left Asheville to pursue her education up east. She never returned to her family—with the expenses of her education there wasn't money to bring her all the way home for a visit. And that is my sole regret, not seeing my beloved daughter before she died."

But the influenza had taken hold quickly, he continued, and before they knew it, she was gone.

He droned on about Adora's brief but significant time on earth, how today was her birthday, and the angels in heaven were welcoming her to a feast in her honor. How even though her life had been tragically cut short, she had gone to a new home and a better place and would always be remembered in their hearts.

Addie tuned him out and let her gaze wander around the sanctuary. Alice and Stuart Dorn were there, flanked by Philip and Marcella. Her mother sat in the front row with her head down and her shoulders shaking, not meeting her husband's eyes. But Tish and Mavis Cameron were nowhere to be found, nor were Big Eleanor and Ellie James, or Mary Love Buchanan. Did they even know about the memorial service? Or had her father kept it completely quiet, burying the notice on page 32 of the newspaper?

Nick stirred in her arms, and she smoothed a hand over his velvety head. This should have been the great reunion, the chance for Mama and Daddy to get their first look at their beautiful grandson—a day of celebration and excitement. But there was no fatted calf for this Prodigal. No feast, no dance, no father waiting on the road to welcome and forgive. Only the declaration that Adora Archer was dead.

Well, she would stay dead. She would get back on the train and return to California, to the surrogate mother who loved and wanted her. She would raise her son in oblivion, never letting him know what kind of man his grandfather was. She would do what she had to do.

As Addie turned to leave, a ray of sunlight pierced through the sanctuary, illuminating one of the stained-glass windows left from the days when Downtown Presbyterian had been a cathedral. Her eyes went to the depiction of another unwed mother—Mary, dressed in a blue gown, holding the infant Christ. She wondered idly what her father would have done if Mary had been his daughter. Probably the same thing—turned his back on her and the Jesus he claimed to serve and left them alone to fend for themselves.

And a sword will pierce her heart . . .

An involuntary shudder ran up Addie's spine. The prophecy, spoken to Mary during the first few days of Jesus' life, seemed to apply to Addie as well. Watching her own father conduct her funeral service was a blade to the soul unlike any she could have ever imagined. And only God knew what further swords awaited her in the future.

She looked back at the stained-glass portrait of Mary and Jesus one last time. The woman, younger than herself, had already been told that the sword would pierce her heart. And yet she bore an unaccountable serenity, a peace that did not rest in circumstance, a hope that looked beyond tomorrow.

Of course. She held Christ next to her heart. Immanuel was with her.

An image rose to Addie's mind—the beloved countenance of Grace Duncan, with her wild red hair and coarse features, whose hard shell covered a tender and compassionate heart. Grace had helped her understand Immanuel, God With Us—not as a doctrine to be adopted, but as a Lord to be worshiped and adored.

She gave a solemn nod in Mary's direction and snuggled little Nick closer against her breast.

Immanuel was with Addie Lovell too.

No matter what tomorrow might bring.

23
ADORA'S DREAM

And so," Addie finished, "I went back to California. Once or twice over the years I considered coming home. But by then Grace was ill, Nick had gotten married, and I had taken over the restaurant." She shrugged. "Besides, my family was all in California. I wasn't about to leave then, not when my first grandchild was just getting ready to start school."

Dee looked up, and Brendan could see the tears in her eyes. "That was me," she explained. "Daddy went into the restaurant business while he was still in college."

Addie nodded. "When Grace passed away, she left the cafe to Nick. He's done quite well for himself too—established a whole chain of restaurants all over the West Coast."

Brendan put a new tape into the recorder—her fourth—and motioned for Addie to continue.

"There's not much more to tell. I still wanted to act—did bit parts now and then, and a few television commercials when they needed a really old lady to sell biscuits or maple syrup."

"Granmaddie! You were never *that* old."

"Well, I felt old. But my biggest acting job was the role I played for years, never letting anyone know—not even your father, Cordelia—what had really happened in those days." She paused and blinked back tears. "I'm sorry, child. I never meant to deceive you. I just, well—"

"I understand, Granmaddie," Dee interrupted. "In those days bearing a child out of wedlock was a horrible taboo. If people had known, it would have marked your life—and Daddy's—forever."

"I told Nick that his father had been killed in a fire—and technically that was true. Whitman Hughes died a year after Nick's birth when his Malibu beach house burned to the ground. But as he grew up, Nick fabricated a whole story around that one idea—that his daddy was a hero who gave his life to save others."

Dee grinned. "Guess we know now where I got my love of fiction."

Addie nodded and patted her cheek, then turned back to Brendan. "He was so set on it, I didn't have the heart to tell him otherwise. I just played out the role of the widow raising a son on her own."

"It must have been terribly difficult," Brendan said. "Even today, being a single mother is one of the most challenging jobs on earth."

"I had a lot of help." Addie smiled and nodded. "I couldn't have done it without Grace—or without God."

Brendan let that last comment sink in. Addie Lovell had been through some terrible tragedies in her life, not the least of which was the knowledge that her own father had declared her dead.

But she could still see the grace in it all, the ways God had led her and protected her and brought love into her life.

Addie reached over to the table and picked up the cobalt-blue bottle. "So many years ago, we put our dreams in this bottle. We fully expected them to come true, every one of us."

"But your dreams didn't exactly come true," Brendan said carefully. "You wanted to become a great actress, and—"

"There are all kinds of dreams," Addie interrupted with a distant gleam in her eye. "There are the dreams we hold in our minds, our plans for the future. And the dreams we cherish in our hearts, the secret dreams we tell no one. But even deeper than either of those are the dreams that fill our souls, the dreams even we don't know about. The dreams God gives us as a gift."

Brendan comprehended Addie's *words,* but she had the unsettling sensation that the *meaning* of those words lay beyond her, just out of reach. And something in her wanted to understand. Usually in situations like this, her ego got the best of her and she pretended to understand whether she did or not. But this time Brendan's desire for Addie's wisdom overcame the compulsion to maintain her image. "Could you explain that? I'm not sure I understand what you mean."

Addie fixed a bright eye on her, and Brendan felt as if the old woman could see straight into her soul. "Good for you, girl," she murmured. She gave a chuckle and went on: "The dream *itself* is the gift, you see—not necessarily the fulfillment. The dream, the longing for something outside ourselves, something greater and finer and nobler, is put into our hearts and souls by the God who loves us. The dreams we're aware of keep us reaching, give us hope, provide a goal to strive for. Whether or not they're ever fulfilled, they serve their purpose. Dreams are like love, child. Love is never lost, even if it goes unrequited. For the very experience of loving makes us tenderer, better people, more capable of receiving and appreciating God's love."

"You keep talking about God," Brendan said. "I don't mean to sound like a skeptic, but how exactly does God come into the picture? It seems to me that you might blame God for the fact that your dreams of becoming a great actress were never really fulfilled."

"No need to apologize for being a skeptic." Addie uttered a lighthearted laugh. "The good Lord loves skeptics—why, they're some of God's greatest triumphs." She gave Brendan a wink. "Sometimes I think the Almighty made people like you just to keep people like me on our toes. But don't you see, dear, it's the dreams we're *unaware* of that are the most important ones. God sees into our hearts and knows our souls inside out. Our conscious dreams may go unfulfilled, but the Lord's dreams—those deeper ones—are always realized. We just have to keep our eyes open to see the miracle when it happens."

She moved closer to Dee and reached out for her hand. "Take my life, for instance. Most folks, looking in from the outside, would say that it was a failure. I lost everything—my family, any chance at a real career—because of one stupid mistake I made when I was too young to know what was good for me. But the Lord has a way of taking the curse and turning it into a blessing." She squeezed her granddaughter's hand, and tears filled her eyes. "The way I see it, God restored it all, with more to spare. Gave me Grace, who saved my life and helped open my eyes to the goodness and mercy in life. Gave me Nick, whose presence made me grow up and understand what real love is all about. Gave me this wonderful granddaughter, and peace in my latter years. All the stardom in the world couldn't have been worth what I've received instead. It's been a very good life. And you can bet that when I go to meet my Maker, I won't be asking any foolish questions about why things didn't turn out the way I wanted them to be."

That night, in her house on Town Mountain, Brendan lay awake gazing out at the lights of the city. The story of the four women who had hidden their dreams in a bottle was turning out to be more, much more, than she had bargained for. It would make a great human-interest series, of course—her instincts hadn't failed her on that point. What she hadn't counted on, however, was the impact the story might have on her personal life.

Brendan had never given much thought to the deeper dreams in her own soul. Her career had always been everything to her, and when it had begun to lose its luster and vitality, she had panicked. Her entire identity was tied up with being the television reporter, the face in front of the camera. Who was she, apart from the persona of Brendan Delaney from station WLOS?

The unwelcome fact was, Letitia Cameron and Adora Archer had caused her to do some serious reevaluating, and she wasn't sure she liked what she saw. When the camera quit rolling and the story was wrapped up, was there anything of significance in Brendan's life that would sustain her?

She turned over in bed and willed herself to go to sleep, but she couldn't free her mind from the tangle of emotions that had been generated by all Addie's talk about God. If the old woman was right—and Brendan wasn't conceding that, mind you—then perhaps God had something more planned for her than a thirty-second spot on the eleven o'clock news and a bit of status as a local celebrity.

Addie's words churned in Brendan's mind, haunting her with the prospect of some deeper truth that still eluded her: *It's the dreams we're unaware of that are the most important ones. God sees into our hearts and knows our souls inside out. Our conscious dreams may go unfulfilled, but the Lord's dreams—those deeper ones—are always realized. We just have to keep our eyes open to see the miracle when it happens.*

When sleep finally claimed her, Brendan dreamed—a troubling image of herself as an old, old woman, lonely and isolated, boring everyone who came near with incessant reminiscences of the glory days long past, when she had been a famous reporter. People listened politely, as most folks were wont to do with the elderly, but she could see that their minds were elsewhere, and at the first opportunity, they made good their escape, returning to their own lives, to more important concerns, and leaving her alone once again.

She awoke just as the first threads of dawn crept over the mountain, jerking to consciousness to find her heart inexplicably heavy and her pillow soaked with tears.

Brendan lay there with her eyes closed, holding very still, trying to recapture the image of the dream. But it, like Addie's truth, eluded her. All that was left was the dull weight in her chest and the nagging suspicion that she was missing something important in her life.

24
THANKSGIVING

November 24, 1994

Brendan sat next to Dee Lovell and gazed around the massive oak dining table at the odd collection of guests gathered for the celebration. At the head of the table, Addie reigned resplendent in a flowing pantsuit of deep turquoise velvet with an enormous peacock feather adorning her platinum hair. To her right, subdued as Addie was bright, sat Letitia Cameron, clad in khaki slacks and a rag wool sweater, with Gertrude Klein, the ever-watchful Doberman, flanking her far side. Across the table, dear old Dorothy Foster beamed over them all as if she were solely responsible for this glad reunion.

"Quite a little family we have here, isn't it?" Dee whispered.

Brendan nodded, and unexpected tears stung at her eyes. Clearly, Dee included her in the "family" designation, as if she belonged. But despite the warm welcome she had received from everyone around the table, Brendan couldn't help feeling like an interloper, a fraud who had wormed her way into their hearts and lives under false pretenses.

Never had she felt so much an outsider as when they clasped hands and each woman around the table prayed, expressing the thankfulness in her heart. Addie and Letitia both offered tremulous gratitude for God's intervention in restoring their friendship. Gert and Dee gave thanks for the Lord's work on behalf of their loved ones, and Dorothy Foster thanked God for bringing Brendan into their lives and using her to accomplish the Almighty's purposes. When it came Brendan's turn, she hadn't the faintest idea what to say. Her heart was full, certainly, but filled with as much confusion and apprehension as thankfulness. She muttered something about being grateful for having friends to share this day with, and when she looked up, everyone was smiling at her as if they were privy to some inside joke she didn't get.

The truth was, Brendan *was* thankful for being invited to this gathering, and especially grateful for the way Dee went out of her way to make her feel included. But still she stood on the outside, looking in on a perspective of faith she couldn't fully understand.

These women—all of them—believed firmly that God had been at work in their lives for the past sixty-five years: leading them, guiding them, intervening to help them fulfill their dreams, or if not to fulfill them, at least to give them new and better futures than the ones they had envisioned for themselves. And just as surely, they believed that she, Brendan Delaney, self-confessed agnostic, was the instrument of the Almighty that had brought God's will to fulfillment in this reunion.

As dinner progressed, the old women chattered among themselves like geese on a riverbank, leaving Brendan and Dee to conversation of their own. Once she no longer felt as if she were on display as the Miraculous Hand of God, Brendan began to relax a little and actually started to enjoy herself.

For one thing, she truly liked Dee Lovell. The young woman was bright and intensely creative, with an amazingly incisive sense of humor. After their first meeting, Brendan had bought the novel, *A Sense of Place,* and read it in a single weekend. The words, the emotions of the book, gripped her. She felt as if she had been immersed in the depths of Cordelia Lovell's mind and heart and come out of the waters a new person.

The novel was the story of a career woman, just divorced after a painful and abusive marriage, who had a bright future ahead of her but did not feel as if she fit anywhere. The woman's struggle to find her place, a spiritual and emotional refuge for the healing of her soul, led her to purchase and renovate a run-down old Victorian house. Her labor to save the house from being condemned paralleled the renovations of her own heart, and by the end of the novel she had discovered herself and cultivated a "sense of place" that not only redeemed her, but brought peace and healing to those around her.

It had been a long, long time since Brendan had experienced that kind of connection—either with a book or with another person. But reading *A Sense of Place* left her with the satisfying feeling of looking down the darkened corridors of her own life and finding hope and light there and with conviction that she and Dee Lovell could be friends—good friends. For the first time in ages, Brendan admitted to herself that she *needed* such a friend. It was a moment of epiphany for her, and a moment of painful self-examination.

Brendan had never had the time or energy for close relationships. A few years back she had been engaged to a handsome anchorman whose lifestyle dovetailed perfectly with hers. She and Steve had so much in common, she told herself—both of them reporters, both able to understand the crazy schedules and incessant demands of the job. But in the end, the relationship turned out to be less about love and more about convenience. The job always came first, and they spent time with each other when nothing else pressed in to sidetrack them. When Steve received a job offer at Turner Broadcasting in Atlanta, there was no question that he would take it, no question that Brendan would stay behind at WLOS. They parted amiably, wishing each other good luck. Brendan hardly noticed when he was gone.

Now, for some reason she couldn't quite comprehend, Brendan had begun to feel the need for people in her life—not fans or coworkers, but people who cared about her for who she was, people who could fill the place of the family she had lost. When the invitation had come to share Thanksgiving with Dee and Addie and the others, she didn't hesitate to accept. And it wasn't for the sake of the story, either—it was for the sake of her soul.

The awareness of her need for others represented a significant change in Brendan Delaney's understanding of herself and, finally, she was able to admit it. She, like Dee's protagonist, desperately needed a sense of place. A sense of belonging. Following this story, meeting these people, witnessing these friendships had opened up a vacuum in her that she had denied for most of her adult life. Subconsciously she knew, even if she couldn't or wouldn't articulate it, that over the years she had gradually shut down—first with her parents' deaths and then with the loss of Gram.

An image swam to the surface of her consciousness, a picture of herself clad head to toe in heavy, shining armor, like a medieval knight. Arrows that flew in her direction bounced off, leaving her unharmed. But the same armor that defended her kept her from feeling the touch of people who drew close to her in love and friendship.

The price of protection was far too high. She had shielded herself against getting hurt, but what had she given up in the process?

Dee reached over and laid a hand on her arm, and Brendan jumped as if she had been burned with a live coal.

"Deep in thought?" Dee grinned at her.

"Something like that."

"Well, come back to earth. Granmaddie has an announcement to make."

Brendan looked to the head of the table, where Addie Lovell stood tapping a spoon on her water glass for attention. The peacock feather bobbed up and down as the old woman began to speak. "I want to welcome all of you," she said formally, "to our little Thanksgiving celebration. Thanks to Brendan Delaney, that sweet young thing, Tish and I have found each other after more than sixty years, and this time we're not losing touch again." She reached out a spotted hand and gripped Letitia's gnarled fingers. "In fact, my granddaughter and I have invited Tish and Gert to come and live with us here. After all these years, it's about time Letitia Cameron got out of that dismal apartment and into a place with a little elbow room."

Brendan turned to see Dee smiling broadly. "You're really doing this? Taking on another one?"

"They'll be so good for each other," Dee whispered. "And Gert can look after both of them when I have to travel."

"You're amazing," Brendan said.

Dee shrugged. "Not really. I just love Granmaddie and want her to be happy."

"And we have a surprise for Brendan too," Addie went on. She motioned to Letitia, who dug in her purse, came up with a rumpled envelope, and handed it over. "Tish received this in the mail yesterday." She passed it across to Brendan.

"What is it?"

"It's a birthday card to Tish from Ellie. From an address in Atlanta." She narrowed her eyes at Brendan. "If you're still interested in pursuing this story, that is."

Brendan's heart gave a little jump. The reporter in her began to salivate, like a bloodhound closing in on a scent. But it was more than a story now, more than just an obsession to reach the end of a fascinating search. It had become personal—a quest not just to find the four women and discover what had happened to their dreams, but to find herself and understand her own secret longings.

She stretched her hand across the table and took the envelope.

"You bet I am," she said. "I'll leave for Atlanta in the morning."

At noon the next day, Brendan pulled the 4Runner to a stop at the curb in a north Decatur suburb. It was a typical neighborhood from the 1940s or 50s—a tidy little row of brick houses, each with its own small fenced yard, single carport, and brick-bordered flower bed around a small front stoop. Number 305 looked pretty much like the rest of them, with the exception of a large Himalayan cat perched on the porch rail.

Across the street, an old man tottered to the curb supported by a walker, retrieved his mail, and waved a shaky hand in her direction. Brendan waved back. She wondered idly if he had lived here all his life and what he'd think if he knew that his neighbor, Eleanor James, was about to become part of the most fascinating story Brendan had ever imagined.

She locked the car and started up the walk, hefting her bag onto her shoulder, but had barely reached the steps when the door opened and a shadowed figure appeared behind the screen. Brendan shaded her eyes. "Eleanor? Eleanor James?"

The screen door opened, and the cat leaped off the rail and dashed inside. "I'm Eleanor."

Brendan regarded her. She had to be in her eighties, but she looked much younger—sixty or sixty-five, at the most. She was tall and slim and wore khaki slacks, a blue denim shirt with kittens embroidered on the pockets, and brown loafers. Her hair wasn't gray, exactly, but a faded blonde, cut short and brushed back from her temples. Her features—high cheekbones and wide brown eyes set in a heart-shaped face—retained if not beauty, at least elegance, unadorned by cosmetics. A web of wrinkles fanned out from the corners of her eyes, laugh lines that gave her a perpetual expression of merriment.

Eleanor ran a hand through her hair. "Forgive my appearance. I wasn't expecting company."

Brendan stepped onto the porch and held out her business card, and the woman scrutinized it for a minute before looking up again. "You're a reporter?" She chuckled and shook her head. "What would the Asheville TV people want with an old gal like me?"

Brendan smiled. "Actually, I'm here wearing two hats. I'm a reporter, yes, and I'm working on a story I hope you can help me with. But more importantly, I—well, I've come on behalf of some old friends of yours."

She reached into her bag and drew out the blue bottle. "Do you remember this?"

The woman extended a hand and took the bottle. "Dear heavens," she breathed. "I'd nearly forgotten." Her gaze locked on Brendan's face. "The others—?"

"Tish and Adora are alive and well and send their love," Brendan assured her. "I have yet to track down Mary Love Buchanan."

"Adora is *alive?*" Tears sprang to the old woman's eyes, and she let out a deep sigh. She blinked hard and peered at Brendan.

"And why, may I ask, are you 'tracking us down,' as you put it, after all these years?"

Brendan hesitated. She wasn't sure she could explain it, her compulsion to find out the end of the story. It had become more, much more, than an interesting profile, a diversion from the humdrum of daily news spots. Now it was more like a personal crusade, a quest to find answers to questions she hadn't even identified yet.

"When the Cameron House was demolished recently, one of the workmen found this bottle and gave it to me, and I discovered the papers inside. It started out as a news story—you know, a personal-interest piece—but it seems to have taken on a life of its own." Brendan paused, searching for words. "I really do need to talk with you, if you have the time. Not just for the story, but for myself."

Eleanor stepped aside and motioned for Brendan to enter. "Old folks like me have nothing left but time," she said with a light laugh. "Come on in; I was just fixing some lunch."

Brendan stepped into the tiny living room and blinked as her eyes adjusted to the dimmer light. The small space was crowded with furniture—a Victorian-era settee, marble-topped tables, an ancient oak pump organ, a set of glass-fronted barrister bookcases. Furnishings, she guessed, from the days when the Jameses owned their big home in Asheville's most prestigious neighborhood.

"The furniture doesn't fit in this little house, I know," Eleanor said as if reading her mind. "But I couldn't bear to part with it all." She snapped on a Tiffany lamp and gestured toward an open doorway. "Let's sit in the kitchen; it's more comfortable."

Brendan settled herself at a round oak pedestal table with huge claw feet and matching pressed-back chairs while Eleanor set out turkey sandwiches and tall glasses of iced tea. "Hope you don't mind Thanksgiving leftovers."

"Not at all. I love turkey." Brendan arranged her tape recorder and notepad on one side of the table, away from the food.

"I suppose I should have just gone to the center and had dinner with the others," Eleanor murmured, half to herself. "But it doesn't seem like Thanksgiving unless the house is full of all those good smells." She took a seat opposite Brendan. "Do you mind if I say grace?" Without waiting for an answer, she bowed her head and offered up a brief prayer of thanks. "I bought the smallest turkey I could find," she went on when she unclasped her hands, "but I guess I'll be eating leftovers until way past Christmas."

"Did you have Thanksgiving here . . . alone?" Brendan felt a pang of remorse as she recalled the large happy gathering in Dee Lovell's massive dining room. Eleanor could have been there with them—

Eleanor shook her head. "I had a few folks in—people from church who had no place else to go." She smiled. "Everybody keeps telling me I should get rid of this old house and move into the Assisted Living Center, where I could have my own apartment and access to help when I needed it. But it wouldn't be the same. I have friends there, but nobody really close. Not like—" She pointed to the blue bottle, which caught the autumn sunlight and glowed as if it had a life of its own. "Not like the friends I used to have."

"Can we eat and talk at the same time?" Brendan reached for the tape recorder. "I'm very eager to hear your story. All I know is what you wrote to put in the bottle—that you dreamed of becoming a social worker and helping those who couldn't help themselves."

"Like Jane Addams," Eleanor sighed. "You know about Jane Addams and Hull House?"

"A little," Brendan hedged. The fact was, she had done a good deal of research on the social services pioneer, but she'd rather hear Eleanor's perspective.

"I read *Twenty Years at Hull House* over and over when I was a girl,"

Eleanor went on. "She was my hero, my idol. Maybe because she stood for principles so completely opposite of the things my own mother valued." She took a bite of her sandwich and chewed thoughtfully. "Life with Mother was very difficult. All she cared about was money and social status and the power and influence she could exert because of her wealth. I often felt like—what was the term Dr. Estes used? *A misplaced zygote.* As if I had somehow been set down in the wrong family."

Brendan held up a hand. "Wait a minute. You've read *Women Who Run With the Wolves*?" The bestseller was a favorite of hers, a book she read and reread, finding her own inner longings in the archetypes the author used to explain human behavior and relationships.

Eleanor grinned. "I'm old, Miss Delaney, not dead. My body may be too decrepit to do aerobics, but my mind hasn't given up on exercise."

Brendan felt a flush of shame creep up her cheeks. "Forgive me," she stammered. "I just don't often meet, ah, older women who would read a book like that."

"Or understand it?" Eleanor held up a bony forefinger and wagged it in Brendan's face. "Beware of stereotyping people, Miss Delaney. You'd be surprised how much people my age understand."

Not anymore, Brendan thought, but she made a mental note to try to keep her foot out of her mouth for the duration of the interview. "So," she prompted, "you felt like a misfit in your own family?"

"I'm afraid so. Even as a small child, I disagreed with my mother's belief that money equaled worth, that poor people pretty much brought their poverty on themselves and deserved the misery they got. As I grew older, I felt increasingly out of place in my mother's social circles. Mary Love Buchanan was my best and dearest friend—you know about her, I assume?"

"A little. The eldest of eleven children, from a middle-class Catholic family."

Eleanor nodded. "Mother despised Mary Love, thought she was a very bad influence on me. Too common, you know. I endured her nasty comments about Catholics in general and Mary Love in particular—it didn't do any good to disagree with Mother overtly—but I always resented having to keep silent. Then Tish came up with the idea of sharing our dreams with each other, putting them in the bottle. It was a defining moment for me."

"What do you mean by that?"

"I was sixteen. Writing out those dreams made me think about myself, about my life, about what I wanted for the future. Everything crystallized, and I was finally able to identify not just what I *didn't* want for my life—namely, to be like my mother—but what I *did* want. I wanted to make my life count for something, to mean more than a bank account or a place on the social register. I wanted to leave a legacy behind, like—"

"Like Jane Addams?"

"Yes. Like that." Eleanor pushed her plate aside and picked up the blue bottle. "I was very young and no doubt very naive," she sighed. "I didn't know, at sixteen, what kinds of things, terrible things, could get in the way of a young girl's dream. . . ."

ELEANOR

25
THE DEATH OF A DREAM

December 24, 1929

Little Eleanor James stood with her mother at the doors of Downtown Presbyterian and scanned the crowd for Letitia and Adora. There—on the second row! Tish was sandwiched in between Adora and Philip Dorn, and there was enough room on Adora's other side for Ellie. Just then Adora caught her eye and waved.

"Mother, I'm going to sit with my friends. I'll catch up with you after the service."

Before her mother had a chance to object, Ellie made good her escape, but she could feel her mother's eyes boring into her back as she made her way down the aisle. A wave of guilt washed over her. It was Christmas Eve, after all. And although Mother would never admit it in a thousand years, she probably was lonely, missing Father, and wanting to share the service with her daughter, the only family she had left.

But she never says that, Ellie's mind protested. Mother never gave any indication of tenderness toward her or her own needs for love and closeness. The sole basis for their interaction was her mother's demands and her own capitulations. All her life, it seemed—or at least since Ellie's father had died when she was nine—Ellie had walked on eggshells, trying desperately to make Mother happy. *No,* Ellie thought, *that's not right. Mother isn't capable of being happy. She's only capable of being less disgruntled.* Despite a life of relative wealth and ease, Eleanor James the Elder did not seem the least bit inclined to enjoy her privileged situation. She depended upon her status but still seemed determined to focus on the bleakest, most dismal aspects of every situation. And thus had fallen to Ellie the responsibility of ordering the circumstances of their lives so that her mother's melancholy would be minimized.

Because Ellie had been named after her mother, their friends had for years referred to them as Big Eleanor and Little Eleanor. Ellie hated the name; it made her feel as if she were destined to become like her mother—a fate she wouldn't wish on her worst enemy. She loved Mother, of course—loved her with the determined duty and suppressed rage of an only daughter. But she had no intention of following in her footsteps. Her whole life, and all her aspirations for the future, focused on a single objective—to prove that she had been wrongly named.

Hidden in a drawer beneath her undergarments was proof of that determination—a statement of her secret dreams, which tomorrow afternoon she would share with her three best friends. They might not understand, but at least they would encourage and support her.

When Tish had come up with the idea that they all write out their dreams and make a commitment to each other to see those dreams fulfilled, everything had come clear to Ellie. For years she had struggled with attitudes she couldn't articulate—the suspicion that she had been adopted, because she was so radically different from the woman she called Mother. The desire to do something—anything—to prove that she wasn't "Little Eleanor." The longing, bordering on desperation, to make her life and future meaningful and significant.

She had begun writing aimlessly, rambling on about her feelings concerning Mother, her hatred of the wealthy social circle that absorbed her mother's time and attention, her feelings of closeness with Mary Love, and how she fit better into Mary Love's middle-class world than she did her own world of wealth and privilege. Then, as she continued to write, something miraculous happened. A vision took shape in her mind and translated itself into words on the page—her calling, her destiny.

Eleanor James the Younger intended to put behind her the entitlements of her station as a daughter of wealth and give her life to helping those less fortunate than herself. She had read and reread her dog-eared copy of *Twenty Years at Hull House* and had taken Jane Addams as her personal hero. That, Ellie thought, was what life was all about—offering a hand to those in need. Voluntarily abdicating rank and privilege in order to live among the poor and be a champion for them. It was a noble cause, and she felt a heady sense of liberty just thinking about it.

Her best friend, Mary Love Buchanan, had already warned her that Big Eleanor would have a fit when she found out. But Ellie didn't care. If she stayed here, in her mother's aristocratic, self-centered world, she would certainly lose her mind before she was twenty. No, Ellie James would go where the greatest need was, and she would make a difference in the world.

December 25, 1929

As Ellie left Cameron House and walked home, a chill wind raised goose bumps on her arms and set her blood racing. She had done it. She had declared, in front of God and everybody—or at least in front of her three closest friends—her intention to immerse herself in the culture of the Have-Nots and do everything in her power to improve their miserable and hopeless lot. She could already envision herself in the teeming city of Chicago, laboring beside Jane Addams at Hull House, becoming a social worker whose commitment to change made a radical difference in other people's lives.

Tish's father seemed certain that this stock market crash would turn around soon enough, that the economy would right itself and things would get back to normal. He kept reassuring Mother that if she would resist panicking and wait it out, she'd come out just fine. But Ellie didn't believe it. And even if the economy did recover, the Crash had already done irreparable damage. She had seen the homeless people standing in line for food, and she was certain it was worse in the big cities. Folks like her mother and the Camerons would no doubt recover, but the little people who had lost their jobs and homes and life savings wouldn't be so lucky. They would need social workers like Ellie and Miss Addams.

A mental image of Mother's pinched, disapproving scowl overshadowed Ellie's noble picture of herself at Jane Addams' side, giving aid and succor to the poor. Mother wouldn't like it one bit, that much was certain. She would undoubtedly accuse Ellie of abandoning her, would load on the guilt with a shovel and leave her daughter feeling as if she had committed some unspeakable crime by not wanting to live her mother's life.

Ellie would have to be strong. She had wasted a great deal of time and effort over the years acceding to Mother's incessant demands, but the time would come—and soon—when she would have to stand up to the woman and refuse to give in anymore. She had already taken the first step by revealing her dreams to her friends, and it gave her a heady, glorious sense of freedom to know that as soon as she graduated from high school—only a year and a half from now—she would be on her way to becoming her own person. No longer Little Eleanor James.

Perhaps she'd be known as Little Jane Addams instead.

Now, that was a shadow she wouldn't mind standing in.

∽

January 1, 1930

Ellie sat in the front parlor of Cameron House and watched with stinging eyes and a heavy heart as Letitia Cameron tried in vain to comfort her mother. She knew all too well what it felt like to lose a father, and she understood the grave responsibility that had been laid on Tish's shoulders, to be her mother's primary source of support. But Maris Cameron was a strong woman, a loving, open-hearted woman—the kind of person Ellie always wished her own mother would be. Maris would get through this, even as difficult and heartbreaking as it was. Ellie wasn't nearly as certain of her own mother's ability to weather the storm.

When Father had died, Randolph Cameron had persuaded Mother to let him handle her finances. It didn't take much to convince her, of course—Mother had never had a mind for business and no intention of developing one. Big Eleanor was quite content to turn it all over to Randolph Cameron, who headed up the most prestigious and well-respected brokerage firm in town. And he had done well by her too, investing so wisely that she had enough to support her for several lifetimes—even in the lavish style to which she was accustomed.

In Ellie's mind, her mother's wealth translated into thousands of children fed, the poor clothed and housed and educated. But Big Eleanor had no such philanthropic notions about the way money should be spent. She lived high and showy—wearing expensive clothes, throwing elaborate parties, and wielding almost unlimited influence in her social circle. The truth was, Ellie was ashamed of her mother and couldn't wait to be free of her expectations.

Mary Love Buchanan stood nearby, fingering a rosary and sending commiserating glances in Ellie's direction. Ellie rarely saw her friend pray, except on those infrequent occasions when she accompanied Mary Love to Mass. Mrs. Buchanan supplied enough prayers for the entire city, Mary Love often complained, keeping God too busy to pay much mind to anyone else. But this situation was different—the suicide of Letitia's father had been enough to drive them all to their knees.

Everyone was focused on Tish and her mother, doing whatever they could by word or presence to bring comfort in this time of shock and grief. All except Big Eleanor. She sat slumped in an overstuffed parlor chair staring at the rug and muttering, "What's to become of me now?"

"Mother, hush," Ellie snapped. Randolph Cameron was dead, for heaven's sake. Tish and Maris's grief was far more important than Big Eleanor James's concern about her finances and her self-absorbed fears for the future.

But when the sheriff and Pastor Archer returned from Randolph Cameron's study with a thick file folder, the expressions on their faces told Ellie that her mother might have reason to be concerned.

"We found something that might help explain this . . . ah, situation," the sheriff began.

Situation. A man was dead, discovered by his only daughter, hanging from the attic rafters, and the sheriff referred to it as a *situation*. Ellie's eyes locked on Tish's hopeless expression, and she cringed.

"Everything's gone," Pastor Archer affirmed with a deep sigh. "Stocks, bonds, everything." He turned toward Ellie and her mother. "Yours, too, Eleanor. I'm sorry."

Mother let out a moan, then began protesting that Randolph had promised her it would get better if she'd only bide her time. "He said to wait," she mumbled over and over again. "Just to wait. He said—"

"He didn't wait long enough," Pastor Archer explained. "The market is recovering, but apparently Randolph panicked. He sold everything, for almost nothing, just trying to keep his head—and yours, Eleanor—above water."

Reality jolted through Ellie's veins like an electric shock. For years—almost as long as Ellie could remember—her mother had been utterly dependent upon her wealth and status. Her position in society defined her; what would she be without it?

"You didn't mortgage your house, did you, Eleanor?" Pastor Archer was asking.

Mother shook her head numbly. "No."

"Then you'll be all right. There's enough to live on . . . as long as you've got a place to live." He turned and gave an apologetic shrug in Maris Cameron's direction. "I'm afraid you're not so fortunate, Maris. These records show that Randolph took a loan on the house—a big one—for investment capital."

"We found a will that leaves everything to you," the sheriff put in. "But I'm afraid it isn't much—only your personal possessions, furniture, and a little cash."

Ellie felt as if she had been hit in the stomach with a cannonball. All her plans for becoming a social worker like Jane Addams, so that she could help those less fortunate than herself, now rose up to mock her. Suddenly *she* had become one of the less fortunate—she and her mother, along with Tish and Maris Cameron. And she hadn't the faintest idea what to do to make it better.

All Ellie knew was that everything had changed in an instant. And she had the sinking feeling she was about to find out what it meant, that old saying that charity begins in your own backyard.

26
LIFE SENTENCE

January 1, 1940

Ellie positioned the calendar on the hook behind the kitchen door and stared at it. January. A new year. No, she thought. Not a *new* year. Just *another* year.

Was it possible that ten full years had passed since that terrible day when Randolph Cameron had taken his own life—and with it Ellie's hopes for the future? It hardly seemed possible, but the calendar didn't lie. *1940.*

Ten years gone, just like that? It had been ages since she'd seen any of her friends. Mary Love had long since moved away. Adora, rest her soul, had died years back of the influenza. Letitia was still in town, but as busy as she was with teaching and helping with her mother's booming catering business, it had been more than a year since she had visited. Life went on, for everyone except Ellie.

Five days ago, on December 28, Little Eleanor James had turned twenty-seven.

Not that it made any difference. The birthdays had passed unnoticed, just like the Easters and Christmases and New Years. Ellie did her best to mark those holidays, making little presents for her mother, baking a ham or a nice hen with cornbread dressing, bringing in fresh flowers. But the gifts went unused, the flowers wilted in their vases, and more often than not Ellie ate alone at the kitchen table.

The doctors had done what they could for Mama, but in the end they threw up their hands in despair and went away. There was nothing physically wrong with her, they said. She had simply retreated into herself, to a place far away where no one could reach her.

Thus the responsibility for everything—the house, their finances, Mama's care—had fallen to Ellie. Fortunately, they had been able to keep the big stone house and had a minimal income from re-investment of the stocks Randolph Cameron had sold at rock-bottom prices. It was enough to get by—to pay for food and utilities, keep up with the taxes—but barely. Sometimes the enormity of it all overwhelmed Ellie so that she could barely breathe. But most of the time she just put one foot in front of the other, marking the unchanging days off the calendar like a prisoner waiting for parole, and all the while pushing from her mind the insistent realization that there would be no release for Little Eleanor James. This was a life sentence, and she just had to make the best of it.

Ellie arranged Mama's breakfast on a wooden tray—orange juice, a scrambled egg with toast, a sliced apple. With heavy steps she pushed through the kitchen door and made her way up the stairs.

"Happy New Year, Mama!" she said cheerfully as she entered her mother's bedroom. The heavy draperies rendered the room almost as dark as night, and a musty smell assailed her nostrils. "Let's get some light and air in here, shall we? It's a beautiful day—a bit cold, but bright and sunshiny."

No response.

Ellie pulled back the curtains and, with a good deal of effort, opened the window just a crack to dispel the stuffiness. Her mother lay with her knees curled to her chest under a mound of tangled bedclothes. Ellie straightened her up, fluffed the pillows, and leaned her against the headboard. "I brought you a nice breakfast, Mama. Maybe we could go for a little walk later this morning. Would you like that?"

It was always the same, day in and day out. Every morning Ellie made the climb up the stairs; every morning she spent an hour or more trying to get a few bites of egg or oatmeal into Mama. Every morning, rain or shine, Ellie suggested that perhaps they might go out today, to take a walk or visit friends or go shopping or have lunch at some little restaurant downtown. She kept up the charade, even though she knew it was hopeless. Mother had not set foot outside this house since Randolph Cameron's funeral ten years ago. But Ellie kept trying, holding on to the slim hope that one day her mother would return from wherever she had gone, would come out of that dark place as suddenly and inexplicably as she had gone in.

"Come on, Mama. Let's get this breakfast into you and then get you up and dressed for the day."

Ellie spooned eggs into her mother's mouth and fed her the apple one slice at a time. Mama chewed obediently and drank a sip or two of the orange juice, but her eyes never registered an awareness that she was eating, or even acknowledged her daughter's presence.

When breakfast was over, Ellie helped her mother into the bathroom, ran water into the tub, and removed her nightgown. Even though she saw it every day of her life, Ellie never got used to the sight of her mother's shriveled, pale body—the sagging, wrinkled skin, the pendulous breasts against jutting ribs. In past years Big Eleanor James had lived up to her name—a tall, robust woman with a full and healthy figure, a flawless coiffure, a rosy flush to her cheeks. Now her flesh hung from a skeletal frame as if all the substance had been sucked out of her. As indeed it had. She never ate unless Ellie fed her, never moved unless Ellie moved her. Wherever she was placed—in the bed, in a chair in the parlor, at the kitchen table—she stayed until she was moved again. It was like living with a cadaver that kept on breathing.

Ellie washed and dried her mother, dusted her body with a sweet-smelling powder, and helped her into a dark cotton dress with a sash. The dress hung on her shoulder blades like rags on a scarecrow, but at least she could cinch it around the waist to give it some semblance of shape.

They moved back to the bedroom, where Ellie placed her in front of the vanity, brushed her hair, and applied a little rouge to her cheeks. "There! You look beautiful, Mama. Like you're ready to go out dancing at a New Year's ball." It was a lie, of course, but it hardly mattered because it roused no response in Mama anyway.

"Now, we're going to go downstairs and you can keep me company while I clean up the kitchen."

Quickly, Ellie made up the bed, shut the window, and gathered up the remains of the breakfast tray. Then, with the tray in one hand and her other arm supporting her mother, they went down to the kitchen.

Ellie had just put away the last of the dishes when a knock sounded on the front door. "Stay here, Mama—I'll get it."

She opened the door to find a strange man standing on the porch, cap in hand. A good-looking fellow—late thirties, she guessed—tall and rangy, with sandy blond hair, piercing blue eyes, and ruddy cheeks flushed by the cold.

"May I help you?"

"Miss James? Ellie James?"

"Yes." Ellie found herself staring and quickly averted her eyes.

"I hope I didn't come at a bad time." He gave a deferential little bow. "My name is Roman Tucker."

Ellie waited, and after a minute or two of awkward silence, the man apparently realized that she had no idea why he was there. He laughed and raked a hand through his hair.

"Sorry. I should have made myself more clear. I'm an acquaintance of Maris and Letitia Cameron, from East Asheville Methodist Church."

"If you're here for a contribution, I'm afraid you've come to the wrong place. If you'll excuse me—" Ellie started to shut the door, but he put his hand out to stop her.

"No, you don't understand. I'm here to help."

"What do you mean, help?"

"I'm a handyman, you see, and—"

Ellie closed her eyes and shook her head. "I'm sorry, Mr., ah, Tucker, is it? We simply can't afford—"

"Listen," he interrupted, "I'm fully aware of your situation. Tish and Maris told me all about it. I'm not looking for money—I have a part-time job as custodian of the church. I'm looking to make a trade."

With fascination, Ellie watched the animation in the man's eyes. How long had it been since she had seen this kind of life in another person's expression? "What kind of trade?"

"Unless I miss my guess, you need someone to help out around the place. I need room and board." He grinned at her, drew an envelope from the inside pocket of his jacket, and presented it to her with a flourish. "Proof, milady, that I am a gentleman of the highest reputation, who in no way will prove a danger or an annoyance to your lovely person."

Ellie knew he was mocking her, but she rather enjoyed it. She opened the envelope and scanned the paper—a letter from Tish and Maris, providing a proper introduction to Mr. Roman Tucker and assuring her that he was a fine man of noble character who would be of great assistance to her. Where they came up with this idea, Ellie had no clue. Still, it was clearly Tish's handwriting. Her eyes filled with tears. She hadn't seen Tish in ages, but it gave her a warm feeling to know that her friend still thought of her, still cared about her.

And the truth was, she desperately needed a handyman. The roof was beginning to leak into the upstairs hall, and the bathtub took forever to drain. The yard was full of weeds, the iron fence could use a coat of paint, and on the north side of the house, the mortar between the stones needed shoring up.

More than that, Ellie suddenly realized how long it had been since she had had anyone to talk to.

She glanced back down at Tish's letter. The girl was right—Ellie did need Roman Tucker's help.

"So, Mr. Tucker, what would you require in the way of accommodations?"

"Very little, actually. Letitia and Maris said you have a small cottage out back that would suit my needs quite well."

"Cottage?" Ellie stifled a laugh. "Mr. Tucker, that 'cottage' as you call it, is little more than a storage shed. It's only one room. It does have a wood stove, but it's full of tools and hasn't had any attention in years. It probably even has mice." She shuddered at the thought.

"I'm sure it will be fine. I'll work first on fixing it up, if that's acceptable to you." He lifted one eyebrow. "As for the mice, I'm sure I can find a cat who needs a home. In exchange for the cottage and two meals a day, I'll do whatever repairs or maintenance you need. Just give me a list."

"When would you begin?"

"Right now, this morning—if that's acceptable with you." He motioned to a battered leather bag at his feet. "I'm ready to move in immediately."

Ellie didn't need to ponder long to come to a decision. "All right. You can take a bed and dresser and whatever else you need from one of the guest rooms," she agreed. "We'll try it for a month. If we're both happy with the arrangement, you can stay. If either of us decides it's not working out, you'll leave without an argument. Agreed?"

"One other thing I'll require," he said as he bent to pick up his bag.
Ellie eyed him skeptically. "What's that?"

"Don't call me Mr. Tucker. The name is Roman—Rome, to my friends.
When anyone calls me 'Mr.' I find myself looking around for my father."

He put out a calloused hand and they sealed the deal with a handshake.
But Ellie let her fingers linger in his grasp, surprised that such rough skin
could have such a gentle touch.

27
THE HANDYMAN

May 15, 1940

Ellie watched through the kitchen window as Rome Tucker pulled weeds from the overgrown garden plot and carefully staked the small tomato plants. His cat, an enormous blue-eyed Himalayan named Mount Pisgah, darted around his ankles chasing bugs.

Shortly after Rome had settled in, Pisgah had arrived out of nowhere, showing up one morning at the door of the little cottage much as Rome himself had appeared on Ellie's doorstep. Barely more than six months old, scraggly and pathetic, she bore no letter of introduction—only a natural gift for hunting, an affectionate disposition, and a purr loud enough to wake the dead. She quickly dispensed with the mice that had taken up residence in the cottage and soon became ruler not only of Rome's heart but of Ellie's as well. In just a few months Pisgah had grown from a scruffy kitten into a well-groomed and elegant feline, her pale silver fur marked with darker gray at the tail, paws, and ears. She carried herself like a princess, with the ruff around her neck fluffed out, her tail erect and crooked like a question mark.

The pleasant sound of whistling came in through the screen door, and Ellie could hear Rome murmuring to the cat, see him smiling as he patted the soil around the roots of each of the seedlings. Rome seemed to find satisfaction in the simplest of tasks, and often Ellie would hear him laugh for no reason at all—except, perhaps, for the sheer joy of living.

Spring had come, and with it new life, and new hope. The hope, Ellie suspected, had more to do with the man than with the season.

Rome had been true to his word. He had spruced up the little stone cottage out back, furnishing it sparsely from a few items gleaned from the house. He had repaired the roof, tuck-pointed the stones on the back side of the house, fixed the plumbing, and done a thousand other things Ellie didn't even know needed to be done. Now he was planting a garden—a nice assortment of vegetables, which would greatly decrease their expense for groceries, and flowers to bring, as he put it, a touch of God's glory to the place.

In one sense, nothing had changed. Mama was still hidden away in the dark recesses of her own mind, still totally dependent upon Ellie. Day passed into day with no improvement, no respite from the endless responsibility, from the awareness that she, and she alone, bore the burden of her mother's life and her own. But from another perspective, everything was different, altered forever by the arrival of Rome Tucker on New Year's Day. Ellie hadn't crossed the threshold of a church since Mama's breakdown ten years ago, hadn't prayed in ages, hadn't given God a second thought since who knows when. But in a strange twist of mind, she was thoroughly convinced that Rome Tucker was an angel in disguise, a messenger of hope sent from heaven to keep her sane and give her a reason to go on living.

"Morning!" Rome's voice called as he came up the back walk. He opened the screen door and stepped into the kitchen with Pisgah close on his heels. "Beautiful day, isn't it?"

Ellie looked up at him and smiled. He had mud caked up to his elbows, and he nodded to the mess and chuckled. "Mind if I wash up?"

"Only if you leave your boots on the stoop."

He looked down and grinned sheepishly, stepped out of his boots, and came over to the sink in his stocking feet. "Something smells great."

"Bacon and eggs and grits." Ellie stepped back, handed him a bar of soap, and waited with a towel while he washed his hands. Pisgah jumped onto the edge of the sink in one graceful leap and stood balanced there, burrowing her head into Rome's ribs. "Pisgah, get off the counter," Ellie commanded. The cat jumped down and twined around her ankles. "What time did you get up this morning, anyway?"

"Don't know. Don't have a clock." He took the towel and dried his dripping arms. "My philosophy is, God gave us sunrise for a reason. Fella gets a lot more done in a day if he doesn't sleep the first half of it away."

"Rome, you don't have to work every second of every day," Ellie chided as she set his breakfast on the kitchen table. "Your cottage and my cooking aren't worth all the effort you put in around here."

He waited until she sat down, bowed his head silently for a moment, then looked up and waved a slice of bacon in her direction. "Your cooking is worth its weight in gold," he countered. "Basic, simple—just the way I like it." He turned a dazzling smile on her, and Ellie felt her heart accelerate. "What's for dinner tonight?"

"Meatloaf and mashed potatoes."

"Perfect." She watched him as he ate, picking at her own breakfast while he devoured his with gusto. When he was finished, he set his plate on the floor, and Pisgah daintily lapped up the remains of his egg and broken bits of bacon. "Is your mama up yet?"

"She's probably awake. When we're done here, I'll take some breakfast up to her and get her bathed and dressed."

"Just like every day," he commented.

Ellie nodded. "Just like every day." She paused and narrowed her eyes at him. "Rome, I want to ask you a question."

"Ask away."

"You've been here four and a half months, right?"

"Yep. Is that your question?"

"Not exactly. I was just wondering—well, in all that time, you've watched me caring for Mama, even helped me with her when I needed to go out. But you've never asked about her—what happened to make her this way."

Rome took a sip of coffee and smiled. "I generally make it a practice not to pry into other folks's business, Ellie, 'cause I don't particularly like folks prying into mine. I try to accept people as I find them, without butting in where I don't belong. It's not that I don't care, and sure I've wondered about her, but I guess I figured you'd tell me about it when you were ready."

He fell silent. Ellie looked into his eyes and found an openness there, an expression of compassion and concern that shook her to the core. Over the years, when people would ask about her mother, she could tell that they were simply nosy, poking around in her misery the way folks will rush to a fire or an accident just to say they had witnessed the disaster firsthand. Rome, however, neither prodded her for information nor turned a deaf ear. He just waited, his calm expression communicating that anything she told him would be entrusted to a soul capable of honor and discretion.

Before she realized what was happening, Ellie was telling him how they lost their money in the stock market crash, how Mama's breakdown had turned her inward and closed her off from the rest of the world. And other, more intimate things, like her long-dead dreams of becoming a social worker and the pain she endured every time she looked at Mama. Like the way she felt trapped, as if she had been buried alive, sealed into a mausoleum with a corpse that still ate and slept and breathed but never spoke.

As the words came rushing to the surface, Ellie realized that she had never told another living soul what she was telling Rome Tucker. There had been no other soul to tell. And she herself had not been aware of the depths of her pain until she spoke it aloud. She should keep quiet. Keep it to herself. Be strong. But the dam had burst, and there was no way to contain it now.

"I've lost e-everything," she gasped. "My life, my mother—all my dreams for the future. I'm twenty-seven years old and I have nothing to look forward to except years of this—this hell." It came out of her in a rush of relief and shame and unspeakable agony, and she pushed her plate away, laid her head on her arms, and wept.

Rome said nothing until the torrent of tears had subsided. Then he placed a hand on her arm—a tender, calloused hand—and whispered, "Ellie, look at me."

She lifted her head and blinked until her eyes cleared.

"I can't possibly understand your pain, so I won't pretend I do. But I know about loss. I—well, I was married once. My wife died. When I lost her, I ran away from everything I had ever known. I thought my life was over. But it wasn't. As long as there is love, there is hope."

"Love?" Ellie stared at him, certain he had lost his mind, and a white-hot rage rose up in her. "What love? I'm not a young girl anymore, Rome, and I have no life. I'm alone here, with a mother whose mind is completely gone, who, according to the doctors, has no hope of ever recovering. I don't even have so much as a prayer of meeting anyone who might, by some miracle, fall in love with me. I'm too old, and even if I weren't, no man in his right mind would take on me and Mama too. I'm trapped, Rome. Stuck. God forgive me, but nothing will change, at least not as long as Mama is alive—and that could be another thirty or forty years. Who will love me then? For that matter, who loves me now?"

She glared at him, challenging him to find an answer, and saw an odd look flash through his eyes. He bowed his head for a minute, and when he raised it again, he was smiling. "God loves you, Ellie," he said in a quiet voice.

Her mind reeled with the injustice of it all, an unfairness she had not allowed herself to dwell on until this very moment. How dare he spout platitudes about God when the Almighty hadn't so much as raised a finger on her behalf? God hadn't healed her mother, brought Mama back to her right mind; God hadn't provided groceries when there was no money or given Ellie opportunity to see her dreams fulfilled. The arguments boiled inside of her, so that she almost missed his next whispered words:

"And I love you."

Ellie snapped to attention. "What did you say?"

Rome smiled. "I said, I love you." He chuckled and glanced down at the cat, who was now dozing with her head on Ellie's foot. "And apparently Pisgah loves you too."

"This is no time for jokes, Rome Tucker."

"I'm not joking." He raised one eyebrow. "Clearly, the cat adores you."

"That's not what I meant, and you know it," she snapped. "I was talking about *you*. You can't possibly love me. You barely know me."

"Of course I know you." He slid his hand down her arm and captured her fingers in his. "I've watched you for four and a half months. I've eaten at your table. I've seen the tenderness and compassion you show in caring for your mother, despite the angry and confused feelings you harbor inside." He grinned suddenly. "Do you remember Ruth?"

"Ruth who?"

"Ruth, in the Bible. When her husband died, she left home and accompanied her grieving mother-in-law, Naomi, back to Bethlehem, to a land that was completely foreign to her. She gave up everything—had no hope for a future, no hope for love. But she found both love and a future, because a wealthy man named Boaz took notice of her loyalty and selfless service to Naomi. He said she was a woman of great nobility and faithfulness." He lowered his eyes. "You are like Ruth, Ellie James. Your devotion and commitment are obvious to anyone who has eyes to see. You are a noble woman. How could I help but love you and want to marry you?"

Ellie looked into Rome's face and saw no trace of mockery or deception. "You really think you might love me?"

"I really know I *do* love you," he answered. "The only question is, can you love me in return?"

Yes! Yes! She wanted to shout it, to throw her arms around him and accept his love without reservation. But something inside held her back. She couldn't answer him—not now, not yet. She had to make sure she wasn't responding to him out of—well, out of sheer desperation.

"Can you give me some time to sort all this out?" Ellie asked, hating herself for her hesitation. "It's so sudden, and—well, I just need to think about it."

She half expected him to get up and stomp out of the house, to be furious at her for her reticence. But he simply grinned and squeezed her hand. "I'm not going anywhere. Take all the time you need."

He got up, took his dishes to the sink, and went to the door. "As long as there's love, there's hope," he repeated as he pulled on his boots. "Don't forget that."

"I won't forget," she whispered to his retreating back.

And for the first time in ten years, Little Eleanor James actually believed it might be true.

∽

August 15, 1940

As the morning sun streamed in, Ellie sat at the kitchen table mesmerized by the prismatic light cascading from the diamond ring that adorned her left hand. It wasn't a large diamond, barely more than a quarter carat, but it was hers.

Rome had presented it to her two weeks ago, exactly nine months from the first day he had appeared on her doorstep. It had been his mother's ring, he explained, willed to him at her death—the sole item of value in her estate. On several occasions he had been tempted to sell it. Times were hard for everyone, and his mother would have understood. But somehow he couldn't bring himself to part with it, even when he desperately needed the few dollars he might get for it at a pawnshop. A hot meal and a dry bed weren't worth bartering his only inheritance. He wouldn't, as he put it, become like Esau, swapping his birthright for a mess of pottage.

Amazing, Ellie mused, what transformations could take place in nine months. Not a long time as relationships go, but time enough. Time enough for hope to germinate, grow, and blossom. Time enough for appreciation and friendship to turn into love.

Ellie leaned back in her chair and sighed. The world around them was in turmoil—war was heating up in Europe, and rumors were beginning to circulate that sooner or later the United States might have to get involved. But here, in her universe, peace reigned. Peace, in the person and presence of Rome Tucker.

She turned her hand this way and that, watching as the diamond caught the light and refracted shards of rainbow around the room. She had never expected this—never expected anything, if truth be told, other than a lifetime of caring for her mother and living in lonely isolation. And then Rome had come, as if by miracle, and everything had changed. No longer did she resent the daily labor of caring for her mother; no longer did she dread the turning of the calendar pages. Every day brought new surprises instead of the grinding sameness: Rome at the door with a butterfly perched on his finger or holding a bouquet of roses nurtured by his own hand. Quiet evenings on the porch, watching the sun set and the moon rise, with Pisgah purring between them on the swing. Eager conversations about the future, plans for a family, for Rome establishing his own business as a carpenter. Tender moments of holding hands and gazing into each other's eyes.

She knew now, as she had not known the day he first proposed marriage, that she truly loved him, a love based on his character, not on her own need for someone else in her life. He didn't care that she had no money, that all she had to offer was this cavernous house. He didn't flinch at the prospect that Mother would always be there, alive but unresponsive, needing constant care and attention. All he wanted, he repeated as often as she needed to hear it, was a chance to live with Ellie and love her for the rest of his days.

The man might not be an angel, but he was definitely a saint.

Ellie jerked from her reverie as the front door creaked open and a dear, familiar voice called, "Ellie? Are you home?"

"Tish!" Ellie dashed through the dining room and met Letitia Cameron in the middle of the front parlor. She flung herself into Tish's arms and hugged her until both of them were breathless, then pulled back and looked into her friend's eyes. Tears clogged her throat, and she gulped them down. "Oh, Tish! I can't believe how long it's been! Let me look at you!"

Ellie held Tish back at arm's length and surveyed her. She had grown older, no longer the teenage girl hanging on Philip Dorn's arm. But she looked good, really good. Happy. Content. "Tish, how are you?"

"I'm fine," Tish said, squeezing Ellie's shoulders. "I'm just fine. Busy. I've missed you, Ellie. And I'm sorry for not coming more often. Time just gets away from me, you know, with teaching and helping Mama, and—"

"It's all right, Tish," Ellie murmured, drawing her friend into another hug. "I know. You've got your own life, and I haven't been able to get away—"

Tish's gaze wandered toward the curving staircase. "How is your mother, Ellie? And how are you?"

"Mother is pretty much the same. But I'm not. Oh, Tish, there's so much to tell!"

Tish smiled wanly and nodded. "I know. Rome . . . well, Rome has told just about everybody at church about the two of you. Let's see the ring."

Ellie thrust out her left hand. "It doesn't rival the engagement ring you got from Philip, but I love it."

Tish grimaced. "The engagement ring I got from Philip paid my way through college. I have no regrets on that score. And it is lovely, Ellie."

"Come on into the kitchen. I made coffee and an applesauce cake. We can talk in there."

Tish followed her and sat down at the kitchen table. "Where's Rome?"

"He's upstairs, reading to Mother. She doesn't respond, of course, but he does it anyway. She seems to rest easier with him around and with the cat curled up at her feet. I think they're about halfway through the new Hemingway. He's so good with her, Tish. Takes a lot of the burden off me."

" I . . . I'm glad." Something about the way Tish said it left Ellie with the impression that a great deal was being left *unsaid*. But Tish just sat there, her eyes darting around the room, while Ellie poured coffee and cut two slices of cake. "That cake looks fabulous—what is it again?"

"Applesauce spice cake, with caramel frosting."

Tish took a bite and closed her eyes. "Mmm. Can I have the recipe? Mama would love it. And so would her clients."

"Sure." Ellie hesitated. "It's Rome's favorite."

An expression flashed across Letitia's features, an emotion Ellie couldn't quite identify. But clearly, the very mention of Rome's name brought something to the surface, something Tish was trying to hide. Maybe she still wasn't over losing Philip Dorn to that pasty little scarecrow, Marcella Covington. Or she might be just soured on marriage in general, or perhaps a little envious. . . .

Well, speculation wouldn't get her anywhere, and Ellie wasn't the type to just sit back and let things ride. If Tish had something on her mind, Ellie might as well know about it. Even though they seldom saw each other any more, they had a history of sharing each other's secrets. There was only one way to find out.

"Tish," Ellie began, feeling a nervous quiver in her stomach, "you've been acting odd ever since you walked in the door. Like you don't want to talk about Rome at all."

"Don't be ridiculous," Tish squeaked in a voice two octaves higher than her normal range.

"I'm not being ridiculous. I'm being honest, and I'd appreciate it if you did the same. Now, what's wrong? Aren't you happy about my engagement to Rome? You and your mother sent him here, if I recall correctly."

A visible shudder coursed through Tish, as if the reminder caused her pain. "Yes, we did. We thought he could be of help to you, but—"

"But what?"

Letitia averted her eyes. "But we didn't know then what we know now, or we never would have recommended him."

Ellie pushed her cake plate away and took a sip of coffee. "What are you talking about? Rome is the gentlest, tenderest, most compassionate man I've ever met."

"That's what we thought too. That's how he *seems*—"

"Seems? That's how he *is*. Letitia, just come out with it. You obviously have reservations about me marrying this man, and I'd like to know why."

Suddenly Tish's face contorted, and tears began to stream down her cheeks. "Oh, Ellie, I didn't want to tell you. But I have to. I couldn't live with myself if I didn't."

Ellie waited, trying to untie the knot of apprehension that had formed in her stomach. At last she said, "Go on."

"It's just that, well, Rome was—was—" She gasped for air. "Did you know he's been married before?"

Ellie released a pent-up breath. So that was it. She smiled and patted Tish's hand. "Of course I know. He told me all about it. His wife died—he lost everything, including her, when their house caught on fire. They hadn't been married very long, and it was devastating to him. It took him a long time to get over it."

"That's not the whole story."

"What whole story?"

"Last week a man came to the church to talk with Reverend Potter. A detective. Seems they've been searching for Rome for years, but he never stayed in one place long enough for them to catch up with him. His wife *did* die in a fire, only the fire was suspected to be arson, and if it was, her death would be ruled"— Tish's voice caught on the word— "murder. She had no family, and her neighbors and acquaintances said that Rome was a drifter who just appeared in her life and swept her off her feet. Once she took up with him, she rarely saw her friends." Letitia's eyes strayed to Ellie's left hand. "But she did wear a diamond engagement ring with her wedding band. It was never recovered after the fire, and Rome was never seen again."

"Are you saying Rome murdered his first wife and plans to do the same to me?" Ellie tasted bile at the back of her tongue and thought she was going to be sick.

"I'm saying that he's still wanted for questioning." Tish reached out a hand and grasped Ellie's fingers. "I'm sorry, Ellie. I had to tell you. I didn't want to, believe me."

A movement arrested Ellie's attention, and she glanced aside as Pisgah dashed through the kitchen headed for her water bowl. Ellie turned her eyes upward to find Rome standing there, his face set like a granite mask. Her eyes flickered to Letitia, who wore an expression of absolute terror.

Ellie rose to her feet and stared at him. "How much did you hear?"

"Most of it," he said in a low, toneless voice. "Do you believe it?" He reached a hand toward her, then drew it back when she shrank from him. "I guess you do."

"Rome, I don't know what to believe." She felt the room beginning to sway, and she groped for a chair and sank into it. "Can you explain this?"

"Explanations will have to wait." He turned his eyes away. "You need to call the doctor."

"What's wrong? Is Mother sick?"

"I was reading to her, and of course she wasn't responding—she never does. I got pretty involved in the book, I guess, and kept on reading for a long time. After a while Pisgah became restless, and when I looked up, your mother was slumped over in bed." He cleared his throat. "She's gone, Ellie."

"Gone?"

"She's dead. Passed away without a sound. I thought she was just asleep, but—"

Ellie's head reeled, and she grabbed at the table for support. She looked down, and all she could see was Rome's engagement ring, winking at her, mocking her. It felt as if it were on fire, burning a hole in her hand, and she jerked it off and sent it flying across the kitchen.

"Call the doctor," she said to Tish. "I'm going upstairs."

"And the police," Rome added as Tish reached for the telephone. "It's time to end this once and for all."

28
LIGHTNING STRIKE

August 17, 1940

Ellie gazed with unfocused eyes at the dark hole in the ground.

Somewhere, as if from a great distance, a man was speaking. "I lift mine eyes unto the hills, from whence cometh my help," the voice intoned in a numbing cadence. But when Ellie lifted *her* eyes toward the mountains, all she saw was the summer haze that turned the Blue Ridge a smoky white, as if the whole world around her were burning, burning.

"Ashes to ashes, dust to dust," the voice went on. Ellie looked again at the black hole. Ashes. Dust. Her ears registered the words about "a sure and certain hope of resurrection," but her mind rejected them. She might cling to the assurance of resurrection for her mother, but there would be no new life for her. All hope had gone up in flames, burned to ash.

Tish nudged her with one elbow, and Ellie jerked back to the present. Obediently, as if sleepwalking, she moved to the pile of raw earth next to her mother's grave, collected a handful of dirt, and dropped it onto the lowered coffin. Her eyes fixed on the tombstone that headed her father's grave, to her mother's left. *Gone too soon,* the epitaph read. She had already decided on the words for Mother's stone: *Finally free.*

When the last "Amen" was uttered, Ellie shook hands with each of the mourners and thanked them for coming. She spoke the words woodenly, like a meaningless ritual, and barely looked at the faces as they filed by murmuring their condolences. Reverend Potter, from the Methodist Church, had performed the simple ceremony. Letitia and her mother, Maris, were there and a number of their friends from the church. Ellie knew that Pastor

Archer and his wife had been notified—they had, after all, been close friends with Big Eleanor back in the days when she had money and social standing and influence at Downtown Presbyterian. But the Archers hadn't come. To them, Eleanor James had died years before she breathed her last breath.

The small knot of black-clad mourners dispersed, and Ellie walked away from them, alone, up to a rise where a cluster of oaks shaded the hilltop. In the shadow of the largest tree, two gravediggers leaned on their shovels, smoking. As she approached, they doffed their caps in a gesture of respect, crushed out their cigarettes, and ambled back down the hill to finish their job.

Ellie settled herself on a rock and stared down toward the river, a ribbon of molten gold reflecting the afternoon sun. Here and there the current ran over boulders in the riverbed, sending off glints of light like tiny diamonds blinding her with their brilliance.

Gold and diamonds.

Instinctively, her gaze dropped to her left hand, her ring finger. Rome's engagement ring was gone, of course—taken by the authorities as possible evidence. Her finger still bore the faint imprint of the filigreed band. The mark would fade in time, she knew. But what of the gaping wound in her heart? Would it heal as easily, closing up without so much as a scar, as if the promise of life and love had never found its way into her soul?

An image surfaced in her mind, a long-buried memory of standing with her father beside a tree that had been struck in a lightning storm. She couldn't have been more than five or six, and she couldn't recall her father's face, but she remembered as if it were yesterday the way he put his slender, manicured fingers into the blackened gash. "Will the tree die, Daddy?" she had asked.

"No, honey, it will be fine," he had assured her. "In time, new layers will grow over it, and the bark will come back so that you can barely tell where the lightning hit. But if somebody cuts this tree down someday, they'll find a spot, right here, that's harder than the rest of the wood, hard as iron."

Was that the way the human heart worked too? Ellie wondered. Did the wound heal up only to leave a knot as hard as iron below the surface?

With a start she realized that she had just buried her mother, and yet the pain that assailed her was not that loss, but the void left by the departure of Rome Tucker.

There had been no time for the explanations he promised her. He had gone with the police willingly, even eagerly, vowing that once things were cleared up, he would be back.

But when? And back from where? She didn't even know where he had come from—Arkansas, Iowa, someplace west of the Mississippi, she thought, but that didn't narrow down the field very much. Rome had been reticent to talk about his past, except to tell her about his first wife's death. How stupid of her, to open her home—and her heart—to a complete stranger, a man who had revealed to her only the barest essentials about his own life.

But he had seemed so honest, so candid. So genuinely in love with her. And he had cared about Mama too, helping lift from Ellie's shoulders the burden of her care. Rome, after all, was the one who had been with her when she . . .

Despite the August heat, a cold chill ran up Ellie's spine.

Rome had been alone with Mother when she died.

The physicians had confirmed, right on the signed death certificate, that Eleanor James had passed on from "Natural Causes." She just gave up, the doctor assured Ellie. Just decided that it was time to go. It wasn't unusual in cases like this for a patient simply to will to die.

But what if they had missed something? What if the suspicions about Rome had been true? If he had killed once, he would have nothing to lose in doing it again. And if they had gotten married, when he grew tired of her. . . ?

"Ellie."

The low voice came, close at her ear, and Ellie jumped up and whirled around. It was Tish, holding out a hand in her direction.

"Ellie, it's time to go home."

The sun was beginning to set behind the western mountains, tinting the summer haze with a glow the color of salmon flesh. Ellie's dark dress was soaked with perspiration, and her hands felt clammy. She removed her hat and ran a hand through her hair. A faint breeze stirred the damp tendrils at her temples, a momentary relief.

"Why don't you come home with us for a day or two?" Tish suggested.

"The fall term doesn't start for another week, and it might be better if you didn't have to be alone."

Ellie shook her head. "I need to be home. And you don't have room. I'd just be underfoot." She sighed. "Besides, Pisgah will be wondering where everybody went. She's not used to being alone."

Tish helped Ellie to her feet, then linked arms with her as they started down the hill. "Then at least join us for dinner tonight. And let me come stay a few days with you."

Ellie hesitated. Part of her mind screamed that she just wanted to be left alone, to think about what had happened, to try to sort out in her mind how she felt about Rome, whether or not she trusted him enough to believe in his innocence. But another part dreaded going back to that vast empty house, filled now only with memories and recriminations.

"All right," she said at last. "But only for a couple of days."

August 20, 1940

Ellie sat at the kitchen table, staring with unseeing eyes as Tish put together chicken sandwiches and leftover green beans for the two of them. Pisgah had scratched at the screen door until Ellie got up and let her in and now lay in her lap, demanding attention and making a strange sound, rather like the cross between a purr and a whine.

Poor cat, Ellie thought as she scratched behind Pisgah's left ear. *She doesn't understand why the house is suddenly empty, why Rome is gone.*

To tell the truth, Ellie couldn't really understand it either. It all seemed like a bad dream—her mother's haggard, lifeless body being carried out of the house on a stretcher; the man she loved, or thought she loved, being led away by the authorities; the burly detective on his hands and knees retrieving her engagement ring from behind the kitchen door. She kept telling herself that if she could just wake up, the nightmare would vanish like mist on the mountains.

Tish set two plates on the table and took a seat opposite Ellie. "Go on, try it. I know I'm not as good in the kitchen as Mama, but I won't poison you. You need to eat."

Ellie stared at the sandwich, took a bit of chicken from the plate, and fed it to the cat. "I'm not hungry."

"I know. It's been years since Daddy died, but I remember."

Ellie looked up and smiled at her friend. Letitia Cameron was exactly the right person to be with her now—someone who understood from personal experience how absolutely horrible it all felt. Tish didn't try to force her to talk or attempt to probe into her grief. She was just here, and her presence had made the last few days, if not easier, at least bearable.

"Thanks for being here, Tish," Ellie said at last. "I don't know what I would have done without you."

"What are friends for?" Tish reached over and patted her hand. "You were with me when Daddy died, remember. And—I don't know, somehow I feel a little, well, responsible. . . ."

Ellie looked up and fixed her friend with a steely gaze. "Let's get one thing straight, Tish. Your father did his best for my mother, and even though it was a terrible time for everybody, I don't hold him accountable for Mama's inability to deal with losing her money. It was more than just the money, anyway. She depended upon her social status to give her a reason to live. She was weak, and when she didn't have her wealth and power to lean on, she simply broke. Your daddy wasn't responsible for it—and neither are you. There's no reason for you to feel guilty."

"I know," Tish said. "But it's not just that. I was the one who brought you the bad news about Rome too. We've been friends for years, Ellie. I hate causing you pain, no matter what the circumstances."

"It's all right." Ellie lowered her eyes and blinked back tears. "I had to know sooner or later. It's certainly better for me to find out now, before I made a mistake that would follow me the rest of my life."

They fell silent for a moment, and at last Tish asked, "What will you do, Ellie?"

"I don't know." Ellie shook her head. "I don't think I can stay here, in this house."

"Remember, years ago, when we wrote out our dreams and put them in the bottle? Back then you wanted to become a social worker, to help people. You could still do that."

The memory swept over Ellie like tongues of fire. She had been so innocent then, so naive. She could still feel the surge of freedom she had experienced when she finally committed those dreams to paper. She had felt noble and strong . . . even invincible.

But the past ten years had smothered that zeal. The flame had died and with it her dreams for making a difference in the world.

"It's too late," she murmured after a while. "I feel old, Tish. Old and tired. I don't have the energy—or the money—to go back to school."

"Can I offer one suggestion?"

Ellie sighed. "Sure. Suggest away."

"Well"—Letitia's voice took on a tone of hesitancy—"you've been cooped up in this house for a very long time."

"It seems like forever."

"Maybe you need to get out a little. You know, meet people."

Ellie blinked. "Meet people? Tish, I've lived in this town my entire life. I know lots of people."

"But you haven't spent time with them in years. You've given your life to taking care of your mother. Now you need to do something for yourself."

"And your suggestion is—?"

"Come to church with Mama and me."

Ellie felt her jaw drop. "You can't be serious."

"You used to go to church."

"Yes, when I was young and didn't know any better. But when we needed support and compassion, where were all those people who claimed to be my friends—and Mother's? You didn't see the great Pastor Archer at the funeral, did you?" Ellie could hear the edge in her voice but couldn't seem to temper it. "I didn't abandon the church, Tish. The church abandoned me."

"I know, I know." Tish nodded. "The same thing happened to us when Daddy died, at least at Downtown Presbyterian. I swore I'd never darken the door of a church again. But then we found East Asheville Methodist— a small church with a real feeling of family. These people don't just *claim* to be Christians, Ellie. They *live* it. It's very refreshing."

Ellie resisted the idea, but she had to admit that Tish and Maris's friends at the Methodist church did seem to be different, somehow. They didn't know Ellie or her mother, but Reverend Potter had conducted the funeral, and a dozen or so of the members actually came to the service. In the past few days, people she had only seen once or twice in her life kept appearing at the door with cakes and pies and casseroles, offering hugs and condolences instead of pat answers and religious drivel. The truth was, in three days she had received more genuine care from simple folks she didn't know than she had in ten years from the society people who had claimed to be her friends.

"A lot of nice people worship there, Ellie. Not rich people or powerful people, but honest, good people who will accept you without question. People who might help make this transition a little easier."

"I don't know," Ellie hedged. "I'll have to think about it."

"All right. You don't have to make a decision immediately," Tish soothed. "You can take your time, get through this, and when you're ready—"

"When I'm ready, I'll let you know," Ellie interrupted. "In the meantime, promise you won't pressure me about it."

Tish lifted her sandwich in salute. "I promise," she said. "No pressure."

August 31, 1940

Tish had been right, of course. Ellie needed contact with people.

She had known loneliness before, during all those years of caring for Mother before Rome came and broke the monotony. At times she had thought she might go mad from the sheer isolation. But back then she had a mission, a duty. She had her mother to attend to, and even in the midst of her isolation, she was never really alone.

Now, the huge old house echoed with every footfall, and the only companionship Ellie had was Pisgah. The big cat never left her side, watching her with enormous blue eyes, purring and rubbing against her at every opportunity, as if to assure her that she had one friend left in the world, a friend who would never forsake her. But even as Ellie grew increasingly attached to Pisgah, she knew, somewhere in the recesses of her mind, that a cat's company simply wasn't enough. If she wasn't careful, she would become one of those eccentric old women who lived with a houseful of felines and never spoke to a living soul.

"You know," Ellie said to the cat one evening as they sat together in the porch swing, "maybe Tish is right. Maybe I do need to get out and meet people, develop some friendships."

"Rrrowww," Pisgah answered, burrowing her head under Ellie's arm.

"I mean, the only real friend I have is Tish, and I can't expect her to be at my beck and call every time I need someone to talk to, now can I?"

"Rrroh-roow-roow," the cat responded.

Ellie stared at the big Himalayan, who sat back and gazed at her, her tail flipping against Ellie's arm. "I'm losing my mind," she muttered. "It sounded like you said, 'No, you can't.'"

"Bbbrrrr," Pisgah purred.

"So, what do you think? Do I dare take Tish up on her offer and go to church with her?"

"Yeowp," the cat answered. She jumped down from the swing and stood by the door, waiting.

Ellie opened the screen and followed Pisgah inside. The cat made a bee-line for the hallway, leaped onto the table, and rubbed her cheek against the telephone.

Ellie shook her head and closed her eyes. "I can't believe I'm doing this."

"Mmoww." Pisgah nudged her arm.

"Now?"

"Mmoww," the cat repeated.

"All right, all right." Ellie clicked the receiver and gave the operator the name of Maris Cameron.

Tish came on the line. "Hello?"

"Tish, it's me, Ellie."

"Are you all right? You sound—I don't know, strange."

"I feel a little strange. Listen, do you remember inviting me to church with you and your mom? A couple of weeks ago, right after the funeral?"

"Sure I remember."

"Well, ah, I've—I've decided to go. Can you pick me up in the morning?"

Silence.

"Tish? Are you there?"

"I'm here. Yes, we'll pick you up. Around ten—is that all right? Wait a minute."

Ellie heard Maris's voice in the background, then Tish came back on the line. "Mama says there's a social after church—a covered-dish dinner. Don't worry about bringing anything. There's always enough to feed a small army."

Great, Ellie thought. *Why did I have to pick this Sunday, of all days?* It was tough enough subjecting herself to an hour of worship; now she was facing an additional two hours, minimum, of small talk, with people she didn't know. What had she gotten herself into?

Pisgah rubbed against her hand and purred.

Tish's voice came through the receiver again. "Just one question, Ellie. What made you decide to come?"

"I'll tell you all about it tomorrow, as long as you promise not to have me committed." Ellie chuckled. "Let's just say I got a gentle nudge from a very good friend."

When Tish hung up, Ellie stood there holding the telephone and shaking her head. After a minute she replaced the receiver and turned on Pisgah. "This is all your fault."

"Bbbrrrr," the cat purred, rubbing against her.

"If this turns out to be a disaster, I'm going to blame it on you, understand?"

Pisgah jumped down from the table and sat on the rug, regarding Ellie with wide blue eyes. Her tail curled upward in its characteristic question mark.

"Rir-rrurrr?" she asked, then stalked off toward the kitchen.

"Yes, yes, I'll get your dinner," Ellie muttered, following. "But you'd better be right about this, or some musician is going to get himself some new violin strings."

29
PROVIDENCE

September 1, 1940

When she walked into the East Asheville Methodist Church close on the heels of Tish and Maris, Ellie's stomach clenched into knots. She suppressed an unaccountable surge of fear—the urge to bolt, to flee for her life. *Don't be ridiculous*, she argued with herself. *These people won't bite.*

In truth, they didn't seem like the biting kind. Everyone was smiling, crowding around her, introducing themselves and shaking hands. Ellie caught a phrase here and there, words intended, she assumed, for encouragement:

"We've heard so much about you—"

"We feel like we already know you—"

"So sorry about your mother, and—"

"We've all been praying for you—"

She recognized a few faces, the strangers who had appeared at her mother's graveside. These friends of Tish and Maris's seemed like genuinely nice people, and yet—

And yet she couldn't shake the feeling that she was being examined, scrutinized like a bug in a jar. She wished they would all just leave her alone.

It was a noisy, happy crowd that filled the little white church—not at all like the somber parishioners at Downtown Pres. No organ music played, no stained-glass windows filled the sanctuary with a soft, reverent glow, no empty crevices reminded her of long-dead saints. Here everything was bright and loud and chaotic, more like a party than a service of worship.

From somewhere else—down the stairs leading off the nave, perhaps—

the aroma of fried chicken drifted to her nostrils. A tantalizing scent, and yet one that set Ellie's teeth to grinding. Not only would she have to endure the actual service, but afterward, she would be subjected to another hour or two of the Christian concern and reassurance she had tasted on her way in. Maris called it "fellowship." Ellie thought of it as torture.

At last Reverend Matthew Potter mounted the two steps to the platform and stood at the pulpit—a small movable lectern, actually, which swayed dangerously when he leaned on it. The congregation showed no sign of coming to order, however. People still stood in the aisles, leaning over the pews. A group clustered behind Maris and Tish continued to pat Ellie on the shoulders and murmur their condolences.

Reverend Potter cleared his throat. No response.

At last he rapped his knuckles on the lectern and shouted, "If you'll all take your seats, please!" The crowd settled down—rather slowly, Ellie thought, and without the least hint of embarrassment—and Potter went on with a chuckle, "You'll have plenty of opportunity to fellowship after the service."

Everybody laughed, and a woman called out, "You just want more time to preach, Matt."

"And you'd preach yourself, Eunice, if I gave you the chance," Potter responded.

"I would," she retorted. "And I'd do a fine job of it too."

More laughter and a smattering of applause. Ellie stared around at the lively congregation in amazement. She had never in her life witnessed this kind of camaraderie among church folks, this kind of down-to-earth banter. She couldn't imagine anyone at Downtown Presbyterian ever talking back to Pastor Archer, and she couldn't recall a single instance in all her years there that anyone ever laughed out loud.

Tish and Maris had spoken truly when they told her this church was different.

Reverend Potter shuffled a few notes in front of him. "I'd like to welcome you all to worship here at East Asheville Methodist Church. As you can tell, we're a pretty close-knit group, but we always want to open our arms to embrace newcomers." He peered over his spectacles and fixed Ellie with a warm smile. "We have with us today Miss Eleanor James, a friend of Letitia and Maris Cameron. You all know abut Ellie's, ah, situation. We've been praying for her for several weeks now."

Please, stop, Ellie pleaded silently. She fought the urge to crawl under the pew. Did these strangers know *everything* about her life?

But Potter didn't stop. "Ellie has recently lost her mother; I conducted the funeral and a number of you attended those services. We want you to know, Ellie, that we love you and support you in your time of grief. Please stand so we can all see you and know who you are."

Ellie froze in the pew, unable to move. Everyone waited. At last Tish grasped her elbow and helped her to her feet, and she stood there exposed while a hot flush of embarrassment crept up her neck and into her cheeks. "Th-thank you," she stammered, and sat down as quickly as possible.

Reverend Potter went on with a few announcements, then reached to the seat behind him to retrieve a worn hymnal. "Let us rise for the opening hymn, a great old song by Charles Wesley—number eighty-six, 'Jesus, Lover of My Soul.'"

Ellie heaved a sigh of relief. The service was finally beginning, and she would no longer have to be the center of attention. As a heavyset woman moved to the piano and began playing the song with great gusto, Ellie leaned over and scanned the unfamiliar words in Tish's hymn book:

Jesus, lover of my soul, Let me to Thy bosom fly,
While the nearer waters roll, While the tempest still is high,
Hide me, O my Savior, hide, 'Til the storm of life is past;
Safe into the haven guide, O receive my soul at last!

Ellie tried to sing, but the notes clogged in her throat and she fought back unexpected tears. It was as if the hymn had been chosen—or perhaps even written—especially for her. In all her years at Downtown Presbyterian, she had never heard anyone refer to Christ as "Jesus, lover of my soul," and the bold, unaccustomed intimacy both shocked and attracted her. But it was the other words that struck a nerve most deeply in her soul. For Ellie James, recent years had been an unrelenting assault of rolling waters and high tempests. The storms of life had overtaken her, and she had found no haven to give respite to her weariness.

A deep, nameless longing welled up in her, accompanied by huge tears that, in defiance of her attempts to contain them, streaked down her cheeks and fell in silent droplets at her feet. All around her, the congregation sang out heartily, oblivious to Ellie's distress.

Her eyes skipped forward to verse two:

Other refuge have I none, Hangs my helpless soul on Thee;
Leave, O leave me not alone, Still support and comfort me.
All my trust on Thee is stayed, All my help from Thee I bring;
Cover my defenseless head With the shadow of Thy wing.

Whoever this Charles Wesley was, he had looked into Ellie James's heart and laid bare her secret pain. *Leave, O leave me not alone,* her mind echoed. She had been alone too long. Alone with Mother. Alone with herself, with her own hopelessness and determination and, yes, even bitterness. Only once had she reached out—to Rome Tucker. She had trusted him, believed him to be the answer to her isolation. But Rome, too, had betrayed her. Who now would cover her defenseless head? Who would be her refuge, bringing support and comfort? Where could she hang her helpless soul and stay her trust?

When the hymn was finished, Ellie sat down and tried to focus her attention on the rest of the service, but with little success. She heard, as if from a great distance, the reading of Scriptures, the voice of Reverend Potter as he preached. But little of it sank in. She cradled the hymnal in her lap, her eyes fixed on the words, her heart crying out for consolation, like a fearful child calling for her parents in the night.

And there, sitting in the pew between Tish and Maris Cameron, Ellie James became a child again, thrust back in time. She wept for her daddy, long dead, who had never been there to wipe away her tears. And for her mama, who had been physically present but too concerned with other things to pay her any mind. Then, in a moment of terrifying realization, she saw herself as her mother had been in the ten years before she died—still breathing, still eating, still going through the motions of everyday existence, but not truly alive on the inside. And she wept for herself, for her irreclaimable childhood, for all the wasted years.

On her left, Maris shifted in her seat, and Ellie became conscious of the conclusion of Reverend Potter's sermon: "In Matthew 23, Jesus mourns over the people's resistance to the truth, saying, 'How I've longed to gather you under my wings, the way a mother hen gathers her chicks, but you refused.' We need God's tender mothering, dear friends. We need God's protective fathering. Let us refuse the call no longer."

The words resounded in Ellie's soul: *God's tender mothering, God's protective fathering.* Could it be possible that the Almighty would do that for her— be the father she had lost when she was nine and the mother she had never really found? Could God, as the hymn promised, provide a refuge from the storm and a place to hang her soul?

Ellie didn't know for sure. She was certain only that her childhood faith, the rituals and social customs she had been brought up with at Downtown Presbyterian, weren't enough. But if there was more, if the God Reverend Potter talked about and Charles Wesley wrote about could really bring her to a place of peace and safety, she was willing to give it a try.

Her eyes drifted to the hymn book, still open to number eighty-six, on her lap. The third verse of Wesley's hymn read:

Plenteous grace with Thee is found, Grace to cover all my sin;
Let the healing streams abound, Make and keep me pure within.
Thou of life the fountain art, Freely let me take of Thee;
Spring Thou up within my heart, Rise to all eternity.

Ellie blinked back the last of her tears and managed a faint smile. *Plenteous grace? Healing streams? A fountain of life springing up within her heart?* It sounded too good to be true. She might simply be setting herself up for another fall, making herself vulnerable to yet another crushing blow.

But at this point, she had little left to lose.

⌒⌒

The rickety, wooden, folding chair swayed every time she moved, and Ellie began to wonder if she would ever make it through this church dinner without dumping an entire plate of fried chicken and potato salad onto her dress. A few tables had been set up in the churchyard to accommodate the food and the diners, but there was not nearly enough room for everyone. As an honored guest, she had been escorted to a chair; now she wondered if she might be better off sitting on the grass.

Once she had recovered from the emotional turbulence generated by the worship service, Ellie actually found herself enjoying the covered-dish dinner. A number of people had come up to her and expressed their sympathy over the loss of her mother, but they didn't, as she had feared, raise the issue of Rome Tucker or try to probe into her private life. Some she recognized as having attended the funeral or brought food to the house afterward, and she did her best to thank them graciously without bringing down an avalanche of gushing sentimentality.

She was awkwardly trying, for the third time, to eat from her plate and at the same time balance her iced tea glass when a shadow loomed over her. "Here, let me help." A graceful hand reached out and rescued the tea glass just before it spilled.

A tall, handsome woman stood before her, clad in a simple but elegant navy dress, with salt-and-pepper hair brushed back from her temples. "I'm Catherine Starr." She smiled, and her brown eyes crinkled with laugh lines. "You're pretty good at this juggling act."

"Not really." Ellie returned the smile. "If you hadn't come along just now, I might have thoroughly embarrassed myself. I'd do better, I think, if I were closer to the ground." She looked around at the parishioners lounging on the grass.

"Then come join me," the woman offered. "I've got a place over there, under that tree." And in a minute or two they were settled in the shade on an old blue and yellow quilt.

Ellie stretched her legs out and propped her tea glass against the tree trunk. "Much better. Thank you, Mrs. Starr."

"Please, call me Catherine." She took a bite of chicken and regarded Ellie. "How are you holding up?"

The question startled Ellie, and she frowned. "I beg your pardon?"

Catherine waved a fork. "We have a wonderful group of folks here at the church," she said. "Except that they can be, well, a bit overwhelming to a newcomer. A little too much compassion and concern sometimes makes visitors uncomfortable, you know?"

Ellie grinned. "Ah, yes. I see what you mean."

"I'll bet you do. I've tried and tried to get Matthew to quit putting new people on the spot like that—forcing them to stand up and be gawked at. But he's convinced it makes them feel special and honored. What it really does is give the members a chance to descend on them after the service with, shall we say, an abundance of goodwill."

Ellie found herself instantly comfortable with Catherine—her quiet voice, her no-nonsense candidness, the way she looked you in the eye without flinching. A quality of trustworthiness and honesty surrounded the woman, and Ellie felt instinctively that Catherine Starr would neither back down from her convictions or try to impose them upon anyone else.

"I must admit, this is a very friendly church," Ellie said at last. "Not at all what I'm accustomed to."

"Which was?"

"Downtown Presbyterian. I was a member there years ago—I'm probably still a member, at least technically. But I haven't been to church in years."

A shadow passed over Catherine's face. "Your mother. Yes. I was sorry to learn of her death. You may not have known it, Ellie, but you've had a lot of prayer support—from this congregation, anyway."

Ellie's first instinct was to put up her fists and fight—at least emotionally. To shout that she didn't need their Christian charity, or their pity. To tell this woman, this whole congregation, that she hadn't asked for their prayers and didn't particularly appreciate them invading her privacy by discussing her troubles behind her back. But suddenly she realized that they meant well, and without warning she was struck with a sense of awe, to think that strangers—people who didn't even know her—had spent time and energy and attention seeking the Almighty's intervention on her behalf.

And their concern hadn't stopped with prayer, either. How many of them had come to her mother's funeral? How many had prepared and brought food for her during the days after Mama's death? One man—she didn't remember his name and probably wouldn't recognize him if he were sitting right in front of her—had even weeded the garden and brought in the vegetables for her. No, they hadn't just sat by idly praying. They had put their faith into action for the sake of a stranger who wasn't even related to any of them.

"I appreciate everything this church has done for me, Catherine," Ellie responded after a moment. "I'm just not certain how to repay all of you. Or even quite how to respond."

Catherine threw back her head and laughed heartily. "But Ellie, no repayment is necessary. Nobody even expects you to respond in any particular way. Don't you see?"

"No, I *don't* see." Ellie's voice came out testy and irritable.

"It's grace," Catherine went on as if she hadn't noticed. "Grace isn't something you earn."

Grace. The words of Wesley's hymn echoed in Ellie's mind. *Plenteous grace with Thee is found . . . Let the healing streams abound. . . .*

"So," Catherine was saying as she set her empty plate aside, "what do you intend to do now, if you don't mind my asking?"

Oddly enough, Ellie *didn't* mind. Coming from Catherine, the question didn't seem intrusive or probing—just interested, and concerned. She sipped her iced tea and considered her answer. "I honestly don't know," she said at last. "I've spent the past ten years caring for Mama and figured I'd go on doing it forever. Then in the last few months everything changed—" She paused. "You know about Rome Tucker, I suppose."

"Yes." Catherine nodded somberly. "I gathered from the things he said that he loved you a great deal."

"Well, that's history now," Ellie snapped, a bit more abruptly than she had intended. "Water under the bridge, or over the dam, or wherever it is that water is supposed to go."

"And so—?"

"When Rome left, he took with him any plans I had made for the future. I'm feeling pretty much at sea now. I only know that I can't stay in that big old house alone. I'm going to sell it as soon as possible."

Until that very moment, Ellie had not made a final decision about selling the house. But as soon as the words were out of her mouth, an invisible burden lifted off her shoulders. It was the right thing to do; she knew it immediately.

"Are you sure?"

Ellie nodded. "I'm absolutely certain, Catherine. The place is far too big for me, and it's too much upkeep. I'm not sure where I'll go or what I'll do. Tish thinks I should go back to school, but I don't think I can do that now. I only know that I have to get out of that house. There are too many ghosts there." She shook her head. "I'm just afraid it might take forever to sell. It's so huge—not the kind of home most families want or need."

A secretive smile crept over Catherine's face, and her expression went hazy, as if she were miles away.

"What's that look for?" Ellie asked.

"Just—just thinking."

"About what?"

Catherine shifted so that she was facing Ellie directly, and her eyes took on a dazzling animation. "Ellie, it may be too soon for you to consider this, and if so, just tell me. But I may have a proposition for you."

"A proposition?"

"Yes. I'm director of a home—a place where elderly people with nowhere else to go can come and live and be cared for. Most of our clients aren't bedridden or terminally ill; they're just old and alone, with no family to take care of them. If it weren't for us, I don't know what would become of them. But here's the problem," she rushed on without giving Ellie a chance to comment. "We have to move. We've run out of space, and the city regulations prevent us from expanding in our present location. If you're really willing to sell, your house would be perfect."

Ellie struggled to take all this information in. If she hesitated, it might be months, even years, before she could find another buyer for the place. But something about Catherine's excitement troubled her. She puzzled over it for a moment, then realized what it was.

"How do you *know* my house would be perfect? You've never been there."

"Of course I've been there. I brought a baked ham and sweet potatoes the day after your mother's funeral—when Letitia was staying with you. And I helped Pete pull weeds and pick tomatoes in your garden."

"You were there? At my house?" Shame washed over Ellie. She didn't recall ever seeing Catherine before. How many others at this church had helped without her knowledge, people she hadn't even known she needed to thank? "Oh, Catherine, I'm so sorry. I didn't know. But I should have remembered, should have thanked you properly—"

Catherine waved a dismissive hand. "That's not important. You know me now, and"—she smiled broadly—"I expect we're going to be great friends. Will you consider my offer?"

"Yes, I most certainly will consider it. I'll consider it quite seriously."

"Oh, and one other thing. Even if you do decide to sell to us, I don't want you to feel forced out of your own home. You probably wouldn't want to be in the house itself—there's a lot of commotion that goes on with caring for a large group of people. But you could stay in the guest cottage—for free, of course—as long as you wanted or needed to. We can even write it into the contract."

Ellie looked up to see Maris and Tish approaching, waving to her that they were ready to leave. "Give me a few days to think about it and to get some legal advice about the value of the house. Could you come by, say, Thursday evening to discuss it?" She got up and brushed the crumbs off her skirt.

Catherine rose. "Until Thursday, then." She grasped Ellie's hand and shook it warmly. "I don't know what you'll think about this, but I firmly believe God sent you here today."

Ellie smiled and looked into Catherine's eyes. "I'm beginning to believe it myself," she said, "for a lot of reasons."

She left Catherine standing under the tree and walked back to the car with Tish and Maris.

"I hope you don't mind us leaving you alone for so long," Tish said. "It seemed as if you and Catherine were deep in conversation, and we didn't want to interrupt."

"I had a good time," Ellie said, realizing that she meant every word of it. "What do you know about Catherine Starr?"

Letitia and her mother exchanged meaningful glances and smiled. "We thought you might have heard of her, except that you've been pretty cloistered for the past ten years," Tish said. "She's a widow, from Richmond. Moved here seven years ago when her husband died. She's become sort of a legend in Asheville—a woman of considerable wealth, who scandalized her high-society family by using her insurance and inheritance money to help a lot of people who had no place else to turn."

"A saint of a woman," Maris added. "A real asset to the community." She opened the car door for Ellie. "There was an article in the paper about her a couple of months ago. What did that reporter call her?"

Tish grinned and got in behind the wheel. "The brightest philanthropic 'Starr' in the Carolina sky," she said. "The Jane Addams of the South."

30
SAINT CATHERINE

November 1, 1940

Ellie awoke with a start to find Mount Pisgah sitting squarely on her abdomen blinking at her with that inscrutable cat stare. The whole bed vibrated as the beast's purr sent tremors, like aftershocks from an earthquake, through Ellie's midsection and down into her hips.

"All right, all right. I'm getting up."

Pisgah stood and began to knead her paws on Ellie's stomach, then moved up, lay across Ellie's chest, and rubbed her whiskers under Ellie's chin. Despite her irritation at being awakened so early—not to mention the discomfort of having a twenty-three-pound feline anchoring her to the mattress—Ellie smiled. Pisgah was, she had to admit, a godsend. A companion who loved her, accepted her, brought her affection and joy, and even a mouse or two now and then.

Ellie could have done without the sacrificial offerings, but you couldn't change a cat's nature, and Pisgah meant well. She always seemed so proud when she laid her kill on the mat outside the door. The first time Pisgah had brought such a gift to Ellie's feet, Ellie had screamed and hurled the dead thing as far as she could fling it into the woods. But the cat hadn't understood; her tail went limp and she had spent the rest of the day yowling morosely every time Ellie came into view.

And so Ellie had steeled herself to the reality of discovering Pisgah's trophies at the doorstep of the little cottage. Clearly, this had been a common occurrence when Rome had lived there; he had simply declined to give Ellie the gory details at breakfast every morning.

Rome.

Ellie still thought about him, wondered where he was and how he was faring, but it had been over two months since he had left, and the pain was gradually dissipating. At first she had thought it would be impossible to take up residence in the cottage he had so recently inhabited, but Ellie discovered that it wasn't difficult at all.

When Catherine Starr had brought her an offer on the house, back in September, the deal included accommodations for Ellie in the little stone cottage. Once the papers had been signed, Catherine had set her own workers to expanding the one-room cottage, adding on a nice bathroom and a small kitchen, as well as a separate bedroom. By the time the renovations were completed, the cottage had been transformed, and Ellie was thoroughly delighted with the results.

Catherine, it seemed, was equally pleased with her part of the bargain. Eleanor James's house had originally been built both as a society showplace and as a home designed to accommodate guests. The downstairs, with its spacious parlors, enormous formal dining room, and ample kitchen, provided more than adequate gathering space. Upstairs, the numerous bedrooms, sitting rooms, and suites had been adapted to the needs of the residents, and two of the large walk-in linen closets had been converted into additional bathrooms. Except for the removal of the back stairway to install an electric elevator, the main house remained pretty much unchanged— right down to the furniture, parlor rugs, and grand piano Catherine had purchased from Ellie in a separate arrangement.

Just enough change, Ellie thought, *but not too much.* She still felt at home in the grand old house, but it no longer held the chill of emptiness.

Ellie nudged Pisgah off the bed and went into the tiny kitchen to make coffee. It was a glorious autumn morning, and when she opened the door to let Pisgah out, she looked across the yard to see Catherine Starr, in flannel pajamas three sizes too big, tossing old coffee grounds into the garden plot. Catherine waved and smiled. "Come on over—the coffee's just about ready."

Ellie picked her way across dew-covered steppingstones to the back door and followed Catherine in. She sat at the table, watching in amazement as one of the wealthiest women in the Southeast puttered about the kitchen like an ordinary housewife, dressed in her late husband's castoff pajamas. "Sugar or cream?"

Ellie shook her head. "No, thanks. Just black, please."

Catherine set a mug of coffee in front of Ellie and settled in the chair across the table. "Better get it now. Rumors are that once we get into this war, we'll be facing rationing—sugar, meat, a lot of things we're used to having."

"Do you really think it'll come to that? War, I mean?"

"I don't know. The last one was supposed to be 'the war that ended all wars,' but apparently it didn't turn out the way people hoped."

Ellie sighed. "Life rarely does." She took a sip of her coffee and changed the subject. "So, are you getting all settled in?"

"Yes, and it's a good thing. The residents are being moved in on Monday. That gives us exactly three days to finish up. The contractor says the elevator will be operational by tomorrow afternoon. That's cutting it close, but—" She shrugged. "It'll all work out. Fortunately, this house was so perfect that we didn't have to do any major renovations. It's a gift from God, Ellie."

"And from you." Ellie regarded Catherine Starr with a mixture of admiration and curiosity. The woman had used her own funds to purchase the house and pay for the renovations. Her offer to Ellie had been more than generous—considerably more than the actual value of the house, and that didn't include the money she had spent to enlarge Ellie's cottage and put in new bathrooms and the elevator. But the biggest surprise of all was the fact that Catherine Starr actually intended to *live* here. She had claimed the library and adjoining music room as an office-bedroom suite for herself, and with the help of a resident nurse, who would take one of the upstairs bedrooms, would provide full-time care for the occupants of what was now called the Eleanor James Home for the Elderly.

Additional paid staff and volunteer helpers would come during the day, but responsibility for the entire venture rested upon the shoulders of Catherine Starr.

And broad shoulders they were too.

Maris Cameron had been right. The woman was a saint. She had given herself, heart and soul, to those who needed a helping hand. Ignoring the protests of her family and society friends, she had single-mindedly determined to use her wealth to do good, to make a place of comfort and security for people who had nowhere else to go. But she didn't just dole out money. She gave herself—her time, her energy, her attention, her love. And she expected nothing in return.

The odd thing was, Saint Catherine seemed to be completely oblivious to her own nobility. Simple and self-effacing, she appeared to accept the calling she had been given as a matter of course, not an opportunity for self-aggrandizement or personal glory. She wore humility like a second skin, taking no notice at all of the praise she elicited from those around her. She never explained herself, not in public, anyway. But Ellie knew, after just a few conversations with Catherine Starr, what motivated her to give herself as she did. She was one of those rare individuals who took seriously God's command to feed the hungry, clothe the naked, shelter the homeless, love the unlovable, and work for justice.

She didn't preach the gospel; she lived it. And in Catherine's case, living it meant emptying bedpans and changing linens and listening to the same stories day in and day out; sitting up all night with the sick, and helping the dying to let go of life and meet their Maker in peace and dignity.

Catherine's voice interrupted Ellie's reverie. "Deep in thought?"

"What? Oh, sorry. I was just wondering what this place will be like when everybody gets moved in."

Catherine grinned. "Sometimes it will be so rowdy that you'll be glad you have the cottage out back." She leaned forward and whispered, "They love to dance."

"Dance?"

"Oh, yes. Burgess Goudge—he's our oldest resident, at ninety-three—has just learned how to jitterbug. He's a corker, I'll tell you. Makes passes at all the 'young gals,' as he calls them. A 'young gal' to Burgess is any female under ninety. He loves the big bands—Benny Goodman, especially. We have to keep him out of the kitchen, or else he gets out all the pots and pans and plays drums along with Gene Krupa."

"Really?" Ellie shook her head. "I guess I figured the residents would be . . . well, rather sedate."

"Some are. But just because they're old and can't live on their own anymore doesn't mean they're finished." Catherine shrugged. "We do our best to keep them active, interested. One of the women, Frieda Hawthorne, was an artist—quite a good one too. She teaches watercolor classes twice a week. Hazel Dennison conducts poetry readings. And of course they like radio drama, especially *The Shadow*."

What would the past ten years have been like, Ellie wondered, if Mother had been exposed to watercolor classes or poetry readings? Rather than just sitting in a chair or lying in bed, dying by degrees, might she have found some reason to come out of the darkness and go on with life? Ellie had no way of knowing. But she did know, beyond any doubt, that Catherine Starr's faith, both in God and in the elderly people she served, was a beacon of light in that darkness.

"So," Catherine was saying, "are you adjusting to your little cottage?"

"There's not much adjusting to do," Ellie responded. "It's just right for me—much better than having this big old house to myself."

"And you think you'll stay a while?"

Ellie considered her answer. The money she had received from the sale of the house and furnishings was more than enough to pay for college. If she wanted, she could start in January, and perhaps someday fulfill that long-awaited dream of becoming a social worker. Months ago, she had told Tish that she had neither the funds nor the energy to start over. Now she had the money, and her energy and optimism were beginning to return. But something else held her back, something she didn't quite understand.

The fact was, although she wouldn't admit it openly, she wondered if God was telling her to stay put.

There were a lot of rational reasons for the feeling, of course, reasons that had nothing to do with hearing God's voice. Ellie had been through a great deal of change in the past months—the death of her mother, the loss of Rome and her hopes for marriage, the sale of her house—and everybody said you shouldn't make major life decisions during a time of extreme grief or emotional turmoil. In addition, she had become increasingly attached to East Asheville Methodist Church and its little congregation of enthusiastic believers. For the first time in years, she was experiencing a sense of belonging, a realization that she was loved and accepted for herself, rather than for what she could do for others. She had found a family, and she wasn't ready to let go of that, even to follow her dreams.

And then there was Catherine.

Catherine Starr was the kind of woman Ellie always dreamed she would become. Catherine, with her worn flannel pajamas and no-nonsense approach to her call from God. Catherine, who knew exactly what she was to do with her life. Secretly, Ellie hoped that Catherine might become her guide, might help her sort through her options and find her way to that same kind of self-confidence and assurance. A role model, perhaps. Or, at the very least, a friend.

Whatever part Catherine was to play in her life, Ellie knew instinctively that it was important. Important enough for her to stay where she was, to watch and listen and learn.

The answer she *wanted* to give to Catherine's question was, *God has put you in my life for a reason, and I need to find out what it is.*

But she didn't have the courage, yet, to be quite that honest. Instead, she said, "Well, I have no place else to go, so I guess I'll stay for a while."

Catherine's dark eyes probed Ellie's gaze. For a minute or two she kept silent, watching, waiting.

"I see," she murmured at last.

I see. Just two words, nothing more. But those two words left Ellie with the disconcerting conviction that Catherine Starr knew more than she was telling.

31
V-E DAY

May 8, 1945

Ellie positioned the calendar on the hook behind the kitchen door and smiled to herself. Just like Catherine, to forget that April had passed into May—and more than a week ago, at that. She took a pencil from the counter and crossed out the first seven days of the month, then circled today's date with a broad stroke.

The eighth of May. Just this afternoon, on the radio, the exultant news had come: The War in Europe was over!

Ellie stared at the numbers at the top of the calendar. *1945.* Five years since her mother had died. Five years since Rome Tucker had disappeared from her life and Catherine Starr had entered it, with her merry band of misfits in her wake. It hardly seemed possible, but the calendar didn't lie.

The past years had risen and fallen, a series of mountaintops and valleys, like the layers of the Blue Ridge. Heights of hope and ravines of near-despair merged together in a lush and awe-inspiring panorama. Those individual moments of triumph and adversity—the death of Randolph Cameron and her mother's descent into darkness, the years of isolation and the hope that came with Rome Tucker's arrival, the chaos following her mother's death, and the slow, uncertain resurrection of her spirit into the light—all seemed to her now merely inevitable stages of the journey.

Strange, Ellie thought, how the darkness and light blended together, like tints on an artist's canvas. When you stepped back, you could no longer see the distinct brush strokes, the separate events that loomed so large at the time. With a little perspective, you saw instead the wider picture, the overall pattern—how the disparate parts fit together, how it all worked.

Five years ago, she had stood too close to perceive any design at all in her life. She had clung to the familiar like a drowning person grabbing for debris, had stayed on at the James Home simply because she didn't know what else to do. Her decision had derived more from fear than faith. And yet it had been the right one—the single most important choice of her thirty-two years.

She would never fulfill the exalted dreams she had crafted for herself as a girl teetering on the brink of womanhood—would never become a licensed social worker or go to Chicago to work at Hull House. Jane Addams had passed on ten years ago, but Ellie's aspirations had died long before that. No longer did she envision herself as making a difference, as having a significant impact on other people's lives. She was no savior to the masses, no champion of the disenfranchised. She was simply Ellie James, spinster, who longed with all her heart to personify the grace of God to those around her.

Catherine Starr had taught her what it meant to live as Jesus lived. Not in words, but in action—in the tender love she demonstrated to the elderly residents of the James Home, in sacrificial, even menial service, in forgiveness of those who harmed her, in the friendship she extended to Ellie herself.

Over the past five years, Ellie had watched and listened and learned. Almost against her will, she had been drawn into the lives of the people who occupied her childhood home. Who, after all, could resist Burgess Goudge's Concerto for Pots and Pans? Or Frieda Hawthorne's rustic watercolor paintings of her beloved mountains? Or Hazel Dennison's epic poem, a parody of *Beowulf*, in which Pisgah the cat went hunting for the giant mouse Grendel?

Ellie shook her head, but the smile remained. This odd "family" of hers, this ragtag collection of old women and old men who had no place else to go, wasn't exactly what she had in mind when, at sixteen, she determined to follow in Jane Addams's footsteps. But these were the people God had placed into her world, and she would do her best to help Catherine care for them.

There would be no glory in such a life, no accolades from the public, no financial rewards. Only the knowledge that she had said "yes" when God called.

A banging at the door leading to the parlor arrested Ellie's attention, and she turned. Burgess stood there stooped over, cane in hand, the bright kitchen light reflecting from his smooth and shiny head. His weathered face wrinkled into a scowl, his eyes bulged behind thick horn-rimmed glasses, and he shook his cane in her direction.

"Hurry it up, will you? The candles are lit, and I'm not about to try to blow them out without your help." He wheezed dramatically. "Less you want to burn the house down around us all, I'd suggest you get a move on." Burgess turned on his heel and began to stomp back toward the dining room. "Catherine says to bring the cake knife with you when you come," he flung over his shoulder as the door swung shut behind him.

Ellie grinned at his retreating back and retrieved the cake slicer from the top drawer. "I'm coming, Burgess," she shouted after him. "I wouldn't miss your birthday for the world."

The door swung open again. "You don't have to yell at me, girlie," he snapped. "Just because I'm ninety-eight years old doesn't mean I'm deaf, you know."

"I know, Burgess. I've got the knife. Let's go."

"All right, all right. But don't point that thing in my direction."

In the dining room, the cake was indeed blazing, a conflagration worthy of the entire Asheville Fire Department. Burgess paused at the head of the table and waited for the singing to conclude. He turned to Ellie. "You make this yerself?"

"I did, just for you," Ellie admitted. "Used two weeks' worth of sugar rations too."

"Tryin' to put me in a coma, are you?" He gave her a toothless grin and winked at her. "It better be good."

"Just blow out the candles, Burgess." Ellie stepped to his side and counted. "One, two, three, blow!"

A great cheer rang out as the last of the candles fluttered out, followed by a round of sputtering and coughing as the smoke dissipated.

Catherine sidled over to Burgess and gave him a kiss on the cheek. "You want to cut it, or shall I do the honors?"

"You cut it. I got too much of the trembles." He raised a shaky hand as proof. "But make mine a big piece, with one of them roses on top."

꙰

An hour later, the party was still going strong. Burgess had insisted on "cutting the rug with all the young gals," and he was doing a pretty fair imitation of a jitterbug to Glenn Miller's "Chattanooga Choo-Choo" when Catherine tapped Ellie on the shoulder and cut in.

"Hey!" Burgess objected. "You're not gonna take my favorite partner away, are you?"

"Sorry, old man, you'll have to make do with me as a substitute." Catherine pulled Ellie close and whispered in her ear, "Hazel's asking for you. I'll hold the fort down here."

Ellie made her apologies to Burgess, wished him a happy birthday, and with a heavy heart climbed the stairs to Hazel Dennison's room. For three years the old woman had put up a valiant fight against the cancer that had invaded her body; now at last, it seemed, the disease was winning.

Ellie had envisioned this moment and believed she was prepared for Hazel's passing. But when she entered the bedroom—the very room where she had cared for Mother every day for ten long years—her resolve failed, and tears blinded her. A musty, acrid odor filled the room. *The scent of death,* Ellie thought suddenly.

"Now, honey, don't cry," Hazel said in a raspy voice. She held out a hand, a withered, palsied claw lined with veins and spotted with age. "It's time. I just wanted to see you before I go."

Ellie settled on the edge of the bed and took Hazel's hand gently in her own. She couldn't stop the tears, but managed to force a little smile for the old woman's benefit. "Let me get you some water, Hazel," she whispered with a catch in her throat. "Your medicine?" There must be something she could *do*—some action she could take that would postpone the inevitable, if only for a little while. She couldn't just sit idly by and wait for the end to come.

"No, my dear. There's nothing to be done."

"But—"

"No buts, child. I beg you, Ellie, not to try to keep me here. The pain is almost gone, and soon I will go too. All I need is for you to sit and wait and listen."

"Are—are you afraid?" Ellie stammered.

"Afraid? Of what?"

"Why, of—of death." The very word, *death,* scraped across Ellie's eardrums like a file on metal, dredging up ancient images of a dark and hooded figure from the world of nightmares.

"What is there to fear?" Hazel responded. Her eyes grew distant and clouded. "To live without regret makes dying easy."

Ellie leaned forward. "I don't understand, Hazel. How can you live without regret?" Her heart filled with pain at the recollection of so many losses. Her parents, the man she loved, the dreams she cherished . . . .

Hazel clutched her hand, a grip surprisingly strong for one so ill. "Listen to me, Ellie James. Regret for what has been—or for what *might* have been—is folly, a waste of precious time and energy. Don't give your future to the past. Don't look back." A ghost of a smile flitted across her face, transforming the wrinkled countenance with its glory. "Only two things are important in this life, Ellie," she went on after a moment. "Love and forgiveness. If you let yourself love, you will never regret it, for even if your love is unreturned, it will enrich you. But to love purely you have to learn to forgive. Only in forgiveness can you be free. Forgive others. Forgive yourself. The path is before you, not behind. You've already made a good start, by putting yourself into the hands of the only One who is capable of guiding you. Trust, child. Trust."

"I'm trying to trust, Hazel. But I'm afraid I'll never understand."

"Understanding is irrelevant," the old woman breathed. "What's important is who you are becoming. Remember Yeats?"

Ellie nodded. Countless evenings over the past few years, she had sat in the parlor and listened as Hazel Dennison read from the works of William Butler Yeats. Much of it she didn't understand, but Hazel's voice made the words sing with an ethereal beauty.

"Then remember these lines, if you heed nothing else," Hazel went on. *"Time can but make it easier to be wise . . . All that you need is patience."*

"What does it mean?"

"It means," Hazel sighed, "that if you wait with hope, you will find wisdom.

Wisdom comes not from the mind, through understanding, but from the heart, through trusting. Have faith, child. With God there are no mistakes, no missed opportunities, no irredeemable failures—only lessons to be learned."

The old woman's breathing grew labored, and she leaned back against the pillows, an expression of wonder and joy on her face. Suddenly Ellie realized she was witnessing a miracle—a woman who could embrace the unknown with the absolute certainty that something greater awaited her.

Ellie's awe at the miraculous quickly dissipated, however, as a different emotion gripped her in a stranglehold—a rage, hot and wild and utterly selfish, at the idea of losing Hazel Dennison so soon. It wasn't soon for Hazel, of course—she had lived a long and fruitful life, rich in wisdom and knowledge and godliness. But Ellie's time with Hazel had been much too short. Hazel had become the mother Ellie had never known, not even while her own mother was alive and well. There was so much Ellie could learn from her yet, so much she needed to know. So much love and appreciation she had yet to demonstrate. . . .

Tears boiled up and coursed down her cheeks, and through glazed eyes she saw Hazel lift her head one final time.

"Trust, child," she whispered. "Let go of regret. Love. Forgive . . ."

Then she squeezed Ellie's hand, smiled, and closed her eyes forever.

❦

Hazel Dennison's funeral, like her life, was a simple ceremony, unadorned by ritual but marked by great depth and faith. The little family from the Eleanor James Home for the Elderly, some in wheelchairs or leaning on walkers, gathered at the graveside to bid their final farewells.

Hazel's grave was only a stone's throw from the massive James headstone, under which Ellie's own parents lay, but she barely sent a glance in that direction. Her real kin were here, beside her, supporting her with love and understanding—almost as if she were the bereaved daughter.

All during the service, Hazel's parting words echoed in Ellie's mind. *Don't give your future to the past. Don't look back. Let go of regret. Love. Forgive.* Ellie couldn't shake the haunting sensation that Hazel had been trying to prepare her for something, to impart a wisdom for her to hold on to.

As the coffin was lowered into the grave and the little crowd began to disperse, Ellie felt an arm go around her shoulders and looked up through her tears to find Catherine standing close beside her. "You loved her a great deal, didn't you?"

Ellie nodded.

"Sometimes giving yourself to God's purposes bears a high price tag," Catherine said gently. "Love can hurt, so much that you wonder if it's worth it."

Fresh tears gathered in Ellie's throat so that she couldn't speak.

"But it *is* worth it," Catherine went on. "She loved you too, you know. Like you were her own."

"I know," Ellie said at last. "I only wish there was something I could have done—"

Catherine pulled her into a strong embrace. "There was something," she whispered into Ellie's ear. "And you did it. You loved her. Your presence made a big difference in her life."

"Are you sure?" Ellie sobbed. "It doesn't seem like enough."

Catherine leaned back and held Ellie at arm's length. "Love is always enough. It's the finest thing we can give to another. Love is God's hand in human flesh."

"But just loving feels so . . . so inadequate," Ellie said. "I always wanted my life to count, to be significant. I wanted to do something—something—" She shrugged, at a loss for words.

"Something important?" Catherine finished. "Your life *does* count, Ellie—only not in the way you envisioned when you were a teenager with big dreams. The significance happens one person at a time."

Catherine linked her arm through Ellie's and steered her away from the mourners, toward the tree-shaded hilltop above the cemetery. The memories of her own mother's funeral flooded over Ellie: the losses, the regrets. But today was different. No longer was she isolated, alone. Now she had love, a place of belonging. And she knew, perhaps for the first time in her life, that whatever the future held, she could face it without fear.

No regrets, Hazel had said. *Only lessons to be learned.*

Catherine pointed toward the grove of trees at the top of the hill. "There's someone here to see you."

Ellie looked. A tall figure stood in the shadow of the trees—a man wearing an army uniform and leaning heavily on a cane. He took a couple of limping steps forward, out of the shade into the spring sunshine. The light glinted off his sandy hair, and he raised his free hand in an uncertain wave.

Ellie shut her eyes and took in a shaky breath. Her mind resisted the truth, but her heart knew better:

Rome Tucker had returned.

32
PLAN B

"Catherine, I can't see him. Not now. Maybe not ever." In the kitchen of her tiny cottage, Ellie propped her elbows on the table and buried her face in her hands. She had thought she had exhausted all her tears at Hazel's bedside and at the funeral. But here they were, forming a knot in her throat again, threatening to overwhelm her once more.

This time not for the dying, but for the living.

Ellie felt Catherine's hand stroking her hair, and she looked up. "I can't do it. Not after all this time. Tell him to go away—please."

"If that's what you really want, I'll tell him," Catherine said evenly. "But before you make that decision, there are a few things you ought to know."

"Such as?"

"I spoke with him at some length. Ellie, he's been absolved of any responsibility for the fire or for his wife's death. The authorities hadn't really counted him as a viable suspect—until he ran away, that is. Only when he disappeared did they begin to question his motives." She looked into Ellie's eyes. "What he told you was the truth. When he lost everything, he just gave up. Began to drift."

"And what about the ring—his first wife's engagement ring?"

"The ring was his mother's, just as he said. The rest was just rumor."

Ellie exhaled a ragged sigh. "So why didn't he tell me all this? Why did he just leave?"

"He saw the expression in your eyes that day, Ellie. You were afraid of him. You didn't trust him."

"No, I didn't. I couldn't help it. And how can I trust him now?"

"A wise old woman I once knew defined trust as 'risk taken and survived.' You won't know for sure, Ellie, until you take the risk."

"But it's been so long, Catherine. Why didn't he contact me? Why didn't he let me know what was happening, where he was . . . something?"

"There's been a war on, remember? Except for ration books and scrap drives, we've pretty much been isolated from the reality of it. But Rome hasn't. By the time everything was settled—the fire was ultimately determined to be an accident, by the way, caused by a cracked stovepipe—Rome was called up for service. He didn't want to try to explain in a letter, he said, but before he had a chance to get back here, he was shipped out. Spent nearly a year on the front before getting wounded, then was in and out of hospitals getting his leg put back together."

Ellie averted her eyes from Catherine's penetrating gaze. "So you think I should just welcome him back with open arms because he's wearing a Purple Heart? My patriotic duty, is that it?"

"I think you have a duty, yes," Catherine replied in a low voice. "But not to Rome. To yourself. If you send him away without ever talking to him, you may live with that regret for the rest of your life."

Something jerked in Ellie's mind, a sharp pain, as if a probe had pricked a sensitive area of her brain. *Live without regret,* Hazel Dennison had told her. *Love. Forgive.*

But how could she forgive someone who had abandoned her without explanation, a man who had professed his love for her and then left her in a heartbeat? She had almost gotten over him, almost begun to forget, and now . . .

"I'm not suggesting that you simply forgive him and pretend it never happened," Catherine went on as if she had read Ellie's thoughts. "But I do believe you owe it to him—and more importantly, to yourself—to give him a chance."

"He had his chance," Ellie snapped. "We don't get second chances in this life."

"Don't we?" Catherine smiled briefly and raised her eyebrows. "Isn't that what grace is all about—getting a second chance, even when you don't necessarily deserve it?"

Catherine's words sent a flush of shame coursing through Ellie's veins, and she felt heat rise up her neck and into her cheeks. Much as she despised admitting it, Catherine was right. Ellie had been given a second chance—an opportunity to make her life count for something, a miracle of hope in the midst of mind-numbing despair. When she had been at her lowest ebb, God had reached into her life and lifted her up on a tide of fresh challenges, new relationships, and an unaccustomed intimacy with the Almighty that had altered her life forever.

The Lord hadn't given up on her, even when she had been angry and bitter and completely hopeless. And she knew, with a sinking sense of inevitability, that she couldn't give up on Rome, either—at least not until she had heard him out.

"All right, you win," Ellie said at last. "I'll talk to him. But I'm not making any promises, understand."

co

Ellie wasn't quite sure what to expect as she followed Catherine into the front parlor, but what she saw certainly wasn't like any reunion she could have envisioned. Rome sat on the sofa, leaning back, his bad leg stretched out on a footstool, surrounded by most of the residents of the Eleanor James Home for the Elderly. Burgess Goudge had "Moonlight Serenade" playing full blast on the record player and was demonstrating his ability to dance like Fred Astaire, with his cane in one hand and a hatrack in the other. Mount Pisgah perched on Rome's chest, kneading his lapels and drooling on his medals. Frieda Hawthorne was squeezed in beside him, chattering about her most recent mountain panoramas and explaining watercolor technique in her high-pitched voice.

Burgess was the first to see Ellie. He abandoned the hatrack and swept her into his free arm for a dance. In the time it took them to make one circuit of the parlor, he had managed to croak into her ear, "Don't let this fella get away, honey. He's a winner."

When the music stopped, everyone, including Rome, was focused on Ellie. Frieda heaved herself off the sofa and tottered over to her. "Such a nice young man you have, child," she squealed happily, patting Ellie on the arm. "Why didn't you tell us?"

Rome pushed Pisgah to the floor, retrieved his cane, and tried to struggle to his feet. "Forgive me, Ellie, I—"

"Don't get up," she said, infusing her voice with as much iciness as she could muster. "I can see your attention is occupied."

"I was just getting to know some of your friends while I waited," he said smoothly. "And hoping you'd see me."

When he got up and began to walk toward her, his eyes locked on hers, Ellie's composure began to slip. His expression was so open, so hopeful, that despite her resolve to keep him at a distance, she felt drawn to him, as if she could see into his soul and witness the love that was still there. By the time he reached her, she was trembling.

"May I have this dance, Miss James?" He put out a hand and grinned. "It's been a long time since this old soldier has had the opportunity to dance with such a lovely lady."

Ellie's eyes went to the cane, to his twisted leg. "Is it all right? I mean, can you—?"

"I'm afraid I don't hold a candle to Burgess," he said with a wink as he tossed the cane onto the sofa. "But I can manage with a little help and support."

Burgess started the record player and the strains of Tommy Dorsey filled the parlor. "*I'll never smile again, until I smile at you. . . .*"

Ellie made a face at Burgess over Rome's shoulder, but the soothing music and romantic lyrics worked their way into her heart, and she found herself relaxing in his arms. His grip tightened around her waist and pulled her close, and his lips brushed against her ear as he whispered, "I've waited so long for this. Give me a chance, Ellie, and I'll explain everything."

"*I'll never love again, I'm so in love with you,*" the Dorsey singers crooned in the background. "*Within my heart, I know I will never start to smile again until I smile at you. . . .*"

When the song ended, wild applause broke out all around them. Frieda clasped her hands to her bosom and shrilled, "Oh, it's so romantic! Just like in the movies!" Ellie felt herself blush.

"Let's get out of here, okay?" Rome said softly.

She hesitated only for a minute. She hadn't wanted to be alone with him, but anything was better than this public display. "All right." She turned on her heel and made for the door, and, amid the laughter and applause, heard Rome's odd little step-scrape behind her.

Alone in Ellie's cottage, they both turned self-conscious. Ellie busied herself making coffee, and Rome wandered aimlessly through the rooms until he came full circle to the kitchen table.

"You've done a real nice job with this place."

"Correction. *Catherine* did a nice job. She had the additions done before I ever moved in here."

"Well, it's nice. Real nice. Hardly looks like the same cottage as it did when I—" He stopped mid-sentence and cleared his throat awkwardly.

"I know. I wasn't sure I could live here until I saw how different it—" Ellie, too, ended abruptly. "Cream and sugar?"

"Just black, thanks." He shrugged. "Like always."

She set two steaming mugs on the table and sat as far away from him as possible, which wasn't far enough, given the small dimensions of the table.

Rome toyed with his mug, turning it this way and that until coffee sloshed onto the wooden tabletop. "Sorry."

Ellie handed him a napkin. "It's okay."

"Ellie—"

"Rome—"

They both spoke at once, then lapsed into silence. Rome held out a hand. "You first."

Ellie shook her head. "No, you go ahead. You said you wanted to talk. I'm listening."

Rome chewed his lip and stared at his coffee cup. "For the past five years I've been planning what I would say to you," he began. "All that time on the front, and afterward, in the hospital. My biggest fear was that I might die before I had a chance to see you again."

"Forgive me for interrupting," Ellie said, "but I'd appreciate it if you'd just get on with your explanations. That's why you came back, isn't it?"

He reached a hand out toward her, and even though part of her longed to take it, to feel the tender touch of his fingers again, she kept her own hands folded in her lap.

"You still don't trust me," he said.

"Give me one good reason to trust," she shot back. "Five years ago you just walked away, and I haven't heard a word from you since."

"Didn't Catherine tell you that I was absolved of any suspicion in the fire, in Amelia's death?"

"She told me."

"But that's not enough."

"No, Rome, it's not enough. I trusted you—once, a long time ago. I gave my heart to you. But then you disappeared. What was I supposed to think? What, in heaven's name, was I supposed to *do*? Keep a torch burning, and rush back into your arms the minute you showed your face again?"

"No. I don't expect that."

"Then what do you expect from me, Rome Tucker?"

"I don't expect anything, Ellie. I just hoped you'd be willing to listen, to give me a second chance. I had to come back. I couldn't live the rest of my life regretting the fact that I didn't try."

Second chances. Regrets. Would she regret it too if she didn't give Rome a chance? Or, more importantly, if she didn't give God a chance to work in this situation?

She sighed and waved a hand. "All right. Go on."

"The day I left, I saw the look on your face when Tish Cameron told you about my past. It was all just rumor and misunderstanding, but I knew I couldn't make you believe that. I had to leave, Ellie. Had to go back and straighten it all out before I could give myself to you as a free man, with nothing hanging over my head.

"Once the authorities had a chance to question me, they immediately took me off their list of suspects. By the time they determined the cause of the fire and declared Amelia's death an accident, Japan had attacked Pearl Harbor and I was called up. I went into the army and got shipped overseas. Then I was wounded and hospitalized. But I never stopped thinking about you, Ellie. Never stopped loving you."

"Why didn't you write? Why didn't you at least give me some indication of where you were and what was going on?"

"I wanted to. I did, in fact, write to you. Dozens of letters."

"I never got them."

"I never mailed them. I'm not very good at expressing myself, Ellie. Everything I wrote sounded so hollow. I had to see you face to face. Had to be able to look into your eyes and see for myself whether you would ever be able to trust me again."

He got up from the table, went into the parlor, and returned with a small canvas bag. "Here," he said, pulling out a sheaf of letters and a file folder stuffed with official-looking papers. "These are the letters I wrote—at least the ones I didn't tear up." He handed them to her. "And this is a copy of the final police report, and a copy of my service record. It's all here—the whole history of the past five years of my life."

Ellie shuffled through the stack, and her heart did a series of flips when her fingers touched the sealed envelopes that bore her name.

"I prayed—every single day—that you wouldn't go off to school in Chicago or New York or some big city where you could vanish forever. That you wouldn't leave until I had a chance to see you again. To see you, and tell you I love you."

Ellie sat staring at the letters and papers, avoiding his gaze. She thought about that moment of decision when she had chosen to stay here and help Catherine with the James Home, rather than pursueing her dreams. Was it possible that other factors besides her fear had played a part in that decision? Factors such as Rome's prayers, or her own need to become the woman she was intended to be? Had God kept her here, waiting, for this moment—for Rome Tucker's return?

Yet she hadn't been waiting, not really. She had never even considered the possibility that he might come back. Instead, she had gone on with her life, had taken her second chance, and had, in the process, found a purpose and significance to her life far deeper than anything she had ever dreamed.

She thought about Catherine Starr, how the woman had helped her learn what it meant to listen to the Lord's voice and follow the Lord's direction. She thought about Hazel Dennison, who even in death had given her one of the great gifts of life. These and other forces beyond her imagining had figured into her decision to stay at the James Home. Was it possible that Rome Tucker was one of those hidden reasons—not the primary motive, perhaps, but one of those secret secondary works of God?

At last Ellie felt strong enough and sure enough to respond, and she raised her head and looked him in the eye.

"You have to understand, Rome," she said quietly, "that I am not the same person you knew when you left here. Back then, I was a girl, uncertain of my direction and willing to cling to any shred of hope for a future. In the years you've been gone, I've become a woman, and I've discovered my own relationship with God—a relationship that has become the most important factor in any decision I make. It hasn't been easy, but I'm no longer lonely or isolated or desperate. I have a life and a calling. I have a family. I have love."

She paused, and as the next words came to her, a sense of peace drifted over her soul like a warm blanket, a power of spirit engendered by the truth that filled her heart. "I don't need you, Rome, to make my life complete. But I am willing to consider the possibility that God has sent you back here for a reason. A very wise and loving woman recently told me that living without regret makes dying easy. I can't make any commitments right now, but I don't want to go to my grave regretting the possibility that I rejected something God might have wanted for me."

She paused and smiled at him. "A long time ago, when you first asked me to marry you, I said I'd need some time to sort it out. I didn't want to accept your proposal out of desperation, the way a drowning person grabs onto the first bit of debris that floats by. Give me time now, Rome. Time to listen to God. Time to listen to my own heart."

"Take all the time you need," he said in a whisper. "I'm not going anywhere."

33
AUTUMN MAGIC

September 22, 1945

Ellie watched from the doorway of her cottage as Rome clipped out the last of the fall flowers from the garden plot. He wasn't as agile as he had been five years ago; he had to bend awkwardly with one knee on the ground and his bad leg stretched out in front of him. But still he hummed and whistled, pausing now and then to stroke Pisgah's silvery fur as she rubbed up against him.

All summer he had stayed, working cheerfully through the sultry days of July and August. He had tended the gardens, coaxing from the stubborn soil enough vegetables to keep them all well fed, had repaired the gutters and downspouts so that the residents no longer got soaked coming in and out of the house. He had even installed an electric attic fan that drew cool air through the big house at night, and he'd put a ceiling fan in the downstairs parlor.

But it wasn't Rome's hard work that softened Ellie's heart toward him, or even his evident love for her. It was the way he related to Burgess Goudge and Frieda Hawthorne—and even Liz Townsend, the newest resident of the James Home, who drove everybody crazy with her incessant chattering and repetition. Always gentle and loving, yet never condescending, Rome lavished each of them with attention and compassion and humor.

Once, when Hazel Dennison was still alive and the two were discussing Ellie's love life—or lack of it—Hazel had told Ellie that you could judge the measure of a man by the way he treated children and animals and old folks. Well, there weren't any children at the James Home, but there were plenty of old folks. And Rome opened himself to them, drew them in, embraced them, and made each of them feel cherished and important.

According to Catherine, this was the way you made a difference in the world—one life at a time. Ellie had difficulty applying the principle to herself and believing her own presence had any significant impact upon others, but she could see it clearly in Rome Tucker. His return had brought fresh hope and life to the members of the the James Home family—and, if she were going to be completely honest, to Ellie herself.

Out of Christian duty—the obligation of forgiveness, the requirement of the law—Ellie had agreed to give Rome his second chance. But inside, she had determined to keep her heart hardened; she had been hurt too much and had no intention of allowing herself to become vulnerable again. Not to him . . . not to anyone.

The problem was, she had *already* become vulnerable—exposed and indefensible against the irresistible power of love. Love in the form of Hazel Dennison, who had become the mother she had never known. Love in the guise of Burgess Goudge, who adored her like his own granddaughter. Love in the unyielding, indefatigable commitment of Catherine Starr. These were Ellie's people, her family. And she loved them with a fierce and holy devotion.

But Ellie had made a mistake—a potentially costly one. She had assumed that different kinds of love came in through different portals of the heart, so that she could fling wide the windows of her soul to embrace the love of God and the love of her newfound family and still keep a part of herself locked and bolted against Rome Tucker's kind of love. Romantic love.

Now, here she stood, watching him from the safety of her doorway, trying to still the pounding of her heart as the autumn sun touched his hair with gold and raised a glistening sheen on his broad forehead. He had proved himself trustworthy. Everyone at the James Home and at East Asheville Methodist had welcomed him home like the prodigal returning from his wanderings. And only her infernal pride was keeping Ellie from doing the same.

She had never thought of herself as a prideful woman. Her own mother's haughtiness, in fact, was one of the characteristics Ellie had spent a lifetime abhorring. Yet here it was, mocking her, like the menacing image of another face, a stranger's face, reflected back when she looked in the mirror.

Ellie didn't like what she saw, but she forced herself to face the distasteful image that loomed before her. Was she so arrogant, so proud, that she had to hang on to the pain of the past rather than forgiving and finding a new place to begin? Was she so holy, so righteous, that she couldn't put herself in Rome's place and understand the hell he had been through in the past five years?

Suddenly the truth struck her, and she recoiled in horror from it. She had been blaming Rome for her own misery, her own hopelessness, when none of it had been his fault at all. He had merely loved her, sought to build a new life for himself and for her, and circumstances had gotten in the way of the fulfillment of that dream. He was no monster; he was not responsible for his wife's death, nor for the war that had come between them. He was simply a man caught in the grip of circumstance—and an honorable man at that, who had faced up to his past and settled his debts before returning to the woman he loved. And she had refused to trust him.

Oh, she had couched her refusal in noble, even spiritual terms—waiting for God's direction, giving Rome a chance to prove himself. But how much proof of his character did she need? Everyone else accepted him—the church, the residents of the James Home, even Catherine Starr, whose opinion Ellie valued above any other. Ellie herself had been the single holdout. And it wasn't for any godly reason, either, no matter how much she might rationalize it in spiritual terms. It was purely out of pride and fear. Pride kept her from forgiving; fear kept her from taking a chance on love.

What had Catherine said about trust? *Trust is risk taken and survived.* There was no way to *know* what would happen if she took that risk and allowed herself to love Rome Tucker. But she was pretty sure she knew what would happen if she *didn't* risk it. Hazel Dennison had told her: *There are only two things important in this life—love and forgiveness. Don't give your future to the past, child. Live without regret. . . .*

As she watched Rome gather up the weeds to take them to the mulch pile, Ellie felt something give way inside her soul. A rush of fearlessness washed through her veins, and she could almost feel the tenderness welling up within her heart. She reached a hand toward him, as if from this distance she could touch him and draw him in. But his back was turned toward her.

"Rome?" she called in a tentative whisper.

No response.

"Rome!" This time her voice was stronger, louder, more certain.

He turned. "Yes?"

"When you're finished there, why don't you come in for a cup of coffee?"

It was a simple request, but—at least for Ellie—one fraught with meaning and laden with promise. Their eyes met, and he stood there gazing at her with an expression of wonder and love.

Suddenly he dropped the mound of clippings, right on the sidewalk, and brushed off his hands. "I'm finished now." He grinned.

"Don't you want to—?"

Rome shrugged. "The weeds will wait," he said as he came toward her. "I'm afraid you won't."

November 3, 1945

The tiny clapboard church was crowded to capacity. White bows adorned the pews, and candles bathed the sanctuary with a holy glow. Bea Whitman sat at the organ, playing and smiling, smiling and playing.

In the small entryway, Ellie adjusted her veil nervously and shifted from one foot to the other.

"Be still, will you?" Tish commanded. "You're going to step on your train."

Ellie fidgeted and grabbed at Tish's arm. "I can't believe I'm doing this."

"I can't believe you didn't do it months ago." Catherine's voice behind her made Ellie jump, and she giggled.

"I feel like a schoolgirl. What if I trip and make a fool of myself?"

"Then everybody will get a good laugh out of it," Catherine said in her no-nonsense tone, "and it will be the most memorable wedding in recent history."

"You're a big help." Ellie pretended to be miffed. "Whatever possessed me to make you my matron of honor?"

"Because you adore me, of course," Catherine countered. "Now, remember, by the time you get back from the honeymoon, we should have the expansion done on the cottage. Are you sure you want to live there instead of getting a place of your own?"

Ellie nodded. "Rome and I talked about it, and there's no place we'd rather be. Besides, you need us." She smiled and gave Catherine a kiss on the cheek. Thanks to the woman's boundless generosity, Ellie and Rome would have a real honeymoon, on the beach in Mexico, and when they returned, the little cottage would have undergone a second transformation. "Now don't get too carried away with the cottage, Catherine," Ellie warned sternly. "I know you. If somebody doesn't keep an eye on you, we'll come back to find the Biltmore House in the backyard."

"The processional is beginning." Tish glanced at the clock in the vestibule. "Right on time. Are you ready?"

"Ready as I'll ever be." Ellie grimaced. "Do I look all right?"

"No, you don't look all right," Catherine answered. "You look beautiful."

"Is Rome here?"

"Rome's been here for hours. I think he arrived at sunrise."

Ellie took a deep breath. "All right. Let's go."

She watched as her two attendants—Tish, the maid of honor, and Catherine, the matron of honor—made their way down the aisle. Craning her neck, she caught a glimpse of Rome, standing beside Reverend Potter at the front of the church. His normally ruddy skin had gone pale, and he licked his lips nervously. *He's terrified,* Ellie thought. *But then, so am I.*

"Scared, honey?"

Ellie turned to see Burgess Goudge, all spiffed up in a gray morning coat and bright red bow tie, ready to walk her down the aisle. Despite her prewedding jitters, she laughed. "A little, Burgess. But I feel better now."

He extended his arm, and they made their grand entrance to the majestic strains of "Joyful, Joyful We Adore Thee." At the end of the aisle, he kissed her, squeezed her hand, and made a grand sweeping bow before taking his seat in the front pew.

Standing alone in the center of the aisle, Ellie experienced a moment of panic. In a traditional wedding, her father would have been beside her, still holding her elbow, waiting until the minister asked, "Who giveth this woman . . . ?" But Ellie had no father, no one to give her away, and after some discussion, she and Rome had decided simply to eliminate that portion of the service. Still, she felt isolated and exposed, and she desperately wished that Rome would move to her side as he was supposed to do.

Ellie looked up and caught his eye. He had made no move to step forward, but was grinning at her. *I love you*—his lips formed the words silently.

Suddenly, Reverend Potter cleared his throat and began: "Dearly beloved . . ."

What was he doing? This wasn't right! The plan was, as soon as Ellie reached the end of the aisle, Rome would come forward and take her hand. But the man hadn't budged, and Ellie wasn't sure what to do next. She wasn't about to get married all by herself.

Then, to her shock, she heard Reverend Potter utter the question that wasn't supposed to be asked: "Who giveth this woman to be married to this man?"

Ellie held her breath, mortified. Well, she should have suspected that something would go awry. Was it an omen, a sign that she had made the wrong decision after all?

Desperately she looked to Rome, who was still grinning at her. And then she heard a shuffling sound behind her, and she turned. All the residents of the James Home were on their feet, along with most of the members of East Asheville Methodist. In unison, they roared out, "We do!"

Tears sprang to Ellie's eyes, and a knot formed in her throat. In an instant, Rome was at her side, cradling her elbow in his hand. He leaned down and whispered, "They love you, Ellie. What a wonderful family you have."

Ellie knew it was true. She glanced around and saw the faces of her family—not blood kin, but people grafted into her life by a divine hand, people with whom she shared a stronger bond than common ancestry could ever create. And then, when she turned and looked into Rome's eyes, she felt a depth of love that shook her to her soul.

Like Job, she had lost everything, only to have it abundantly restored by the hand of a gracious and compassionate God. Although she would probably never understand all the *whys,* she recognized the source and was thankful.

Understanding is irrelevant, Hazel Dennison had wisely told her. *Only love matters.*

Ellie smiled and took Rome's outstretched hand.

"Do you, Eleanor James, take this man to be your lawfully wedded husband?" Reverend Potter asked.

Ellie blinked back tears and took a deep breath. "I do," she said. "I most certainly do."

34
MRS. TUCKER

November 25, 1994

I always thought it was ironic," Ellie concluded as she cleared the dishes from the table. "Jesus' earthly life ended at thirty-three. At thirty-three, I was just beginning mine. A newlywed at that advanced age—can you imagine?"

Brendan twisted her face into a grimace. "I'm thirty-three and not married."

"Forgive me, dear." Ellie resumed her place at the table and patted Brendan's hand. "I didn't mean to hurt your feelings. But times are different now, you know. People wait much longer to marry and have families."

"With the kind of job I have, I'll probably be waiting forever."

Ellie smiled gently. "Is there a special person in your life?"

"Hey, I'm the reporter. I should be asking the questions." Brendan grinned. "Just kidding. There was someone once, a while back. But it didn't work out. Our jobs took us in two different directions. And to tell the truth, I didn't miss him all that much once he was gone."

"And what about your family?"

Brendan paused. She really didn't want to dredge up the details of her past, but if anyone could truly understand, it would probably be Ellie James Tucker. "I have no family," she said after a moment. "My parents died when I was quite young. My grandmother raised me, and now she's gone too. I'm alone."

"Ah." Ellie peered at her with questioning eyes. "But are you, really?"

Brendan frowned and tilted her head. What was the old woman getting at?

"Don't you have someone?" Ellie went on. "Someone who has become family for you, even though you're not actually related?"

To Brendan's surprise, the first name that came to her mind was not Vonnie Howells, who had been her best friend for years, but Dee Lovell. Dee and Addie, Letitia Cameron, and even the old German battle-ax of a nurse, Gertrude Klein. At the Thanksgiving gathering yesterday, Brendan had experienced a sense of belonging unlike anything she had known since her grandmother died. Dee had even referred to the group as "our little family." It was a good feeling, to know you were welcomed and included. Yet Brendan felt herself holding back. She didn't want to become some Tennessee Williams heroine, "always dependent upon the kindness of strangers." She had always been strong and independent, convinced that she didn't need anyone. It was far too frightening to open herself to some-thing else—something that, in the long run, might prove deeply hurtful.

"Family is based on spirit, not on genetics," Ellie was saying. "The people your soul connects with, the people who fit into your heart. That bond can be just as strong as—in some cases, even stronger than—blood."

"And you found your family in Rome Tucker and in the residents of the James Home," Brendan said, steering the conversation back to Ellie.

"I did." Ellie nodded. "It wasn't always easy, you know. We endured a lot together—cancer, stroke, Alzheimer's. They all died, one by one. But for the most part they passed on peacefully, because they knew they were loved. They knew they were not alone."

"And what finally happened with the Eleanor James Home for the Elderly?" Brendan asked.

"Rome and I continued to live in the cottage and gradually took over more and more of the duties of running the home and caring for the resi-dents. For a number of years we had a full house, with new people com-ing all the time. When Catherine died, she left the entire operation to us, knowing that we would be true to the calling. Eventually other care facili-ties began to spring up, however, and our numbers dwindled, so we finally sold the house and moved here."

"But why Atlanta? Why leave your roots?"

"Remember Matthew Potter, the pastor at East Ashville Methodist?"

Brendan nodded. "He had moved here to take a church that was comprised mostly of elderly folks. When he heard we were thinking of selling the house, he urged us to come to Georgia and help out." She smiled. "We just couldn't get away from it, I guess. A couple of miles from here is one of the largest nursing homes in the Atlanta area. Rome and I helped get it established—nearly thirty years ago, now."

Elllie sighed and gave a little shrug. "Rome was in his sixties when we moved here. His heart finally gave out—oh, about ten years ago. I miss him still, but we had a good life. A long life. A life filled with love."

Brendan felt a movement at her ankles and reached down to pick up the big Himalayan cat. The beast purred contentedly and settled into her lap.

"That's Stoney," Ellie explained. "Named for Stone Mountain. He's the last offspring of our dear old Mount Pisgah—four generations removed." The old woman reached out a hand and scratched the cat under his chin. Without warning, he leaped onto the table and began rubbing his whiskers against the blue glass bottle. Brendan caught it just as it toppled off the edge, and Ellie grabbed the cat and set him firmly on the floor.

"You break that bottle, and your name will be Mud Cat," she scolded.

"Mrrow." Stoney glared at her and stalked off into the kitchen.

Brendan held the bottle up to the window and regarded it solemnly. It was just an old piece of glass, but for over sixty years it had guarded the dreams of four young girls. And, in an odd way, had led Brendan herself on a quest for her future. "What do you think of your dreams now, Ellie, after so many years?"

The old woman's face creased into a smile. "I suppose you could call me a failure," she answered. "I never really fulfilled my dreams. Never went to college or became a social worker or got to work with Jane Addams. Never even set foot in Chicago." She paused. "But sometimes your dreams are not as important as your calling. So, in a way, perhaps I did accomplish what I set out to do. Maybe I helped people. Maybe, as Catherine would say, I made a difference—one life at a time."

She stopped suddenly and regarded Brendan with an intense gaze. "And what about you, Miss Brendan Delaney? What of your dreams?"

Brendan shook her head. She couldn't respond to Ellie's question. Not yet. The pieces were all beginning to fit together, but there was one final segment she needed to discover before she could find her answer. "There's one more dream I have to track down before I can concentrate on my own," she said. "But nobody seems to know what happened to Mary Love Buchanan."

"None of the others were as close to Mary Love as I was," Ellie responded. "Yet even I haven't heard from her in years. It may be a wild-goose chase, but I can give you one place to look."

The old woman went to a kitchen drawer, rummaged, and came up with a pen and a used recipe card. She wrote something on the back and handed it to Brendan.

"Let me know what you find."

Brendan looked at the address. "Minnesota?"

Ellie nodded. "Last I heard. They should be able to tell you something, at least."

"Whew. That's a long way."

"When you're committed to your dreams, distance hardly matters," Ellie said cryptically.

"Tell that to my boss, who will no doubt have some choice words to say about my expense account." Brendan said, then shrugged. "I may get fired, but it's a risk I'll just have to take."

35
PASSAGE TO THE TUNDRA

November 28, 1994

"Y ou want to go *where*?" Ron Willard, station manager of WLOS, kept his voice low, but his face was beginning to turn a bright shade of crimson.

"Take it easy, Ron," Brendan urged. "You'll block your arteries."

"I'll have a full-blown coronary if Chedway gets word that I authorized a trip to—where is it? Alaska?"

"Minnesota." Brendan tried to maintain a semblance of calm. Marcus Chedway, owner of the station, was a notorious tightwad. True, when he had purchased the station it was deeply in debt and now operated in the black, but everybody complained about his penny-pinching.

"Have you forgotten that this is a *local* station?" Ron shook his head. "Not this. No way."

"That's your final word?"

"Final. Absolutely. Kaput." He raised his head and glared at her. "I warned you not to run over budget on this story. Have you seen your expense account totals lately?" When Brendan didn't answer, he went on. "I didn't think so."

"But honest, Ron, this is going to be a wonderful story. It's got a great local angle, and—"

"I'm sure." He didn't sound sure, and Brendan winced inwardly.

"Ron, please—"

He held up a forefinger and shook it in her face. "Nope. Don't try that abandoned-puppy look on me, either. It won't work. I've known you too long."

"All right." Brendan sighed. He was right, and she knew it. Chedway would have both their heads if he found out the station was paying for her to traipse off to Minnesota on a story that might or might not pay for itself in the long run. But she had to go. As hard as she might try to still the voices in her head, she kept hearing echoes that urged her on: *Take the risk. Trust. Don't give your future to the past. Live without regret.*

Brendan wasn't sure what kind of future she was seeking, but she was absolutely certain what she *didn't* want that future to be: a never-ending loop of sameness, reporting meaningless stories that faded into oblivion as soon as the camera panned away. Although the thought left her distinctly uncomfortable, she found herself identifying with Ellie James Tucker, longing for her life to count for something, to have some significance beyond herself. She couldn't be a social worker, or a teacher; she did not, in fact, have any clear picture of what form that significance might take. But something deep inside her—in her heart, in her soul—she had responded to Catherine Star's advice to Ellie: *Change happens one life at a time.*

Suddenly Brendan realized that Ron was staring at her, waiting for something. "What?" she snapped.

"I was just wondering if you were going to stand here in my office daydreaming all day."

"Sorry, Ron. I was just thinking." In a flash of insight, Brendan knew what she had to do. "I've got some vacation time coming, haven't I?"

Ron nodded apprehensively. "Yes, but—"

"Then I want to take it. Now. Today."

"What part of *no* don't you understand, Brendan? As of this moment your expense account on this story is closed."

"I'll take care of the expenses myself. Just approve the vacation. Three days, maybe four. I'll be back before you know it."

"You can't just go flitting off to the tundra on a moment's notice. Didn't you watch the weather channel this morning? The whole Midwest got a snow dump—about a hundred feet, I think—over the Thanksgiving weekend."

"Did you ever hear of snowplows? Unlike our nearsighted city fathers, Minnesota is prepared for that kind of weather. I'll survive."

Ron sighed and waved a hand. "I give up. Go. Make your trek into the arctic wilds. But don't call me if you get snowbound until the spring thaw."

Brendan grinned at him and made for the door, then stopped and turned. "Oh, one more thing."

"What now?"

"I'll take a Handycam with me, if you don't mind. I might need it."

"Sure. Whatever." Ron shook his head. "Check it out from the supply guys—and don't drop it in a snowbank."

"It's already in my car." At the sight of Ron's upraised eyebrows, Brendan shrugged. "I knew you'd give in, one way or another."

"Get out of here. And be careful."

"If Chedway notices my absence, tell him I'm on vacation."

"Right," Ron said. "Just a little igloo holiday. R and R in a dogsled."

◦⁄∽◦

November 29, 1994

By the time Brendan got to the rental car counter at the Minneapolis–St. Paul airport, she had begun to wonder if Ron might have been right about the foolishness of this trip. Her fifty-minute layover in Cincinnati had stretched into three hours, and now, at dusk in the Twin Cities, it was snowing again, blowing icy pellets into her face as she listened to the Avis manager's instructions for the third time.

"Take 494 west to 169," he repeated, pointing at the map. "Puts you right into Mankato."

"Is 169 a main highway?"

"Trunk highway," he said. Brendan didn't know what that meant, but didn't ask for fear of looking stupid. "'Bout as main as you get, going that way."

Brendan squinted at the yellow lines on the map and felt a knot of apprehension form in her throat. She had driven in snow plenty of times, but in North Carolina she had her 4Runner, and she generally knew where she was going. This little compact she had rented didn't even have snow tires, much less the security of four-wheel drive.

"You sure I'll be all right in this car?"

"Plow's been through. Should be pretty clear." He peered into her face. "Not from around here, are you?"

Brendan grimaced. "North Carolina. How'd you guess?"

"Accent." He opened the door for her and smiled. "Not much of a snow, really. Usually get a big clipper this time of year. Take it easy, now."

"I will." She started the car and buckled her seat belt. "Thanks."

"You betcha. No problem."

Brendan eased out of the snow-packed parking lot, testing her brakes. The back end skidded a little, but by the time she got off the airport road onto 494, the road seemed clear and fairly dry. Still, she kept to the right lane, taking it slow while eighteen-wheelers whizzed past her at a dizzying pace.

When she reached the turnoff to 169, however, conditions worsened. She nearly missed the turn because the road sign was packed with snow and discovered almost immediately that 169 wasn't nearly as well-traveled—or as well-plowed—as the interstate loop around Minneapolis. For over an hour she gripped the wheel in a white-knuckled panic as snow clogged the wipers and piled up on the hood of the car. Darkness had closed in, and she could see only a foot or two beyond her headlights.

Then, out of the woods to her right, a shadowy form dashed onto the highway. Brendan gasped and hit the brakes as a deer—a big buck with a huge rack of antlers—leaped across the road, crashed one shoulder into her fender, and went sliding off on the other side. She had no time to see what happened to the animal. The little compact skidded on a patch of ice and made two complete revolutions before thudding to a stop with both right tires in the ditch.

For a minute or two, Brendan simply sat there, shaking. Her heart pounded painfully in her chest, and her hands, still gripping the wheel, trembled uncontrollably. When the initial shock wore off, she made a quick inventory. No broken bones, no lacerations. Just a throbbing ache across her shoulders from muscle tension and the beginnings of a migraine.

She got out of the car and picked her way to the edge of the highway. The compact leaned precariously into the ditch, and both the front and rear wheels were lodged in a snowdrift up to the axles. If she had been in her 4Runner, she probably could have driven out, but without four-wheel drive, there was no hope.

Brendan looked around and made a quick assessment of her situation. She could see no lights anywhere—just the eerie blue glow of snow across the fields, interrupted by dark patches of woods.

Unexpected tears rose up to blind her, and she suddenly felt overwhelmed with loneliness. She wasn't accustomed to such a vast, open landscape unbroken by the familiar mountains of the Blue Ridge. It made her feel small and insignificant and totally isolated.

What was she supposed to do now? She had no way of getting the car out of the ditch, and the highway was completely deserted. There was no place within sight where she could walk to for help, and she could freeze to death before anyone found her. She needed a phone.

Of course! How stupid could she be? She never went anywhere without her cell phone!

Shivering, Brendan dashed back to the car, slid in behind the wheel, and cranked the engine to get some heat. When warm air began to course through the vents, she removed her gloves and fumbled in her big leather bag. Her hand closed over the phone, and she breathed a sigh of relief. She wasn't exactly sure where she was, but she did know the highway number, and a few miles back she had passed an enormous billboard bearing a huge Jolly Green Giant and the words, "Welcome to Le Sueur"—enough information, surely, to get help coming in the right direction. She flipped open the phone, dialed 911, pressed SEND, and waited.

Nothing happened.

Brendan jerked the cell phone away from her ear and peered at the display. The dim green message read: LOW BAT.

Murphy's Law, Brendan thought grimly. *If anything can go wrong, it will.*

Well, there was nothing to do but wait. Wait and hope . . . and maybe even pray.

Brendan awoke to a pounding in her head. She peered groggily through the windshield, trying to get her bearings. She felt strangely disconnected from her body, as if she had been drugged. She was chilled to the bone, and her stomach lurched uneasily.

The pounding continued.

After what seemed like an eternity, Brendan realized that the pounding was coming not from her head, but from *beside* her head. Then she became aware of lights behind her and a voice shouting and turned to see a dark form the size of a bear beating on the window with a huge fist.

She rolled down the window and found herself face-to-face with a burly man in a brown hunting cap, with flaps pulled down over his ears.

"Trouble?" he asked, as if a car in the ditch might be there by choice.

"I—I—yes," Brendan stammered.

"Stuck here long?"

"I—I don't know."

The massive hand opened the car door and took Brendan by the elbow. "Get on up in the cab where it's warm," the man said, pointing behind him. "We'll tow her out."

Numbly, Brendan followed him back to an enormous green tractor with an enclosed cab and the words "John Deere" painted on the side. With some difficulty she clambered up into the cab.

A young boy, not more than fifteen, sat behind the wheel. The man looked up at her from the ground. "You okay?"

"I think so."

"Name's Sven Hanson," the man said. "That's my boy, Lars."

Lars nodded and pulled at the brim of his baseball cap but said nothing.

"Hand down that chain."

Lars reached behind the seat, then leaned over Brendan and dropped a thick length of chain with S hooks on both ends at his father's feet.

"Pull her up in front."

The tractor roared to life, and Brendan held on while Lars steered the lumbering machine to the side of the road in front of her disabled rental car. Within minutes, the car was out of the ditch with all four tires on the icy pavement.

"Thanks," she said when Sven returned. "What do I owe you?" She started to get out of the tractor, but he shook his head.

"Lars, go steer. We got to pull her in."

Lars jumped down and went to the car while Sven took his place at the tractor controls. "Not from around here, are you?" he asked as he ground the gears and started off.

"No," Brendan sighed. "Why?"

"Car's outta gas. Ran it to keep warm, did you?"

"It was better than freezing to death."

"Maybe. Dying by gas isn't much better." He turned toward her in the dim light. "Tailpipe was clogged full of snow. Carbon monoxide."

Brendan stared at him. No wonder she felt drugged and sick to her stomach. "You mean—?"

"Yep. Not a good idea, running the engine when you're in a drift."

She fell silent as the full impact of the situation registered. This man, this stranger, had saved her life. "How did you find me?"

"Wife saw you when she crossed the bridge over the highway. Sent me and the boy back to check on you."

"Well, I do appreciate it, Mr. Hanson. If it hadn't been for you, I might not have lived through this night. I don't know how to thank you."

Sven shrugged. "No problem."

They chugged on through the darkness, the high headlights on the John Deere cutting a swath through the night. "What time is it?" Brendan asked after a while.

"'Bout midnight, I guess."

"Where are we going?"

"Home. Got a farm up a ways, near Norseland."

"Does Norseland have a hotel? I mean, I'll need a place to stay."

"Wife'll make up a bed for you. In the morning we'll gas up the car and get you on your way."

"I couldn't possibly—" Brendan stammered. "I mean, I don't want to impose."

"No problem." Sven turned the tractor off the main road onto a narrow gravel driveway and pulled up in front of a rambling two-story farmhouse. "Go on in," he said.

While Sven and Lars unhooked the chain and pushed the rental car into the barn, Brendan climbed awkwardly down from the tractor cab and picked her way along a shoveled path to the porch. She was greeted at the front door by a round, ruddy-cheeked woman in a stained apron and navy cardigan sweater.

"Come in, come in!" the woman said cheerfully, as if greeting a long-lost friend. "Are you all right, dear? It's getting colder, I think. Wonder if we'll get more snow?"

The front door opened directly into a large living room. The rug was shabby and the furniture worn, but a welcoming fire blazed in the fireplace, and a tall blue spruce, decorated with lights and ornaments, filled one corner.

"Let me take your coat. I've got hot chocolate on the stove and a fresh batch of kringla and krumbkakke. Do you want a sandwich? You must be hungry after your ordeal."

Brendan handed over her coat and sank onto the chair nearest the fire. Mrs. Hanson, apparently, had inherited all the gregarious genes in this family. She chattered her way into the kitchen and back, returning with a tray of mugs and a heaping platter of cookies.

"Thank you, Mrs. Hanson," she said as the woman handed her a steaming mug of cocoa.

"Call me Elke. And your name is—?"

"Oh, sorry. Brendan. Brendan Delaney."

"What an interesting name. Is it—?" Elke paused, thinking.

"Irish."

"Irish. How fascinating. We don't hear many unusual names in these parts. Most of us are just plain old Hansons and Erdahls and Bjornsens and Rollenhagens—"

The door opened, and Sven and Lars entered on a blast of frigid air. "Kinda chilly out there," Sven commented as he stomped his boots on the rug. Lars stomped as well but said nothing.

Once he had doffed his heavy coat and hat, Sven Hanson didn't look nearly so much like a big bear. He was tall, certainly—over six feet—but thin, with a wide forehead, blondish-gray hair, and pale blue eyes. Lars, a younger, blonder version of his father, had the same lanky build, a buzz cut, and a bashful smile.

While the males chugged down their hot chocolate and devoured cookies by the handful, Elke kept up a running commentary about the weather, Brendan's midnight rescue, and the process involved in making kringlas—which, Brendan had deduced, were the pale, pretzel-shaped cookies with a distinct anise flavor.

At last Sven stood up, cleared his throat, and declared, "Time for bed."

"Oh, wait!" Brendan scrambled for her bag and retrieved her checkbook. "Let me pay you for your trouble. And for the room."

Sven frowned and shook his head. "No need."

"But you came out in a snowstorm at midnight! You saved my life—"

"Ya."

"But you won't let me repay you? Not even for the gas?"

"This is Minnesota," he said curtly. "People help each other." With a shrug he disappeared up the stairs.

Brendan turned to Elke, who was putting sheets and a thick down comforter on the sofa. "We don't have a guest room, but you'll be pretty comfy right here."

"Elke, why won't your husband let me pay him for his trouble? I mean, you've all been so generous—towing my car, putting me up for the night—"

The woman turned and gave Brendan a look of sheer amazement, as if anyone with a grain of sense would never even raise such a question. "In this part of the country, everybody helps everybody else. If a farmer gets sick or hurt, his friends and neighbors bring in his crops and feed his live-stock. When a person gets in trouble, like you did tonight, whoever's nearby comes to help. If it hadn't been us, it would have been someone else." She paused and smiled. "It's nothing we need payment for, or even thanks. It's just our way. You'd have done the same."

Brendan wasn't so sure. Would she have put herself out so much to aid another human being, a stranger, who had been stranded or hurt or needed help? Was this what Ellie James had meant by changing the world one life at a time? The question haunted her as she stared into the dying embers of the fire and snuggled under the heavy down comforter.

But Brendan Delaney's self-examination didn't last long. Exhaustion overtook her, and just as the mantel clock struck one, she drifted into a deep and dreamless sleep.

36
THE MOTHER HOUSE

November 30, 1994

By the time Brendan left Norseland at ten the next morning, the storm that had stranded her had given way to blue skies and blinding sun on the new snow. Highway 169 had been plowed, and traffic had melted off the last of the ice glaze into harmless rivulets of water.

Elke had insisted that she stay for an enormous, artery-clogging farm breakfast consisting of ham and bacon, potatoes, eggs, and thick slices of toast made from homemade honey wheat bread. Now, in the car headed south, Brendan fought to keep her eyes open and wished she could take a nap.

In the quaint little town of St. Peter, she stopped at a convenience store and got coffee. She had intended to buy gas too, but Sven Hanson had filled the tank from his pump at the farm. Brendan wondered for the hundredth time what would possibly motivate these simple farm folk to treat a stranger so well. The only answer she could come up with was the answer Elke had given: "It's just our way."

South of St. Peter, huge rocky cliffs rose on Brendan's right, and to her left, low-lying fields swept down to the river. A cave in those cliffs, Elke had told her, once provided refuge to Jesse James when he was on the run from the authorities. The woman had said it with pride, as if the outlaw had been an honored ancestor.

Brendan drove on, enjoying the unfamiliar, snow-covered scenery, until she reached the outskirts of Mankato, Minnesota, where she stopped to get directions to the address Ellie had given her. The fellow running the gas station—a gray-haired man with a distinct stoop—stared at the slip of paper and nodded.

"You know where it is?"

"Yep."

"Is it nearby?"

"Yep." He motioned to her to follow, went out the door, and pointed to a high hill in the distance. "There she is."

Brendan squinted and saw an enormous building that looked like a small castle. "There must be some mistake."

"No mistake. It's the Mother House." The man said the words quietly, and his face bore an expression of awe and reverence. "Take the bypass here and get off at the next exit. Go left, and then another left on the first road. It's a ways up the hill, but you can't miss it."

Brendan thanked him, got back in the car, and followed his directions. All she had to go on was an address on a slip of paper, but the man had seemed to know the place immediately. The Mother House, he called it. What did that mean?

As the rental car labored to the top of the hill, Brendan found herself confronted with a sprawling brick building. It had to be at least a hundred years old—three stories high with towers and turrets and two enormous wings going off from the center. A sign at the crest of the hill read: *School Sisters of Notre Dame.*

Brendan knew she had to be in the wrong place, but there was nothing to do but go inside and ask for directions again. She parked the car, got out, and wandered toward what seemed to be the only entrance—a set of double doors covered by a black awning. As she pulled the door open, she nearly ran headlong into a pleasant-faced young woman in a down jacket and fur-lined boots.

"May I help you?" The woman smiled and took a step back.

"I—I don't know," Brendan stammered. "I'm looking for someone."

The woman pointed. "Up the stairs and to the left. Where the sign says, *Office.* Someone should be able to help you."

Upstairs, Brendan found herself in a long hallway. The place was eerily silent except for the distant tapping of a typewriter. She found the office and knocked timidly.

"Come."

Brendan opened the door and stuck her head inside. A rotund woman of about fifty, with graying hair and ruddy cheeks, sat behind a desk. "I'm sorry to disturb you," Brendan began. "I'm trying to find someone, but I'm afraid I'm in the wrong place."

The woman grinned broadly. "That depends on who you're looking for."

Brendan held out the slip of paper Ellie James had given her. "Is this the right address?"

"Yes indeed. And the person's name—?"

"Mary Love Buchanan. She's an elderly woman, in her eighties."

The woman rose from behind the desk and went to the door. "Follow me." She moved noiselessly down the hallway, with Brendan close on her heels, until they reached a set of oak doors. "She's been very frail of late," the woman warned. "We don't like to see her overtired."

Brendan reached out a hand and laid it on the woman's arm. "What *is* this place?"

"Why, it's the Mother House. Of the School Sisters of Notre Dame."

"And Mary Love *lives* here?"

"Many of our elderly come here when they retire." The woman fixed her with an odd gaze. "Come. You'll see."

She opened the door and ushered Brendan into what seemed like a different world. It was a chapel, with high vaulted ceilings and two steps up to a broad stone altar illuminated by the dim light from stained-glass windows. On the altar, a perpetual flame burned, and in a corner to the right, a statue of the Virgin Mary was fronted by a bank of burning votives. The candles cast a wavering light over the Virgin's feet and threw moving shadows into her face. In front of the shrine sat a wheelchair, occupied by a nun in full habit.

Brendan's guide went directly over to the nun and waited, then cleared her throat quietly. "Sister? You have a visitor."

Gnarled hands reached out from the folds of the black habit and grasped the wheels. The chair pivoted, and Brendan found herself staring into the face of an ancient woman. Her skin was wrinkled and seamed, but her eyes shone like chunks of pale aquamarine. The old nun squinted and peered at Brendan.

"Do I know you?"

Brendan hesitated. "Mary Love Buchanan?"

"No one has used that name in years," the elderly nun whispered. "Who are you?"

"I'm Brendan Delaney. I've come to see you, all the way from Asheville, North Carolina." She paused. "An old friend of yours sent me. Ellie James."

A shadow passed over the old woman's face, and she crossed herself. "She's not dead, is she?"

Brendan smiled. "No." She turned to the gray-haired woman. "Is there someplace we can talk?"

"Upstairs, in the day room. Do you feel up to it, Sister?"

The nun turned a scalding look on the woman. "How many times do I have to tell you, Janelle? I'm not infirm, and I don't need pampering." She rolled her eyes at Brendan. "This one looks hale and hearty enough to give me a push. You go on back to your work."

Janelle smiled and patted the old nun's hand. "All right. I'll see you later." Then she was gone, as silently as she had come.

"Young nuns!" the old woman spat out. "You get old, and people start treating you like a child again." She looked up at Brendan. "What did you say your name was?"

"Brendan Delaney."

"Ah. A good, strong Irish name. Catholic, are you?"

Brendan shook her head. "I'm afraid not."

"Well, too bad for you, Brendan Delaney. Now, let's get going."

Brendan took control of the wheelchair and pushed as the nun gave directions. Down the hall, up the elevator to the third floor, and into a bright, spacious room with windows overlooking snow-covered woods. When they arrived, the nun set the brake on the wheelchair and transferred herself to a high-backed wing chair facing the view. She waved a hand in Brendan's direction. "Get that thing out of my sight, will you? I need it to get around—spinal degeneration, you know. But I hate seeing it. Reminds me I'm getting on in years, even if I don't like to admit it."

Brendan moved the wheelchair to a corner by the door and returned to find the nun with her feet on the coffee table. She was wearing white sweat socks and Nike running shoes under her habit.

"Sit," the old woman commanded, waving a hand at the chair next to her.

Brendan sat.

"So Ellie sent you, did she? Guess you didn't expect to find a *nun*."

"No, ma'am, I didn't," Brendan admitted. "I have to say it was a bit of a shock. I—I don't even know what to call you."

"Call me Mary Love, of course. *Sister* Mary Love, if you like."

"So you kept your own name?"

"I have another, the name I adopted when I donned my first habit. Nuns these days keep their baptismal names, you know. And I rather like being called Mary Love. I've worn this habit for over fifty years, but I never could get away from thinking of myself as that little Buchanan girl from Asheville."

"All right, *Sister.*" The word felt foreign on Brendan's tongue. "Do you mind explaining to me what kind of place this is, what you're doing here?"

"This is the Mother House of the School Sisters of Notre Dame. We are an order of teaching nuns, and this house—our central headquarters, if you will—is an administrative center. The activities of the order are organized from here. A lot goes on here—spiritual direction, training, counseling. It's also a home for retired nuns. Those who are physically able still work—making clothes and quilts for the homeless, for example. Sister Janelle, the nun who brought you to me, is the Reverend Mother's administrative assistant."

"That woman was a *nun?*"

"You obviously watch too much television. Times have changed; the church has changed. Most nuns these days don't wear habits any longer. In my day, we all wore them, and some of us older ones have retained the traditional garb." She grinned broadly. "Force of habit, I suppose you'd say."

Brendan chuckled at the joke.

Sister Mary Love shifted in her chair. "Now, just why is it you've come all this way?"

Brendan reached into her bag, drew out the blue glass bottle, and set it on the table.

"Lord, have mercy." The old sister shut her eyes and crossed herself.

"You recognize this bottle?"

Mary Love opened her eyes. "I could never forget, not in a thousand years."

"That's why I've come." Briefly, Brendan sketched out the story of finding the bottle during the demolition of Cameron House, and how the idea had gotten into her blood, leading her to track down the four young women who had committed their dreams to the bottle.

"Good heavens—that was sixty years ago."

"Sixty-five."

"Sixty-five years. I remember it as if it were yesterday."

"Do you remember this?" Brendan laid a page in front of her, a photocopy of the pen-and-ink drawing that had been left in the bottle. "You said, years ago, that your dream was to be an artist. You showed a lot of promise, even as a young girl."

"Yes, promise," Mary Love murmured, half to herself. "But promise has a way of getting diverted. Dreams change, you know. They carry us for a while, they die, and then—if we're fortunate enough to have eyes to see— they're reborn. The path we choose for ourselves isn't necessarily the path God chooses for us. . . ."

MARY LOVE

37
AND IT WAS GOOD

December 25, 1929

Yesterday had been mild—milder by far than the usual Christmas Eve in the mountains—but this afternoon winter had reasserted its hold. Mary Love Buchanan walked home in the gathering gloom of dusk, clutching her portfolio to her chest to block the wind.

It wasn't a *real* portfolio, of course—not the kind that actual artists carried. She had made it herself from two big sheets of cream-colored cardboard salvaged from a dress box from her father's store. With an awl she had painstakingly punched holes and sewn it together with an old leather bootlace, then decorated it with colorful prints from magazine covers and cut slits in the top for a handle.

Someday she'd have a real one, burnished brown leather with a brass clasp and pockets inside. But for now the makeshift folder served its purpose—protecting her cherished drawings from getting folded and dog-eared.

Despite the chill December wind, Mary Love walked slowly, dragging her scuffed shoes along the sidewalk and pausing now and then to gaze at her surroundings. She committed to memory the black outline of a bare elm tree stark against the setting winter sun, the contours of the mountains in the distance behind the tall silhouette of the Flat Iron Building. Rich images, she thought, for paintings in oil or watercolor—paintings that would make her famous someday.

This very afternoon, she had declared herself an artist. The idea both excited and terrified her.

She had actually sat there, in Letitia Cameron's attic, surrounded by her three best friends, and revealed the secret dream she had savored since she was a little girl. From the time she was four or five and got her first set of paints and pencils as a Christmas gift, Mary Love had determined that she would be an artist. And yet it wasn't so much a decision as a discovery—the deep awareness of a gift, a calling that could not be denied or suppressed.

The nuns at school, especially Sister Francis, talked a lot about a person's calling. True to her name, Sister Francis held a firm belief in the holiness of all God's creation and urged her charges to open the eyes of their souls to God's presence in the world around them. Most of the kids rolled their eyes and yawned with boredom when Sister launched into one of her sermons on vocation, but Mary Love hung on every word. It made her feel special, this realization that the creative Lord of the universe had endowed her with a portion of that same holy creativity.

And Mary Love didn't often feel special, not in a household of eleven children. As the eldest, it fell to her to care for the young ones, to cook and clean and help with homework, to bring peace and order amid the chaos. Heaven knows Mama didn't do it. She was too busy going to church, praying all hours of the day and night, attending every single Mass and lighting every candle in sight.

Except for the fact that Mama was so efficient at producing babies, Mary Love often wondered if the woman hadn't missed her calling. Perhaps she should have become a nun, a vocation in which devotion to prayer and meditation didn't interfere with everybody else's life and make other people miserable.

Mary Love sat down on a low stone wall bordering the sidewalk and watched as a late-migrating flock of geese flew overhead, honking madly and steering their V toward points farther south. Even through her wool coat, the cold seeped from the stones into her behind and up her back. But still she sat, unable to force her feet to walk the last few blocks home.

It was always this way, every time she left the house. She dreaded going back to the noisy, crowded conditions in which her family lived. There was always something to *do,* some child to tend, some chore that awaited her, when all she really wanted was to be left alone to think and daydream and draw. She could never be alone in that house. Even her own room was no refuge, since she shared it with Beatrice and Felicity, the two sisters closest to her in age. The two of them were constantly bickering, and when they weren't at each other's throats they were prying into Mary Love's private things, conspiring to embarrass her by reading her diary or drawing mustaches on the pen-and-ink portraits she had sketched of her classmates.

Her friends didn't know how good they had it. The three of them, especially Ellie, who should have known better, talked a lot about how awful it was to be an only child and how wonderful it would be to have brothers and sisters to share with and confide in. But they didn't have to live with it on a daily basis.

Mary Love would have traded places with any of them in a heartbeat. And it wasn't because their families had money, while hers struggled to pay the bills every month. To her, just the idea of solitude seemed like heaven itself. She could only imagine what it would be like to have a room of her own, a place to spread out, a real desk at which she could draw to her heart's content. A little privacy.

Lights were beginning to come on in the houses up and down the street, and with a sigh she struggled to her feet and walked the last few blocks home. When she reached the front stoop, she took a deep breath, braced herself, and opened the door.

"Mary Teresa Love Priscilla Buchanan!" her mother yelled as the door closed behind her. "Where have you been?"

Mama always used her children's full names when she was angry or annoyed, a habit Mary Love found insufferable. Still, given the fact that the woman had eleven children with four names each, the simple achievement of remembering them all was little short of miraculous.

"I told you, Mama, that I was spending the afternoon at Letitia's."

"Hmph. What you find to talk about with those highfalutin society girls, I'll never understand. Are you sure they invited you, or did you just tag along on your own?"

Mary Love suppressed a sigh. "Of course they invited me, Mama. They're my *friends*."

This was one of Mama's pet subjects, the class distinction between Mary Love and her friends. Hardly a day went by that Mama didn't rail on them, accusing them of every sort of snobbery. Occasionally Papa even got in on the act, questioning why his eldest daughter seemed so intent upon remaining in school when so many of the other girls her age had long ago gone to work or gotten married. Middle-class young ladies, he insisted, didn't need the luxury of education; it just made them want what they could never have.

But on this one issue Mama had come to her defense. Mama thought that if Mary Love stayed in school, under the daily influence of the nuns, some of that spirituality might rub off. And Mary Love didn't tell her any different. Let Mama think what she wanted, as long as she could stay in school—the one place that provided a welcome respite from duties at home and the opportunity to explore her calling. Mama removed baby Vincent from her hip and handed him over. "The baby needs feeding, and the twins need a bath. I'll be late for Mass if I don't hurry along."

"Where's Papa?"

"At the store. He said he had some bookkeeping to catch up on."

"On Christmas Day?" Mary Love felt unwelcome tears spring to her eyes. She knew, of course, that times had been getting increasingly difficult since the stock market crash, and she ought to be more understanding. But it wasn't fair. Papa's response to the tightening economic situation was to work harder, to keep the store open longer hours and do the accounts himself. Mama's approach was to pray more, to entreat every saint in the book to look with favor upon their most faithful intercessor. That left Mary Love to run the house, feed the children, and do her best to keep order.

"I'm gone. Be good, and don't forget to do the dishes." With a parting wave, Mama rushed out the door and slammed it behind her.

Fighting back a surge of despair that threatened to overwhelm her, Mary Love took the baby into the living room, sat down with him, and slid her portfolio under the sofa, where it would be protected from prying eyes and grasping hands. Vincent shifted restlessly in her arms; he needed changing and was obviously hungry. "In a minute," she crooned, rocking him gently against her shoulder.

What would it be like, she wondered, to be able to fulfill the dream she had revealed this afternoon in Tish Cameron's attic? To live alone, to have only herself to be responsible for, to have uninterrupted time to paint?

Was this truly her calling—her vocation, as Sister Francis would say? Or only an idle fantasy? Could she make a living at it? Or even make a name for herself?

If she had been Mama, she would have prayed about it, would have moved heaven and earth, would have lit a thousand candles and stormed the gates of glory asking for a sign from above. But Mary Love wasn't her mother. She had quit praying long ago—except when she had to during Mass, and that didn't count because she didn't mean any of it. None of the trappings of her mother's religion held any significance for her. She didn't sense God's nearness in the candlelight and the incense and the liturgy. She didn't feel the Spirit when she knelt for Communion or chanted the *Kyrie*.

And yet there was one situation—only one—where she *did* experience God's presence. When she poised a pencil over a sheet of art paper and began to draw. In those moments, creativity flowed out of her hands, and she felt as if she understood, just a little, how the Almighty must have felt when the clay took shape, inhaled its first breath, and stood up a living soul.

That was faith. That was divine intervention.

And it was good.

An acidic odor assailed her nostrils from baby Vincent's soiled diaper, and she grimaced. Art would have to wait. There were dishes to do and children to bathe and a dozen other chores that demanded her attention.

But someday, she swore to herself, things would be different.

Someday.

38
THE CALLING

May 8, 1931

Mary Love sat in the back of Sister Francis's classroom with her head on her desk. It was almost over. Two more weeks, and she would stand in the commencement line, receive her diploma, and . . . and then what?

What did it mean to graduate—even to graduate with honors—if her future only held more of the same? Papa already had it planned that she would work for him, another Buchanan at the store that bore their family name. Mama wanted her to stay home and be a full-time house slave. Mary Love was quite certain that if she had to choose either option, she would undoubtedly go mad.

The only other alternative was marriage, and there wasn't much chance of that looming on her horizon. Mary Love knew the truth about herself. She was chubby, average-looking, and probably too smart for her own good. She refused to play the coy games other girls engaged in to get the attention of the opposite sex, and even if she had been interested, she rarely had much time to do anything about it. The long and short of it was, boys didn't pay much attention to girls like Mary Love Buchanan.

Faced with those unacceptable options, Mary Love had secretly applied to an art academy in Minneapolis, Minnesota—just about as far away from North Carolina as you could get. Even as she filled out the application, she had known that her parents would be furious, and everyone would say that she was abandoning her family. But that couldn't be helped. She had to follow her dream.

Now, she held in her hands the answer to her application, and when she had opened the envelope and read the response, her heart had sunk like a stone. Yes, they were certain she had promise and potential as an artist and would welcome her as a student in the academy. But times were difficult and scholarship money was scarce. If she could manage her expenses, they would waive half her tuition.

Even half the tuition, however, was an enormous, insurmountable barrier. There would be no art school for Mary Love Buchanan. Not now. Maybe not ever.

She could almost hear her dream of being an artist shattering into a thousand shards, like a piece of crystal stemware toppling to the floor. The only saving grace of this moment was that she had told no one. No other human being, not even her best friend, Ellie James, would witness her humiliation and despair. She would simply go home, keep her grief locked up, and get on with the business of fulfilling everyone else's expectations.

It wasn't that she didn't love her family. She loved them deeply and would have missed them if she had gone away to school. But her love had long ago been overshadowed by the grim inevitability of duty, by the constant demands on her time and attention. Was it so horrible, so utterly selfish, to want just a little corner of her life for herself?

"Mary Love?"

She raised her head. Sister Francis had returned to the classroom and stood there staring at her, obviously puzzled to find her still here.

"Are you all right, child?"

"Of course, Sister," Mary Love muttered. "I'm fine." A hot prick of conscience seared through her brain, and she averted her eyes. Everyone knew you didn't lie to a nun. It might not be a mortal sin, but they had some kind of sixth sense that ferreted out untruth like a terrier sniffing out a rat. She looked up again and waited.

Sister Francis's eyebrows shot up, nearly disappearing under her wimple. "Are you sure?"

Mary Love sighed. She couldn't do it twice in a row and expect to get away with it. She might as well tell the truth and get it over with. "No, Sister, I guess I'm not."

Sister Francis glided to the back of the room and perched on the edge of the desk next to Mary Love's. Amazing, how nuns could change positions without ever seeming to move their feet. A lot of Catholic children grew up

with the notion that nuns didn't even *have* extremities—that they were dis-
embodied heads and hands held together by some miraculous work of God.
Mary Love knew better, of course—her own Aunt Belva had become a nun
years ago and taken the name Sister Consummata. No one in the family had
seen Consummata for a long time, but Mary Love was pretty sure her legs
were still intact. Still, it was a wonder, this atmosphere of peace and serenity nuns exuded. As if they were above being burdened by the petty concerns that consumed ordinary people.

Sister Francis's mellow voice pierced Mary Love's consciousness. "Tell me
what's troubling you, child."

"I'm graduating in two weeks," she said, looking into the nun's wide
hazel eyes.

"I know. And with honors. We're all very proud of you."

"Thank you. But I—well, I'm having some struggles about what comes
after."

"After graduation?"

Mary Love nodded. How could she tell this woman—this *nun*—that she
would abandon her family in a minute if she only had the money to go to
the art academy? How could she communicate, in ways Sister Francis could
understand, her dreams and longings for the future?

"Do you have a family, Sister?" She blurted the question out before
thinking, then wished she could take the words back. It was an unspoken
law that one did not talk to a nun about her former life; when a nun
entered the convent and took vows, she left behind all vestiges of worldly
association.

Sister Francis's eyebrows arched a second time, and a rosy flush crept
into her cheeks. But instead of reprimanding Mary Love for asking, she simply nodded. "Why, of course," she said. "A mother, two brothers, and a sister. They live in Minnesota. My father died several years ago."

Encouraged by this uncharacteristic show of openness, Mary Love
pressed on. "Do you miss them?"

"Sometimes. We keep in touch."

Mary Love felt her jaw drop open. "You do?"

"Of course. My life is here, in my vocation. But I write to them regularly."

"I—I thought you would have to give that up."

"A nun's vow of poverty, chastity, and obedience means that we give up worldly wealth, ambition, and self-determination. It doesn't mean we cease to be human." She smiled and laid her hand over Mary Love's. "Why are you asking these questions, child?"

Mary Love hesitated. Her eyes fixed on the slim gold band that adorned Sister Francis's ring finger—the symbol of her marriage to Christ and the Church. All the nun's words about vocation, about the calling of God on a person's life, came back to her in a rush. She knew beyond any doubt that God had called *her* too—called her to be an artist, empowered her with the ability to interpret with pen and paints what she saw with her eyes and her heart. She had felt it, that overpowering intensity that came with creativity. Perhaps becoming an artist was a lot like becoming a nun—the willingness to give up everything for the summons to something greater.

"I've listened to what you've said about calling, Sister. About vocation. And I think that maybe—maybe I have a calling too."

She was going to go on, to explain about the desire that burned in her heart, about her dream of giving her life to her art. But Sister Francis interrupted her before she could get another word out.

"Why, Mary Love, that's *wonderful*! To tell the truth, Father McRae and I have talked about it, wondering if you might eventually discover your own religious vocation. It's a holy thing, you know, to be chosen by God to give your life to the Church. And your parents will no doubt be thrilled. Your mother is such a devout woman."

Mary Love started to protest, to tell Sister Francis that becoming a nun wasn't exactly the sort of calling she had in mind. But then an idea began to form: This might be the answer—not to her prayers, since she hadn't prayed any, but to her dilemma. A way for her to leave the chaos of home behind and still keep her reputation intact. If she couldn't do it by getting married to a man, maybe she could do it by another kind of marriage. Sister Francis was right: No one would criticize her for abandoning her family if she was going away to become a nun. Having a priest or nun in the family was a badge of honor, one her mother would show off like the crown jewels. And Mary Love could easily imagine herself in a quiet convent, living in blissful solitude and introspection, having all her needs met. What better situation to nurture her creative spirit?

"Would you like to talk with Father McRae about this?" Sister Francis was asking.

"Yes," Mary Love said with a firm nod. "Yes, I believe I would."

August 23, 1931

Mary Love stood on the platform at the depot, gripping a small bag of personal items in one hand and holding her makeshift portfolio under the other arm. The whole Buchanan clan—Mama, Papa, and all the kids—stood in a semicircle around her, watching her with expressions of awe and wonder on their faces. Even baby Vincent beamed beatifically from Papa's arms. Nearby, Sister Francis and Father McRae stood smiling and nodding in her direction.

The train pulled in, and Mary Love felt her stomach rumble. For a moment she battled against the temptation to tell them that this was all a terrible mistake, a misunderstanding. Once she got on the train to Minnesota, there was no turning back.

But everyone seemed so pleased with her decision. Mama was weeping into her handkerchief, fingering a rosary and uttering fervent prayers between her sobs. Papa stood straight and stoic and said nothing, but his chest was puffed out with pride so that she thought his buttons might pop off at any minute.

Father McRae and Sister Francis approached. "Father wanted to have a prayer with you before you go," Sister whispered.

Mary Love nodded, set her bag down, and knelt awkwardly on the wooden platform, still gripping her portfolio under her left arm. Father McRae placed his hands lightly on her head. "We commit into your keeping, O Lord, this our sister Mary Love Buchanan," he prayed. "Watch over her, and endow her with the gifts of wisdom and obedience. Let her heart be always turned toward you, O God, and may she find in you what her spirit seeks. In the name of the Father, the Son, and the Holy Spirit, Amen."

Mary Love made the sign of the cross and struggled to her feet. She hugged each of her brothers and sisters in turn and reminded Felicity and Beatrice not to pick on each other, then kissed her parents and turned to board the train.

"Go with God, my child," Sister Francis whispered, squeezing her hand and giving her a quick embrace.

With a hiss of steam the train began to move, and Mary Love leaned out the window, waving and watching until they were merely specks in a vanishing distance. Then she sat down and let out a shuddering sigh.

Well, it was done. She was on her way.

As the train picked up speed, the click-clack of the wheels settled into a steady rhythm, the kind of sound that lulls the mind into giving up the secrets it has held in hiding for years. In a chaotic, illogical collage of images, Mary Love went back through her childhood—what there had been of it—with its never-ending cycle of new babies coming and chores to be done and Mama leaving her in charge while she went off to Mass. She remembered that horrible night when Tish Cameron's father died and Ellie's mother began to slide into the darkness of her own mind. She relived the knife thrust of envy she had experienced when Adora Archer announced her intention to go off and follow her dream in Hollywood.

But most vividly, she remembered that Christmas afternoon in the Camerons' attic, when the four of them revealed their dreams and vowed to support each other forever. What earnest eagerness had filled her soul that day! She had believed that anything was possible if you just wanted it enough. All of them had.

But life seemed to interfere with the fulfillment of those dreams, the way the wind caught autumn leaves and scattered them far and wide. Letitia would never marry Philip and have his children. No one had heard from Adora in months. And poor Ellie, locked away in that house with her mother, had been condemned to a living death.

Ellie. The thought of her best friend brought tears to Mary Love's eyes. Ellie had always been the one to stand with Mary Love, to defend her, to draw her into the circle and believe in her. What would Ellie say now, if she knew that Mary Love was on a train bound for Minnesota, taking the first steps toward a lifetime of religious service?

She hadn't told Ellie, hadn't even said good-bye. She couldn't bring herself to do it. Ellie was the one person who would know better, who would call her to account for this decision. Ellie wouldn't believe for a minute that she really had a vocation; she would know that Mary Love was simply running for her life.

And so Mary Love had avoided the confrontation. Just as soon as she got settled, she reasoned, she would write to Ellie, let her know where she was and what she was doing. Things had been so busy these last few weeks, getting ready to go; there had been so much to do. But that was rationalization, and Mary Love knew it. The truth was, she couldn't take the chance that Ellie James might be able to talk her out of it.

Mary Love laid her head back on the leather seat and listened as the wheels pounded and the car swayed gently beneath her. *Click-clack. Click-clack. . . .*

Her eyes grew heavy. She leaned her head against the window, and as sleep began to overtake her, she heard in the deep recesses of her mind the prayer Father McRae had offered on her behalf:

May she find in you . . . click-clack . . . what her spirit seeks . . . click-clack . . . may she find in you . . . click-clack . . . what her spirit seeks . . . .

39
TIME ON HER KNEES

January 20, 1932

Mary Love leaned forward and tried in vain to stretch the kinks out of her aching back. The soapy water she was using to scrub the sacristy floor had already frozen in a puddle around her knees. The stones themselves were as cold as the icicles that hung like enormous stalactites outside the tiny mullioned window.

No one had warned her—not Father McRae, not Sister Francis, and certainly not the Reverend Mother who had so warmly welcomed her on her first day at the convent—that the life of a postulant was nothing short of slave labor, or that winter in Minnesota was only one step removed from the frozen pit of hell in Dante's *Inferno*. Of course they didn't tell her. No person in her right mind would have willingly volunteered for such service if she had known the truth.

And yet, here she was, on her knees in a tiny cubicle off the cavernous convent chapel, scrubbing away as if her very soul depended upon it.

The convent, called Our Lady of the Immaculate Conception, wasn't really so bad. It was, as Mary Love had expected, a quiet place, conducive to contemplation. The only problem was, everything—absolutely *everything*, except sleeping—was done in community. At five the bell would sound to awaken them, and again to call them to meditation in the chapel. Then Mass, then breakfast, then work assignments. Every minute of the day was rigidly scheduled, and the postulants were expected to fall in like little soldiers. Obedience and discipline, after all, were inherent in Holy Rule.

But Mary Love had found a way around the rules. In the mornings, she would race through her chores and sneak off to her cell, where she pulled out a secret stash of art paper and sketched. At night, after lights out, she would slip away to the bathroom—the one place in the convent where the lights burned all night—hide in a bathtub, and continue her drawing. Once, when the temperature dipped to −40, she nearly froze her behind. But it didn't stop her. After that, she took a blanket with her, with her pencils and paper rolled up inside.

It was against the rules, of course, and if she got caught, she would undoubtedly spend the next six months cleaning toilets and peeling potatoes. But it was worth the risk. She had left behind the familiarity of home and family for this opportunity to find herself in her art, and she would take the chance while she had it. As a postulant, she was supposed to be seeking her identity in God, but the religious exercises never brought her any nearer to the Almighty. She felt closer to God when she was drawing than when she knelt in forced prayer. Wasn't that what a religious vocation was about, after all?

A shadow fell over her. She looked up to see the scowling face of Mother Margaret, the Mistress of Postulants, glaring down at her.

Mother Margaret—as she herself told the story—had taken her name from St. Margaret, who defeated the devil in the form of a dragon, was beheaded, and later spoke to Joan of Arc. Evidently Mother Margaret thought martyrdom a glory much to be desired. She couldn't have it for herself, however, so she did her best to impose it upon her charges. She mustered the postulants like a drill sergeant, barking orders and examining their work with the critical eye of a perfectionist. She tolerated no idleness, and if so much as her shadow came into view, all the postulants went into a flurry of nervous activity. Even the Reverend Mother, Mary Love suspected, fell victim to Mother Margaret's intimidation.

"Woolgathering again, I see." The nun towered in the doorway between the sacristy and the chapel. Her voice was cold, colder than the floor by several degrees.

Mary Love had been at Our Lady for five months—long enough to know that levity of any sort, under any circumstances, was strictly forbidden in Mother Margaret's book of religion. She was pretty sure the woman's face would shatter into a thousand pieces if that dour countenance ever attempted so much as a hint of a smile. Still, she couldn't help herself.

"It seems to me, Mother, that a little extra wool might come in handy, as cold as it is."

The joke fell flat, and Mother Margaret's eyes narrowed. "Idle hands—"

"Are the devil's workshop," Mary Love finished. "I know, Mother."

"Then get back to work. You should have been finished by now." She pulled a hand from the folds of her habit and pointed a bony finger at Mary Love's nose. "You," she said ominously, "are one who bears watching."

Mary Love lowered her eyes. "Yes, Mother." The cold crept up her knees and numbed her legs, but she didn't dare move.

"Self-denial," the old nun muttered. "Self-control. We die to self, that Christ may reign supreme."

"Yes, Mother." Mary Love was fairly certain that her legs had already died, but she doubted that a piecemeal martyrdom was quite what Mother Margaret had in mind. She waited, frozen in place like the statues in the chapel and the ice under her kneecaps, until the nun turned her back and moved noiselessly down the center aisle and out the door.

✑

"So she caught you daydreaming, did she?" Adriana Indergaard whispered in Mary Love's ear as they set the refectory table for dinner. "The Dragon Mother?"

Mary Love suppressed a chuckle. Behind their hands, most of the postulants laughed over that disrespectful nickname for Mother Margaret—a reference to the saint's victorious encounter with the devil. The original St. Margaret might have *overcome* the dragon; their Mother Margaret, on the other hand, had incorporated many of its less attractive traits into her personality.

"Don't let her hear you call her that," Mary Love warned. "She's already belching out fire today."

"So I've heard." Adriana rolled her eyes. "So we've *all* heard." She grinned at Mary Love. "She was standing in Reverend Mother's office complaining about your 'woolgathering'—and your audacity—at the top of her lungs. Did you *really* tell her that the wool would come in handy to give us a little extra warmth?"

Mary Love nodded. "I'm afraid so."

"And she was not amused."

"She's never amused."

"Well, I thought it was funny," Adriana admitted. "And just between us, I suspect Reverend Mother did too. I don't think she agrees with Mother Margaret's attitude that you have to be miserable to be a Christian—or a nun."

Mary Love watched as Adriana deftly laid out plates and silverware. The girl was a corn-fed beauty, straight from the tiny burg of Guckeen, Minnesota—a town that Adriana herself described as "a bump in the road." Every time Mary Love saw her, she wondered what a girl like that was doing in a convent. With her blonde hair and flawless Nordic complexion, Adriana was the image of a Midwestern beauty queen, and she had the brains and good sense to match her looks. She had, Adriana had confessed in a moment of candor, been chosen Sweet Corn Princess in her home county two years in a row and had left behind not one but two up-and-coming farm boys eager to marry her. Adriana, however, would accept no suitor but Christ. She had been aware of her vocation since the age of six, and nothing would deter her from that calling.

Adriana handed Mary Love a stack of plates and whispered as she passed by, "What do you daydream *about,* Sister?"

Mary Love hesitated. She couldn't tell Adriana the truth about her obsession with painting, or that art, not religious service, was her true vocation, the passion that fired her soul. She suspected that it might be a sin—maybe even a mortal sin—to take vows under false pretenses. But then, she was a long way from her final vows, and coming to Our Lady had provided a refuge for her, a place of quietness, an escape from a life that held no promise at all for the future.

"I don't know," she hedged. "What do *you* think about when no one's around?"

Adriana didn't blink an eye. "God," she said simply. "I think about what a privilege it is to be able to give my life in God's service. I pray to become more like Our Lady and more like her son, our Savior. I dream about that wonderful moment when I will take my vows and become a Bride of Christ."

Of course. Adriana Indergaard would spend her free time in the pursuit of holiness.

In truth, Mary Love envied her—a sin that didn't threaten her soul, but gave her something to talk about every week at confession. Adriana was so certain of her direction, so absolutely sure that God had chosen her. She would be the perfect nun—chaste, obedient, cooperative—a paragon of all the qualities Mary Love struggled with on a daily basis.

Mary Love, on the other hand, would *never* be the perfect nun. And if she kept crossing Mother Margaret, there was a good chance that she would never become any kind of nun at all.

○

Mary Love was in her cell, frantically sketching out an idea that had come to her the day before while emptying the kitchen garbage. It was a landscape, a breathtaking snow scene, with moonlight coming down from behind the clouds. Hidden in the trees at the edge of a clearing, a face looked out on the scene—a luminous, beatific countenance—which was at once the source and the recipient of the beauty of the night.

The bell sounded for evening prayer, but Mary Love couldn't stop. She had to get the face just right or she would lose the mystical ambiance of the entire drawing. In a frenzy she sketched on, possessed by an intensity beyond herself.

And then, suddenly, Adriana Indergaard stood beside her, looking over her shoulder.

"Sister?"

Mary Love jumped up, sending her pencils flying, vainly attempting to hide the sketch. Adriana, with her single-minded focus on God's will and purpose, would undoubtedly frown upon this pursuit of worldly ambition. It was unspiritual, ungodly . . . and most certainly a violation of Holy Rule.

But Adriana didn't look displeased. She looked . . . transported. She stared down at the drawing, crossed herself, and breathed, "It is the face of God!"

Mary Love gaped at her, dumbfounded. Then, following Adriana's gaze, she looked for the first time at what her own hands had created. Even in a black-and-white pencil sketch, the picture held an ethereal quality, an otherworldliness. The face within the forest watched over the scene with an expression of profound love and protective passion. Instinctively, without words to express it, Mary Love identified the feeling. It was what she experienced in her art.

"Please, don't give me away," she begged. "I couldn't help myself—I just had to—"

"Of course you did."

Four words, nothing more. But the tone and the words told Mary Love that Adriana Indergaard, the Sweet Corn Saint from Guckeen, Minnesota, understood.

"I know it's time for prayers, but—"

Adriana nodded, and a single tear streaked down her cheek. "You *were* praying. This is the most profound prayer I have ever witnessed."

Their eyes met, and in that moment a bond was forged between them, an unspoken connection that Sister Margaret would undoubtedly have forbidden as one of the "particular friendships" expressly prohibited between postulants.

Adriana reached out a hand and touched the face in the woods gently, with a sense of awe and reverence. "Perhaps it is a sin," she whispered, "but I envy you this gift. God has given you the ability to see and re-create a vision of what is holy. It is the stuff saints are made of."

The words lodged in Mary Love's soul: *a gift . . . the stuff saints are made of.* For months she had thought of the time she spent drawing as stolen hours, pilfered from the Almighty and deserving of punishment. She had hidden her sketches away furtively, dreading the inevitable day when someone would discover them and her guilty secret would be revealed. But now the truth was out, and to her surprise, Mary Love felt not guilt, but liberation. A new sense of purpose rose within her, as if, despite her disobedience to the rules of the order, the Lord had somehow smiled upon her.

She looked back at the drawing, at the benevolent, compassionate face behind the trees. *The face of God,* Adriana had called it. Was it possible that the Creator of the universe truly was present in her art, that every stroke of the pencil was a wordless prayer?

Perhaps. If so, maybe it wouldn't matter so much that Mary Love Buchanan would never be the perfect nun.

40
DISCOVERY

May 13, 1932

Through the window of her cell, Mary Love looked out on the broad sweep of lawn behind the convent. After what seemed an interminable winter, spring had dawned bright and beautiful.

Less than a month ago, the transformation had begun. Crocuses, exactly like the ones back home, had poked through the snow, their hardy colors signaling the beginning of new life. As the snow melted, shocking patches of bright green appeared, followed by daffodils and the slender yellow-green leaves on the weeping willow trees. The ice on the river broke up and floated downstream, and soon baby rabbits browsed alongside their mothers in the deep grass at the river's edge.

Everywhere she looked, Mary Love saw one miracle after another, sign upon sign of the Creator breathing life into the world again. Like a tuning fork lifted and struck, her soul vibrated with wonder, with the promise of tomorrow. Even the Mass had taken on fresh meaning, the familiar prayers and hymns infused with vitality. The dark days of Lent had given way to the light of Resurrection Morning.

Mary Love smiled wryly to herself as she sat down to draw. She was even beginning to *think* like a nun. And, to tell the truth, she was beginning to *feel* like a nun as well. Not a conventional nun, full of religious fervor and holiness like Adriana, but at least more at home within herself, more at peace. No longer did she envy Adriana's sense of calling or feel guilt and shame over her own passionate intensity. She had found her place, and it was good.

With careful hands she smoothed the wrinkles out of a sheet of butcher paper and poised her pencil over it. Months ago she had run out of art stock, but that hadn't stopped her from drawing. She had shocked Mother Margaret by volunteering for extra duties in the kitchen, and when the good-hearted Sister Cecilia had her back turned, Mary Love had filched the paper and stowed it under her postulant's dress. But the old nun was too quick for her; she saw the furtive deed and confronted Mary Love.

"I need it for prayers, Sister."

Sister Cecilia raised an eyebrow and smiled slyly. "Take it, then. But next time, ask."

For prayers, she had said, and Sister Cecilia had accepted the reasoning without question. It hadn't been a lie, either. Not even a small one. Since the day Adriana had seen her drawing of the face in the woods and declared it to be the countenance of God, Mary Love's sketching had become her "prayer and meditation." This was no longer a rationalization, but a reality.

It had come upon her gradually, like winter melting into spring, until one day she realized that another presence filled the room as she worked, a nearness close as her own heartbeat but quite distinct from what people usually called inspiration. She felt the power in her mind, filling her heart, overflowing into her hands. And the result was surely not of herself, but a cocreation between Mary Love the artist and God the Creator.

Her subject matter hadn't changed. She still drew landscapes, nature scenes, and the faces of people around her, but there was a dimension that had not been there before. One of her favorites was a sketch of Sister Cecilia standing over an enormous soup kettle. She had transformed the nun into a peasant woman, her wimple replaced by a scarf tied over her forehead. In the drawing, Sister Cecilia's broad, homely face took on a heavenly light, as if in her poverty she had found the source of true wealth. It was the portrait of an ordinary woman touched by God's grace.

And there were others too. A sketch of Adriana, in all her pristine beauty, cradling a small child in her arms. Sister Terese digging joyfully in the garden. Her baby brother Vincent sitting in a bed of flowers with a butterfly perched on his finger. All different images, but with one common thread— the glory of God manifested in the humble experiences of life.

Mary Love didn't know, in artistic terms, whether her drawings were any good or not. And most of the time she didn't care. It had become more important simply to render faithfully the images that presented themselves to her mind, to work and learn so that each new drawing was better than the last.

A surge of anticipation shot through her veins as she began to rough in the outlines on the butcher paper. She could see the picture in her mind— a garden in springtime, not fully blossomed but just on the verge of bursting into bloom. An image, she thought, of the state of her own spirit, hovering in preparation for some wonderful, unexpected miracle.

Without warning, the door burst open, and Mary Love found herself staring into the scowling face of Mother Margaret.

"So! This is what you do when the Holy Rule commands you to prayer!"

In two strides, the Mistress of Postulants crossed the room and slammed the window shut, blocking out the pleasant sounds of birdsong and water rippling in the river.

"Mother, I—" Mary Love stopped. It was no use to explain. The Dragon Mother would never understand how a worldly pastime such as drawing could be a type of prayer. Self-indulgence, she would call it. Or worse.

The old nun ripped the butcher paper from Mary Love's hands and examined it. "There are more of these . . . these *profanities*, I assume?"

Terror gripped Mary Love's heart, but she wouldn't lie. "Yes."

"Show me."

Mary Love went to the wardrobe, pushed aside her nightgown and extra postulant's dress, and drew out the makeshift portfolio, now bulging with a year's worth of drawings. Some were on art stock, some on butcher paper, and still others on odd sheets of cardboard or paper bags.

"Bring them and come with me. Immediately."

Head down and eyes burning, Mary Love followed Mother Margaret down the corridors until they stood at the door of the Mother Superior's office. The old nun rapped twice, then opened the door and walked in without being invited.

The Mother Superior, the undisputed head of Our Lady of the Immaculate Conception, was a stout, broad nun with pink cheeks, a prominent nose, and clear brown eyes with deep crow's-feet fanning out from the edges. Younger than Mother Margaret by ten years or more, she nevertheless exuded an air of authority. All the postulants respected her, but they didn't fear her. She had a reputation for unflinching integrity, but also for compassion.

Reverend Mother looked up from her desk, and Mary Love saw an expression of irritation flash across her face. "Sister, one usually waits for a response before barging in." Her tone was calm, even, but the rebuke was clear.

Mother Margaret didn't seem to notice. "A matter has come to my attention, Reverend Mother, that you must attend to immediately."

"Must I?" Reverend Mother slanted a glance at Mary Love, who stood outside the doorway, and Mary Love thought for an instant that she might smile.

"Indeed." Mother Margaret snaked out a hand and hauled Mary Love into the room. "This postulant has been disobedient and deceptive. She is consumed with worldly thoughts and self-indulgence. I only thank God we discovered her true nature in time."

Reverend Mother peered over her glasses at Mary Love. "Come in, child. Sit down before you fall down."

Mary Love sank into a chair. Her legs wouldn't stop trembling, and she thought she was going to be sick, right there on the Reverend Mother's carpet.

"Now, Sister, what is the nature of this alleged infraction of Holy Rule?"

The Mistress of Postulants jerked the portfolio from Mary Love's grasp and spread it on the desk before the Reverend Mother. "*This*," she said with emphasis, "is what this postulant has been doing when she should have been working"—she slanted an acid glance in Mary Love's direction—"or sleeping."

Reverend Mother held up a hand. "*This postulant* has a name." She shot a compassionate glance in Mary Love's direction. "These are your drawings, child?"

"They are. I caught her in the act, and she admitted it," the Dragon Mother interrupted. "I had been suspicious of her for some time—rumors have been circulating about her, you know. Then Sister Cecilia let it slip that she asked for butcher paper from the kitchen. When I couldn't find her at her work assignment, I went to her cell and discovered her with these . . . obscenities . . . blasphemies!"

Reverend Mother shuffled through the portfolio and said nothing for a long time. Finally she raised her head and fixed Mother Margaret with an inscrutable gaze. "If you don't mind, Sister, kindly point out to me where you perceive blasphemy or obscenity in these works."

The Mistress of Postulants stepped behind the desk, her beady eyes searching through the sketches. "Here!" she crowed triumphantly. "This one of a little boy in the flowers. He is"—she shuddered—"*naked*."

"I believe he is," Reverend Mother agreed. "Exactly as God made him."

"And this one! She's turned our own Sister Cecilia into a *peasant*."

"Sister Cecilia *is* a peasant," the Mother Superior countered. "A fact of which she has never been ashamed."

"Well, what about this one? Isn't this the face of Adriana—who is, if I might remind the Reverend Mother, the most promising and spiritually astute among our postulants? This picture shows her in the guise of a mother—an *unwed* mother."

Mary Love cringed. She was doomed, and she knew it. The truth was, she *had* been deceptive, and she *had* violated Holy Rule—not once, but many times. She deserved whatever punishment she got. But it nearly broke her heart to hear Mother Margaret twisting her work into something profane, accusing her of blasphemy. Of that, she was not guilty.

Suddenly the Reverend Mother stood to her feet and banged the portfolio shut. "I've heard enough," she snapped. "Sister Margaret, you may leave us now."

"But-but—" the old nun sputtered.

"I said, you may leave us. I will take care of this matter, you may be sure."

"Yes, Reverend Mother." In an attitude of uncharacteristic submission, the Mistress of Postulants lowered her eyes and made her exit.

When the door closed behind her, the Mother Superior came out from behind her desk and perched on the edge, directly in front of Mary Love.

"Look at me, child." It was an undeniable command, yet the voice was gentle and entreating.

Mary Love raised her head. Her eyes stung with tears, but she bit her lip and answered, "Yes, Reverend Mother?"

"Your year of postulancy is almost at an end. Within a few months, you will stand before the bishop and exchange a bridal gown for the habit of a novice. If, that is, you decide to continue pursuing a religious vocation."

Mary Love nodded.

"So let me ask you just one simple question: Why did you want to become a nun?"

Mary Love knew the "right" answers—answers that would please Reverend Mother and get her off the hook: That she had been given a vocation. That she had been called by God. That she desired to live her life in service to Christ and the Church. But as she looked into the Mother Superior's face, she realized that she could never succeed in misleading this woman—nor did she have any desire to try.

"I come from a large family," she said with a sigh. "I'm the oldest of eleven children, and all my life, as far back as I can remember, I bore the responsibility of caring for my brothers and sisters. My mother was very . . . ah, religious. Went to Mass every day, prayed incessantly. And left me to do all the work and care for the younger children."

She paused, and the Mother Superior motioned for her to continue.

"All I ever wanted," Mary Love confessed, "was quietness and peace, time to draw and paint. I dreamed of being an artist, of living alone, of having solitude—something I never got at home. I felt called to it, like a—" She stopped suddenly.

"Like a vocation?" Reverend Mother supplied.

Mary Love lowered her eyes. "Yes."

"And—?"

"I wanted to go to the Academy of Art in Minneapolis—even got accepted and was awarded some scholarship money. But I didn't have the funds for the remaining tuition. Then one of my teachers at school—my favorite nun, actually—misunderstood when I talked about my calling to art; she thought I was saying I had a vocation to be a nun. I grabbed onto the idea, believing that might be my answer, a way to get away from the responsibilities of the family and have the chance to find my direction."

"And so you entered the convent under false pretenses, knowing you did not have a religious vocation?"

"I'm afraid so."

"The religious life is not intended to be an escape from unpleasant reality," Reverend Mother said sternly. "Do you understand that?"

"Yes, Reverend Mother."

"Nor is it a place where deception and duplicity can be tolerated."

"I know, Reverend Mother. I'm sorry."

"Tell me, Mary Love," the Mother Superior said, using her given name for the first time, "what have you learned during your year with us?"

Mary Love thought about the question for a moment. She had nothing to lose by telling the truth, so she took a deep breath and plunged in. "I've learned that God comes to people in many different ways. You don't have to live on your knees in order to pray or light a million candles to get the Lord's attention. God comes to me when I draw, Reverend Mother. I know I was wrong to shirk my duties, but I can't seem to get to God without a pencil or paintbrush in my hand. When I'm working—when an image fills my mind and demands to be released—I feel the nearness of my Creator in a way I never experience through any other means."

"I can see that in your artwork."

"Is it true, Reverend Mother, what Mother Margaret said about my drawing? Is it blasphemy?"

"What do you think?"

Mary Love gazed into the woman's eyes and found there an openness, a willingness to listen. She took a deep breath and considered her next words.

"I think it's the truest expression of the faith that is growing in me," she said at last. "I think it's the way God speaks to me, and through me, and the way I speak back to God."

The Mother Superior smiled, and her crow's-feet transformed into deep laugh lines. "Mother Margaret and I have, shall we say, different perspectives about many issues. Would you like to know what I discern in your drawings?"

Mary Love nodded. "Very much, Reverend Mother."

The Mother Superior reached behind her and picked up the portfolio off the desk. "This one—" She held up the sketch of the little boy with the butterfly on his finger.

"My baby brother, Vincent," Mary Love explained.

"To you, perhaps. To me, it is a portrait of the Christ Child discovering the wonders of his Father's world." She retrieved the drawing of Adriana. "Mother Margaret looks at this and sees a blasphemy, turning a Christ-centered postulant into an unmarried mother."

"And what do you see, Reverend Mother?"

"I see the Madonna and Child. I see a holiness of love unparalleled in history. I see a woman who risked everything to be obedient to the purposes of God." She flipped through the portfolio and picked out the snow scene, where the face Adriana had identified as God looked out from the forest. "And here," she said, "I see the sum of your spiritual experience. I see the Lord God admiring the beauty of creation with joy and passion and fulfillment." She paused. "You obviously know what that emotion feels like. Few of us ever even get a glimpse of it."

The tears Mary Love had been holding back spilled over and fell onto her hands, which were clasped tightly in her lap. "Thank you, Reverend Mother."

"I cannot condone your deception in this matter, Mary Love, but I think I understand it. I have just one more question for you: If you had to take your final vows tomorrow and commit yourself to a lifetime of religious service, would you do it?"

Mary Love sat back, shocked beyond words at the question. For a full minute she couldn't speak.

"Well?" Reverend Mother prodded.

"I don't know if I could give up my art."

"I'm not asking if you are willing to abandon your art. I'm asking if you wish to go forward with your training."

"But what would I *do*?" Mary Love blurted out. "As a nun, I mean?"

Reverend Mother's brown eyes crinkled, and she burst into laughter. "Child," she said when she had regained control of herself, "our primary purpose in this life is not to *do*, but to *become*. To grow in Christlikeness, to become more like our Lord. To draw near in the Spirit. To glorify God with whatever our hands touch." She shook her head. "It takes most of us years to discover our path. You have already found yours. Don't you think the Church needs artists, people who can catch a vision of God and translate it into a form the rest of us can benefit from?"

"You mean I could continue to draw? And paint?"

"It would be the grossest kind of disobedience, child, if you did not." She held up one of the drawings. "Despite Sister Margaret's rather negative viewpoint, I believe your work has the potential to bring us all closer to the Creator who made and loves us."

"So you'll allow me to go into the novitiate? You won't be sending me away?"

Reverend Mother considered this in silence for a moment. "It will be two more years before you make your Temporary Profession. That should be time enough for you to discern your true calling." She stood up and held out a hand in Mary Love's direction. "Come with me."

Mary Love followed her until the two of them stood at a small doorway to one side of the chapel. "Have you ever been in here?" Reverend Mother asked, pointing toward the door.

"I don't believe so. What is it?"

The Mother Superior pulled a key ring from the folds of her habit, selected a key, and unlocked the door. The ancient oak creaked open to reveal a large storage room, filled with odds and ends of broken furniture, office supplies, and, much to Mary Love's surprise, a tall angled desk that faced three enormous windows.

"It will take some cleaning up," Reverend Mother said. "But some of the other postulants can help. It will make a fine studio, don't you think?"

Tears blinded Mary Love, and the room began to swim. "Reverend Mother, you can't mean it!"

"I never jest about discipline for my novices," she countered. Then she gave Mary Love a broad wink and squeezed her shoulder. "Although I *have* been known to enjoy a good joke now and then. Your response to Mother Margaret about woolgathering was one of my favorites. But don't tell her I said so."

She removed the key from the ring and placed it in Mary Love's trembling hand. "I'll authorize a cleanup detail, beginning tomorrow morning."

Tears clogged Mary Love's throat, and for a minute she couldn't breathe. At last she croaked out, "Yes, Reverend Mother. And thank you, Reverend Mother!"

But before she could get the words out, the Mother Superior was gone, leaving her alone with her miracle.

41
THE STILL SMALL VOICE

May 14, 1932

Mary Love rolled up her sleeves and ran a hand across her sweating face. Reverend Mother had been right. The storage room would make a marvelous art studio—but not until it had been thoroughly scrubbed. She turned and looked at Adriana, then began to laugh.

"What?" Adriana gave a puzzled frown.

"Nothing. It's just that, well, you usually look so—so perfect, even when you've been digging in the garden or scouring pots in Sister Cecilia's kitchen. I wish I had a mirror. You've got hair sticking at all angles out of your veil, and a huge cobweb hanging from your shoulder. You look like a refugee from a haunted house."

With a wicked gleam in her eye, Adriana grabbed the sticky cobweb from her arm and wiped it across the front of Mary Love's black dress. "Well, Sister, you don't look so great yourself."

"If cleanliness is next to godliness," Mary Love shot back, pounding her with a dustrag, "I think somebody needs to go to confession!"

They struggled furiously for a minute or two, smearing each other with dirt from the storage room until both were covered with grime, then collapsed, laughing themselves breathless, on a couple of packing crates.

"What is the meaning of this?"

The stern voice shocked them both into silence, and the two postulants scrambled to their feet to stand at attention before the glowering face of the Dragon Mother.

"Mother Margaret!" Mary Love stammered. "We were just—just—"

"I can see with my own eyes what you were doing. Wrestling on the floor and yowling like alley cats is not proper deportment for a nun. And you, Adriana!"

"Yes, Mother?"

"I thought better of you, of all people." She turned toward Mary Love. "What are you doing in here, anyway?"

"Cleaning, Mother Margaret."

"By whose authority? This storeroom is not on the work schedule."

Mary Love hesitated. "By, uh—by the Mother Superior's authority." She reached into the pocket of her habit and held out the key. "This room is to become my new studio. For my artwork, you see. Reverend Mother gave it to me."

A thundercloud passed over Mother Margaret's hawkish countenance. "Reverend Mother *gave* you this room?"

Mary Love nodded and slanted a glance at Adriana. The girl had her hands folded and her eyes cast down in an attitude of humility, but a tiny smile tugged at the corners of her mouth. "I gathered she was quite pleased that you brought my work to her attention," Mary Love said quietly.

The Mistress of Postulants opened her mouth to speak, but no words came out. For a full minute she just stood there, her jaw gaping open. Her face flushed red, then white, then red again. At last she turned on her heel and stormed away.

When she was out of sight, Mary Love heaved a sigh of relief, and Adriana let out a nervous giggle. "Did you see the look on her face?"

"I thought she was going to have a fit of apoplexy," Mary Love whispered.

"You can bet she'll give the Superior an earful. I hope Reverend Mother doesn't change her mind."

"I can't imagine that she would," Mary Love answered. "Adriana, if you could have seen the look on her face when she was examining my sketches! She saw something in my work. Something wonderful. Something—"

"Spiritual?" Adriana supplied. "I'm not surprised. I told you. The face of God shines in your drawings."

"And I have you to thank for all of this."

Adriana screwed her pretty face up in a frown. "What do you mean?"

"You were the first one who ever understood. In fact, you understood it better than I did myself. You may not know this, but you helped me discover the faith in my own work."

Adriana shrugged. "The countenance of God was always there," she said simply. "It's everywhere, all around us. We just have to open our eyes to see it."

⁓

August 2, 1932

Mary Love knelt in the chapel, her eyes fixed on the flame that cast a wavering light over the altar. Her mind seethed with conflicting emotions, and her stomach churned. Reverend Mother had sent word that today, after midday prayers, she was to report to the office to discuss the issue of her reception as a novice.

Reverend Mother had already indicated that she could stay on at the convent, continue with her training, and use her novitiate years to discern whether or not she truly had a vocation. Until her Temporary Profession, two years from now, she could leave at any time. And even after that, a special dispensation could release a nun from her vows.

The problem was, Mary Love had had her fill of deceit and duplicity. She wanted to stay, of course, but she wanted to make sure her motives were right in doing so. For days she had searched her heart, prayed, meditated, and scoured the Scriptures for a glimpse of the truth that lay in the deep recesses of her heart. The closest she had come to an answer was that "only God knows the heart." And God hadn't told her what was in hers.

Mary Love knew that some changes had taken place in her spirit. No longer did she sneak time from her chores or after hours to sketch in secret. Now that she had a studio and her work had the blessing of the Superior, she found herself looking forward to the assigned prayer hours for meditation and contemplation. Her painting and sketching were always with her, of course—seeping from her subconscious and coloring even her prayers with new ideas. But now she no longer had to hide her passion for art, and she discovered that her passion for God had moved to a new dimension. She just wasn't sure if that passion represented a true religious vocation.

Lord, she prayed, *show me the direction you want me to take.*

It was the simplest of prayers, unencumbered by ceremony or ritual, but it came from her heart, and she knew instinctively that God heard. She waited, hoping one last time for a clear answer to her present dilemma. No reply came, at least not in any audible form, but by the time prayers were ended, her mind had settled down a bit and her heart was a little more at peace.

When the bell sounded, she crossed herself, gathered up her prayer book and rosary, and made her way through the convent corridors to the Mother Superior's office.

The door stood open, and Reverend Mother sat at her desk, her hands folded in prayer. Mary Love waited quietly, and at last the nun raised her head and motioned for her to enter.

"Come, sit, my child."

Mary Love perched nervously on the leather chair across from Reverend Mother's desk.

"You have been praying about your decision to be received into the noviatiate?"

Mary Love nodded. "Yes, Reverend Mother."

"As have I. But before I tell you the conclusions I have reached, I'd like to hear what God has spoken to your heart."

Mary Love had no idea how she would answer Reverend Mother. In this morning's Mass, the Gospel lesson had been from Luke 12: "When they bring you unto the magistrates," Jesus commanded, "take no thought how you shall answer, or what you shall say: For the Holy Ghost shall teach you in the same hour what you ought to say." It was a wonderful promise and certainly applicable to Mary Love's present situation, but would it work for her?

I'm counting on it, she thought grimly. The Mother Superior was waiting, and she did not yet have her answer. Finally she took a deep breath and blurted out, "God has spoken nothing to my heart, Reverend Mother. Not a single word."

"Excuse me?"

"I'm sorry, Reverend Mother. I didn't mean to sound flippant. But I have prayed fervently, asking direction concerning the decision that lies before me, and the Lord has responded with silence."

The Mother Superior lowered her eyes, and Mary Love could see that she was fighting to suppress a smile. She could afford to be amused—it wasn't *her* future they were talking about. At last she lifted her head and regarded Mary Love with a calm appraisal.

"And what, my child, do you interpret this silence of God to mean?"

Mary Love stared at the woman's mirth-filled eyes. Was Reverend Mother actually suggesting that no answer might be an answer? Before she could stop them, the words tumbled out: "Only God knows, Reverend Mother, and he hasn't seen fit to tell me."

The Superior pressed her lips together, and the corner of her mouth twitched. Then she burst into laughter, loud enough to set Mother Margaret into a frenzy of disapproval for a week. At last she regained her composure. "Oh, child," she said, wiping her eyes, "that is one thing I do love about you. Few of us are courageous enough to be so honest with God."

"Thank you, Reverend Mother—I think," Mary Love stammered. "But that still doesn't answer the question."

The older woman sobered and fixed Mary Love with an intense gaze. "God's will doesn't often come to us in a blaze of illumination, like fire on Mount Sinai," she said. "Look into your heart, child. What does it tell you?"

Mary Love thought about that for a moment. "I realize, Reverend Mother, that the further I go in my training, the more certain I'm supposed to be about my vocation. But the fact is, I'm not sure."

"Can you tell me what your hesitations are? Do you wish to leave us?"

"Oh, no, Reverend Mother. I don't want to leave. You've been so good to me, and I'm learning so much. I just—well, I don't understand why I'm hesitating." She paused, and silence stretched between them. "Is it possible that God hasn't spoken to me because I'm not ready to make a decision right now?"

The Mother Superior nodded. "Perhaps."

"And," Mary Love hurried on, grasping for reasons, "maybe with more time, I could become the kind of person a nun should be. Like—like Adriana." The truth was, she despaired of ever becoming as holy or committed as her friend, but she wouldn't tell her Superior that. Not now, anyway.

Reverend Mother raised a hand to stop her. "The Lord makes no such comparisons, Mary Love. We are not judged by how well we imitate someone else, but by how fully we reflect the image of Christ as individuals." She shrugged. "You will never be like Adriana. And Adriana will never be like you. Each of you is a creation of God, made in the divine image, but as different as one snowflake is from another."

"Yes, Reverend Mother."

"Still, you are wise not to pretend a level of commitment you do not feel." The Superior smiled. "Indeed, you have grown in wisdom since you came to us."

"I hope so. It's all right, then, for me to go forward with my training as a novice? Even though . . . even though I'm not completely sure whether or not I'll be led into a religious vocation?"

"The bishop is coming to speak with the postulants. I will discuss your situation with him, and if he agrees, you will be received with your sister postulants. You will spend the first year, the canonical year of your novitiate, in instruction, meditation—and painting. You will devote yourself to reflection, the study of theology, deepening your own spirituality, and improving your art. But there will be no more shirking of duties or drawing in the bathtub at night, is that understood?"

Mary Love gaped at her. "How did you know about that—the bathtub, I mean?"

Reverend Mother's eyes twinkled, and she tried vainly to suppress a smile. "I was a postulant once myself—a long time ago, in the Dark Ages, you understand—but not unlike you, Mary Love. I had my moments of rebellion."

"You? I can't believe it."

"Believe it, child. All of us are, beneath this habit, quite human." The Superior paused and gazed at Mary Love—an expression filled with tenderness and compassion. "Tomorrow you will submit three names to me for approval. Together we will choose one, the name you will be given at your reception. Have you thought about what name you should take?"

"I have, Reverend Mother. I'll be ready."

The Superior stood, indicating that the interview was over. "Go with God, my child."

Mary Love knelt to receive Reverend Mother's blessing, and as the woman's hands touched the crown of her head, she felt peace flowing through her, like a river of warmth in her veins. She still did not know what her future held, whether she would ever wear the wedding band that would signify a perpetual profession. But that decision—the taking of her final vows—was still a long way off. She had time. Time to study and meditate, time to paint and seek the will of her Creator.

God had not spoken . . . yet. But much to her amazement, it seemed that even in the silence, she had heard.

42
SISTER ANGELICA

September 1, 1932

Mary Love stood next to Adriana, waiting for the moment when she would walk down the aisle and take on the full habit, with the white veil and wimple, that signified reception into the novitiate. She was anxious to get the ceremony over with, but not for any deeply spiritual reasons. The high lace collar of the bridal gown she wore scratched at her neck and made her uncomfortable. The small anteroom off the chapel, where the postulants had dressed for the ceremony, was stuffy and stifling hot, and a trickle of sweat ran down her back.

Mary Love looked over at Adriana, who seemed totally calm and collected, her face radiant with a beatific smile. Adriana had chosen the name Jeanne, after Joan of Arc. Appropriate, Mary Love thought—a name that reflected piety, spirituality, prophetic vision, and unflinching commitment to God. The Perfect Nun would be named after the Perfect Martyr.

Reverend Mother had laughed when Mary Love had informed her of the name she had chosen. Most people would assume that the choice was a derivation of St. Angela or one of the several beatified hermits who went by the name of Angelo. Only Mary Love and her Superior knew better. The name actually came from a man who wasn't an official saint at all—Fra Angelico, the fifteenth-century artist whose work manifested God's creativity in all its glory. Despite the fact that the man hadn't been canonized by the Church, Reverend Mother heartily approved of the choice. For Mary Love, she said, taking the name of a maverick non-saint was probably the best reflection of the way God had worked in her life.

From this day forward, she would be known as Sister Angelica.

November 1, 1932

Mary Love sat at her desk, staring out the wide windows of her studio across an expanse of snow-covered lawn. The first substantial snow of the season had come last night, blanketing the convent grounds with huge, soft flakes. Now the sun shone against the new snow and cast back prisms of light, as if God had showered the world with diamonds.

She wasn't sure if she would ever get accustomed to the Minnesota winters. Unlike the milder seasons back home in the Blue Ridge Mountains, winter here began early and lasted long. Mary Love didn't mind the snow—it gave her an ever-changing scene to paint, full of subtle colors, shadings, and minute detail. But she dreaded the numbing cold, when the temperatures dipped into the minus column and the wind whipped across the prairie. Even in summer the convent was cool; in winter, it became downright frigid.

She blew on her fingers and applied a little more azure paint to her palette. But before she could load her brush and begin again, the door opened to reveal Adriana.

Sister Jeanne, Mary Love reminded herself. *Adriana is now Jeanne.* It was hard, getting accustomed to the new names the postulants had adopted when they had been received into the novitiate.

"A blessed All Saints' Day to you, Sister Angelica."

Mary Love looked around, wondering who else had wandered into her studio, and then realized with a start that *she* was Sister Angelica! Even her own new name would take some getting used to. She still thought of herself as Mary Love, the chubby little Catholic girl from North Carolina. Flustered, she laid down her brush and palette and rose. "Sister! Come in!"

Jeanne folded her hands and shook her head. "Reverend Mother sent me to tell you that you have a visitor, Sister." She raised one eyebrow. "His Excellency is on his way to see you."

"The Bishop?" Mary Love let out a gasp. Bishop Reilly was making rounds, visiting the convents throughout the state, she knew, and had honored them by celebrating All Saints' Mass for the nuns at Our Lady of the Immaculate Conception. But why on earth would he want to see *her*?

In dismay she stared down at the paint-smeared smock that covered her work habit. "Thanks for warning me." She ripped off the smock and replaced it with a clean one. "I'm such a mess." With stained fingers she pushed stray wisps of hair back under her wimple. "Is that any better? Do I have time to go change?"

"No change is necessary," the Mother Superior's voice came from behind Jeanne. "Sister, may I present His Excellency, Bishop Reilly."

Jeanne disappeared and the Superior entered with the bishop right behind her. He was a tall, handsome man with gray hair and bright blue eyes. His bulk seemed to fill the studio, and as he stepped forward, the hem of his cassock swiped a new painting that leaned against the wall. Mary Love grimaced as she saw the black fabric smudge the wet oils.

"Careful, Excellency—that painting is still drying," she blurted out. She ran and knelt at his feet, rubbing at the stain with a rag. "Mineral spirits should get it out." But the rag wasn't as clean as it might have been, and her attempts to tidy up the mess just made it worse. The small streak of paint seemed to grow with every stroke of the rag, until what had been a tiny stain became a three-inch swath of smeared paint.

The bishop looked down, first at her groveling at his knees, then at the ruined painting. "Never mind the cassock," he said as he raised her to her feet. "But I am sorry about the painting. I should have been more careful."

"It's all right," Mary Love stammered. "I can fix it."

At last she raised her eyes to his and remembered her manners. "Forgive me, Your Excellency." Awkwardly she genuflected, grabbed for his hand, and kissed his ring.

His crow's-feet crinkled, and he laughed. "I should be the one asking forgiveness for barging into your studio and making a mess."

Mary Love liked this affable man immediately. He seemed so normal, so down-to-earth. The kind of person she could be herself with. Her gaze went to Reverend Mother, who was smiling.

"When His Excellency heard about your rather unorthodox work assignment, he had to see for himself." She turned to the prelate. "Her work is quite good, don't you think?"

The bishop didn't answer. He was stepping carefully around the perimeter of the room, peering at Mary Love's paintings. At last he turned.

"Reverend Mother, you are to be commended on your encouragement of this novice's talent."

The Superior nodded. "Thank you, Your Excellency."

"And you, young woman—"

"Yes, Your Excellency?"

"I'm no expert, but I think you have great talent. Talent that you are obviously using to the glory of God."

"Thank you, Your Excellency."

"Your Mother Superior tells me that you have some hesitations about going on with your training."

Mary Love lowered her eyes. "That's correct, Your Excellency."

"Do you mind telling me why?"

Mary Love slanted a glance at Reverend Mother, who nodded reassuringly. "Tell him."

"Well, sir, I—ah—" Mary Love paused, then took a deep breath and continued. "When I first came here as a postulant, Excellency, I came under false pretenses. I used the convent to escape. I hid my artwork, doing sketches after hours and when I was supposed to be working." She shook her head. "Reverend Mother has been gracious enough to encourage my art, and I have learned a great deal about myself and about faith in the process. But when the time came to be received into the novitiate, I wasn't sure my motives were pure. Reverend Mother allowed me to continue, with the understanding that I would use my novitiate years to explore my vocation—and my art. I want to be honest about what is really in my heart, but I've had a hard time discerning whether or not I truly am called to the religious life. God may have hidden reasons that I don't know about; but for myself, I do not want to continue my training in deception, or by default."

"A wise choice, my child—and a godly one," said the prelate. He turned back to the paintings. "This one in particular I find very moving." He pointed to an oil, rendered from Mary Love's original sketch of Adriana with a child in her arms. "The Madonna," the bishop continued, "not as we often see her, so holy and removed, but as a real person, an ordinary young girl chosen by God for an extraordinary mission." He peered more closely at the face. "She has a purity that shines from within, like a celestial light. And yet she looks familiar somehow."

Mary Love shot a glance at Reverend Mother, who was smiling. "She should, Your Excellency," the Superior answered. "That is the face of the young nun, Sister Jeanne, who escorted us here this morning."

Much to Mary Love's surprise, the bishop did not criticize her for using Adriana's countenance to represent the Holy Mother. Instead, he nodded thoughtfully. "A very good choice. Michelangelo took his faces for the Sistine Chapel from ordinary working men in the tavern. He was much maligned for making saints out of sinners, but isn't that what God does all the time?" The prelate looked up at Mary Love and grinned. "You're in good company, I'd say, with both the Lord and Michelangelo on your side."

Bishop Reilly came back to Mary Love's desk and sat down, being careful not to swipe his sleeve in the wet paint. "Would you be willing to sell one or two of your paintings?"

"*Sell* them?" Mary Love gasped.

"Yes. You know, for money."

"I—I—don't know," she stammered. "I've only just begun, Your Excellency. I have lots of sketches and a number of works in progress, but only a few that are finished. Besides—" She turned in a panic to Reverend Mother. "Is that allowed—to take money for my work?"

"The money wouldn't come to you directly," the prelate went on, "but to your order. And your paintings would hang in the offices of the diocese, where many people would have the opportunity to view your work—and give glory to God, of course." He paused. "The Scripture is very clear that the laborer is worthy of payment."

"Well, I—yes, I suppose so." Mary Love's heart was pounding, and she wiped her sweating palms on the sides of her smock. "If Reverend Mother approves, of course."

The Superior folded her hands and nodded.

"I'd like to take this one—" The prelate pointed to the Madonna. "And I'm fascinated by that one—" He indicated the snow scene where the face of God looked out with pride over creation. "I'd like that for my own office."

At last Mary Love found her voice. "I'm honored, Your Excellency."

"No, child, you've got it backward. The diocese will be honored. And more importantly, God will be honored."

Bishop Reilly made his way to the door with Reverend Mother on his heels. "You have a great gift, Sister Angelica," he said in parting. "Use it wisely."

43
THE CHANGE OF A LIFETIME

April 28, 1934

Spring was late in coming—or at least in staying. An early melt the last week of March raised everyone's hopes, only to dash them when April brought more snow and ice. The poor bulbs, deceived into budding by the unseasonable warmth, now lay shivering and rigid as sleet coated their tender shoots.

It was bad enough, Mary Love thought, when winter stretched on and on. But when the fickle weather teased them, then thrust them back into a gray and frozen wasteland, it was almost too much to bear. For days now, the entire convent had labored under the gloom. Everyone was snappish and irritable. Meals were taken in glum silence, and Masses were mumbled and uninspiring. For herself, Mary Love hadn't painted in a week. She just stared out the window, waiting for some sign of life. Waiting for resurrection.

A faint knock sounded on the door of the studio, and she turned. "Come in."

The door opened, and Sister Jeanne stood there, but even her radiant Nordic countenance seemed less bright than usual. "Sister Angelica, Reverend Mother would like to see you."

Mary Love sighed. "All right. Tell her I'm coming."

When she reached the Superior's office, the door was shut, and she could hear voices inside. She waited, trying not to listen, but she was certain that one of the voices—the one raised loudly in protest—was that of Mother Margaret. The Dragon was roaring, and it was impossible not to overhear.

Mary Love caught snatches of the conversation: "... *never a word of thanks from anyone ... when I discovered her ... good riddance, is what I say.*"

The door slammed open, and the Mistress of Postulants nearly bowled Mary Love over in her haste to leave. When she saw who it was, the nun scowled and shook her head. "Eavesdropping?" she hissed. "I should have known. No good comes from coddling a novice." She brushed past, leaving Mary Love standing in the hallway.

"Come in, child," the Superior called.

Mary Love entered cautiously, as if walking on eggs. She could still feel tension in the room, an almost palpable atmosphere of discord.

"I don't know how much of that you heard—"

"Reverend Mother, I wasn't eavesdropping. Honestly, I wasn't."

The Mother Superior raised a hand. "I know you weren't, child. Anyone in the county could have heard Sister Margaret without half trying." She rolled her eyes. "You might as well know—I'll announce it tonight at dinner anyway. Sister Margaret will be leaving Our Lady tomorrow."

"Leaving?" Mary Love stammered. "What do you mean, leaving?"

"She's not forsaking her vows, if that's what you're asking." Reverend Mother exhaled a heavy sigh. "She's transferring to another convent—one where, in her words, 'Holy Rule is followed to the letter and discipline is valued.'"

"Is it because of me, Reverend Mother?"

The Superior hesitated for a moment. "Sister Margaret has never been happy under my authority," she said at last. "She feels that I am not strict enough. Your situation simply added fuel to the fire. At first she was angry because I didn't send you packing when she first discovered your deception. Now she's angry because the bishop values your work and she hasn't been given credit for discovering you." She shook her head. "I pray she finds a place of peace."

Mary Love stared at the Mother Superior. "She wants credit for *discovering* me?"

Reverend Mother nodded. "Ironic, isn't it?"

"It would be, only I haven't exactly been discovered. I just do my work and seek God for enlightenment and inspiration."

"Your humility is commendable, child," Reverend Mother said. "But I fear it's a bit more complicated than that." She held up a letter. "The fact is, you *have* been discovered."

"Excuse me?"

"I have here a letter from His Excellency, Bishop Reilly. It seems that an old friend of his, a priest from New York, came out to visit and happened to see your painting of the Madonna in the diocese office. This friend, Father Conroy, has a number of people in his parish who are part of the art community on the East Coast. He was so taken with your work that he sent for a Mr. Douglas Eliot, who is curator of a gallery in Manhattan."

Mary Love frowned. "This is all very interesting, Reverend Mother, but what does it have to do with me?"

"When Mr. Eliot saw your Madonna—and your other work that the diocese has acquired—he was apparently very impressed. He asked Bishop Reilly's permission to invite you to New York for a showing in his gallery. He thinks you may have a promising and lucrative future, if the rest of your work measures up to that same quality."

"I can't go to New York. I'm a nun."

"You're a *novice*," the Superior corrected gently. "You can go, and you will."

Mary Love's heart constricted. So that was what Sister Margaret was referring to when she said *good riddance, if you ask me.* "You're sending me away? Please, Reverend Mother—"

"Do you remember our little talk concerning your reception into the novitiate?" the Superior interrupted.

Mary Love nodded.

"You said, then, that God had not spoken a word to you. You have been waiting and working and listening for nearly two years. Perhaps God is speaking now."

"No, Reverend Mother," Mary Love protested. "I was waiting for God to assure me that I had a vocation, that I could, in good conscience, take my vows. I'm only four months away from my Temporary Profession. God would never tell me to *leave*."

"Do not be too certain, child, about second-guessing the Almighty. The Lord has ways that are beyond our understanding."

"But I'm—I'm—"

"Frightened?" Reverend Mother supplied. "I know. But as we've discussed in the past, the convent is not a refuge from the world. You have not found the answers you seek within these walls. Perhaps you will find them out there."

Tears sprang to Mary Love's eyes. She felt as if her heart, her very soul, were being ripped in half. She wanted to stay at the convent, protected, surrounded by the familiar, where she had begun at last to develop a faith of her own. But as much as she hated to admit it, Reverend Mother was right. This was the chance of a lifetime—the chance to fulfill her dreams. Maybe this was why she hadn't been sure about her vocation. Only one thing was certain: If she rejected this opportunity, she would never know.

"So you think I should go to New York, Reverend Mother?"

"I think you should listen to your heart."

"But what if I make a mistake?"

The Superior smiled and cocked her head to one side. "Do you ever make mistakes while you're drawing or painting? You know, get the shape of a face or the curve of a tree trunk wrong?"

"Of course, Reverend Mother." Mary Love felt herself blush. "Lots of them."

"And then you throw the whole sketch away?"

"No. If it's a pencil sketch, I erase the error and correct it. If it's a painting, I paint over it and rework it until I get it just right."

"And do you imagine our Lord is any less committed to the work of our lives?"

Mary Love thought about that for a minute. "You mean," she said at last, "that even if we do make mistakes, go the wrong way, God has a way of correcting our path?"

"Even more than that," Reverend Mother said. "I believe that if our hearts are devoted to God, whatever path we take leads us ultimately back to the One who created and redeemed us." She paused for a moment, then continued. "The Lord is just as present in Manhattan as in this convent, and the vocation of an artist is no less holy than that of a nun. Each of us fulfills God's call by becoming what he designed us to be."

"Then I'll go to New York," Mary Love said with a conviction she didn't really feel. "And I'll trust that, one way or another, God will give me direction."

44
REBIRTH OF A DREAM

May 5, 1934

Mary Love stood on the sidewalk and craned her neck, looking up and up and up. The buildings were so tall, rising so high that they threatened to scrape the sky. She clutched her gray wool coat, and a fleeting anxiety coursed through her veins. Was this what the Tower of Babel was like, that ancient monument to the pride of humankind?

The streets teemed with traffic, and everywhere she looked were crowds of people. The spring wind whipped through her stockings and stung at her legs. She felt naked and exposed in her civilian clothes and kept reaching into her pocket for her prayer book, but it was packed away in her suitcase at the hotel.

"Come on, honey—we don't have all day!"

A firm hand grabbed her by the elbow and hustled her into a waiting taxicab. Douglas Eliot squeezed in beside her. "New Morning Gallery, Forty-sixth Street," he told the cabbie, then turned to face Mary Love. "Now," he said briskly, "the gallery owners have seen your work and are *extremely* pleased." He exaggerated the word *extremely* and adjusted his pink silk ascot. Were all art people this flashy? Mary Love had no idea, but if Douglas Eliot was representative of the lot of them, she was in for a wild ride. Eliot talked with his hands, making grand gestures and calling everyone *darling* and *honey*.

"Most of the major critics will be there tonight," he went on. "Absolutely everyone who is anyone. Believe me, darling, they are going to *adore* you."

His hands flitted over her coat, adjusting her collar. "The exhibition is all set up. When we get there, if you see anything you want changed, just speak your mind."

"I'm sure it will be fine, Mr. Eliot."

"Call me Dougie, darling. Absolutely everyone does." He settled back in his seat. "Now, we'll have an hour or two at the gallery to meet everybody, check out the arrangements, schmooze a little."

"Schmooze?"

"You know, chitchat, play up to the owners, make everybody happy." Eliot peered at her. "You can do that, can't you?"

"I—I think so."

"Then we'll whip back to the hotel, give you a chance to change, and meet the owners at Chez Franzia for dinner. You do like French cuisine?"

"I have no idea," Mary Love said frankly.

Eliot let out a tittering laugh. "Oh, my dear, you are too much! You will captivate the entire city—you'll see!"

The taxi screeched to a halt, and Eliot jumped out. "Here we are." He pointed to a narrow stone building with a lavender door. "New Morning Gallery—the site of your imminent conquest."

Mary Love followed him into the building and up a flight of stairs into a wide, well-lit exhibition hall. A series of partial walls had been erected, forming a kind of maze, and as she walked through, every turn brought her face to face with her own work. She was amazed at the sheer volume and at the creative arrangement of her paintings. When the bishop had first come into her studio, nearly two years ago, she had only a few finished paintings to show him. Now the partitions were covered with oils and watercolors, and Mary Love felt as if she had fallen down the rabbit hole into Wonderland. Maybe she *had* become a real artist, after all.

The Madonna had been brought from the diocese office, as had the snow scene now called *The Face of God*. She gazed at the paintings as if someone else had done them—the peasant countenance of Sister Cecilia smiling benignly in her direction, and over on the far wall, Sister Terese laboring in the garden.

It seemed so long ago that she had stolen work time and given up sleep to do these frantic sketches, and now that they were transformed into oils, she felt awed, as if some divine Spirit had breathed into them a life of their own. She went to the Madonna and peered at the lower right-hand corner.

Sure enough, there were her initials, tiny, almost invisibly worked into the grass at the figure's feet: MLB. It was her painting, all right. On display in a big New York gallery!

Douglas Eliot stood in the corner talking animatedly to two men in dark business suits. He motioned her over. "Gentlemen, meet your star attraction, Mary Love Buchanan. Miss Buchanan, may I introduce Daniel DeVille and Patrick Langley, owners of the gallery."

She shook hands with the two men, and they continued talking with Eliot as if she were invisible.

"Great job, Doug," Daniel DeVille was saying. "This'll be a smash."

"Where on earth did you find her? In a nunnery, you say?" Langley chimed in.

"My priest at St. Pat's saw her work in the diocese office in Minnesota. When they told me she was a nun, I couldn't believe it."

"She doesn't look like a nun."

"She's a novice, actually," Eliot explained. "She hasn't taken final vows yet; that's why she's in street clothes."

"Well, can you put her in something a little less dowdy, then?" DeVille asked. "Maybe dab a little makeup on her? She's not bad looking, but that getup isn't likely to impress the critics."

Eliot cut a glance at Mary Love. "I'll take care of it."

Mary Love stood there, listening to them talk around her as if she were a commodity to be bartered on the trading floor. She was flattered, certainly, by their obvious respect for her work, but she was exhausted from her trip, and she didn't think she could stand much more of this speculation about how to make her look more presentable.

"Mr. Eliot?" she interrupted. "I don't think you need me here. If you don't mind, I'd like to go back to the hotel to rest before the showing tonight."

"Of course, darling, how boorish of me!" Eliot gushed. "I'll put you in a cab this minute." He escorted her to the street, flagged down a taxi, and opened the door. "Plaza Hotel," he told the driver, then turned back to Mary Love. "Get a good rest, and I'll pick you up at seven."

♑

At six, Mary Love was just stepping out of the bath when a knock sounded on her door. She wrapped herself in the plush terrycloth robe provided by the Plaza—dazzling white, with a gold P emblazoned on the pocket—and went to the door.

"Who's there?" she called timidly.

"Delivery for Miss Buchanan," a crisp voice answered.

The moment Mary Love opened the door, a brisk bellman pushed past her carrying an enormous box. "What is this? I didn't order anything."

He looked at the delivery slip. "Delivered from Macy's. Compliments of Mr. Douglas Eliot, Esquire."

Mary Love opened the box and let out a gasp. It was a dress—the most beautiful dress she had ever seen. A floor-length black satin with long sleeves and a beaded bodice. Along with it there were black satin low-heeled pumps and, much to her embarrassment, silky black under-things.

She held up the dress, and the folds of black satin draped around her legs. "I can't possibly wear this."

The bellman surveyed her with a critical eye. "Looks to me like it will be a perfect fit."

Flustered at his attention, Mary Love thrust the dress back into the box. "All right. You can go now."

The bellman stood smiling at her with his hand extended, but didn't move a muscle. Mary Love stared at him, then finally figured out what he wanted. She reached out and shook his hand heartily. "Thank you very much."

The smile vanished, and the bellman turned on his heel, nearly bumping into a large, frowsy-looking woman who had just come to the door.

"Miss Buchanan?" the woman said. "Mary Love Buchanan?"

Mary Love glanced at the clock and sighed. *What now?* It was almost six-fifteen, and if she didn't hurry, she wouldn't have a prayer of being ready when Douglas Eliot showed up at seven.

"I'm Flossie Forrester, the hotel hairdresser," the woman said with just a touch of pride. "I'm here to get you ready for your big night. Hair, makeup—the works."

Mary Love started to protest, then ran a hand through her short, damp hair. Even in her preconvent days, she had never been very adept at hair-styles. She had always looked a little—well, dowdy, as Mr. DeVille from the gallery had described her. When she had overheard him say that, it stung a little, but she had to admit it was the truth. And nuns, after all, did not give in to the sin of pride where fashion was concerned.

Still, this was an important night, not just for her, but for the gallery and for Douglas Eliot and for the diocese. She still had reservations about the dress, but she might as well give it a try. *When in Rome . . .*

"All right," she conceded. "I guess I could use some help. But nothing too flashy."

The woman tugged the padded stool away from the vanity. "Have a seat, hon. When I'm done with you, you won't recognize yourself."

That's what I'm afraid of, Mary Love thought. But she sat down obediently, with her back to the mirror, while Flossie Forrester pulled out a curling iron, combs and brushes, boxes and bottles, and went to work.

At fifteen minutes before seven, Flossie declared herself finished. "You're gorgeous, hon. A real transformation. Take a look."

Cautiously, Mary Love swiveled around on the vanity seat and ventured a glance into the mirror. A stranger stared back at her—a young woman who might have been a more sophisticated cousin, perhaps. Her brown hair curved softly in short curls around her face; her aqua eyes had been accentuated with a sable-colored shadow, and her cheeks heightened with just a touch of rouge. It didn't look like her face—the plain, unadorned novice's face surrounded by a white veil and wimple—but the effect was quite pleasing, in a worldly sort of way.

"Now, the dress." Flossie handed her the black undergarments and pointed toward the bathroom. "Put those on, then come back."

When Mary Love returned, clasping the white robe against her chest, Flossie was holding up the dress, shaking the wrinkles out of it.

"That dress will never fit me," Mary Love declared. "I'd better stick with my suit."

The suit was a puce-colored dress and jacket someone had donated to the convent's charity box for the poor, an outfit the word *dowdy* didn't begin to describe. It had seemed all right when Mary Love had chosen it from the charity box, but now that she was in New York, surrounded by a style of living totally unfamiliar to her, she realized how completely inadequate it was.

"Just try it," Flossie urged.

Mary Love slipped the dress over her head and Flossie buttoned up the back. When she turned toward the mirror, she couldn't believe her eyes.

"It does fit," she hedged, "but I don't know—"

"It's perfect." Flossie fiddled with the hem as Mary Love stared at her reflection. She had always been pudgy, with a round face and plump arms and legs. But somehow, without her realizing it, her body had transformed itself from the chubbiness of childhood into the sleek curves of a full-grown woman. The habit had hidden the metamorphosis. And, to be perfectly honest, Mary Love hadn't given a second thought to her body since she had entered the convent.

She pulled at the sparkling bodice, trying to bring it up in front a little. "Don't you think it's a little, ah, daring?"

Flossie let out a high-pitched laugh. "Daring? It's beautiful, it's chic, it's *outrageously* expensive. But daring? No."

"Then you don't think it's too revealing?"

"What could it possibly reveal?" Flossie countered. "The neckline doesn't show a thing, you've got those long sleeves, and the hemline goes all the way to the floor. Unless you're Queen Victoria, there's not much else that could be covered up. Honey, you could be a nun in that dress."

Mary Love suppressed a smile. "It does look nice, doesn't it?"

"It looks stunning. What's the occasion?"

"The opening of my first show, at the New Morning Gallery."

"You're an *artist*?"

Mary Love nodded.

"Well, congratulations, honey. There aren't many women who can do that—make it in the art world, I mean. Knock 'em dead, sweetie—for all us working gals."

Flossie gathered up her supplies, and as she headed out the door, Mary Love thought, *What a wonderful saint's countenance that woman's face would make.*

⌒つ

"You look absolutely fabulous, darling," Douglas Eliot crooned as he steered Mary Love toward the refreshment table. "That dress is a knockout."

Mary Love assumed this to be a compliment, but she didn't respond. "Are all these people here to see *my* work?" she asked, looking around at the milling crowd. One man was taking notes on a small clipboard as he studied each of the paintings. Others simply pointed and commented. One gentleman in a clerical collar stood before the Madonna with his hands folded and a look of rapture on his face.

"Every single one of them," Eliot assured her. "By tomorrow morning you're going to be the toast of the city."

Mary Love wasn't sure being the toast of New York was exactly what she'd had in mind when she sat in Tish Cameron's chilly attic and placed her dream of being an artist in the blue glass bottle. She had never thought for a minute about becoming famous; all she had wanted—then, and now—was to be free to do the one thing she loved most.

Reverend Mother was right—God certainly did work in mysterious ways. Who would have thought that a lowly novice hidden away in a Minnesota convent would have her talent discovered and put on display in New York City? This was, she had to admit, the culmination of her dreams, the answer to prayers she hadn't even dreamed of praying. Still, something was missing. Something wasn't quite right.

"Smile, darling. Mix. Mingle. Let the people see you." Eliot squeezed her elbow and gave her a little push toward a crowd of people who were staring at her. "I've got some business to attend to. Ta-ta."

One of the women in the group stepped forward—an elegant-looking matron with upswept hair and enormous diamonds dangling from her earlobes. "Tell me, Miss Buchanan," she said, "what is your background? Where have you studied?"

"I—I haven't studied at all," Mary Love stammered. "Actually, I'm a novice."

"A novice!" A sandy-haired young man laughed. "Miss Buchanan, you may be untrained, but your work clearly shows monumental talent and great complexity. No false humility now. There's not an art critic here who would call you a novice."

Mary Love opened her mouth to explain, then thought better of it and kept silent. How could these cultured and sophisticated people understand the simple faith that inspired her work, the simple lifestyle that had engendered it? They expected her to be as cosmopolitan as they were. Tonight, she looked the part, but an expensive beaded dress and a pair of satin pumps couldn't change who she was on the inside.

"Miss Buchanan, may I speak with you?"

Mary Love turned to see the gentleman with the clerical collar standing next to her. Perhaps here was someone who could understand the spiritual significance of her art. Someone who would know what it meant to be inspired by a source beyond yourself.

"I'm Father Conroy." He held out a hand, but Mary Love just stared at him blankly. "Tim's friend—your Bishop Reilly?" he prompted. "I came to Minnesota to visit the diocese and saw your work."

At last the name connected, and Mary Love nodded. "Of course. You're the priest who sent for Douglas Eliot." She shook his hand. "The one who started all this."

He threw back his head and laughed. "Guilty as charged. I see that Doug has been doing some work on you personally as well as on this exhibition."

Mary Love looked down at the dress and ran a nervous hand over her hair. She felt a flush run up her neck and into her cheeks. "I guess I don't look much like a nun, do I?"

"Not even like a novice." His warm brown eyes crinkled with delight. "But don't worry. You look just fine. Very"—he groped for a word—"modest."

"Thank you, Father." She gripped her hands together. "I feel like a fish out of water."

"Well, you don't look out of place. And believe me, everyone is quite impressed with your talent."

"I'm glad—I think."

"Tim—Bishop Reilly—told me that you had some misgivings about your vocation. Do you think this might be why?" He waved a hand in the direction of the crowd. "You obviously have a bright future in the world of art, if you want it. And, if the prices I've heard are any indication, a rather lucrative one."

Mary Love gaped at him. "You mean people are *buying* my paintings?"

"Except for the two that belong to the diocese and are not for sale, I believe almost every piece in the exhibition has been bid on." He chuckled at her amazement. "When I walked by a few minutes ago, two women were haggling over the one of the little boy with the butterfly, trying to outbid each other. DeVille was grinning like a Cheshire cat. He stands to make thousands tonight, just on his commission."

"What do you mean, thousands?"

"Didn't Doug Eliot tell you that the gallery takes a ten percent commission on any sales?"

"Yes. But—"

"Miss Buchanan, let me make this very plain. Your paintings are selling for very high prices, particularly considering the fact that you're a newcomer to the art scene. These people are collectors, critics. They know what's good when they see it and what's likely to appreciate in the future. You will leave here tonight with enough money to support you for years."

"But why do I need it? When I return to the convent—"

"The larger question is, *will* you return to the convent? Unless I miss my guess, Bishop Reilly and your Mother Superior very wisely encouraged you to come to New York to find out whether or not that's what you really want."

Mary Love hesitated. "It's what—what I've *thought* I wanted."

"Then I would counsel you to consider your options carefully. There's nothing wrong or unspiritual about being successful. Besides, you may not have a convent to go back to."

Mary Love felt her heart lurch into her throat. "What are you talking about?"

Father Conroy scratched his head and looked away. "I probably shouldn't tell you this, but it's something you need to know. When I was in Minnesota, Tim—Bishop Reilly—told me that the diocese is considering shutting down Our Lady of the Immaculate Conception. Money is tight everywhere, and the church is going to have to make some sacrifices. Our Lady, even though it is a small convent, has become a drain on the diocese budget. A cloistered order simply doesn't pay its way. There's talk of transferring your Mother Superior to Florida and assigning the other nuns elsewhere."

"They can't do that!"

"They can, and they will. Your Reverend Mother wants to start a school where the nuns could teach, and that could eventually solve the financial problem. But the start-up costs are prohibitive; there's just not enough money to do it." He patted her on the shoulder. "I'm sorry to be the bearer of bad tidings, Miss Buchanan, but I thought you should know. It might make a difference in your plans."

Mary Love's mind swirled with a hundred questions, but before she could ask even one of them, Douglas Eliot reappeared, preening in his tuxedo like a penguin. "This is fabulous!" he gushed. "Darling, I simply must speak with you. Father, you will excuse us, won't you?"

"Of course." Father Conroy tapped Eliot on the shoulder. "Bring her to Mass in the morning, Doug."

"I'll do that."

The priest backed away, and Mary Love was left alone with Douglas Eliot.

"It's just the most marvelous showing ever," he said. "I expected it to go well, but darling, this is beyond my wildest dreams! People are fighting like junkyard dogs to see who can pay the most for your paintings. Now, we have to talk about your future."

He backed her into a secluded corner and lowered her into a chair. "Do you want something to eat? A drink? The champagne isn't exactly Dom Perignon, but it's not bad."

Mary Love shook her head. "No, thanks."

"All right, then, let's get down to cases. Your showing, my dear, has the potential of putting New Morning Gallery at the center of New York's artistic community. DeVille and Langley are in heaven. They want to know what else you have, or how quickly you can produce it. Anything you paint, they can sell. At a modest commission, of course."

"Of course."

"They want to set you up in a studio—overlooking Central Park, if you like. A nice big loft with fabulous light and lots of privacy. Anything you need."

Mary Love closed her eyes and tried to still the churning in her stomach. "You mean they want me to live here—in New York City?"

"Where else would you live?"

"At the convent, of course. I can do my paintings there, can't I? Wouldn't Mr. DeVille and Mr. Langley want them, no matter where I painted them?"

"Yes, but why in heaven's name would you *want* to? This city is the hub of civilization, the most exciting place in the world for an artist—second only to Paris, perhaps. You wouldn't even have to go back to Minnesota at all. We can set it all up in a matter of a week or two, and in the meantime you can stay at the Plaza." He gripped her hands. "You'll adore it, darling— parties, night life, fantastic shopping. Anything your heart desires."

Mary Love looked beyond him, where the milling crowd was beginning to disperse. Past the shoulders of a tall fellow in a tuxedo, she could see the face of Sister Cecilia peering down at her from the wall. A little farther over, Adriana's countenance, captured in the Madonna, radiated with an ethereal glory. Their presence comforted her, brought a familiar warmth in the midst of this alien culture.

"I'll need some time to think about it," she said. "To pray."

A startled look crossed Douglas Eliot's face, as if he had forgotten that she would consider prayer part of the equation. "Certainly," he said at last. "Can you give me an answer tomorrow?"

Mary Love sighed. "Yes. Tomorrow." She smoothed her hands over the beaded satin of the dress. "Let me ask you one question, Mr. Eliot."

He drew up his face in a grimace. "Dougie. Not Mr. Eliot. Please."

"All right"—she forced the name out—"Dougie."

"Much better. Ask your question."

"Exactly how much money are we talking about?"

A gleam shot through Eliot's eyes. "Well, let's see. We've got, what—twenty-five or thirty paintings?"

"Twenty-eight. *The Madonna* and *The Face of God* belong to the diocese, remember?"

"Oh, yes. It's too bad too. Everybody wanted that Face of God thing." He shook his head. "So. Twenty-eight paintings. Just for a rough figure, I think we're averaging about ten thousand apiece—some less, of course, but some a good deal more."

"Twenty-eight thousand dollars?" Mary Love gasped.

"Math isn't your strong suit, I take it," Eliot quipped. "No, darling, not twenty-eight thousand. Two hundred eighty thousand, minus the gallery's ten percent." He gave her a sly wink. "And more where that came from."

"I—I don't know what to say."

Eliot grinned at her. "It makes a difference, does it, in your decision about your future?"

"Yes," Mary Love admitted. "It makes a big difference."

She stood in the dark overlooking the lights of Central Park. A misty rain was sifting down, coating the streets and walking paths with a glaze like sugar candy. Above the trees, the moon hung suspended in a bank of clouds. The orb itself was invisible, but its rays pierced through, an angle of light, a path that stretched from heaven to earth.

Mary Love gazed, transfixed, at the tranquil scene. Her subconscious mind assimilated the details: the subtle colors, the slant of the moonbeams, the hidden face of the source of the illumination. But her consciousness focused on one wonder alone: that on a chilly, rain-soaked spring night, the Almighty was present in New York City.

As she watched the rain drift down, peace settled into the deep places of her soul. At last she understood her calling and vocation—how she could use her gift for the glory of the One who had given it. How she could fulfill those dreams, so long ago written out and hidden away in a blue glass bottle.

Prayer evaded her, but it didn't matter. As full as her heart was, words were unnecessary. Besides, she already had her answer.

Once more, in the silence, God had spoken.

Once more, Mary Love Buchanan had listened.

45
THE GIFT

September 2, 1935

"Sister Angelica?" The voice drifted through the heavy oak door. "Sister Angelica? It's time to go."

Mary Love frowned at the interruption. This was a *convent*, for heaven's sake, not a barnyard. Why couldn't people be just a little quieter when she was trying to work?

The voice came again, this time followed by an insistent rapping. Suddenly Mary Love jumped to attention. *She* was Sister Angelica! Would she ever get used to that name?

Exactly twelve months ago she had stood in the chapel of Our Lady of the Immaculate Conception, received her black veil, and made her Temporary Profession—the vows of poverty, chastity, and obedience. It would be another two years before her final vows, when she would receive the wedding band that marked her as a perpetually professed Bride of Christ. But time no longer mattered. The true confirmation of her vocation had come that rainy May night in Manhattan. Not in a blaze of glory or a thundering affirmation from the sky, but in a still small voice, in that secret place in the heart where God can most often be heard. On that night, with the fulfillment of all her dreams spread out before her and a future of fame and fortune awaiting her, Mary Love had made her choice and knew it to be right.

"Angelica!"

"All right, all right, I'm coming." Mary Love opened the door.

The smiling face of Sister Jeanne greeted her, and Mary Love grinned in return. "Oh, it's you. Why didn't you just come in?"

"I didn't want to disturb you. Reverend Mother has made it very clear that you're not to be bothered."

"Great." Mary Love swung into step beside her. "Now I'm going to be treated with kid gloves."

"That's not what Reverend Mother intends, and you know it. But face facts, Sister Angelica. You are—"

"I know. I'm the convent's greatest commodity."

"What you are," Sister Jeanne corrected, "is a gift. A gift to us, and to God, and to the children."

They stepped out the front door of the convent into a crisp autumn morning. Across the road, where once had been a vacant field full of burrs and thistle, a beautiful two-story stone building shone in the sunlight.

Mary Love and Jeanne joined the ranks of nuns who were making their way toward the crowd gathered around the door. When they reached the front sidewalk, Bishop Reilly, with a smiling Reverend Mother at his side, motioned for Mary Love to come forward. He raised his hand, and the murmuring subsided.

"This is a glorious day in the history of our diocese," he said. "A year ago, the convent of Our Lady was on the verge of being shut down. But today, thanks to Divine intervention in the person of our own Sister Angelica, Our Lady begins a new venture. A new life."

He pointed above the double doors, where a massive stone was engraved with the words: *See, and know . . . and understand . . . that the hand of the Lord hath done this, and the Holy One of Israel hath created it. Isaiah 41:20.*

Mary Love's eyes wandered to one side, where a group of children in little plaid uniforms looked on with wide eyes and slack jaws. So innocent, so open. Who among them, she wondered, would have the gift? Which one of them would enter the art room of this new school, pick up a paintbrush, and discover a lifelong passion and calling?

The bishop waved her to the front, and all eyes turned upon her. She went reluctantly, uncomfortable with being the focus of attention.

"God has worked in mysterious ways to bring us to this place," he said. "Sister Angelica is an accomplished artist, as most of you know by now. But rather than seek fame and fortune for herself, she has followed the call of God into a life of poverty, chastity, and obedience. The proceeds from her paintings have made this new school possible, and future earnings will help to maintain it for many years to come. May the Lord bless you, Sister, and prosper your work."

Mary Love nodded her thanks and lowered her eyes.

"And now, on behalf of the diocese, I wish to make a presentation. Reverend Mother?"

The Mother Superior stepped forward.

"When she was only a postulant, Sister Angelica began a journey that was completely unknown—and, if truth be told, a bit unorthodox." A ripple of laughter coursed through the crowd, and the bishop continued. "But you, Reverend Mother, had the vision to encourage her and to allow her to find her own way. When I first saw Sister Angelica's paintings, I was overwhelmed with the vision this young woman had of God's presence in all things, and I purchased two of her early works on behalf of the diocese. At this time, we give back to the convent—and to the school—the magnificent painting that has come to be known as *The Face of God*.

"That painting," the prelate went on, "is now hanging in the central hallway of the school, where it will remain as a reminder to all of us that God does not always operate in the way we expect and that the Lord Christ is present in every aspect of our lives."

Amid a smattering of applause, Mary Love took the scissors he handed her, cut the ribbon, and threw open the doors. His Excellency then led the procession, offering blessings of consecration on the new building. The children shoved and jostled to get inside, dashing through the halls and squealing with excitement as they inspected their new surroundings.

One child, however, held back—a lean, wiry boy of about ten, with deep-set eyes and a shock of black hair falling over his face. He stood in the central hallway and stared up at the painting on the wall. Mary Love watched him as his eyes took in every detail, and one hand reached out longingly, as if he wanted to trace the contours with his finger.

Finally he looked at her. "Did you really paint this, Sister?"

Mary Love nodded. "Yes, I did."

"I didn't know nuns were allowed to do stuff like this."

She smiled at the child. "What's your name?"

"Francis. Francis Fabrini. Everybody calls me Frankie."

"Well, Frankie, I'll tell you the truth. I was a very rebellious postulant."

His head jerked up, his eyes round as saucers. "Really?"

She nodded. "Really. But God was gracious to me. And so was the Reverend Mother."

He grinned. "You mean you weren't supposed to paint, but you did it anyway?"

"Something like that."

His countenance grew somber and contemplative. "You know what, Sister? I think you're wrong. I think you *were* supposed to paint this. Just everybody didn't know it."

"Maybe you're right, Frankie."

"Can you teach me to do it?"

Mary Love hesitated. She had been through this discussion with Reverend Mother a hundred times during the construction of the school. All the other nuns would be teaching, but Reverend Mother had relieved her of that responsibility. Her assignment was to paint, to create. The walls of her studio were already filled with sketches, and every three months or so that sweet, eccentric Douglas Eliot in New York called, clamoring for more paintings for the New Morning Gallery. She didn't have time to teach, Reverend Mother insisted. Not if she was going to get her work done.

Her mind drifted to that wild, confusing week in New York, when critics had hailed her and collectors had poured money into her lap, vying for the chance to own one of her paintings. The doors of opportunity had opened to her, and the world had been laid at her feet.

Then, at last, she had understood. The real challenge of life was not fulfilling one's dreams, but being willing to give them up for the sake of a greater call. God had not asked her to lay down her art—that was a Divine gift and would not be revoked. God had only asked her to lay down her pride.

Poor Dougie had been devastated at first, but it hadn't taken him long to begin making plans to capitalize on her anonymity, to make the most of her "mystique," as he called it. Mary Love could not have cared less about his promotional schemes. All that mattered was that she could return to the convent, knowing, finally, that when the time came, she could take her vows with integrity. She could follow in the footsteps of Christ and become an invisible servant. She could, forever, be Sister Angelica—not by default, but by design.

"Sister?" The boy's voice drew her out of her reverie, and she looked down to see him gazing up at her.

"I'm sorry, Frankie. What did you say?"

"I asked if you would teach me. To draw like that. To paint." He pointed at the snow scene, and his narrow little face held an expression of awe and wonder.

Mary Love knelt down beside him and took his hands. "Where do you think art comes from?" she asked.

He frowned for a minute, then his countenance cleared. "From God," he said firmly. "And from in here." He laid a hand on his chest. "I think it's like a fire that needs to get out. Something burns inside. Like being hungry, but not for food."

Mary Love rocked back on her heels. "Yes, I'll teach you, Frankie." No matter what she had to do, she would convince Reverend Mother that a few hours a week wasn't much to sacrifice for a ten-year-old who already knew that creativity was an inner fire blown to flame by the breath of the Almighty.

A light came on in the boy's eyes. "Thank you, Sister. Thank you."

"You're welcome, Frankie."

He ran off down the hall to join his schoolmates, leaving Mary Love standing alone in front of the painting that had set her on this journey. The hidden face in the woods stared back at her, with just the hint of a smile around the eyes.

Everyone had marveled at how much she was willing to sacrifice for the sake of her vocation, how much she had relinquished to be obedient to God. But no one could understand, unless they had done it themselves, that it wasn't a sacrifice at all. She had let go of her dreams, but in return, she had been given passion and fulfillment, vision and direction. Not to mention a little boy named Frankie, who felt the fire burning inside him.

All things considered, her so-called sacrifice was a bargain. And a very good bargain at that.

46
THE ARTIST

November 30, 1994

"For years, then, I taught and painted and lived at the convent of Our Lady," the old nun concluded.

Brendan leaned back in her chair and smiled. "And found your vocation," she added.

"Indeed I did." A faraway expression filled the old woman's eyes. "After a while, the initial excitement over my work—all that hoo-ha in New York—died down somewhat. But by then, my paintings had made enough money to see the convent school through for many years. And Frankie—my very first student—that boy went on to become quite an artist in his own right, working as a cover designer for a big New York publishing house."

She paused and smiled. "Odd, isn't it, how God works sometimes? I often think that if I hadn't become a nun, I would have been just one more obscure artist struggling to find a niche in the market. Dear old Douglas Eliot, God rest his soul, used to tell me that it didn't matter how much talent you had, you needed a hook, something to get people's attention. The habit did that for me, I suppose." She smiled, and the crow's-feet at the corners of her eyes deepened. "No one expected a nun to paint with such passion and life. I rather suspect people think we abdicate our humanity when we take our vows."

"No one who ever met you would believe that." Brendan took the blue glass bottle in her hands and stroked its contours with her fingers. "Looking back, do you see yourself as having fulfilled those dreams you put in this bottle?"

"Yes and no," Mary Love answered. "An important part of the dream, as you know by now, was to live alone, to have solitude." She grinned broadly. "A nun has times of solitude, certainly, but mostly it's a life lived in community—a bigger community, even, than my family. I never got away from the responsibilities of that kind of life, and ironically, I found myself with a lot more children than I had to take care of at home. But by then I had grown up a little, and the dream had changed. My values had changed."

"So you don't regret entering the convent?"

"Heavens no, child. Sometimes we do the right thing for all the wrong reasons. And somehow, the Lord manages to sort it out and make it work." She chuckled. "If we have our eyes open to see the miracle, we find our dreams fulfilled in ways we could never have imagined."

"Someone else told me almost exactly the same thing," Brendan mused.

"And do you believe it?"

Brendan smiled. "I'm trying, Sister. I'm afraid my eyes have been shut for a long time. It takes a while to get them open and working again."

"So, now that you've got the final piece of your story, what are you going to do with it?"

Brendan set the bottle down on the table and clenched her hands in her lap. Since about halfway through Mary Love's story, an idea had been niggling at her. It might not work, but she had to take the chance. "I've been thinking about that. How would you feel about going back to North Carolina for a few weeks?"

The old woman's eyes flashed with interest. "North Carolina?"

Brendan nodded. "It would take a while to put it together, but I'd like to do more than just a personal interest story on the four of you. If I can convince my boss, I'd like to put together a whole hour's program—have all of you there, interview you on camera—"

"Like a Barbara Walters special?" Mary Love let out a cackling laugh. "That sounds like fun—as long as you don't ask probing questions about my romantic life." She gave Brendan an exaggerated wink and nodded. "They don't need me here. Count me in."

"Then you could get away?"

"I'm due for an extended retreat. I'll have to clear it with the Reverend

Mother, of course, make sure it's all right with her. But she's a marshmallow. It shouldn't be a problem."

"Can you leave, say, on Monday? That's December 5. For about six or eight weeks."

"I'll check my Day-Timer." At Brendan's quizzical look, she grinned. "Just kidding. It should be fine. But where will I stay?"

"I'll take care of everything." Brendan smiled to herself. She would call, of course, but she had no doubt that Dee and Addie would be delighted for Mary Love to stay with them. Then she'd go back to Atlanta and bring Ellie up for the occasion. What a Christmas it would be, with the four of them reunited.

"All right, Monday, then. I'll make the arrangements." Brendan stood and gathered her equipment. "Thanks so much, Sister, for your time." She pointed toward the wheelchair. "Do you want me to take you back downstairs?"

"No, leave me here." The old nun waved an age-spotted hand. "I need some time to myself. You've given me a lot to think about."

Brendan nodded. She had some thinking of her own to do. "If you need me," she said, "I'll be staying at the Holiday Inn. I'll call you later and let you know our flight times."

She headed for the door, only to be arrested by the nun's voice: "One more thing, child."

Brendan turned back. "Yes, Sister?"

"I'll say a prayer for you. Keep your eyes—and your heart—open."

December 3, 1994

Brendan sat at the small table in the cramped hotel room, her laptop computer open and her tape recorder at her elbow. She had just finished transcribing the last of Mary Love's tapes, and she had a sketchy outline of the story all ready to fax to Ron Willard, but she didn't feel any sense of accomplishment.

For the past three days she hadn't set foot out of this room. The bed was a rumpled mess—a testimony to her sleepless nights—and a stack of dirty dishes from room service stood next to the door. She probably should let the maid in to clean up. But housekeeping was the last thing on her mind.

There was more, so much more to this story that couldn't be communicated even in an hour's worth of film. It would be a great personal-interest piece, certainly. Ron was going to love it. This story would draw people in, compel them, the way she had been compelled at the outset of her research.

It wasn't just a story about four friends who, despite all odds, found each other again after sixty-five years. It was about *dreams*—the fulfillment of dreams, and the death of dreams. That was the common denominator, the factor that would make viewers identify with these women. Everybody had dreams, and most people, Brendan thought, never had the chance or took the risk to fulfill them. Failure was the great human leveler—the dreams that never came true. This story had everything—love, loss, pathos, fulfillment. And it raised one of the great universal questions of life: *What are your dreams? And what are you willing to sacrifice to see them realized?* But there was something else—something that nagged at Brendan and wouldn't let her go. Something that kept her awake and then invaded her sleep when she finally fell exhausted into bed. Something that she didn't know how to address in the story—or in her own life.

It was the God factor.

Every one of these women—despite the disappointments and pain of their lives, despite the odd turns their paths had taken—acknowledged that even in the darkness, when they were unaware of it, God had somehow been at work in their lives. Letitia never married, but God gave her many children. Adora never became a star, but God brought great love and contentment into her life. Ellie never became a social worker, but God enabled her to make a difference in her world. And Mary Love—Sister Angelica voluntarily gave up fame and fortune, only to have God use her talent in a totally unexpected way.

None of these women had found their dreams, at least not in the way they had originally envisioned. And yet all of them had been given a great gift—the ability to see beyond the surface, to find significance and purpose in the calling placed on their lives.

This truth now stared Brendan squarely in the face, and her evasive maneuvers no longer worked. For years she had closed her mind and soul to the possibility of God because life hadn't turned out the way she expected. Her entire life—past, present, and future—had been defined by a single moment of disaster: the untimely deaths of her parents.

Yes, it was a horrible, senseless tragedy. But now, faced with the story that had consumed her attention for the past two months, Brendan was forced to realize that she wasn't the only person in the world who had faced tragedy and sorrow. What about Letitia, who had found her father's body after he committed suicide? Or Adora, who had faced pregnancy out of wedlock and watched as her own father declared her dead? Or Ellie, who stood by helpless and trapped while her mother descended into madness? Yet none of them interpreted their sorrows as the result of the callous indifference of an uncaring God. On the contrary, they had discovered a loving God in the very midst of their struggles, a God who brought them out of the darkness into the light.

A phrase floated through Brendan's mind—the deathbed advice Ellie James had received from Hazel Dennison so many years ago: *The path is before you, not behind. Don't give your future to the past.*

Was it possible, she wondered, that some power beyond herself—God, perhaps—had brought her to this story for reasons she could never have imagined? You could call it chance, she guessed, doing the demolition story and finding the blue glass bottle. Just one of those quirky things that can't be explained. But she suspected that the four women who had become so important to her would call it something besides mere coincidence.

Brendan let her mind drift, and a series of images begin to rise to the surface. Seemingly unconnected events from her past began to take on a pattern. Her parents' deaths, which led to her living with Gram, which led to her becoming best friends with Vonnie Howells. It was Vonnie who had encouraged her to take journalism classes in college and to apply for the job at WLOS when Brendan didn't think she had a prayer of landing it. And it was ultimately the job at WLOS, and her dissatisfaction with the mundane daily grind, that had compelled her to explore the blue bottle story, where one piece of information led to another, and another, and another. Now the completion of the story had brought her full circle, face-to-face with herself—and with God.

Too many coincidences, she thought. If she had been tracking a story that had this many chance encounters, she would suspect a conspiracy—or at the very least, a plan.

But if there was a plan at work in her life, where was it leading her? She hadn't a clue. Yet for the first time in many years, she was willing to find out. Willing to explore the possibilities. Willing not to be in total control.

Keep your eyes—and your heart—open, Mary Love had said.

It was wise advice. Advice that, at long last, Brendan Delaney just might follow.

47
WHAT SHALL I BRING HIM?

December 25, 1994

Inside and out, Dee Lovell's big house was a fairyland of greenery and tiny white lights. In the corner of the library, a massive Christmas tree brushed its topmost branches against the high ceiling, and a golden angel with gossamer wings peered down over the scene.

The gifts had been opened. A first edition of *The Secret Garden* for Letitia, a rare publicity cel from *Gone with the Wind* for Adora. Ellie cradled in her lap an autographed copy of *Twenty Years at Hull House,* and Sister Angelica—who insisted upon being called Mary Love—gazed with wonder at a fine reproduction of Giotto's *St. Francis Feeding the Birds.*

The aroma of turkey and dressing wafted in from the kitchen, and Brendan's stomach growled. It was a perfect day—just perfect—with a light snow sifting down, a fire blazing in the fireplace, and carols playing softly in the background.

Mary Love stood up, leaned on her walker, and cleared her throat. "Before we get caught up in the wonderful dinner I smell cooking in the other room, I want to take the opportunity to thank Brendan Delaney for everything she has done to make this day a reality." A murmur rippled through the room. "I know she didn't do this just for us—she has a report to do, and from everything I've heard, she's going to work us like pack mules in the next few weeks. But if it weren't for her, we wouldn't be together today."

Brendan gazed around at the now-familiar faces—women she hadn't even known existed at this time last year. She could hardly believe how dear they all seemed to her—like four grandmothers, all doting on her. And Dee, of course, who had become like a sister. For the first time since her grandmother died, she felt as if she truly had a family. Tears sprang to her eyes, and she bit her lip.

"Now, child, don't go blubbering all over the first editions," Mary Love scolded. "Besides, I want your undivided attention." She motioned to Dee, who went into the office off the library and returned with a large package wrapped in brown paper. "I've kept this for years," she said. "It was one of the first paintings I ever did, but I never showed it to anyone. And now I want you to have it, Brendan—not just from me, but from all of us."

She pulled the wrapping off and, when the framed portrait stood revealed, a gasp went around the room.

"It's called *Four Friends*," Mary Love explained. "As you know, my life took some unexpected turns, but like all of us, I never forgot that Christmas Day so many years ago, when we met in Tish's attic and shared our dreams."

It was a portrait of Letitia, Adora, Eleanor, and Mary Love, gathered in a dimly lit room with high gables and exposed beams. On the table stood a candle and a blue glass bottle. But the four weren't young girls, as they had been that Christmas Day in 1929. They were adults, and the illumination from the candle cast their faces in an amazing contrast of light and shadow.

"This isn't a painting," Letitia said solemnly. "It's a prophecy."

Brendan gazed at the faces. Tish was right; it was much more than a portrait. In the painting, Letitia stood to one side, alone, with a number of small children in the shadows behind her. Adora was dressed for the stage, but she held a tiny baby in her arms. Ellie was reaching out to a group of old men and women. And Mary Love herself, in a long black dress, sat at an easel in the right-hand corner, painting the entire scene onto a miniature canvas. She had caught them all—not as they had imagined their dreams would be fulfilled, but as those dreams actually had been realized. Letitia with her school children; Adora giving up acting to care for little Nicky; Ellie with the residents of the James Home; Mary Love in the habit of a nun. And in the center of them all, the blue glass bottle was glowing from within as if illuminated by a light all its own.

"It's amazing," Brendan whispered. "How did you do it?"

"I have no idea," Mary Love answered candidly. "I just painted what I saw in my mind's eye. But when I went back to it later, it seemed very different than what I had first envisioned."

"I can't accept this," Brendan protested. "It's much too valuable."

"You don't want it?" Mary Love's face betrayed her disappointment, and Dee gave Brendan a swift jab in the ribs.

"Take it!" she hissed. "It's a gift, for heaven's sake!"

Brendan held the painting up. "I can't tell you how much this means," she began, but tears choked her and she couldn't go on. She was completely overwhelmed, not just by Mary Love's presentation of the portrait, but by the love and acceptance she felt from these dear women. "I'll tell you what," she said when she had regained her composure, "why don't we hang it here, over the mantel, so we can all enjoy it?"

Dee gave her a nod of approval, and within minutes Mary Love's *Four Friends* gazed down at them from above the fireplace. As stunning as it was, it left Brendan with an eerie feeling, like looking into the past and the future at the same time.

Ellie went to the piano and began to pick out a song. "Mary Love's painting reminds me of an old Christmas carol. Remember the last verse of 'In the Bleak Midwinter'? *What can I give him, poor as I am . . . ?*" she began.

"*If I were a shepherd, I would bring a lamb,*" the others chimed in. Brendan didn't know the song, so she just listened. "*If I were a wise man, I would do my part . . .*" The lyrics wrapped around her soul and gripped her with a strange sensation of longing. "*Yet what I can, I give him—Give my heart.*"

Brendan thought she would strangle from holding back the tears. When she could stand the pressure no longer, she let them go, and they spilled over and ran down her cheeks. Dee noticed and drew her aside.

"Is anything wrong?"

"I—I don't know," Brendan stammered.

"Let's go into my study for a few minutes." Dee led the way, and before she knew it, Brendan was sitting in the burgundy leather reading chair sobbing into a soggy tissue.

"Now, give," Dee commanded.

"It was—I'm not sure. The song, the painting. This story. Everything."

"You mean it's stirred something inside you that you don't understand?" Dee translated.

"Maybe. I've never had a story get to me like this. It's made me reexamine everything. My life, my purpose. My future."

"And your dreams?" Dee prodded gently.

"Before this, I never even thought about my dreams. I just did my job, made good money. But—but—nothing in my life has ever *lasted*!" she blurted out. "My whole life, my career, is sound bites, ninety-second spots on the news. Even this story, which has been an obsession for almost three months, will be a sixty-minute program. A good one, I can feel it. But then what?"

She took a deep, ragged breath and looked up into Dee's face. "When all of you were singing that carol—'What can I give him?'—I kept thinking: *Nothing*. Not a blessed thing. I have nothing to give."

"Yes, you do," Dee corrected softly. "You can give your heart."

"My heart's not worth giving. There's nothing there. It's a stone."

"I don't believe that."

"When my parents were killed, I turned away from God—and from love. I didn't let anybody close, except my grandmother, and then she died too. I've survived by keeping people at a distance, by being independent. Then all of you came into my life, talking about dreams and how God is still present even in darkness and sorrow. It's been very confusing—and yet I can't seem to block it out."

"Maybe you're not supposed to block it out," Dee suggested. "Maybe you're supposed to let it in."

"It's too late."

Dee shook her head firmly. "It's never too late." She pointed toward the door. "Look at them. They've gone through some terrible experiences in their lives, and yet they've found a reason to go on . . . a purpose. A dream— a hope that can't be killed."

Fresh tears rose up in Brendan's throat. "And where do I find my dream? My reason, my purpose?"

"The same place they found theirs," Dee said quietly. "Within your own soul." She paused, and for a moment silence engulfed them, broken only by the faint sounds of laughter and the background of Christmas music coming from the library. "Tell me the truth, Brendan—what is it about this story that's got you so agitated?"

Brendan thought for a minute. "There's something important in this story, Dee—something that has the potential of touching a lot of people's lives. Everyone has dreams—" She stopped and grinned through her tears. "Well, *almost* everyone. And everyone has known what it's like to see their dreams crumble. But these women—your grandmother and the others— have found something more stable to hang onto. They're not content and fulfilled because circumstances turned out the way they hoped, but because of their faith in a God who is above circumstance. For a while I tried to pass over it as denial or some kind of Pollyanna religion. But it's not. It's real, and it shows."

She sighed. "The sixty-minute special will be good, don't get me wrong. It'll probably earn me a promotion. But the story's too big for the time slot. Most people, when they go through difficult times, get hard and bitter and angry. Trust me, I know. If people could only experience for themselves what these four women went through, how they managed to come out stronger and wiser and nobler, it would make a difference in a lot of people's lives."

"And that's what you want to do? Make a difference?"

"I guess so. I'm tired of giving my life to throwaway journalism. I'd like to leave something a little more permanent behind—something that might make the world a better place. Does that sound stupid?"

"It sounds like a dream worth pursuing." Dee squatted down beside Brendan's chair and peered into her face. "Brendan, was there ever something you wanted to do with your life that would have that kind of permanence?"

Brendan knew the answer immediately, but she averted her eyes and didn't respond. She felt a flush run up her neck.

"Come on, tell me."

"Writing," Brendan mumbled.

"What did you say?"

Brendan shook her head. "I feel like an idiot saying this to you, Dee. You're a Pulitzer novelist. A professional. But that's what I wanted, a long time ago. To write books. Not news reports, books."

A broad grin broke out on Dee's youthful face.

"You think that's funny?"

"Funny, no. Ironic, yes." She went to her desk and rummaged in the top drawer. "I was going to talk to you about this later, after you had finished production on the special. I kind of—well, did something behind your back."

Brendan jerked to attention. "Like what?"

"I—ah—" Dee shook her head. "When you first came here to talk to Granmaddie, I couldn't get the story out of my mind. The four old women, the blue bottle, the dreams. You could probably tell how fascinated I was with it."

"So?"

"So, I had a little talk with my publisher. Strictly confidential, you understand—sort of testing the waters. And he thinks this would make a great novel—a fictionalized account, based on the true story. He said when you're ready to discuss it, you can contact him."

"I can't write a novel! I'm a journalist."

"Right," Dee said, her tone laced with heavy sarcasm. "Heaven forbid that you should try something you haven't done before. It might be a risk."

Brendan's stomach knotted, a mingling of anticipation and absolute terror. "Do you really think I could do it? And you'd be willing to help me?"

"I'd be willing to do more than that. It's your story, of course, and your decision. But one option might be for us to collaborate, as cowriters—"

It took a minute for this suggestion to sink in. Then reality hit her: Cordelia A. Lovell, Pulitzer Prize–winning author of *A Sense of Place,* was offering to lend her name and her expertise to a project they would do together.

The very idea shook Brendan to the core. Not just because Dee was willing to work with her on a book project, but because somehow, in the midst of all the confusion and turmoil, she suddenly found herself faced with the answer to a prayer she had never dared to pray. All the events of her life—good and bad—seemed to converge in a pattern that brought her to this place, this time, this opportunity. And she knew, finally, that through all the years of darkness, she hadn't been alone.

A sense of joy and purpose welled up in her soul, a passion unlike anything she had ever known. So this was what it felt like, having direction, knowing peace. Brendan had always assumed peace to be some kind of nebulous cloud of passivity, like being on massive doses of painkillers. But this peace was active, alive, a palpable presence. She wanted to *do* something—to run, shout, find some tangible way to mark this moment, to capture and hold the reality in her soul forever. Some way, unaccustomed as she was to gratitude, to say *thank you*.

What I can, I'll give him—Give my heart. . . .

"We can talk about the details later, when you've finished the sixty-minute special," Dee was saying. "But think about it, will you? My publisher is very enthusiastic."

"I don't have to think very hard," Brendan laughed. "But there is one little detail we'll need to attend to right away."

"What's that?"

Brendan pointed toward the library. "Getting their permission."

"I doubt that will be a problem," Dee said with a chuckle. "I have an in with one of the principal players."

Brendan stood up and dried the last of her tears. "Shall we go tell them the good news?"

"And what, exactly, are you going to tell them?"

Brendan hesitated, groping for words. "That Somebody has answered their prayers," she said at last, "and given a rootless journalist a sense of purpose and direction. That one more dream is about to come true."

Dee lifted her eyes toward the ceiling. "It happens," she said with a shrug. "More often than you might imagine."

EPILOGUE

February 11, 1995

Dreamers wasn't exactly an earth-shattering journalistic exposé, a candidate for the Emmy nomination. But it held its early prime-time slot—just after the evening news—moderately well, generating a mild flurry of local interest.

"A sweet story," the *Citizen-Times* called it. "A tiny beacon of hope in a bad-news world."

Brendan, for her part, couldn't have cared less about the reviews. She was proud of the story—proud of the work she had done. For the first time in recent memory, she had produced a piece worthy of airing, a story that wouldn't be forgotten as soon as the closing credits rolled.

She pressed the pause button on the remote and chuckled to herself as Dwaine Bodine's face filled the screen. Ron Willard had pitched a fit when she told him she intended to use the gregarious demolition worker in the opening and closing scenes.

"You're going to let that redneck camera-hog get his fifteen seconds of fame in *our* film?" Ron shook his head in disbelief. "What's happened to you, Brendan? If I didn't know you better, I'd think you'd gone completely soft."

Brendan had done her best to contain her amusement, albeit unsuccessfully. "Dwaine's not a redneck," she had insisted. "He's a sweet guy, really. Just wants to help. And besides, he's the one who started this story in the first place, by finding the bottle and giving it to me. He's a crucial part of the whole plan."

"What plan? What are you talking about?"

"What I'm saying is that I want to show him a little appreciation," Brendan had said firmly. "All right?"

"All right," Ron conceded. "It's your show. But try to keep a lid on him, will you?"

Dwaine, as it turned out, had been absolutely brilliant. Humble and self-effacing, he fairly emanated the kind of "aw-shucks," homespun philosophy Brendan was looking for. A common, uneducated person, but one whose dreams were every bit as valuable and important as the grand schemes of the educated and elite.

She pushed the play button, and Dwaine's boyish face came to life. "I found it up in the rafters, y'know?" he was saying. "It was a purty thing, that nice blue color. Thought it might make a real good souvenir for you, Miss Delaney." He grinned broadly into the camera. "Just goes to show that you never know what you're gonna find when you keep your eyes open."

Brendan clicked the television off and went into the next room. Everywhere she looked, boxes were piled up—some sealed and ready to go, some still open. She really ought to finish packing.

Tomorrow morning she was moving into the guest house behind Dee Lovell's big home in Hendersonville, and together they would begin work on the new book. The house on Town Mountain had sold in one day, along with a lot of the furniture and other possessions she had acquired over the years. It was time to scale back, to simplify, to streamline. Time to give herself to the new direction her path was taking. She wondered, briefly, if she would miss the old life.

Her laptop lay open on the desk, pulsing a blue light into the dimly lit room. She sat down, poised her fingers over the keypad, and began to type—a dedication for the book that was yet to be written:

> To the Blue Bottle Club,
> Letitia, Adora, Eleanor, and Mary Love,
> whose faith, strength, and determination helped me discover my dreams.

An appropriate inscription, she thought, for the women whose lives had touched her own so deeply. They could never have imagined, on Christmas Day in 1929, that their dreams, their lives, would turn out to be a gift beyond price to a young woman who had not yet been born. But Someone Else knew—the One whose birth they celebrated that day, the One whose hand had guided the four of them through the years, even when they were not aware of the Presence.

Brendan gazed at the words on the screen. It wouldn't be easy, this new life she had chosen. No regular paychecks, no paid vacations, no insurance benefits, no expense account. But it was the opportunity of a lifetime, the chance to find out if she could really make it as a writer. And amid all the conflicting emotions—the fear, the exhilaration, the apprehension, the sense of adventure—Brendan Delaney knew that, no matter what the outcome, the dream itself was worth the risk.

It was all a gift. A frightening, uncertain, bewildering gift—but a gift, nevertheless.

"Thank you," she breathed into the darkness.

As she uttered the words, the fear began to dissipate, replaced by a warm infusion of something else. Peace. Assurance. Confidence. Not in herself, in her abilities, but in the One who had brought her to this place and time. She smiled, and then, almost instinctively, added one final line to the dedication:

And to Dwaine, whose profound insight taught me an important bit of wisdom:
"You never know what you're gonna find when you keep your eyes open."